Evelyn Anthony began v ⟨ **P9-EEP-267** of successful historical novels before she turned her talents to creating the superbly crafted thrillers for which she is now so highly acclaimed. Her last two novels, *The Doll's House* and *Exposure*, were both published by Corgi. She is married with six children and lives in Essex.

Critical acclaim for Evelyn Anthony:

THE DOLL'S HOUSE

'Anthony is an arch-exponent at crafting high tension mixed with romance . . . The novel is both gripping and highly enjoyable' Elizabeth Buchan, *Sunday Times*

'A well-crafted yarn with an intriguing twist at the end, just like all great spy stories' *Company*

'A compulsive new thriller . . . The plot is good, the characters well drawn, it's fast-paced and involving' *Woman and Home*

'Again, Anthony melds romantic suspense and espionage thrills for a spirited diversion – this time involving a love affair that bobs crazily around a plot to rub out an Arab prince . . . Seamlessly styled entertainment – with tight action and a wry, inronic close' *Kirkus*

EXPOSURE

'She has carved out a niche of her own as the Queen of contemporary thrillers . . . many will find this Evelyn Anthony's best thriller yet' Maureen Owen, *Daily Mail*

'Evelyn Anthony's narrative power – electric suspense as the veils of mystery peel away – makes it absolutely gripping' *Daily Telegraph*

'Evelyn Anthony writes a cracking good thriller . . . It is high class, pacey and beautifully plotted' *Publishing News*

Also by Evelyn Anthony

THE DOLL'S HOUSE
EXPOSURE

and published by Corgi Books

BLOODSTONES

Evelyn Anthony

CORGI BOOKS

BLOODSTONES
A CORGI BOOK : 0 552 14241 7

Originally published in Great Britain by Bantam Press,
a division of Transworld Publishers Ltd

PRINTING HISTORY
Bantam Press edition published 1994
Corgi edition published 1995

Set in 10pt Linotype Sabon by Kestrel Data, Exeter.

Corgi Books are published by Transworld Publishers Ltd,
61–63 Uxbridge Road, London W5 5SA,
in Australia by Transworld Publishers (Australia) Pty Ltd,
15–25 Helles Avenue, Moorebank, NSW 2170
and in New Zealand by Transworld Publishers (NZ) Ltd,
3 William Pickering Drive, Albany, Auckland.

Reproduced, printed and bound in Great Britain by
Cox & Wyman Ltd, Reading, Berks.

To my darling Michael,
with all my love.

1

'Darling,' Elizabeth Hastings reminded him, 'if you don't hurry up we're going to be late.' It was unlike James to sit with a drink when he should have been dressing to go out. She came into the handsome drawing-room, and stood beside his chair. He looked up at her and smiled.

'You look terrific,' he said. He held out his hand and she grasped it.

'I heard you come in, I was getting ready upstairs and I thought you'd be up. Anything wrong?'

He shook his head, touched by her anxiety for him. He was so lucky. He couldn't believe it sometimes. His beautiful, sweet-natured wife, the prize he had won from so many contenders.

'What's the matter?' she repeated. 'You look tense.'

He got up, finished his gin and tonic and held her in his arms.

'Not tense, sweetheart. Excited.'

'What, tell me?' She waited expectantly. 'Something good?'

'It could be,' James Hastings answered. 'Kiss me, and I'll tell you all about it while I get into my monkey-suit.'

He disliked wearing a dinner jacket. He liked being casual when he got home from the office. Open-necked shirt, sweater, loafers. He wore belts with designer buckles, which Elizabeth thought vulgar but didn't say so. Such tiny differences of taste between them. James wasn't hidebound like her father and her poor dead brother, conventional, hedged in by custom instilled in them by family and tradition. She was still inclined to be

7

old-fashioned, even after five years of marriage to her human dynamo. She teased him with the nickname, mocking the restless energy and seeking mentality that didn't know how to sit still and take time off to look at life.

James had to be in the centre of things, he had even jazzed up the pace of her own interior decorating business. Since their marriage it was flourishing, with commissions for private houses and an office block. Elizabeth was swept along on his enthusiasm; she worked harder, became more positive, and the small one-woman business she had started with a legacy at twenty-one was now expanding daily.

'Darling,' he said, 'before I tell you my news, how was your day?'

'Busy,' she said. 'I had a call from Mitchels; the chairman loves his office! Everybody kept saying how difficult he was, always wanting changes, but not this time.'

'You're a clever girl,' he said fondly. 'Of course he liked it. Any news on the quotes for Westminster?'

Elizabeth said, 'No, not yet. It'd be a miracle if I got it. All the names are after that one.'

'I'll bet they are,' he said. 'But don't underestimate yourself. If you get that job, sweetheart, you're made.'

There was a new Lord Chancellor, and his apartments at Westminster were due for complete redecoration. Encouraged by James, Elizabeth had submitted designs and quotes in competition with the grandest household names in the world of interior decoration and design. The impudence appealed to Elizabeth, who had a mischievous streak.

'Colefax and Fowler, Nina Campbell . . . God, wouldn't it be a joke if I pipped the lot of them?'

'And why not?' he insisted. 'You're every bit as good and half the price.'

They went upstairs together, and she sat on the bed

8

while he showered quickly and then began to dress. He had a lean, virile body, and she loved the feel of him; she had a few cheerful love affairs behind her when they first met. Nothing serious, just encounters that were fun, with men she liked but didn't fall in love with. She was unprepared for making love with James. She was twenty-two and she discovered what sexual passion between two people really meant. And not just physical fulfilment . . . but tenderness, humour and a sort of painful joy in being together.

They were so completely different as people; she was country born, a sportswoman who rode and fished, and loved long walks with the family dogs. He loved the theatre, modern art, classical music. He also swam every day and played squash, but she realized later that this was merely to keep fit, and not an enjoyment for its own sake.

He taught her to appreciate things she would have dismissed as boring before she met him. She knew her self-confidence had developed and she was richer for it. There had been a price to pay after they married, but she shrugged it off. Life in a big London house in Thurloe Square, fewer and fewer weekends with her family in Somerset, new friends with money and business interests, or politicians like the Chichesters who had invited them to dinner that evening, a more aggressive approach to her own career. She adapted to James's lifestyle without much difficulty because she loved him so much and she was so happy with him.

'Now come on,' she said. 'You know I'm dying to hear all about it . . . What's happened?'

He had tied his tie, grimacing because he never succeeded at the first attempt and he hated failing at anything. 'Julius Heyderman's coming over on Tuesday night. He's called a special meeting of the whole Board for Wednesday. Kruger's coming back from France, the Wassermans are on their way from New York, and Reece is coming via Spain. The office is really buzzing. Arthur had gone down to the country, so his secretary was running round like a blue-assed fly trying to get in contact. It must be some kind of trouble; Heyderman never comes at this time of year. He's down at the Cape. Oh damn . . . darling, can you do this for me?'

He pulled the tie loose in exasperation.

'Calm down,' Elizabeth told him. 'And keep still or I can't do it. There. I'll get you one on an elastic band if you make such a fuss. Go on . . . why should it be trouble?' She watched him as he pulled on his jacket, and checked that he had his keys and an Asprey cigar case she'd given him as an impromptu present one day. Then she said suddenly, 'It's not something you've done, is it?'

'Oh God no, darling. I haven't cocked up. I'm not important enough to justify Heyderman making more than a telephone call.' He loved her for thinking that he was. 'My guess is, it's either a crisis blown up in South Africa that's going to affect the mines – the political situation is so bloody unstable it must be like sitting on a timebomb – or it's our Arthur Harris.' Arthur Harris was the London Managing Director of Diamond Enterprises.

She turned the big oval cut diamond round on her finger. That ring had been the only jarring note in her engagement. Elizabeth wanted a nice sapphire with a diamond each side, something she could wear every day of her life, as her mother wore hers, even washing-up or feeding the dogs. But James had been adamant. As the fiancée of an employee of Diamond Enterprises her ring had to be a statement. When she first heard that he worked for D.E. she asked him if he was a jeweller, and giggled because he didn't look like one. He had explained that he didn't know one stone from another; his job was strictly executive. She had never liked that big vulgar ring, but it upset him if she didn't wear it.

She pushed back the long silky blond hair that tended

to fall over her face. James wouldn't let her cut it or pin it. He was crazy about her hair; loved to smooth and twist it between his fingers.

He often held her and looked at her. Just looked, and then told her how beautiful she was. And how incredibly lucky he was to be married to her.

'Why should it be Arthur?' Elizabeth asked.

'Because Heyderman hates him; he'd jump at the chance to kick him out. Arthur won't enjoy waiting for brother-in-law Julius to walk in on Wednesday!'

'I'd much rather have Heyderman than Arthur,' she said. 'I've always liked him.'

'You've never crossed him,' James said. 'Or failed him. You know . . .' He paused, about to put his most secret ambition into words. 'You know if Arthur did get the elbow, it might open the door for me . . .'

Elizabeth stared at him. 'You? For his job? But you're the youngest, what about Kruger and Andrews . . . ?'

'Kruger's past it. That business with the secretary didn't do him any good.'

'I hate that woman,' she said coldly. 'She deliberately broke up that marriage. After thirty years. She's a bitch.'

He shrugged. Nobody liked Ruth Fraser. Especially other women. She was just too clever and sexually attractive for her own good. He went on. 'Andrews is the only one. He should be in line . . . but . . . I just get the feeling Heyderman might be tempted by new blood.' He grinned at her. 'Mine.'

He looked at his watch. Another present from Elizabeth. She was so generous with money. She was always giving him surprises. He had been brought up to be careful, not to indulge in needless extravagance. But, unlike his wife's family, the Hastings money was very new.

He stood up. He said, 'I've been there twelve years. I reckon I'm ready for the top job if it's offered to me. Come on, darling, we'll be late. I hope you won't be bored – they're not very exciting, the Chichesters. I'll make it up to you later.'

'I bet you will,' Elizabeth said. They had a wonderful love life; it had got even better as they grew together. And now there was the added incentive of the baby they both wanted. Two years of waiting and hoping, no medical reasons except the prolonged use of the Pill. 'You can't expect Nature to oblige immediately,' the gynaecologist had said. 'You'll have to be patient. It'll happen. Most likely just when you want to go skiing.' They had laughed and gone away reassured.

But so far Nature had remained obdurate and Elizabeth would cry with disappointment as her hopes were dashed again.

James was kind and supportive, comforting her. 'It'll be all right,' he soothed. 'The more you fuss, the longer it'll take. You're twenty-seven, sweetheart, for Christ's sake . . . we've all the time in the world.'

He was an aggressive driver; Elizabeth winced as he shot over a changing traffic light. She looked at him and bit back a protest. She knew he was impatient, consumed with that amazing energy she found so exciting. He had given her so much love, so much enthusiasm for life. He'd made her grow up. 'Jamie,' she said, using his pet name, 'you've got more brains than the rest of them put together. If Heyderman gives you the chance, you go for it!'

He drew into the kerb by the Chichesters' house in Lancaster Gate. Chichester was a rising Tory politician. He could be very influential. James put his hand on her knee. *Go for it*. She could say that with the self-confidence that comes from living in the same house in the same place for generations, and never having to worry about money or what other people thought. Such a different background from his own.

The politician and his wife were good hosts; James

carefully noted the signs of affluence, like good claret, superb food, and some very expensive antiques. The wife was tailor-made for constituency work: rather plain, jolly, no threat to the ladies of the local Association, with two bouncing blond sons and an appetite for charity committees. She would help her ambitious husband reach his goal. James was no fool; he recognized a steely gleam in the eyes. As usual, Elizabeth charmed everyone. She was so naturally nice, he thought, feeling proud of her. Strangely she was no threat to other women either. She was so blatantly in love with her own husband, and she didn't flirt. He often wondered how she managed to be so beautiful and so unselfconscious about it. Confidence again, he supposed. That precious commodity he had acquired so painfully and with such determination.

His father had made money, that and his son's advancement were his only interests. His mother was unhappy in a silent way and drank in secret. When James was up at Oxford his parents finally got divorced. They had only stayed together because of him, and he knew it. He wasn't grateful. He only felt guilty.

He had learned how to cultivate people who would accept him and ignore the ones that never would. He was a brilliant scholar, and he left Oxford with a first and a fine record of academic achievement behind him. He was popular and handsome, and he knew everybody. When he joined Diamond Enterprises it was a surprise to some of the people who knew him. He had been marked down for politics. But D.E. knew their men; they knew what to offer to entice the best potential and they knew how to push them aside and forget about them if they failed in their promise. James hadn't failed; he had got his seat on the London Board at an age when most men were just coming up to the managerial level. He had loved every moment of the climb. And he had studied his colleagues very carefully. They were all possible rivals and he knew they viewed him from the same angle.

He focused upon Dick Kruger, South African born, clever, a man who had failed to fulfil his promise because of his obsession with his secretary. James didn't like Kruger because he was loyal to Arthur Harris. Whatever his ambitions had been in the past they were finished now, and he had settled for loyalty. He was shrewd and could see through people. James felt that Kruger could see through him more clearly than someone like Andrews with his English lack of imagination.

If Arthur fell eventually, and James's ultimate ambition was realized and he succeeded him, then Kruger would have to go, because he had showed himself to be an enemy; there was always danger in keeping someone on when they'd once shown you the knife. The founder of one of the great armaments industries once said of fights in business, 'Never wound, kill.' James took that seriously. He knew his own reputation from the Board down: Hastings is a ruthless bastard. And they were right, he was proud of it.

A year ago Heyderman had drawn him aside after a meeting in England and suggested that he might come out to Johannesburg for a trip. The invitation hadn't come to anything, but it was very significant nevertheless. It was a sign that Heyderman had noticed James.

So he had tried to make an ally of Reece. Reece had signed the cable. He would be coming with Heyderman. Reece was the alter ego of Julius Heyderman. His private secretary, personal assistant, and God knew what else. Reece was the X quantity, completely unknown. There was the one point that united all the members of the Board of the London office; from the Managing Director Arthur Harris down to Andrews, who didn't really hate anybody: they all loathed Reece. Reece was Heyderman's spy. Everyone knew that, but nobody could ever catch him out. Reece spent half the year in London and half in South Africa. He had worked with Heyderman in Johannesburg for many years. James wished he knew a little more about the man, because he felt certain it would give him an entrée to the way Julius Heyderman's mind worked. He had tried hard to cultivate him, asking him to lunch away from the boardroom lunches where it was impossible to talk privately, but Reece never accepted. He wasn't intimate with anyone; no-one had ever seen him smile or heard him laugh, or make any remark except of the most general nature. He was dull and sinister at the same time, and James gave up trying to make contact with him.

He glanced across at his wife and made a signal that it was time they went. She was talking to the politician's wife, and the older woman was obviously enjoying herself. It was extraordinary how well Elizabeth got on with people with whom she had nothing in common. It was part of that alien background of hers that you were always polite and took trouble with people.

They said goodbye to their hosts, and James reminded the politician that he had promised to come to lunch with him and meet some of his fellow directors. They'd be so interested to hear his views on monetary union.

They drove home in silence, but when they stopped outside their own house in Thurloe Square, James put his arm round Elizabeth and kissed her.

'Sweetheart,' he said. 'Wasn't a bad party, was it?'

'I enjoyed it.' She smiled the warm, fond smile which was only given to him. 'I always enjoy things when we're together.'

James said, 'You seemed to be getting on very well with Sally Chichester. What on earth were you talking about?'

'Oh, where to take the boys skiing – she couldn't make up her mind, didn't really want to go to Switzerland. I suggested Austria – it's lovely, and much cheaper. I thought she was quite tough – so was he.'

'You've got to be if you want to get off the Back Benches,' he said. 'He could be very useful. I've asked him to lunch with the Board. Come on, darling, let's go in.'

He wanted to sit on in the car for a bit, holding her and talking, going back to the days before they were married, but it was nearly one o'clock in the morning, and he had a heavy day in front of him. Everyone in the office was keyed up. His fellow director Kruger was expected back from France tomorrow, and the day after was the twenty-fifth. He could hardly wait to see what it was all about. He had wanted to make love to Elizabeth, but he had to be fresh for his work. When they made it to bed at last, he turned on his side and went to sleep.

The tugs drawing barges on the East River were hooting, and all along the waterfront the lights were springing up in the Manhattan skyline, forming the pattern which had come to mean America to every tourist. The tall skyscrapers winked and gleamed and the cars flashed by in streaks of light on the East River Drive. It was the view that had sold Clara Wasserman the apartment. She loved sitting by the window watching the sun set and the light fading and New York turning on the lights until it glittered and sparkled like a magic city. She also loved this bit of river because she had been born within the sound of those hooting tugs and steamers, in an overcrowded tenement on the West Side, which was home to twenty families and where everybody knew everything about everybody else. Even as a child Clara had hated the public life; you couldn't have a row, or make love or be ill or have a child or die, without everyone sharing in it whether you wanted them to or not. But that was fifty years ago, and now she and David had their apartment on East 52nd with its magnificent view, and it was so private and exclusive that the elevator never took more than two passengers at a time, and when it stopped you were at your own front door. The apartment had cost them 1.8 million dollars, and the one thing David complained about was that they spent so little time in it. But then the diamond business involved a lot of travelling; David was always making trips to Johannesburg to see the boss, Julius Heyderman, or to London to see the Managing Director, Arthur Harris, and that wasn't counting the out-of-town trips all over the States. When he and Clara married, David was apprenticed to one of Tiffany's suppliers; he was training to be a cutter. That was a long time ago; they had been married thirty years, and now he was on the Board of Diamond Enterprises. As Clara liked to say to him, you can't go higher than the top.

Everyone in the diamond world knew two things about David Wasserman: he was the world's greatest living expert on rough stones, and he was one of the very few men left who had worked with D.E.'s founders, Jan Heyderman and Pat Harris, in Johannesburg when the gold and diamond empire was being built after the death of Rhodes. He also had a wife who knew nearly as much about the industry as he did, and he never made a decision without talking to her first. They had no children and they were so close mentally and physically that they were like Siamese twins.

Clara turned away from the window. She shouted to her husband, who was in the next room, just as all their families shouted to each other above the din of children crying, neighbours yelling and street noises. She had not lost the habit of her early years.

'David! Aren't you finished yet?'

He came into the room, a little man with a lined face, seamed with years of concentration, his bald head fringed with grey hair. He was a dedicated and immaculate dresser with a passion for English clothes, beautifully cut suits from Savile Row and shoes by Lobb of St James. When he was in London he always carried an umbrella, and he had a dozen, all made for him by Brigg. Even his underwear came from Sulka in Bond Street, and this was something Clara had given up trying to understand.

They had been in bed watching TV when the cable arrived from London the night before:

CONFERENCE CALLED LONDON 25TH. ARRIVING EVENING 24TH. IMPERATIVE YOU ATTEND. KRUGER, ANDREWS, JOHNSON ALSO NOTIFIED. REGARDS, JULIUS.

If Heyderman was recalling the whole London Board of Directors, then there must be a major crisis. The last time there had been trouble Heyderman made the trip to London from South Africa: both the Wassermans remembered it well. Ivan Karakov was one of the biggest jewellers in Europe and America, and he could make a valid claim to occupying the late Harry Winston's throne as the king of the retail jewellery trade.

They had known him for years on a personal as well as a business basis, because he was one of D.E.'s biggest customers for super-quality gems. A little over a year ago he had begun arguing with Arthur Harris about the quality of the diamonds he was buying from them, and the prices he was being charged. As a diamond man himself, Wasserman could sympathize with Karakov's objection to the system of regular diamond sales. Dealers from all over the world came by invitation only, and each one was allotted a parcel of goods at a fixed price. If he argued or complained about the price of the stones, he got a worse parcel next time or no invitation at all. It was as simple as that. David had never pretended that it was a nice way of doing business, but it was certainly effective. It kept the price of diamonds pegged, and controlled the supplies, even if it meant breaking the backs of mining companies and retail firms alike who tried to go outside it. D.E. had so many interests in all branches of industry that it was like an octopus, and, whether you liked him or not, it needed a Chairman like Julius Heyderman to control it properly. He had come on to New York and seen Karakov personally to persuade him to accept his allocation of diamonds, promising they would be of better quality. They had worked out a kind of compromise which satisfied Karakov for a while. It was an indication of just how important Karakov was in the industry that Julius had crossed the world to see him.

'Packing,' David Wasserman said. 'Always packing! I don't know why we don't sell this apartment and live in a hotel!'

'Because you like it here,' his wife said. 'I like it, too. Why don't you quit grumbling? Isn't it better to be home for a few months in our own place? I'll get Martha to finish the packing for you, if you're tired.'

'You overwork that woman,' David said. 'I keep telling you, Clara, one day she'll leave. Then what will we do, eh? You want a drink?'

'Not right now. I'll go tell Martha to finish up for you.' Then she said suddenly, 'You think this London meeting is something to do with Ivan Karakov?'

'I don't know,' David shrugged. He was mixing himself a gin and tonic from the bar at the other side of the room. The decorator who did their apartment had made the bar in the top half of a Chippendale bookcase. All the Wassermans' furniture was eighteenth-century English with a few Early American pieces of great rarity. By contrast, their pictures were modern. There was a Braque hanging above the mantelpiece and a very fine Buffet in the dining-room which they had bought quite cheaply in Paris when he first began exhibiting. Their taste was faultless.

'I don't know for sure, but I just have a feeling, that's all.'

'But Ivan's been happy lately, hasn't he?' Clara said. 'When they were over last July, they were so friendly –

we went to the theatre, they took us to dinner. Ever since, Laura kisses me when we meet . . . Why should it be him?'

'I told you,' David said, 'I don't know. OK, so he's friendly, and his wife kissed you. You ever heard of the kiss of death, Clara?'

'You don't like her.' His wife smiled and made a little gesture with her hands. A blue-white diamond cut in the famous Karakov style, a long baton, blazed like a meteor on her hand. 'You don't like the woman, that's all. You think Ivan's been nice with us because he's up to something, is that it? You could be right. But you got any other reason you haven't told me? You know something I don't know?'

He never kept anything from her, and she knew it. But he was uneasy about Ivan Karakov, and not just because he thought Laura Karakov was pure poison. Which she was, of course.

Clara returned to the attack. 'Well,' she said, 'you know something. Tell me.'

David shrugged. 'OK, OK, but it's just a hunch, that's all. I got nothing really to go on. Someone saw that guy Mirkovitch coming out of Karakov's office when he was here last month,' David said. 'I wondered what he was doing there. I still wonder.'

'Maybe Ivan wants to do a deal with Mirkovitch,' Clara said.

David dismissed the idea, with contempt. 'He wouldn't touch the Russians. He wouldn't dare, behind our backs. Change your mind, Clara, have a drink. We got another hour before we go.'

'All right.' She said it over her shoulder as she went out, and he heard her calling to the maid to finish his packing and put the cases in the hall for the doorman to take down.

He always grumbled that they were over seventy, and long journeys were for young men. But it didn't matter.

He couldn't have resisted that cable if he'd been on his deathbed. He'd still have caught the plane to London for this meeting. Next to the imponderable, shining beauty of diamonds, the fascination of the endless struggle for power would hold him in the business until the day he died. Diamonds were the real secret. The others fought over them, looked for them, dug them up, cheated and lied and intrigued to get control of them, but only men like David Wasserman loved them for themselves. He loved all diamonds, even the poor little stones.

A few hours later, the 747 streaked ahead in the night sky, and he slept beside his wife in the first-class section. Up in the forward lounge, the duty hostess read a novel.

'You're sure you want to come? It shouldn't mean more than a couple of days.' Dick Kruger reached out for her hand. They were side by side on mattresses, baking in the sun round the pool at the Hotel Du Cap. They went there every year; his wife Valerie had hated it, disliking the ostentation and vulgarity of the super-rich clientele. But she could never criticize the hotel itself. The setting, food and service were superb.

Ruth was not like his wife. She loved the money and the luxury. She smiled at him, her fingers twining in his. She was very dark, with curiously cat-like green eyes; she was small and slim, but the nut-brown body, barely covered in a brief bikini, was voluptuous, with a full bosom and rounded hips. She was thirty-three, unmarried, and she had been his secretary for eight months before she caught him. The affair had begun on one of his long trips abroad. He'd taken her with him because she was tri-lingual in French and German, and more than fluent in Spanish and Italian. There had been the possibility of a deal in Guinea, where illicit diggers had moved on to a rich alluvial field. Kruger had set up a number of small buying offices under the control of

Diamond Enterprises which offered top prices for cash and thus plugged a major leak on to the free market. Guinea was a primitive country with few facilities, but Kruger had got tired of Valerie's refusal to travel to places like Sydney or even New York. She was bored by business trips, and didn't make a secret of it. So he took his new secretary along, because of her facility with French, which was the common language, and because she was eager to go. He had felt lonely on a lot of trips, and he was pleased to have the company. Someone to talk to when the day's business was done, rather than sitting alone drinking in some fifth-rate hotel with dodgy air-conditioning.

He hadn't meant to go to bed with her. They'd had a lot to drink, the hot spiced food had made them both sweat, and suddenly she had looked at him and said, 'I think you're the most attractive man I've met in years. I must be pissed . . . I'm sorry.'

And Dick Kruger had looked into the green eyes and heard himself say, 'That's what I've been thinking about you . . .'

'So, why don't we do something about it?' She had a husky voice, and she ran a hand down his bare moist arm. 'Let's go upstairs,' she said. 'We can take a shower.'

Kruger had stood up. She had hold of his hand and her finger caressed his palm. 'If there's any water,' he muttered, pulling her from the table.

'Even if there isn't,' Ruth Fraser said, and she laughed.

It was the most revealing sexual experience of his life, and he was a man who liked women and enjoyed having sex. Ruth was different. She called up a virility he'd thought was diminishing with middle age. She aroused him, satisfied him, then brought him back to a peak again and again, until he marvelled at himself.

The next morning, she was business-like and in control

of the situation. All she said was, 'Thank you for the best night of my life. Now I have your schedule here. You're meeting the Minister at ten o'clock.' She smiled at him. She had white, beautiful teeth. And they were sharp, as he now knew.

'Which probably means any time up to eleven. And they're sending a car for you to go to the mining area at around three-thirty.'

He'd said, 'I want you to come with us. You've never seen the sharp end of the business. And if they get too technical you can translate.'

'I'd be fascinated,' she said, and he knew that she meant it. 'Thank you, Mr Kruger.'

That touched him. She wasn't going to take advantage. 'Dick,' he said.

She smiled and nodded. 'Dick,' she repeated in that silky voice.

They made love every night, and often during the blistering afternoons. By the time they travelled back to England, he was addicted. They stopped off for a break in Paris, making some excuse to the London office, and he bought her some expensive clothes and a gold bracelet from Boucheron. He took her out to dinner at the Crillon in her new dress and everyone stared at them. It gave him a real glow to be seen with her.

He had felt guilty about cheating on Valerie, but, as time passed and he shared his business life and his sex life with Ruth, that guilt changed to resentment. He was childless, because his wife had had an abortion before they married, and couldn't have a baby because of complications. For years he had suppressed his disappointment and his anger, now it surfaced. What, he asked himself, was he getting out of this marriage?

Valerie had become a woman he no longer wanted. A woman who wouldn't travel because she found his business boring, who spent money on entertaining people with whom he had little in common and kept an expensive house which he didn't regard as home any more. Home was Ruth Fraser's flat, where he talked over the day's problems with someone who shared his passion for Diamond Enterprises, commiserated with his disappointments or frustrations, and encouraged him to believe he still had a big future. And then there was the marvellous invigorating sex Ruth gave him, making the middle years drop away till he felt as potent as a bull. She had said to him one evening when they'd been together for a year, 'Why don't you move out? We can have a place together. Why do we have to go on lying? Valerie won't care. You spend nights away and she doesn't even bother to check up. Why don't you talk to her?'

And he had said, 'You're right. I'll do that.' He had been so relieved.

Prepared to be generous, he had offered his wife anything she wanted if she would let him go gracefully. But she wouldn't. She'd fought. She'd pleaded, she'd reproached, she'd refused a divorce under five years . . . He didn't see her reaction as love for him because he didn't want to. He saw it through Ruth's viewfinder: Valerie was spiteful and holding out for money. They bought a Chelsea house and were openly living together. And working together. In the office Ruth still called him Mr Kruger. Then, as hard as she had resisted, his wife suddenly gave in. She agreed to a divorce in two years, accepting the settlement he offered. She wrote a sad and dignified letter, saying he was making a mistake but she accepted that he didn't love her any more. There was no point in fighting for him. He had read it and thrown it away. He was damned if she was going to make him feel guilty as a parting shot.

Beside him, rubbing sun oil into her legs, Ruth looked at him and frowned. Their holiday in France was over; she accepted that. He talked soothingly of a couple of days' interruption as if she was a fool and didn't know the implications of an emergency meeting with Julius as well as he did.

She said, 'It's trouble, isn't it? And I'm coming back with you, darling.' She stopped the sun oil and smiled at him. 'I'm not missing out on the drama. I'd go crazy sitting here not being part of it.'

He was so grateful. Another woman would have complained, or looked martyred. Valerie would have simply exploded at the intrusion. But Ruth understood. She was with him every step of the way. He talked everything over with her; he listened to her opinions and often followed her advice. 'I love you,' he said. 'It's time we got married.'

She lay back, stretching in the hot sun. 'No hurry,' she murmured. 'Let's see what the hell Heyderman wants first.'

And he knew that she meant every word.

Ray Andrews had been a director of Diamond Enterprises for five years. He was still under fifty and he had started work in the accounts department of the London office twenty years ago with a wife and one child, and no private income or expectations. He was a quiet man with a brilliant accountant's brain, and he had begun to rise steadily after the first year. It was not just a genius for figures that brought him to the notice of the management, but an acute political sense which could forecast the economic trends in Europe, America and the Far East; trends which controlled the price of metals and soft commodities in places as far from each other as Tokyo and the Ivory Coast.

Whenever there was a tax problem, or a question of economic aid to a country where D.E. had interests, Andrews packed up and flew off to sort it out. He and his wife Susan had married very young, and they had three children. They were a united family; early financial struggles had brought them very close together, and, though he was now in the £150,000-a-year bracket, they still lived modestly in a house in Swiss Cottage, and saved as much of his salary as they could. Their daughter was at home; and their elder son was in Canada, teaching, and his brother was reading Economics at Reading University.

Their small circle of friends didn't include anyone connected with Ray Andrews' business, because Susan didn't feel at home with the smart wives of the other executives. She was a gentle, homely woman, passionately interested in her brilliant husband and her children, but painfully shy with strangers. On the rare occasions when she had to meet the Harrises at some official party or dinner, she was nervous and gauche, and Julius Heyderman himself absolutely terrified her.

Ray had therefore never become intimate with any of his fellow directors except Dick Kruger, who was slightly older, and Susan had made a genuine effort to like him for her husband's sake. Kruger had been a tough, ambitious man in the early years, but now his star was fixed, and there was no surer proof of this than Arthur Harris's close friendship with him. He had left his wife after thirty years for his secretary, Ruth Fraser, and this had made Susan feel uncomfortable when she met them together. The girl was typical of the tough career woman, hard as nails and quite without embarrassment.

The scandal was an old one now, and the position between Kruger and his secretary was generally accepted, but Ray said it hadn't done him any good to get found out. His wife Valerie had been well liked, and people were sorry for her.

There was a new director, James Hastings, whom Ray and particularly Dick distrusted and disliked. Kruger's suspicions of him were pathological, he was so jealous of the up-and-coming men. Susan, meeting Hastings and his wife once or twice a year at the usual office functions, thought him smooth on the surface, but hard and supercilious underneath. He was definitely on the make. His wife had a title. Dick Kruger said nastily, 'She would,' and that was enough to tie Susan up in knots of shyness before she opened her mouth. Her own background was middle-class professional; her father had been a small-town estate agent, and her entire life was sheltered and, in modern parlance, distinctly unsmart. But, on the whole, the business didn't intrude much into the Andrews' private life, except when it took him away on trips, and then she was miserable and moped, and wrote long letters asking when he was coming home.

He sat back in the Underground, and opened his *Evening Standard*. He went halfway through the newspaper without taking in a word, then he folded it and put it away in his overcoat pocket. Heyderman was coming, and nobody – not even Arthur Harris himself – knew what was wrong. Everyone was being dragged back for this special conference no matter what they were doing or where they were, and there were a lot of worried people in the London office.

Ray Andrews was worried too. He had a very keen instinct for trouble, which was part of his business acumen, but what he couldn't decide was what relation it might have to the only major mistake in his career. Five years ago he had gone out to Russia to get a concession for the rights to a new discovery in Archangel. The team of investigating geologists had been encouraging, and then enthusiastic; kimberlite rocks had been found, and while this didn't prove diamonds existed on that site, diamonds in depth were never found without that particular rock formation. Later reports indicated several kimberlite pipes, and by this time the team was really excited. Andrews' negotiations had been successful; the only minor point of delay was the Minister for Nuclear and Mining Development's insistence on coming to London to sign the agreement, but this was the usual way of getting a trip to London at the company's expense. Andrews came home to get Arthur's agreement to the final draft, and left an assistant in Moscow to keep a watch. A week later the whole thing blew up in his face. The Minister was arrested, charged with corruption in office, and the negotiations stopped dead. Andrews flew back on the next plane to take over, and forwarded the relevant papers to the Minister's successor. The papers were returned to him after a fortnight when all his attempts to see the new man were frustrated, with a curt note explaining that negotiations on the concession to mine the area had been suspended indefinitely while the financial links of his imprisoned predecessor with Western companies were being correlated prior to his trial. Andrews had been escorted to the airport.

They had never succeeded in getting a foot in that particular door. The Soviet Union broke up, and when the political situation stabilized, Moscow supplied the technical expertise to deal with exploration and development. Westerners were not invited. Andrews had lived with that shadow over his career ever since. It wasn't lifted by rumours that the deposits in Archangel were very rich indeed.

The tube train pulled into Swiss Cottage, and he pushed his way on to the platform. It was Monday the 23rd. Less than forty-eight hours to wait, then he would sit round the big table in the boardroom on the top floor of Diamond House and find out if that one unlucky incident, forever viewed as his blunder, was connected with the summons from Heyderman. He had a wretched feeling that it was. He checked his watch. He and Susan planned to take their daughter to the cinema to see the latest Spielberg epic. He decided not to mention his worries to his wife. She took everything to heart, fiercely loyal to him and unable to be of any help because she couldn't master the complexities of his business. He made up his mind to put his fear aside and enjoy the evening.

Thank God for his family. He had always kept his priorities right.

'Why do we *always* have to interrupt our holiday?' she demanded. 'Last year he called you back after ten days. He does it on purpose!'

She looked up at him, scowling. Reece didn't want her to be upset; he'd broken the news to her tactfully, assuring her it wouldn't be for long, dreading her temper and the sulks that would follow. Her bad moods lasted for days sometimes, and he had no defence against her. He loved her so much and he couldn't bear it when they were at odds with each other. They had been enjoying their holiday in Malaga; there were so many beautiful places to visit, and they were keen sightseers. They toured the ancient villages, staying a night or two at small hotels, then moving on. It was their perfect holiday; neither liked swimming or lying on beaches in the sun. They were so happy together, so ideally suited. She had taken the news that he had to go to London for a Board meeting very calmly, and he had imagined there wouldn't be a storm. Now, as he was undressing, and she lay naked on the bed, her body silvery in the shuttered gloom, she began to abuse Julius Heyderman and complain angrily about the disruption of their holiday. He knew she was jealous because he was so loyal to his boss. She accused him of putting Heyderman's interests before her happiness; he always denied it angrily. It was the only cause of their infrequent rows. They agreed on everything else, shared everything else.

'Darling,' he protested. 'Don't spoil our evening. I've got to go. You'll be all right here, it'll only take a few days then I'll be back.'

He sat on the edge of the big bed beside her. He stroked her gently in the way she liked.

'Come on,' he wheedled. 'We've got our lovely siesta time . . . then we'll go for a drive, it'll be nice and cool by then. I've looked up a new place to eat, and we can have some good wine. You know how much you enjoy that . . .'

She turned her head away, and said, punishing him, 'I don't feel like going anywhere. What am I supposed to do on my own? You know how lonely I get – I won't wait around here, I'll go home.'

He spoiled her, he admitted that, but then he liked to indulge her, pander to her silly whims. It made him feel strong and protective. She had jerked away from his caressing hand.

'Don't,' she said. 'I don't feel like that, either.'

It was useless to stand against her; he wanted her so much, the sight of her lying there, her legs drawn up against him, roused him till he was ready to beg. He had to make peace. 'I'll do it the way you liked last time,' he whispered, capitulating. 'I can't go away with you feeling angry with me . . . You'll be miserable, too, you know you will.' He put his hands on her and shifted her on to her stomach. She was very thin and light. He stroked her back and buttocks.

She turned her head to look at him and sighed. He was right. She'd fret and suffer if they parted without making it up. 'I hate the Heydermans,' she muttered, more to herself than to him. 'Especially him. He rules our lives . . .'

Reece woke first. She slept like a child, her mouth ajar, exhausted and sated. He'd known how to win her round. He smiled fondly and slipped out of bed to shower the sweat away. He hoped she'd hear him and come to join him, splashing and laughing under the water. Or she could sleep on and he'd wake her later. He'd made a note of the best restaurant some ten kilometres away in the next town. They'd make it a special evening, the best food, plenty of the strong Spanish wine she loved. She always wanted sex after she'd been drinking wine. They were abstemious at home, careful with money, leading quite frugal lives. On holiday they splurged. It would be the best evening of the holiday so far. 'And there'll be more like it when I come back,' he promised. 'We'll stay a few days longer, so you won't miss out. I'll ring every day. Mind you don't fall for any Spaniard while I'm gone . . .'

2

Arthur Harris was a small man; he had a full head of greying hair that grew back from an intelligent forehead and the forehead was part of a sensitive face. The nose was too long and the lips too thin; he had never been good-looking, and now his skin had the same greyish tinge as his hair. His very dark eyes looked out on the world with sadness. Socially, he possessed great charm. Outside his role as Managing Director of D.E. London Arthur led a varied life; he loved sailing, and was a member of the Royal Yacht Squadron. He had a fine Carolean house near Hamble, and sailed most weekends. He collected pictures, mostly seventeenth-century Dutch landscapes; he chose them with care and love of beauty. He read a great deal; there were few subjects he was unable to discuss, and he was an erudite and witty conversationalist.

From the moment he came through the big, glass-fronted doors of the offices in Blackfriars Road, he changed completely. He sat in his office behind a fine eighteenth-century French desk and conducted the operation of Diamond Enterprises London with the ruthlessness inherited from his grandfather. Pat Harris had left Canada where he had been prospecting and settled in South Africa. There he teamed up with Jan Heyderman from Holland. Secretly, Arthur hated the great man; he seemed to the boy an oversized Dutch bully with a bellowing voice that could be heard from one end of a mine shaft to the other. And he had always hated Julius. They had grown up together, two ill-assorted characters, bound to one another by the association of their grandfathers. Arthur's grandfather Pat Harris was the junior partner. The disparity in the two heirs' positions carried over into adult life, when the boys went into business and found their adult feelings were embittered by the added friction of power politics.

Physically they were poles apart. Julius was very tall, built like a heavyweight, his personality so strong he dominated any gathering. He had always made Arthur feel inadequate. They were natural enemies even before he had married Julius's sister.

Arthur knew that only his enormous stock-holdings in Diamond Enterprises prevented his brother-in-law from throwing him off the Board. He also knew that, in spite of the seeming impossibility of doing it, Julius Heyderman was determined that one day he would succeed.

In retaliation, Arthur was equally determined to stay as Managing Director of the London business until the last moment of his working life.

Arthur got the news that his brother-in-law Julius was arriving when he returned from a trip to the boat yard. He was thinking of having a new boat built for Cowes next year. He hadn't mentioned it to his wife, because he never told her anything if he could help it. She was as keen on sailing as he was, and very competent, but she made their only common interest a weapon to use against him. If he mentioned the new boat, she would sneer, humiliating him. He had long guarded against her tongue by keeping her at a distance.

Christina Heyderman Harris was a good-looking woman in her early fifties, who had once been beautiful. She had shared her brother's blond colouring and she had the same remarkably clear blue eyes. But disappointment and hatred for her husband had soured her looks as it had distorted her character. Her mouth was thin and turned down, her expression set in a habitual sneer as if she had just seen him make a fool of himself. She was twenty-two and the biggest catch in South African society when she fell in love with Arthur. Arthur was slight, sensitive in looks and manner, so different from the hearty sports-mad friends surrounding her brother that she was fascinated by the contrast. She indulged in a romantic fantasy about the quiet, reserved young man, convinced that she had found a soul-mate. He talked about art, about the theatre, about books.

Unlike her other admirers, Arthur assumed that Christina had a brain, which was true. Not till they married did he discover that she had a voracious sexual appetite which he was expected to satisfy. He couldn't. He tried, and the birth of their only child held out some hope, but the decline was rapid, as his self-confidence suffered repeated failure and her dissatisfaction turned to contempt. And then to loathing. Everything Christina had once found attractive – his gentle manner, his artistic and intellectual interests – grated upon her as evidence of his feebleness and lack of virility. But she would never leave him because of the boy. She adored her son. He was a big, brawny child who grew into a strapping Heyderman clone. Good at all forms of athletics, dim at school, cutting a swathe through the women, regardless of age, but always dominated by and devoted to his mother. He despised his father because from babyhood he sensed that Christina did. He modelled himself on his uncle, but failed because he hadn't inherited the intelligence of either set of genes. For his sake, Christina had denied herself the lovers she would have taken without a qualm of conscience about Arthur. Nothing must upset her boy. No divorce must interfere with his education and development. His life must never be blighted by a broken home. Instead it was blighted by his parents' mutual hatred, and his own role of manipulator. She had taken the message from Arthur's secretary, and felt elated at the arrival of her brother. She had been very close to Julius from childhood, right through to the time when she defied him and married Arthur. She had refused to listen to him, and paid the penalty of nearly thirty years' unhappiness. She had never told him what went wrong, she didn't need to; she was sure he guessed. He'd said at the time of her engagement, 'He's a bloody little wimp! His balls are in his brain, Christa . . . he won't make you happy . . .' She was sure he knew why the marriage was so patently wretched. Now he was coming to London, and that must mean trouble for Arthur.

She had been reading when Arthur came back. She put the book down and said, 'There's a message for you. By the telephone.' She didn't say what it was. She just watched his face as he read it. He recognized her writing. He couldn't keep that a secret. He nerved himself.

'Julius is coming over,' he said.

'I know,' she slipped a marker between the pages of her book. 'I wonder why? Something your end must have gone wrong.'

'Why my end!' he demanded irritably. 'Why must you assume that I'm at fault? But then you can't help it.' He turned away, threw the scrap of paper in the waste-basket.

'Because Julius wouldn't come over at this time of year and bring all the others back from holiday unless there was a real crisis, and it's not back home, or I would have heard. So . . .' she lingered on the word, '. . . it must be London. And that's you, isn't it?'

He had been playing this game for so many weary years. He was tired. 'If you say so,' he shrugged. Indifference was his best defence. Christina thrived on arguments. 'Anyway, I shall know in two days' time.'

'I see those Americans are coming over,' she said. His secretary had volunteered answers to all her questions. She had always been charming to Arthur's staff. That way they told her things he didn't want her to know.

'The Wassermans . . . Yes . . . you know, he's a director.'

'I hope you're not going to ask them down here,' she said. 'Dreadful old bores. I couldn't think of anything to say to either of them . . . and you asked them to *stay* . . .'

'I won't do it this time,' Arthur said quietly. 'You made them so uncomfortable that they wouldn't want to again. I shall take them out in London.'

Christina picked up her book. She felt that she had won that round. 'Thank God for that,' she said. 'I am surprised Julius didn't call you personally. Just sending a message by that awful Reece seems rather offhand. Or don't you think so? I do. Very casual, as if you didn't count more than any of the others . . .'

In spite of himself, Arthur's pale face flushed. She knew the weak spot and she dug into it without mercy. Julius despised him, and treated him accordingly. Arthur believed, wrongly in this instance, that his wife had confided their domestic differences to her brother. He bore her a deep, cold hatred for that betrayal.

'He's busy,' he said coldly. 'Probably doesn't want to come over. He doesn't mean to hurt intentionally. He's not like you.' He turned and walked out. He never slammed a door. He heard her laugh as he closed it.

Trouble. She was right, of course. He had an instinct for things going wrong. It had never failed him. He was a quiet man, but could fight as hard and dirty as Julius Heyderman if he had to; he prepared himself for battle. The same instinct whispered to him that their loss of the mine in Archangel had come back to haunt him.

The boardroom of the London office was a strange anachronism in an ultra-modern building. It was a long room with a low ceiling, and the walls were panelled in genuine sixteenth-century linenfold panelling. The table was a magnificent single-piece Elizabethan refectory, fourteen feet long, and the chairs were of the same period.

With some regard for comfort, they had cushions and seats of crimson velvet. Overhead, there was an early Dutch brass chandelier, a museum piece in itself, like the Persian carpet on the floor, and the superbly carved oak court cupboard, which was full of liquor. The room was dark and restful; everything in it had cost a fortune and it was an exact copy of old Jan Heyderman's office in Johannesburg when he was at the height of his power. When his grandson Julius succeeded, he had stripped the original boardroom down to its walls and had it redecorated by one of the most advanced designers in the Union. Julius didn't want people coming to his boardroom and thinking of his grandfather.

All the directors were there, sitting on each side of the narrow table. In front of each there was a note pad, pen and pencils, a small bottle of mineral water and a crystal glass, and the print-out minutes of the last meeting. In the middle of the table, where Julius would sit in a rather larger chair than the others, there was a small decanter of whisky and a jug of water. For the last few minutes the door had been opening; first to come in was Dick Kruger, and then James Hastings; they nodded to each other and were spared the trouble of talking because Ray Andrews arrived, followed by David Wasserman, and for a minute or two the conversation was general. It paused as Arthur appeared; he looked round him and went over to David Wasserman. He was always very courteous to people.

'Very good of you to make the trip, David,' he said. 'I hope Clara's not too tired.'

The old man shrugged and smiled. 'You know Clara – business never tired her yet. I left her sleeping like a baby.'

'Gentlemen,' Arthur said, 'Julius will be here in a moment; I suggest we sit down.'

He went to the end of the table; he had mineral water in front of him like everyone else. He watched the rest of the Board taking their places. Senior men like Kruger and Wasserman were on his right and left, Ray Andrews sat next to the other director, Johnson who was European Sales Director and a mining engineer, then, nearer the end, sat Hastings. There were two empty places; they were waiting for the Chairman, Heyderman. When Julius came in everybody looked up. Then they stood up, casually, so as not to make it appear more than a wish to give the Chairman a personal welcome, but he walked past them without stopping and Reece was behind him, pulling out his chair. Reece sat down on Heyderman's left. If there had ever been any doubt how close Reece was to the Chairman, it was answered now.

'Good morning, gentlemen.' Julius Heyderman looked round the room and nodded to them all. He seemed even browner and fitter than when they had last seen him, a handsome, blue-eyed giant, with the trim athletic figure of a young man. He always wore blue; it was almost a trademark. The sky-blue shirt and dark blue suit were part of the Heyderman image, part of the legend of the international sportsman, crack shot, champion water-skier, scratch golfer. The legend was quite true. Everything Julius did had to be done better than anyone else; he had always lived to the limit of his capacity, and he worked at the same pace as he played games. Everyone in the room seemed to shrink by comparison. James Hastings watched him intently; here was power personified. He was like a god, with health, magnetism and good looks seldom found in millionaires, and Julius couldn't have counted his millions. James felt an odd excitement rising in him; he felt as he supposed the corps commanders under Napoleon or Wellington must have done when they sat in on the final conference before the battle. Heyderman glanced down the table towards his brother-in-law Arthur, who looked slighter and greyer, by comparison.

'We had better get down to the real business straight

away,' he said. 'That all right with you, Arthur? We can go into the routine stuff later.'

'Of course,' Arthur said mildly.

'Right. Now, gentlemen, I've come a long way in a hell of a hurry; some of you know me well enough to realize I wouldn't do this myself or ask it of you unless there was a very good reason. Some two weeks ago I received word that the new mine near Archangel is in full production. It's a bonanza!'

Ray Andrews glanced quickly at Arthur Harris. His instincts had been right. Five years later that one mistake had caught up with him.

'This, gentlemen, is a big mine. I needn't remind you that it should have been ours.' Julius's blue eyes stared down at his brother-in-law.

'I don't think that's relevant.' Arthur's voice was calm and cold. Inwardly he was shaking with anger. The great bastard – sitting there, rebuking him publicly. 'We've never depended on the ownership of every mine. We control the outlet for the stones. We will in this case, if the Russians want to sell on the world markets.'

Julius ignored him. 'This looks like a mine with a long life and there's no reason to suppose that their output will decrease. But that's not all.' He looked round at them, searching each face, and even David Wasserman began to feel uneasy. Heyderman cleared his throat. 'I said the mine was a bonanza. It's much more. It's not just yielding top-quality gemstones, but fancies.'

They all looked up at that. 'Fancies' – the trade name for the coveted coloured diamonds. Julius went on. 'They're bringing up some of the biggest, cleanest brown stones, Canaries, and blues ever mined. But, more than that, they're bringing up these.'

As he spoke, he plunged his hand into his breast pocket and brought out a clenched fist. He opened it. A two-inch square of white paper lay in his palm. He unwrapped it slowly. The stone blazed on the white surface like a big drop of blood. The fire and colour danced in the light as he held it out in front of them all.

'My God,' David muttered. 'My God . . .' He could hardly speak. He reached out and Heyderman put the diamond into his hand. It trembled. 'Never . . .' He was shaking his head. 'Never in my life . . .'

'Five carats,' Heyderman announced. 'Flawless. There's never been a red diamond like it in the history of diamonds. And,' his voice rose, 'this is not the biggest. This is a *sample*! This is the appetizer for the biggest investor of gems in the world.'

Abdullah Bin Saladin, Chief Minister and blood brother of the King of Saudi Arabia. His collection of rare stones was unique, beyond price. He had tried and, through the error of a telephone bidder, failed to buy the only red diamond to come on the market in half a century. It had weighed under a carat. It had gone to a private collector in Japan.

'There are greens, too,' Julius told them. 'Big stones, marvellous colour and purity. But these . . .' He took the red diamond from David and held it between thumb and forefinger. 'These are beyond calculation, beyond price.'

Kruger said, 'But they can't sell them. Not without us. They're valueless if they can't market them . . .' He left the rest unsaid because he had seen the sick expression on Arthur's face.

'Karakov can market them,' Julius Heyderman said. 'And my information is that he's about to sign an agreement with Moscow which makes him their sole outlet onto the world markets. By-passing us and breaking the cartel that's held the industry together since my grandfather bought out Barnato. We have a monopoly on distribution, gentlemen, and that monopoly is vital if diamonds are to keep their value. The trade doesn't like us, but without us they wouldn't have survived. The bottom would have fallen out of the market for industrials and gems when the world went into recession

40

in the Thirties. We *are* diamonds. If our grip on prices is broken by Karakov or any other bastard, we go down and the whole industry falls with us.'

There was a silence then.

Finally David Wasserman said, 'He could try it and he'd enjoy the risk. He's an egomaniac.' He said it again, 'He just could try it—'

'And succeed,' Heyderman said harshly. 'He is to the jewellery trade what we are to the rough trade. He cuts, sets and sells everything he buys. He's the only real heavyweight since Harry Winston, and Christ knows, he gave trouble enough . . . Reece, you have the figures for Karakov's turnover for the year?'

Reece got up, taking a sheaf of papers from his briefcase. 'I have them here, Mr Julius.' He always addressed his employer in the terminology of a past generation, before the false chumminess of Christian names became common usage. He cleared his throat slightly. 'The house in Paris and the secondary establishments in London, New York and Hong Kong sold nearly a billion dollars' worth of goods last year. The big Middle East clients, like Prince Abdullah now like to buy direct from Paris. I haven't got the exact figures but I expect to get them in the next few weeks, and I'll let you have them immediately.'

God knows, Hastings thought, how he managed to get copies of Karakov's company accounts.

Industrial espionage was widely practised in all the major industries throughout the world. Morally indefensible, but one of the hard facts of business life. That was Reece's sphere of operations. He produced the results, and nobody asked him how he got his information. Someone in Karakov's organization, in a senior position in the accounts department, had passed on those figures, and only Reece would ever know who it was.

'We'll stop Karakov, of course,' Arthur Harris said. 'The thing I propose is to fly to Paris this evening and see Ivan myself. Talk to him face to face. I'm sure I can make him see reason. He can't be unaware of the long-term consequences of this deal with Russia.'

'He's Russian born,' Kruger remarked. 'He'd like to be back in the fold now capitalism is the new creed. I think David's right; he's all ego.'

He was trying to warn Arthur Harris not to take on something that would fatally damage him if it failed. Harris understood the warning, but he had to do something to regain the initiative. So far Julius Heyderman had completely dominated the meeting. He said, 'I think he'll talk to me. We've always had a friendly relationship.'

For a moment, Hastings saw Heyderman glance at his brother-in-law, and then, with a slight shrug, turn to Reece.

'Have you got a copy of that confidential letter Karakov sent to Mirkovitch in July?'

Again the briefcase opened and the photocopy was in his hand; it was like watching a magician doing card tricks.

'Read it,' Heyderman said flatly. 'Just the relevant paragraphs.'

Reece slipped on his glasses; they gave him a sinister aspect, thick rimmed with wide black side pieces.

He scanned down the page. 'It's here,' he said, not looking up at Arthur Harris. ' "It's been such a pleasure to negotiate with you; my frustrations with D.E. over the years have been brought to breaking point by the devious and short-sighted attitude of Harris in London, whose word simply cannot be trusted. I look forward to a long and fruitful partnership with you, the Archangel Mining Corporation and the Russian government. I look forward to meeting President Yeltsin and to visiting the site . . ." etc.' Reece stopped and slid the paper back into his briefcase. He knew he was called a spy, a creeper who did the Chairman's dirty work. Too often Arthur Harris had vented his feelings about Heyderman on his underling Reece; this was Reece's moment. He looked down at his hands folded on top of the desk and allowed himself a slight smile.

There was absolute silence in the room. Ray Andrews lit a cigarette. It was so still the lighter rasped like a hacksaw. Arthur Harris's pale face had flushed. Kruger came to his defence. He glared at Reece aggressively. 'Are you sure that's genuine?'

'Absolutely,' Reece answered. 'It has the same provenance as the other documents. It came out of Karakov's personal correspondence file. It was an informal letter, not a company memo. It wasn't intended for general viewing.' He said it very softly, as if he were apologizing.

Arthur Harris didn't look at him, or at his brother-in-law, who had just humiliated him in front of them all. Deliberately. He said, 'In view of this, I should not try to negotiate. I'd like to say that his personal opinion does not concern me in the least. My only concern is what is best for our business.'

James Hastings had to admire him for that. He had shown quiet dignity in the face of a calculated and brutal insult, orchestrated by Heyderman. But it wasn't any good being dignified when you couldn't strike back.

Heyderman made a gesture, which didn't fool anybody, least of all his victim. 'We should have taken a tougher line with him in the beginning,' he said. 'Don't worry, we'll nail the old bastard. As I see it, we've got to plan this like a battle. Attack the problem on two fronts. First, someone's got to go to Moscow and get to the Minister of Mining Development. And, if necessary, to President Yeltsin. Someone with the know-how and the weight to undermine their confidence in Karakov, and persuade them that he doesn't have the resources to market their stones properly without us. Point out what a trade free-for-all would do to the market and to their hopes of substantial foreign currency.'

He looked at Ray Andrews.

'You negotiated with them five years ago. You know the country and the set-up. You may be able to rectify that mistake when you lost us the mine. Will you take it on?'

Ray Andrews was not a coward; his moral principles had sometimes caused embarrassment. He had boobed, and he accepted the responsibility. Even though he knew it was a poisoned chalice.

'I will,' he said firmly. 'I'll fly out to Moscow and report back on the situation, if introductions can be arranged through our Embassy. I'll need all the diplomatic pressure I can get if I want an interview at the top.'

'I'll put that in train,' Arthur Harris said quickly. 'We have excellent relations with the Foreign Office; they'll be glad to help.'

'Good,' to their surprise Julius Heyderman pushed back his chair. 'We'll break for an early lunch. I've got an appointment. Reconvene at one forty-five. Then we can discuss how to deal with Karakov and who's going to do it.'

They lunched in the directors' dining-room. Arthur did not believe in the canteen culture, as he described it. He didn't lunch with his employees. He wouldn't have enjoyed it, nor, he maintained, would they. James hesitated. He didn't want to sit with them, to listen to enemies like Kruger and yesterday's men like Andrews and Wasserman, picking over the bones of the meeting. He wanted to go to his office, order a sandwich sent up from the canteen, and think things through. Arthur Harris didn't want to eat lunch anyway, but he knew he was among friends and he could speak his mind. But not with Hastings listening. He paused and said pleasantly, 'Are you joining us, James, or are you busy?'

James was glad to take the hint. 'I am,' he said. 'I've got a heap on my plate at the moment . . . If you'll excuse me I'll grab something and work through till the afternoon. Interesting development, I must say.'

'Very interesting,' Arthur Harris agreed. 'But it's just another problem. We'll solve it.' He gave James his sad smile and went through into the private dining-room.

'See you at quarter to two,' Ray Andrews said, following him. He was good natured, and he wasn't jealous of Hastings. Dick Kruger went after him without saying anything. He couldn't hide his feelings, and with James he didn't even try.

They had a drink before lunch. 'Who's Julius going to suggest takes on Karakov?' Ray Andrews asked. He answered his own question. 'You're the obvious choice, David. If you'd be prepared to do it. You've known him for years, you're a diamond man from way back.'

Arthur Harris sipped his gin and tonic. 'I don't think he has David in mind,' he said slowly. 'Or you, Dick. He wouldn't give you the chance to make a success of something so important. You're too loyal to me.'

'I'd kick Karakov's fat arse,' Kruger said violently. 'That's what he needs, a good hard kick where it hurts. I'd ban him from all "sights", as a start.'

Ray shook his head. Kruger's Afrikaans temper had been a handicap all through his business career. Cutting off Ivan Karakov's supply of gemstones by refusing him the right to buy at the monthly 'sights' in London was not just too drastic, but ineffective. Karakov had a huge stockpile of fine gems. He might welcome exclusion from the obligation to pay big prices to Diamond Enterprises.

'Let's eat, shall we?' Arthur suggested. 'We haven't that long before the meeting. The Game Pie is good – I had it yesterday. I think Julius is going to spring a surprise on us.'

He said to the waitress, 'I'll have the claret. I think,' he went on, 'he's going to suggest young Hastings. No potatoes, thank you.'

Andrews stared at him. Kruger went red with rage. David Wasserman gave nothing away.

'That's what I think,' he continued. 'It will be the opening shot in the war he's decided to declare. Not just on Ivan Karakov, but on the whole top management structure in London. Starting with me.'

James let his coffee get cold, and ate half his sandwiches without even tasting them. Who would get the Paris assignment? He went over the probable candidates, even including some of the up-and-coming men at management level, only to discard them, along with Kruger, old Wasserman and Arthur Harris whose attempt to take control had been so brutally thwarted in public by Reece and that damned letter. Devious, short-sighted Reece could never be trusted. Christ, he muttered, Heyderman doesn't play by the rules when he's out to get someone. That's why he's at the top of the heap and Arthur Harris is on the way down . . . It always came back to himself. He must be the one marked out for stardom. If he succeeded. Failure would mean he'd have to resign before an excuse was found to fire him. He wouldn't think about that. He wouldn't fail, why should he? He never had from the time he decided he was going to become a prefect at his prep school and went on to be Guardian at Radley. He saw what he wanted and he went for it. *Go for it*, his wife had said. 'By God,' he murmured it aloud, 'she doesn't realize what it could lead to, but I'm going to win this one if I get the chance.'

Elizabeth was meeting her mother for lunch. Jill Fairfax seldom came to London; she found the city noisy, dirty and full of bad-mannered people. It was all pushing and shoving, and dreadful traffic jams. Nowhere to park. She and Liz's father made two or three trips a year when he watched cricket at Lord's and she had her hair permed and bought some clothes. In the summer they stayed with their daughter in Thurloe Square. The next visit was before Christmas to buy presents, and they stayed at Brown's Hotel.

This trip up from Somerset was exceptional. She was worried about Elizabeth, and had made an excuse to come to London to see her. By train, and not staying overnight as Liz suggested. She didn't really like staying in James's house when he was there. He was always welcoming, but she felt an intruder, as if he didn't like her imposing herself on them. She had taken Elizabeth to Claridges Causerie, a great treat she felt, and settled down to probe. She was a large, gaunt woman, weather-beaten from a life spent in the open air; she hunted, showed working spaniels, and lived a busy life serving the village community. Her husband was a magistrate, Chairman of the Parish Council and active on local committees. Their only son had been killed with the Scots Guards in the Falklands campaign. That had made Elizabeth even more precious to them.

'Now,' Jill Fairfax said. 'What shall we have?' She thought her daughter was too thin; undeniably beautiful with a polish acquired since her marriage – everyone stared at her when they came in, and Jill was proud of that, but surely she'd lost weight since they last met.

She didn't mince her words. Another trait she sensed her son-in-law disliked. 'You look far too skinny, darling. Not been dieting, have you?'

Elizabeth smiled. 'No, Mum,' she said firmly, 'I haven't. I'm the same weight I was in June, give a pound or two. If I ate a lunch like this every day, I'd be bursting out of my clothes!'

'Working too hard then,' Jill Fairfax insisted. 'You told me about the new office block in Richmond, for Everlife Insurance, that must have been exhausting.'

'It was a challenge and it was fun,' Elizabeth protested. 'I'm still hoping against hope I might get the Lord

Chancellor's commission. I went to see him last week, and he was such a nice man.'

'He was at school with Pop, wasn't he?'

'Very likely,' Elizabeth said. 'But I didn't mention that. If I get this, it'll be on my own merits. All he knows about me is that I'm Elizabeth Hastings Designs.'

Jill shrugged. Her daughter had always been touchy about making use of social contacts. Jill Fairfax's generation saw no harm in it, but Elizabeth had been determined to succeed as a person, rather than as her father's daughter.

Her mother laughed. 'Trouble with you, Liz, is you're a bloody inverted snob.' Jill was very much an open book and she didn't much care whether people liked what was on the page. She had always spoken her mind. 'All right, you're not dieting and you're not overworking. But Pop and I didn't think you looked too happy last time. That's why I came up specially: to see you and to find out if everything's all right.'

Telephones, she insisted, were bloody useless. You had to talk to people face to face.

'Everything's fine,' Liz insisted. 'Except the one thing. I'd just been disappointed, yet *again* in June. And since. I don't know what to do. You never had any trouble.'

'No,' her mother agreed. 'Poor Nick was a honeymoon baby. You came along three years later, just as planned. But you'll never hit the bull's-eye if you keep worrying. Everyone's told you that.'

'I know,' she said miserably. 'But I can't help it. I know how much Jamie wants a family. And he's so good about it.'

'Well so he should be!' Jill said sharply. 'It's just as likely his fault.'

'Mum,' Elizabeth warned, and her mother shrugged.

'I wasn't criticizing. Look, Lizzie, that'll come. Just try not to concentrate on it so much. It screws up everything inside. Apart from the bloody pregnancy business, you're happy?'

'I'm very happy,' Elizabeth said simply. 'I love him and he loves me. He's so good to me about everything. I wish you'd believe that. After all, it's five years.'

'I know.' Jill Fairfax finished her wine. 'It's just that you're such different people. We always *liked* him—'

'No you didn't,' Elizabeth interrupted. 'And you said so. You wanted me to marry someone like Pop and live in a nice house in Somerset and breed dogs. I'm not like you, Mum. I love our life here, and Jamie's the most exciting man I've ever met. Or ever will. We have everything in common and he spoils me rotten. So no more nonsense, please?'

'I'm sorry,' her mother said. 'I worry about you, that's all. You come down once in a blue moon, and it's such a hassle getting up here for us . . . I'm sorry,' she said again. 'It's just that after we lost Nick, we clung on to you a bit too much . . .'

Her eyes filmed for a moment. Elizabeth reached over and held her hand. 'Mum,' she said. 'Mum darling, don't . . . It's all right. I understand. That's another reason I want a baby. For you and Pop. You'd love a grandchild, wouldn't you? It might make up a little bit . . . I didn't mean to snap, but Jamie's a really wonderful husband. You've nothing to worry about. We're happier than we've ever been. Truly. I'm the one that gets moody. It's quite hard on him sometimes.'

Jill Fairfax smiled. 'I'm sure it is. When you sulked as a child, the whole household was upset. Now, darling, changing the subject. Prue Langham has left her husband. Run off with a local farmer. Can you imagine the gossip? We're absolutely riveted, of course.'

Elizabeth slipped easily into the talk about people she knew and had grown up with, while a corner of her mind recognized how bored James would have been, not knowing anyone. One of the reasons why he resisted going down for weekends to stay with her family was not just boredom, but the feeling he was left out when they were all together; her aunt and uncle were half an hour's drive away, with married children and grandchildren. The Fairfaxes tended to gather like a tribe, immersed in local gossip and mutual friends. Generalities were not discussed. World affairs, politics, business – God forbid *business* – such topics were touched on briefly, if at all, and quickly changed to something comfortable like the price of land, or the difficulties of the Hunt in coping with the antis. Elizabeth had seen him withdraw, and sensed his discomfort. It pained her because she loved them all and she was part of them. But much more part of him. On her own initiative she cut down on the visits to her home.

She looked up and interrupted her mother in full flow. 'Oh . . . that's Valerie Kruger . . . sitting down over there in the corner table.'

'Valerie who? Do I know her?'

'No, she's the wife of one of D.E.'s directors. Probably ex-wife by now. She's very nice.' Elizabeth caught her eye across the room and gave a little wave and smile. 'I liked her. She had a good sense of humour. She made some of those ghastly company parties bearable.'

Jill Fairfax studied her. A very good-looking woman, probably middle to late forties, very dark and chic – she used the old-fashioned word to describe such women with immaculate clothes and hair.

'Divorced? Oh well, nobody stays the course these days. No bloody backbone, that's the trouble.'

James Hastings disliked women who swore, and his motherin-law seldom let a sentence go by without the word bloody creeping in. His own mother would never have used such a word in conversation.

'It wasn't her fault,' Liz said. 'Her husband started an affair with his secretary.'

'How common,' her mother remarked. 'So she left him,

I suppose. Silly woman. Should have got rid of the secretary. I would have done.'

'Yes, Mum,' her daughter agreed, smiling. 'Set the dogs on her, no doubt . . . no, it wasn't quite like that. This girl made a real go for Dick Kruger. And she was the sexiest thing you've ever seen. Tough as old boots and determined to get him. Jamie said he made a complete fool of himself. Ruth Fraser, that's her name. Thirty years he'd been married, and she broke it up. Just for money. He's years older than she is, and not anything special. Rather ugly, very South African. I never liked him. But so far,' she said with satisfaction, 'he hasn't married the little bitch. She still works for him, though, and they live together. Mum, I think I'll just go over and say hello. Some people dropped Valerie after they split up. Keeping on the right side of *him*.'

She went over to the table. 'Hello, Val,' she said. 'How are you?'

Valerie Kruger looked up and smiled. James Hastings' lovely wife, always so friendly and good natured. A pearl cast among swine, she had thought privately as soon as she met her. With a prize swine of a husband, according to Dick. 'Hello, Elizabeth. You're looking great. As always. How nice of you to come over. My friend is late, as usual. Is that your mother over there? I see a family likeness.'

'Yes, it is,' Liz said. 'I'll tell her, she'll be pleased. Look, let's have lunch one day. Are you still in Phillimore Gardens?'

'Yes; Dick moved out – I stayed put. Do call. I'd love to see you again.'

Elizabeth went back and sat down. Another woman was making her way across the restaurant towards Valerie Kruger. They had seen Valerie once at the theatre with a man. James had been embarrassed and tried to avoid them. Elizabeth couldn't understand why and had been angry. 'I just don't want to get involved, that's all,' he'd explained. Elizabeth couldn't see how being friendly to someone they both knew was anything more than an ordinary kindness. She had made a point of moving up the aisle to talk to Valerie, while James hung back. It had clouded an otherwise enjoyable evening at a very good play.

After lunch she and her mother went to an exhibition at the Waddington Gallery. Pop's birthday was coming up, and they decided a nice animal in bronze of horse and jockey would be a joint present for him. He had been a talented amateur rider in his youth. They all rode as a matter of course. James was terrified of horses and only watched them on a racecourse at Royal Ascot. Invariably, to Liz's chagrin, he won money.

It had been a happy day spent together. She dropped her mother at Paddington Station; they kissed briefly, Jill Fairfax was not a demonstrative woman. 'Goodbye, Liz darling, thanks for a lovely day.' She had the bronze packed up under her arm. 'I'll have to hide this when I get home. I'm sure he'll love it. Pity you couldn't come down, just for the night. We're planning a dinner party of all the old cronies.'

'I'll try,' Elizabeth said. 'Even if James can't get away, I'm sure I can . . . Bye, Mum, and thanks for a super lunch.'

'Good luck with the Lord Chancellor thing,' Jill said. 'I must say it would be such fun if you got it. I can make everyone at home livid boasting about how my daughter's doing up the Palace of Westminster . . . they won't know the difference.' She saw Elizabeth's face and said seriously, 'It means a lot to you, doesn't it? I wasn't being funny, darling . . . I really do hope you get the commission.'

'Yes,' Elizabeth answered. 'I wouldn't admit it to any-one else but it does mean a lot to me. Since I don't seem able to have children I'd like to succeed at something!'

Her mother turned to look at her. 'Don't be ridiculous,

Liz. If you stop worrying you'll have a houseful of bloody children in the end and wish you'd never started! Let me know if you can come down for Pop's birthday. Bye . . .'

When Elizabeth got home she found a message on the ansaphone. It was from James. 'Darling. Cancel everything tonight. We're going to Annabel's. I've got great news. We're going to celebrate, just the two of us . . . See you around seven-thirty.'

Cancel everything. Dinner and bridge with friends. What could she say to excuse them? And what great news? He'd seemed breathless with excitement, whatever it was . . . a new job . . . he'd been so keyed up about the Board meeting, and she remembered that remark about Arthur on the way out . . . new blood, he'd said, half joking in self-defence, mine . . .

It couldn't be *that*. No, Elizabeth dismissed the idea. But something very prestigious and important. She looked up the address book, found their friends' number, and, hating to lie on principle, decided to tell the truth. 'I'm so sorry, Pam, we can't come tonight . . . No, I've just got a message from Jamie. He's asked me to call you and say can we have a rain check . . . Something mega's come up in the business and he's planning a wild celebration. Just the two of us.' Yes, she agreed, it was rather romantic. Pam said her man would have taken himself off to Boodles and got drunk with his mates . . . Next week, maybe, they mustn't miss out on their bridge. They had to win their money back after the last time.

Elizabeth went up and had a bath, looked out the dress he liked best – a black silk jersey sheath, very short and cut low at the back. He said it made her look madly sexy. She had beautiful smooth skin, pale as a lily in winter, and tanning to a deep golden brown in the sun.

There was some colour left after their summer holiday in Portugal. She wore no jewellery except the mammoth diamond, and some extravagant fake paste earrings that danced and jangled in her blond hair. Gardenia scent, high-heeled black ankle-strap shoes, bare legs shown off by the wickedly brief skirt, and she was ready. He kissed her hard, smearing the pale lipstick, eager and possessive. 'You look gorgeous,' he said. 'I've been watching you, didn't you realize?'

'No,' she held him off, laughing, sharing his urgent desire, knowing that unless they broke away they'd end on the bed and never see Annabel's. 'We're going out,' she whispered. 'Remember . . .'

He took a deep breath. He let her go. 'I haven't told you,' he said. 'Heyderman offered me the plum job this afternoon. If I make it work, the sky's the limit for me. Reece said it in so many words. I want to tell you all about it. I didn't want to share tonight with anyone else. Just us, darling. I've messed up your lipstick . . . kiss me again, then put some more on and we'll go.'

It was a long, deep kiss. 'We'll make love,' he whispered to her. 'We'll make love all night when we get home. You wait . . .'

He had left when Elizabeth woke the next morning. She lay in a contented haze, remembering the wonderful night they had spent together.

First, dinner at Annabel's, with too much champagne, holding hands and whispering like two new lovers instead of old marrieds with five years' distance run. Then dancing with him, feeling the rhythm change to a slow sensual courtship, holding each other, oblivious to their surroundings. It was as if they'd turned back time, to the first evening they met. Another nightclub, Tramps this time; she was one of a noisy party of young men and their girls, her brother Nick was with them, and the girl everyone expected him to marry; she danced like a wild thing, leaving her partner to fend for himself, swept up in the thrilling beat of the music.

When she went back to the table, laughing and

breathless, James was sitting there. He had been watching her, ignoring his own date, just watching the lovely blonde letting rip on the dance floor. He had told her about it afterwards. He knew one of their party and deliberately crashed their table to meet her. He had known from that first sight, that she was the one he wanted. He had reminded her of it as they danced.

'You were the sexiest thing,' he murmured. 'I was out of control just watching you . . . I am now,' and he'd pulled her even tighter against him.

They came back soon after midnight, and he had kept his promise. There wasn't much sleep, only interludes before they came to each other again. Before they fell asleep in each other's arms, Elizabeth had drifted on the thought that surely, surely, they had made a baby . . .

That morning she got up, bathed, examined herself in the bathroom mirror, as if some miraculous change had already taken place. None had, of course. She had a fine, slender body. She placed both hands on the flat stomach. She wanted to be pregnant so much that it was a physical ache. It had seemed so easy when they abandoned contraception. Two years to get adjusted, have fun, find the right house. It was all planned and ready, but nothing happened. Nothing in the last three years but endless monthly disappointments. There was no medical reason. She was healthy, James was fertile. He had undergone the test just to set her mind at rest. He was so understanding, so patient with her. He had insisted, and she recognized the wisdom of it, that they didn't make love just by the calendar. That mustn't lose its spontaneity. He loved her because he wanted to; a child would come, or not. He didn't mind. But Elizabeth knew that he did, and that made her more anxious. He might deny it, laugh it off, but he'd planned the top floor as a nursery when they bought the house. She hadn't forgotten that.

It was easy for her mother to counsel patience. Her maternal longings had been quickly satisfied. And they had transferred to the breeding of her much-loved spaniels. Elizabeth was empty; she had never experienced the feeling in that way to anyone, but she said it to herself that morning. So much in love with her husband, everything going for both of them, but empty, unfulfilled. 'Oh please,' she said it aloud. 'Please make it happen this time . . .' She found herself blinking back tears. It wasn't a prayer. She hadn't been to church for years, not even when she went home to Somerset.

She didn't think you could deny something, and then ask it to help when it suited you. She made a resolution not to think about it. Not to worry, not to look for early signs. Not to hope. They were moving to Paris before the end of the month. There were a million things to be organized. She had an efficient team in her small shop in Walton Street; there were no major jobs in hand at the moment, she had deliberately turned down two smaller commissions, for a house in Kensington and a flat in South Molton Street, in case, just in case, the miracle happened and her scheme and competitive quotes were accepted by the Lord Chancellor. It would be a miracle, Elizabeth insisted. She and James had talked about it briefly the night before; she was touched that in his own exuberance he hadn't forgotten that she too had a career to run. She had been too warm with champagne and desire to do more than say it could tick over for the next couple of months while she was away. After all, if something came up urgently, she could always fly over for the day . . . even the job at Westminster, she had said blithely, knowing it wasn't true, and at that moment she hadn't cared. James meant everything to her. Loving him, wanting him more than ever.

A million things to do. The house to close up. Packing, ringing her friends, going to Walton Street to sort out any details on the current job which was so nearly finished it could run to the end without her supervision . . . Letting her father and mother know. Oh God, she thought, Pop's birthday . . . I hope I don't have to miss that . . . no, three weeks away, it was just all right.

James would have to go over to Paris for a few days before they made the final move. She'd be able to get down to Somerset and see her father. Better ring and tell them the news first. No, better not. They hated upheavals. Her mother once told her that after her brother Nick's death, her father wouldn't answer the telephone for weeks . . .

She bathed and dressed, her mind full of plans. The letter was in the morning post when she went downstairs. She saw the official seal on the envelope and tore it open.

She read it and the colour ran up into her face. The miracle had happened. Her scheme and quotes had been accepted in preference to the top names in London interior design. She took the letter into the kitchen and sat down to read it over again.

A commission that would establish her among the top rank of the profession. Exciting, demanding, time consuming. Months of work, preparation, constant supervision on a day-to-day basis, with a tight schedule for completion.

She put the letter down and tried to think clearly what the choices were. Her own dismissal came back to her, whispered to James in the intimacy of the night-club.

'Even if I did get it, darling, I could cope. It's only two hours door to door from Paris to London. If it happened, which it won't . . . come on, I love this music, let's dance . . .' She couldn't accept the job *and* go to Paris with him. It was a straight choice. As a professional she couldn't compromise and hope to fulfil the contract properly. At that moment the telephone rang. It made her jump.

She picked it up and heard James's voice. 'Liz? How's my girl?'

They'd been so close, so radiantly together last night.

57

They'd only been apart for a few hours and he was ringing her . . . 'I'm fine,' she said. 'How's my superman?'

He laughed. 'Bushed! What a night, my darling. I just wanted to say thank you and tell you how much I love you . . .' She felt the sting of tears in her eyes.

'I love you too,' she said. The choice was made. 'I had a letter this morning. I didn't get the Westminster job. So I'm really looking forward to going to Paris.'

'Oh, sweetheart, I'm sorry. Don't be too disappointed, will you?'

'I won't have time, I'm going to be so busy.'

'I wish I could take you out to lunch but I'm flat to the boards What are you going to do today?'

'Start making lists, see what we need to take with us, stuff like that. We can have a quiet evening tonight, darling. I'm bushed too.'

'Well,' he drew the word out. 'Well . . . you might drop by Cartier sometime this afternoon. I've ordered a little something for you. No, darling, I'm not going to tell you what it is. But it'll cheer you up, I promise. I just wanted to give you a surprise. So go along and get it. Bye, sweetheart . . .'

Elizabeth put the phone down and picked up the letter. There hadn't really been a conflict. She had learned her priorities from her own family. Her husband and her marriage would always come first with her. And she had the comfort of knowing that she had, in fact, succeeded. James wouldn't see it like that. Business success meant so much to him. That was why she had lied . . . it was her decision, her choice. She didn't want him feeling guilty because of what she'd missed.

3

'I think James should go to Paris and make contact with Karakov.'

Julius Heyderman had opened the Board meeting with that sentence. He was met by a shocked silence, and then Kruger burst out, 'Hastings? Why him? He hasn't the experience, or the weight, to talk to someone like Karakov. No offence,' he added, turning towards James, 'but it'll look as if you're sending the office boy!'

Arthur Harris winced. Kruger was making it worse; you could try persuading Heyderman, and he might listen. Bluster or question his judgement like that, and he'd see you in hell first.

'David is the best choice; he's a diamond man, Karakov knows him . . . Even me, if you follow it through. We've been on the Board for years. We're serious players. I say again, no offence to you, James, but you're too young and too new—'

'Which is why I'm sending him,' Heyderman cut in. 'Karakov won't listen to David, and certainly not to you, Dick. We heard this morning how he feels about the London office . . . that certainly includes you. Hastings is young, he's new and Karakov will drop his guard, because of those factors. He'll think you're easy meat, James,' he spoke to him directly. 'And you'll let him think so. Let him think he's in control. He's such a vain bastard he'll believe it. Anyway, gentlemen, if Hastings is prepared to take it on, then I say he joins the Paris office on a three-month secondment. Longer, if necessary. Arthur? You support me in this?'

It was a command, not a question.

'Only if I register my reservations,' his brother-in-law said. 'Yes, conditionally I support you, but I draw the line at more than three months. You said yourself that time was of the essence to stop this agreement with the Russians.'

Julius looked at him with dislike. 'If Andrews doesn't cock it up again, Hastings won't need three months,' he snapped. 'Agreed?'

Nobody dissented. Kruger had shot his bolt.

'Good.' Almost as an afterthought he turned to James. 'You happy about this? Feel you can make a success of it?'

The bright blue eyes were fixed on him, shrewd and probing. He hadn't flinched.

This was his chance, his golden moment. He took it as he'd taken every opportunity on offer to rise up in the world.

'I'll give it my best shot,' he said clearly. 'And I don't expect to fail. Thank you, Julius. When do I go?'

'See Reece,' Heyderman closed the subject. 'With Andrews. He'll brief you both. Now, to the rest of business.'

The meeting ended an hour later. Heyderman went out first, followed by Reece and then Arthur. Ray Andrews and James found themselves behind Kruger and David Wasserman. Johnson went off without wasting time; he had a lot of work to do.

In the corridor, Wasserman stopped. 'Well, Ray my boy, you got a dirty job ahead of you,' he said.

'Bloody impossible,' Andrews said shortly.

'You'll bring it off,' James piped up.

'Ah, the wonder boy.' Kruger stopped and faced him. 'How come you managed to crawl up Julius's ass without anyone noticing?'

Wasserman laughed; it was not so much a laugh as an

old man's cackle, malicious and dry. 'Now, Dick, don't be like that. You had your chance, like James here. Good luck to you, my boy.' He patted James on the shoulder. 'You'll need it, won't he, eh?' He laughed again.

'You'll need a bloody miracle,' Kruger snapped. 'If you make a mess of it, Hastings old son, Julius'll chew your balls clean off. That's if you've got any left when Ivan Karakov's finished with you!' He turned and walked away. The old man looked after him and shrugged. Andrews looked embarrassed, James Hastings showed nothing except that he was white-faced, and Wasserman knew what that meant in some men.

'Don't pay any attention to him,' he said. 'He don't mean anything nasty; just forget it. He's edgy, that's all.'

James gave him a look that was quite impassive; his colour was still very pale.

'Most people are edgy when they know they're past it,' he said. 'I'll give you a ring, David; perhaps we could have lunch before you go back? Fine, I'll do that then. Come on, Ray. Let's go and see what Reece has to suggest.'

Reece stood up as they came into his office. It was furnished in ultra-modern style, with sepia-coloured walls and white wood furniture. There was a large reproduction of a Chagall abstract and a small drawing, which Hastings recognized as an original by Paul Klee; those two pictures and some framed photographs of his family were the only decorations in the office. Functional was the word that leaped to the mind; efficient, up to date, expensive, and quite without atmosphere. But the room wasn't a reflection of Reece's personality. The key to that lay somewhere in those two paintings and those dumpy figures in the photographs on his desk. As they sat down, James identified him as the sullen little boy with a little girl standing, he guessed, between their parents; the background was indeterminate, the group was windblown, and Reece's father looked self-conscious in a panama hat. Reece wasn't married, and that was all anybody knew about his personal life. A negative. James took a cigarette from the onyx box and looked into the man's dark, flat eyes. God, he was a creepy little bastard.

'Mr Hastings, I think we'll have a general run-through with your side of the problem first. Then we'll deal with Mr Andrews; is that all right?' He looked from one to the other and smiled. He knew them very well, these two men, and his summing up had decided their present assignments, though they would never know it. He had first advised Heyderman to watch Hastings; Reece could smell ambition, and it was so strong in Hastings that it stank in Reece's nostrils the moment they met. He had an animal instinct for certain things; he knew if someone was afraid, and how far they could be pushed. That had been very useful on occasions when he had been left to distance the company from some awkward situation. He knew when threats were useless, and it was necessary to use other means, like money or promotion to close a mouth or stifle a pang of conscience. Hastings would have very little conscience. There wasn't much he'd balk at, if the prize was big enough, and that was why the Chairman had selected him to take on Karakov; he'd chosen him because Reece said he was the man, and Julius trusted Reece's judgement as much as he did his own. Reece knew this, and he was very gratified. If you happened to be a small man, and not much to look at, and with certain things to hide, it was a great satisfaction to be the right hand of a man like Julius Heyderman. They said there was a woman behind every great man; Reece didn't believe it. He knew there was usually a Reece. If Hastings had no conscience, then Ray Andrews had too much, and that was why he was going down while Hastings was going up. He had thought very seriously about Andrews. Julius had been inclined to dismiss him; he was Arthur Harris's man, competent but lacking the final flair which distinguished men destined for the top. In Reece's view that was unfair and unwise. Andrews was brilliant, it was just bad luck that his one mistake should have caught up with him now; but it seemed as good a time as any to begin the long-planned operation against Arthur by bringing down one of the men who could be counted on to stand by him. Andrews was being given the Russians to deal with, and though it looked impossible, Reece felt there was a remote chance that if he got to Yeltsin, they might come to terms. It wasn't essential that Andrews should fail in order to get the chocks from under Arthur. If he succeeded, they would change tactics. He must have a price; Reece didn't worry about that too much. Everyone had one.

'Now, Mr Hastings, let's put you in the picture.' Reece buzzed his secretary. 'Bring in the Karakov file.' He never said 'please' to subordinates. When the file arrived he began leafing through it. 'We don't have a proper agreement with Karakov. It's not a formal thing, just a letter of intent. He wanted an agreement, and we went through the formalities of letting his lawyers talk to ours, just to humour him, but naturally we can't let our clients have anything which might be interpreted as rights over us. Now, Karakov has been getting about half his total requirements from us, and the rest he has to go out and buy from the trade. What he does get from us is a far higher proportion of the large special stones than anyone else. He gets these stones very cheaply, as he takes so much of the poorer quality goods which are more difficult to sell.' Reece paused for a moment, and then went on. 'As you know, there's an element of risk in the big special stones. You can pay a hundred thousand for a wonderful-looking piece, and then cleave it and find it's lost all its promise and life. You find yourself with two or three moderate stones worth about twenty thousand and a lot of small stuff at the end of it.

'But, on the other hand, if you get a good one . . .' he

shrugged. 'Karakov likes the big stuff; he takes the risk. He's had some bad buys but overall he's made a great deal of money. If he gets a monopoly on these red diamonds, he'll be strong enough to cause us *serious* problems. As Mr Wasserman said, he's an egomaniac.

'Now, Mr Hastings, Mr Julius feels you should go to the Paris office as soon as possible. Get established there. Rent a nice apartment. You'll make contact with Ivan Karakov – Mr Wasserman can arrange that. I suggest your approach is friendly, even ingenuous. Be nice, be a little bit pained about the rumours that he's falling out with D.E., but give the impression that you're not as clever as you think you are. You don't mind me saying this, do you? It's all just a suggestion – you'll handle it in your own way, of course. Get to know him socially. Entertain. Be friendly. Of course, you'll be taking your wife. Don't just stop on a business footing.'

James nodded. He didn't see the point of the lecture. Cheeky bastard, telling him what to do . . .

Reece continued, 'Oh, and Mr Julius wants you to take a secretary/personal assistant from this office. Someone who knows the business at first hand and can be trusted with highly confidential material. Ruth Fraser is the obvious choice.' He looked expectantly at James. 'I'm sure she'll agree to go,' he added.

'You're not going! You ring through to that bastard and say you've changed your mind!' Dick Kruger was yelling at her. He'd lost control of himself halfway through her explanation and stood over her shouting.

'For God's sake,' Ruth protested. 'Half the office can hear you . . . Stop screaming at me!' She had never seen him lose his temper and she didn't like it. She didn't like being yelled at either, seeing how his fists balled up as if he were going to hit her. Under the South of France tan, she was quite pale. 'Stop it, Dick, calm down . . .'

He took a very deep breath. In a lower tone, he said,

'You're not going to Paris with Hastings. So don't let's argue about it, it's a fact. You just call Reece and tell him. Now.'

Ruth Fraser looked at him. 'Sit down,' she said. 'Just sit down and listen to me, will you please?' She got up and came to him. She put her arms round his waist. His body was rigid. Tact, she told herself, handle him carefully. Of course he's upset. He hears it from Reece first, then I accept before he gets a chance to hear my side of it . . . 'Sit down,' she urged, pressing herself against him. Body contact never failed. It failed then. He pushed her away. He swallowed, in control of himself at last. The hurt showed in his eyes. That hurt her, too.

'Why didn't you wait? Why didn't you talk it over with me first?' He sank into the chair behind his desk. 'Why did you just say "Yes" right off?'

'Because Reece wanted an answer,' Ruth told him. 'If not me, then someone else . . . probably Judy Palmer. You know how ambitious she is . . . and she's no friend to you. Darling,' she lowered her voice, pleading with him, 'you've been worried about Hastings from the start. Now he's got a top-level job from Julius. So where does that leave you, if he brings it off? Out!'

She paused. She came round the desk and stood beside him. She laid a hand on his shoulder. 'But he won't,' she said very softly. 'Not if I go with him. That's why I said yes. Because I can protect you.'

'I don't need protecting,' he said. She felt him respond to the pressure of her hand. She knew she was going to win. 'I don't want you living in Paris. I don't give a toss about Hastings or anyone else. I want you with me.'

She leaned against him, slipped an arm around his neck. 'We can be together every weekend,' she said. 'I can fly home or you can fly out. If Hastings screws up quickly, I'll be back before you know it.'

He sighed. He reached for her and brought her round

to sit on his knee. She was very small and her feet didn't touch the ground.

'Christ,' Kruger muttered. 'I love you so much, Ruthie. I need you . . .'

'I know,' she said. 'We need each other. Darling, I want to do this for you. For us. I don't want that smug little shit to win. I'll let you know every last detail, so you can tell Arthur. And I'll pull the rug from under him if I get a chance. And I will. Reece said I would have access to all the confidential material. That's what got to me. I could see the opportunities.' She reached up and touched his mouth. 'And you see them too. You're too good an operator to pass this up. Say I can go . . .'

Kruger didn't answer. He loved the feel of her, the scent of her. His stomach lurched at the thought of separation. Weekends together. That wasn't so bad. Paris was no problem. And she was right. She'd keep him ahead of the game, primed against Hastings and able to arm Arthur Harris.

The idea that Ruth could actually wreck any deal Hastings might negotiate with Karakov was far-fetched . . . typically feminine. But not impossible, with an adversary like Ruth. She was as clever as a grove of monkeys. And what she didn't know about Diamond Enterprises and the way it operated, was literally not worth knowing.

'Say yes,' she prompted. 'We can get married if you really want to. Will that make it better? No-one in the office has to know.'

He'd asked her often enough, and her lack of hurry had surprised him. It pleased him too, because a lot of his and Valerie's friends had said bluntly that she was after marriage and his money. But she wasn't. She wasn't anxious to tie him down. Or herself. That aspect had made him uneasy, and he had started pressing her for an answer. Now, unexpectedly, she had given it. Proof of her good faith. Proof that, as she said, what she was doing in taking on the job of assistant to his enemy, was for his sake.

He said, 'I'll get a special licence.'

'Would you like a drink first?' Julius Heyderman hesitated. He'd never visited this girl before. She came out of Reece's little book of useful names and addresses. She was very pretty, ash blond, very full breasted – he couldn't bear skinny, flat-chested women – and she had magnificent legs. The fee was five hundred. It included tickets for the new hit musical in the West End, if the client wanted a night out, with sex afterwards at his choice. Julius didn't feel like going to the theatre. 'I've got whisky, gin, vodka and a bottle of champagne on ice if you'd like that.'

She was very well dressed, nothing cheap or tarty about her. She spoke well, was poised and friendly. The flat was nicely furnished, with decorator stamped all over the nick-nacks and colour schemes. Nobody would have imagined she was a very high-class prostitute.

'Whisky, no ice, just water please,' Heyderman said. Reece knew he liked women straight. Once he made a mistake, with a sullen brunette who offered special services. Heyderman had walked out. He had never needed sexual deviation. Reece was left in no doubt of his error.

Heyderman liked the look of her. She was elegant and she knew how to sit still. He hated women doing what he described as a bloody Salome dance when they poured a man a drink.

'Mind if I have a whisky with you?'

'Why should I? It's your whisky.' He was in a bad mood; he had been irritable and restless back at his hotel, unable to relax. He was worried, and he knew the antidote for that. So he told Reece to make a date for him, and there he was in a walk-up flat in Mount Street, drinking whisky with a whore. For five hundred pounds flat rate.

'You haven't been to me before, have you?' she asked. 'I'm sure I'd remember you. Are you just visiting London?'

'Till the day after tomorrow,' he said, sipping his whisky.

She had beautiful ankles and small feet. He liked a woman to be voluptuous but never coarse. It was a physical beauty that had attracted him to his first wife, Eileen. She had the translucent Irish skin, and the deep blue eyes associated with the Celtic race. She was graceful and pretty in an elfin way, and he swept her into marriage a month after they met. She was on a trip to South Africa with her uncle and aunt. Julius learnt that she lived with them in County Cork; her parents were dead. She was at teacher training college. He fell in love immediately, and for the first time. He had lost count of the girls he'd taken to bed in his teens and twenties. He hadn't wanted to marry any of them; the chime of wedding bells, however faint, sent him on a convenient trip abroad. But the shy, country-bred Irish girl filled him with a frenzy of passion and possessiveness. He roared into her life like a golden lion, and she was whirled into a huge wedding in Johannesburg, showered with diamonds, clothes, a new Bentley convertible which she didn't dare to drive, and a place in South African society that she had no idea how to fill. Julius hadn't given a damn. He let her find her own way, always protective in the background, confident that she would win hearts on her own merit. And right in his judgement, as usual. He was popular, courted because of his power and the great industry he was destined to lead when his father died, but Eileen Heyderman was loved by everyone. She had a mischievous sense of humour and a hugely kind heart, without an ounce of conceit or self-importance. He adored her. As she adored him in return, and was as disappointed as he was that their first born, a daughter, resembled neither of them.

She was a difficult, fretful baby, and a fractious toddler. As she developed, it seemed as if some wayward Irish gene had by-passed the Dutch ancestry, and produced a throw back. Stella had black hair and dark blue eyes. She was a pretty child, but the wayward streak made her troublesome and unpredictable. The coloured nannies spoiled her, giving in to every tantrum. It was Eileen who named her Stella. Julius thought it a beautiful but inappropriate name for such an unruly little girl. Had she been a son, he would have been proud of the self-willed nature and fierce independence. He didn't understand this female child, and he left her upbringing to her mother. In turn, Eileen, embarked on a succession of pregnancies which ended in miscarriage, left it to the servants. She wanted to give Julius a boy and she refused to listen to medical advice and give up hope.

And then she went full term. How careful they were, how anxious not to lose this precious baby, which both were convinced was a son and heir for the Heyderman empire. The child Stella watched them and felt herself ignored, displaced as the centre of attention in the nursery where everyone chattered about the coming baby. Instinctively, she hated this unseen thing that confined her mother to bed for days on end. The god-like figure of her father had no time for Stella at all, he hardly saw her now. In revenge for this neglect, she terrorized her nanny and the nursemaids and longed for something to happen that would stop the horrible intruder being born. As the time for the birth approached, Julius had the best gynaecologist flown out from London with his personal nursing staff. Everything his love and money could devise was done to help Eileen carry their child to full term.

At three days past the date, she went into labour. It was a little boy. It lived for a few hours and died of a congenital heart defect.

Stella saw the weeping maids and heard that she had lost a baby brother. Briefly, she exulted, and then fell into a screaming fit induced by a terrible sense of guilt. She had wished the baby dead, she had made it happen. She was uncontrollable and nobody understood why. The guilt took root and flourished. Julius, grief stricken, had still another blow to suffer.

His adored wife Eileen, only thirty-two years old, had a mental breakdown. He didn't know what to do or how to cope. Anguish for her suffering mingled with impotent rage at his own helplessness. Nothing brought her out of the pit of depression. It was a pit so deep that she couldn't bear daylight, and lay in semi-darkness, silently weeping and refusing to speak.

There were times in the early months when he drank himself into oblivion, only to reject the coward's option and try yet another doctor, another remedy. In the end, after a dreadful day when Eileen tried to saw through her wrists with a pair of nail scissors, Julius admitted defeat. After twelve months he accepted that it was neither safe nor possible to keep her at home, or right to have a daughter growing up in that atmosphere. So Eileen went into a private nursing home. Stella blamed herself for that, too.

Eileen survived for ten years. Julius visited her every day and sent flowers daily when he was abroad. He had *affaires*, because sex was a necessity to stay sane in mind and healthy in body, but he never brought any woman into Eileen's house. He was at her bedside when she died of cancer. The disease consumed her rapidly; she hadn't realized what was happening and he insisted that she wasn't allowed to suffer pain. He held her hand as she died, and closed the eyes which had filmed over without a sign of recognition for him. Then he set out, heavy in heart, but determined to rebuild his life. He buried his personal tragedy with the coffin; he respected his wife's Catholicism and refused cremation, although he loathed the idea of burial and physical decay for her.

Then he steeled himself to forget the past, with the strength of a naturally powerful will, honed and hardened by pain.

He had his business empire and it absorbed him more and more. He had married again, hoping to provide a stepmother and a family background for Stella, who showed every sign of running wild, but it was a dismal failure. His choice was a widow, a divorcee near his own age. She had hated his daughter and divorced him after five years for mental cruelty. He was always travelling and paid her no attention. She was a stupid woman, but he admitted that his endless business trips left her trying to cope with Stella unsupported. His daughter was the epitome of teenage rebelliousness. Her personality was far stronger than her stepmother's, whom she set out to torment and defy at every opportunity. After the divorce, she claimed responsibility for the breakdown to her father's face. Julius retaliated by sending her to a well-known Swiss boarding-school. He hoped that a strict regime, coupled with a good education, would tame Stella and keep her out of serious trouble. Instinctively he recognized that trouble and his daughter were mutually attractive. His attempt to find a mother substitute had cost him a fortune in the divorce settlement, and left Stella the victor in the contest. He consigned her to what he believed was a safe place, and buried himself in his business.

He had met his present wife, Sylvia, just before Stella was expelled for getting drunk and smashing up her room. She was seventeen. She was flown home in disgrace, and he had no idea how to cope with her. She was a striking girl, bold and sullen looking, with the light of the devil in those smutty blue eyes. She had stood up to him, and that took courage. Stella was never short of that. She admitted being drunk. She taunted him with her abuse of the school's trust; she had deceived them from the beginning and done what she liked. He had come close to hitting her. Instead he slammed out of the room. When he had gone, she collapsed in tears, overwhelmed by the sense of guilt and rejection that drove her from one destructive act to another. In despair, Julius had turned to Sylvia for advice. They were lovers, but there had never been any mention of marriage. She was a widow, rich in her own right. When she offered to talk to Stella, he accepted, but with little hope. Sylvia pointed out that she had brought up three children through their teens after her husband died. She might just get through to his daughter.

It took quite a time, but she displayed a stoic calm that Stella couldn't shake. She couldn't gain her confidence, but she told Julius that his daughter was a confused, unhappy girl who needed to focus on something. She needed a challenge. She was very intelligent. That, she felt, might be the key. At Sylvia's suggestion, he arranged for tutoring and entered Stella for Witwatersrand University. He was so impressed and grateful that he asked Sylvia to marry him.

She didn't tell him till afterwards, that she had gone to his daughter's room and found her passed out drunk, the night before the wedding.

He had never blamed Sylvia's practical, well-intentioned advice for what happened to Stella. She had supported him through the trauma of the years that followed. She loved him, he knew that, and in his way, he returned that love.

Sitting opposite the girl that evening, he thought of Sylvia and missed her very much. He had come for sex from this paid tart, as a means of working off his rage and frustration with the situation that had arisen, threatening his precious industry.

He needed to talk about his problems with this uncomprehending audience, because it might help him to focus. Arthur Harris, he thought bitterly, the weedy enemy of his boyhood, inheriting his power through a Canadian roughneck, marrying Christa and making her miserable. His sister. She could have had any man in the country at the lift of a finger. He hated Arthur because he had a son, even though that son was stupid and oafish. He was still Julius's only heir. Families. Jealousy, rivalry, tragedy. The bombshell that was Stella, ticking but not defused . . .

Scowling at his thoughts, he held out the empty whisky glass for a refill. The girl gave him her bright professional smile, and brushed his hand with her fingertips as she took it. He noted that the second drink was stronger than the first.

'Have you had a good time here?' she asked. She had taken her seat again, and her skirt had ridden so high he could almost see her crotch. It didn't arouse him.

'No,' he said, suddenly angry at the invitation. 'I hate this bloody country; it's cold and wet and on its last legs . . . everyone looking for handouts, and whinging. But I had to come here. I've got a stupid bastard running my business and he's made such a balls up I've had to come over and sort it out.'

'Why don't you sack him if he's no good?'

'Because he's a big shareholder. And he's married to my sister. I'm going to get him out, but it won't be easy.'

He swallowed hard on his whisky. He never used his real name; she had no genuine interest, she was just going through the motions.

That had begun to irritate him, too.

'What kind of business is it?'

How those impersonally smiling eyes would brighten if she knew, he thought. How she'd sparkle and lean forward at the mention of that magic word. *Diamonds*.

'I deal in jute,' Heyderman said.

'Oh, that's interesting.' She was too efficient to try and hurry her clients. Some of them sat with her half the night, getting drunk and talking. It was such an insult to think she was interested in their piddling business worries or their old cows of wives who didn't understand them. She was twenty-four and she had never liked men or had a moment's enjoyment out of them. She had a girl friend that she was very fond of, and they had a lovely time together, making fun of the men. Girls didn't need them for anything but money. This was a good-looking one; she supposed he'd make his mind up soon and they'd go in and she'd go through the motions. Sometimes they gave a lot more than the fee if they thought you'd had fun out of them. She put up a marvellous show, nails and teeth and all. But he was talking again, and she resigned herself and sat down with another drink.

'I've got to vote him out,' Heyderman said. He had a mental picture of Arthur, looking grey and pained, being eased off the Board, and it delighted him. 'I've got to weed out his supporters and win over the others to my way.'

She'd heard this sort of monologue many times before, and she knew what to say by heart.

'Who will you put in his place, then?'

'I think I've got a man,' Julius said slowly. 'I've had my eye on him. He's young, and he's bloody clever. He's got flair, this fellow. He could run the thing my way.'

He was almost talking to himself, following his train of thought.

'He's got no financial interest in the business – I've given him a job to do, and if he brings it off, well, I think he'd fit the bill. He can have some decent share options . . . Am I boring you?' He shot the question at her and for a moment the smile slipped and he saw the hostility in her eyes.

'You like to talk, I'm happy to listen,' she said. 'I don't have to understand it all, do I?'

She decided that this was the moment, and she stood up, smoothing her skirt over her thighs.

'Wouldn't you like to come to bed, sweetie? I'm ready, if you are.'

Julius Heyderman stared at her; he looked at her deliberately, from the pretty face, past the superb figure with its film-star breasts and little waist, to the long supple legs. And suddenly he knew what she was.

As he was fond of saying, he didn't run a business worth four hundred million without knowing something about human nature.

'No,' he said. 'I wouldn't. I wouldn't touch a lesbian like you with a barge pole. Here's fifty in notes. That's for the whisky.'

He heard her screaming after him as he left the flat. Five hundred pounds for that. Thank God she hadn't fooled him. The idea of touching her turned his stomach. Some men were titillated by the idea of normal sex with a lesbian. The thought revolted him. He hated deviants of both sexes. He had long abandoned the strict principles of his Dutch Reformed upbringing, but his prejudices remained.

He would have a few words to say to Reece. It was time he checked the names in his address book. He drove back to his hotel, feeling invigorated, as if the row with the girl had purged his frustration over Arthur Harris. Harris could wait, Julius decided, ordering sandwiches and a bottle of excellent claret. He only drank whisky and the very best wine. He believed that gin and vodka rotted the gut, and poor wine damaged the brain. Good wine, he maintained imperiously, never gave anyone a hangover. He put through a call to his wife Sylvia at their house on the Cape. The manservant said she was out with friends. Julius felt deprived. He not only missed Sylvia, he missed his own beautiful sun-drenched country; with all its problems and uncertainties, it was his homeland and the only place in the world he wanted to live.

He finished his sandwiches and enjoyed his wine. He

had set the pieces on the board. Andrews to Moscow. Reece was right, he was a good man, a valuable ally for Arthur who would be detached if he succeeded, and retired if he failed. Hastings to Paris. *There* was a ruthless operator; he had a jungle smell about him that Julius recognized. The wife was a lovely girl; he wasn't impressed by British titles, but he admired her for refusing to trade on hers. He liked her; he thought she was too good for Hastings, but that was not his business. She'd be a great asset in Paris. Karakov loved beautiful women and was a snob.

He employed a Romanian prince as one of his salesmen; he also used a well-endowed Argentinian to bring in the older rich women as clients. He was tough as steel and crafty as a fox. Julius wondered how James Hastings would measure up against such an opponent.

He was surprised by Reece suggesting that Hastings take Kruger's secretary as his personal assistant. He had met her briefly, summed her up as a common little sexpot with ambition to better herself, and pointedly ignored her. But she was clever; she had a very good business brain which was under-used, according to Reece, who knew everything about everyone. Nauseating little creep, his wife Sylvia said whenever Reece was mentioned. Julius agreed, but oh how valuable when you had the second biggest operation of your business run in London by an enemy . . . Reece had smelt out more in his yearly stint in Blackfriars Road than Julius could have discovered from a dozen other sources. He said Ruth Fraser had potential, and that she would be better employed helping Hastings than bailing out Kruger when he made mistakes. He had quoted several instances. So Julius said she was to go. As predicted, she accepted on the spot. Interesting, he thought. Puppets on strings, all of them, and he was the puppet master, pulling this one, jerking another. He didn't enjoy manipulating people. But he had to protect Diamond Enterprises, and the whole diamond industry, from the mines down to the cheap high street jewellers who depended upon him and his power to fight off market forces and recessionary swings. They stood or fell together; only a megalomaniac like Karakov would put so much at risk. But he would learn. The hard way.

4

'Darling,' James said, 'I've got a list of apartments, take a look and see what you think . . . Here,' he handed the brochures to her, flipped some pages and pointed, 'that sounds rather nice. The rue Constantine is a very smart address.'

Elizabeth smiled. She couldn't resist teasing him for being what she called a postal district snob. 'Do we have to be smart? I'd like to live on the Left Bank . . .'

'Maybe, but that wouldn't impress Karakov. And that's what we're about. He's got to see the youngest member of the D.E. Board lighting up the Paris social scene with his beautiful titled wife. He'll love the Lady Elizabeth bit.'

'Balls to that,' Liz said rudely. 'I never use it, and I'm not going to start now. So you can forget *that*. I mean it!'

'All right, I was just getting a rise. For a change. Seriously, look through these and if you see one you like, maybe you could take a day and fly over and view. I'm too busy, and I'll like what you like. I always do. Get yourself some clothes while you're there. Givenchy?'

'That wouldn't be a bribe, would it?'

'It might,' he agreed.

'Then make it Christian Lacroix and I'll go.'

He looked at her and smiled with sheer pride and happiness. What lucky star had led him to that night-club where he saw her first, and knew by the end of their first dance that this was the girl? She had a naturally gay temperament, in the real sense of that purloined word.

78

She was always finding something ridiculous to laugh at, usually at her own expense. She was devoid of sham or conceit; he thought she was the most natural person he had ever met. Generous to a fault, she'd give anything to anyone who told her a sad story. She had little or no physical fear.

Those dreadful nags she used to ride down in darkest Somerset. He'd weaned her away from the clodhopper set, thank God. Her parents still hadn't really forgiven him. She was going down for her father's birthday; she hadn't pressed him to come. He grinned, remembering how he'd tried bullshitting about being so sorry to miss it, but with the move to Paris . . . Typically Liz had cut him off short with her devastating frankness. 'You're not sorry, darling, you'd hate every minute of it – all Pop's cronies from the Army and the Hunt Committee.'

And, because he found it impossible to put on an act with her, he'd said simply, 'An absolute nightmare, sweetheart. You go and get an extra nice present from me. And have fun.'

It was a wonderful marriage. They understood each other, each gave way about things that didn't matter and talked their way through things that did. She had brought a new dimension into his life: honesty and trust. Into his private life. The business world was not made up of people like Elizabeth. He judged this the moment to tell her about Ruth Fraser. Immediately Liz forgot about going to Paris. She dropped the glossy estate agent's brochure on the floor and stared at him.

'You're taking her with you? I don't believe it! Whatever for?'

'Confidential secretary-cum-personal assistant. That little rat Reece was adamant. Fraser was Julius's choice. Not even preference – choice! I made it absolutely plain I didn't like the idea or see the necessity, but he insisted. I even suggested that Palmer girl – you don't know her, darling, she's in the finance department – but Reece had already asked Fraser, and she'd said yes. I don't know what Kruger felt about it. Pissed off, I should think—'

'Not as pissed off as I am,' Elizabeth said. 'She's awful. God, I'm not having her round my neck, I promise you—'

'You won't have any contact at all,' he protested. 'She's strictly office hours. We don't have to mix with her socially. Look, you don't think I like the idea, do you? Kruger's bimbo stuck under my nose, watching everything and running back to him with details. Why Julius picked her I'll never know.'

But he did know. Because she was the most competent, business-orientated woman in the London office, and also, without her at his elbow, Dick Kruger would be less effective. He decided not to labour the point with Elizabeth. She had few faults in his eyes, but one of them was a difficult temper when it was roused. And strong prejudices, which ruled out women who broke up thirty-year marriages. He sighed, 'Don't make an issue, Liz, please. I've told you, you don't have to see her . . . I had to take her. It was an order, not a suggestion.'

'All right.' Elizabeth shrugged. 'I don't mean to be difficult . . . it's none of my business who acts as your secretary. Sorry, darling. It's just that I saw Valerie Kruger when I was lunching with Mum. Now, let's have a look at this palace you've picked out for us to live in . . .'

All was harmony again between them.

Ray Andrews had booked into the hotel in Moscow. He had an appointment to see the British Ambassador at eleven that morning. He had slept badly, he had indigestion from the heavy and over-spiced Russian food he'd eaten the night before, and he'd rid his comb of yet more of his thinning hair. Susan was always going on at him, saying not to wear a hat because he was going bald. He had told her very calmly that, for that very reason, he preferred to cover his head with a trilby or a cap. She hadn't listened, because she still said the same thing afterwards. In her mind hats and hair loss were synonymous. They'd spoken on the telephone when he arrived. She'd sounded cheerful, which relieved him, and there was nothing gone wrong in the few hours since he'd left home. He loved her, and he knew she hated being on her own. He wondered sometimes what she'd do if he died, then put the thought away. He was sick of travelling himself, now. He'd spent such a large part of his working life on planes. He knew every major airport and a lot of minor ones. He'd travelled dusty pot-holed roads in Africa and twelve-lane highways in the States, stayed at luxury hotels and rat holes where there wasn't enough water to wash in, and malarial mosquitoes buzzed round the room all night. He had enjoyed it then, he was young and filled with a sense of adventure; he didn't enjoy it any more. He had come to a career stop, and his home and family life were more important now, perhaps because of that. He was honest enough to admit the likelihood. Moscow held no charms for him. Five years ago he'd done the tourist bit and walked through the riches of the Kremlin – day after day of them – when he was waiting for an appointment with the senior trade official in the Russian Nuclear Energy Ministry, the ministry responsible for all mining development.

The negotiations had ended in disaster, casualties of the upheaval in Russian political affairs; now he was expected to resurrect them. He felt a lack of confidence in his own ability to deal with people in a bureaucracy like the one that was strangling Russia. It had been hard enough in the days of Gorbachov; now conditions were chaotic in the new Russia under Yeltsin. They already had their guaranteed outlet into Europe and the Middle East through Ivan Karakov.

Why the hell should they listen to him? He made an effort, telling himself that just because he was upset about losing so much hair, he mustn't anticipate failure. Failure carried its own aura. He had to walk into the Ambassador's office, and impress him with his confidence and self-belief. He had the power and influence of Diamond Enterprises behind him. In the early years, he had seen them topple governments . . . He twitched at his tie, jammed a brown trilby on his head, and set off for the Embassy.

'As you can appreciate, Mr Andrews, the situation here is so volatile, it's extremely difficult to get anyone to make a decision about anything.' The Ambassador was a distinguished career diplomat, a lifelong Russophile who was liked and trusted by the new men in power and many of the old ones trying to wrest it back.

'I think', he said slowly, 'your best bet is to see D. V. Borisov. He's not the nominal head of the Ministry, but he has the final yea or nay about what happens in that department. He's been up to Archangel to see the mines recently.'

'Borisov . . .' Andrews frowned. 'That name rings bells . . .' The Ambassador looked at him with respect. He wasn't just a businessman with a lot of international muscle. He had wider knowledge.

'It should do,' he said. 'Igor Borisov was head of the KGB under Brezhnev. This is the son. He's a scientist and an engineer. He's said to be a liberal in spite of the family background. Shall I put in an unofficial word for you? I've met him several times. He's a remarkable man.'

Andrews said, 'I'd be most grateful, Sir Peter. I haven't got an easy job ahead of me.'

The Ambassador smiled. 'Well, you'd be the judge of that. But one thing I can tell you: nothing is for ever in Russia at the moment. Anything can change, with or without reason from our point of view. Yeltsin or Rostopchine. Personally I put my money on the President. They don't come any tougher or more cunning. Perhaps I should have said clever.'

Andrews knew the interview was at an end. 'One last thing,' he said. 'Whose man is D. V. Borisov?'

The Ambassador got up. Andrews did the same. 'No-one knows,' he answered. 'That's what makes him so interesting. If you find out, please let me know.'

They shook hands. 'Goodbye, Sir Peter, and thank you. I know my Chairman will be very grateful for your help.'

'I only hope it can produce a meeting for you. We'll do our best. Good luck, and don't hesitate to call on us if you feel we can do anything more. We'll be in touch.'

Andrews waited for two days. He bought some presents for Susan and the child still at home; he wrote to their son in Canada, and sent postcards to the university student who he knew wouldn't have bothered to read a letter, but would love the view of Lenin's tomb. He was going through the Socialist Worker phase. And, late in the morning of the third fruitless day, when he was starting to despair and wondering whether to chase up the Embassy, he got an invitation to visit D. V. Borisov at the Nuclear Energy Ministry Mining Division on Upinsky Street. He had been given exactly twenty minutes' notice.

5

Paris was hot and empty in August. Elizabeth flew into Charles de Gaulle, and the estate agent met her with a car. He was a tall man, hair slightly greying, and he had a most attractive smile. 'Madame Hastings? I am Jean Pierre Lasalle. How was your flight?'

'Perfect,' Elizabeth said. 'It took longer to go through all the hassle at the airport than to fly over. What a scorching day.' The sun was brassy overhead as they walked out to his car. He opened the door for her to sit in the rear. 'Oh no,' she said. 'I'd like to sit in the front.'

She saw him smile. 'I'd like that, too. Do you know Paris well?'

'Quite well; we've spent several weekends here . . . usually in the spring. It's such a beautiful city.'

'It is,' he agreed. 'I prefer it empty as it is now. All the world goes on holiday in August.'

'Except you,' she remarked.

'Except me. I have a house in Normandy and I go there at weekends and stay in the city during the week. Which is why I am having the pleasure of showing you the apartments. I suggest we go straight to rue Constantine, which is a very impressive apartment.'

'And the most expensive,' Elizabeth added.

'When you see the interior, you won't think so,' he assured her. 'And then I will take you to lunch, and we can see the house in rue de la Perle and the other apartment on the Place de la Concorde. That has a wonderful situation, but is smaller than the other two.'

'I'm booked back on the six o'clock flight. Will we have enough time?'

'I'll make sure you're not late,' he said. They drove through empty streets, except for batches of foreign tourists, slung with cameras and dressed in the uniform of American travellers – track suits, or sweatshirts and jeans with trainers, guidebooks in hand. Elizabeth thought privately, No wonder the French exit *en masse* . . .

'I'll park here,' he said. 'The apartment is in that corner building.'

Elizabeth followed him. It was on the first floor. He unlocked the front door and stood aside for her. 'The owner is in Monaco,' he explained. 'Working there for two years. He's prepared to take short lets of three or six months, that is why the rent is so high. But it's very beautiful.'

Elizabeth couldn't disagree with that. The main salon, as he called it, was a magnificent room, with floor-to-ceiling windows that looked out over the Esplanade des Invalides. The furniture was eighteenth century, rather stiff and formal, fine pictures . . . she recognized quality because she had grown up with it on the walls at home. The regal atmosphere was duplicated in a long cream and gilt panelled dining-room, with seating for fourteen. She walked through to the bedroom; whoever the gentleman working in Monaco was, he wasn't the type to put his feet up and relax when he came home.

She turned to Lasalle. 'It's lovely,' she said. 'But I find it a bit overpowering. I think it would be wonderful for entertaining, as you said on the telephone, but I'm not sure I want to live in it . . .'

'Then let's have lunch and then go to rue de la Perle. That is also beautiful, but quite a contrast. I have booked a table in a little restaurant I know. I hope you like it.'

Elizabeth smiled at him. He hadn't tried to pressure her or resented her criticism of the flat. She liked him, and she was looking forward to lunch. The restaurant was small and modest, the sort of place patronized by native Parisians. The food was excellent. She refused more than a glass of wine. 'I'm useless if I drink during the day,' she explained. 'And I've got to keep a clear head. The trouble is it's all happened so quickly. I really have to make a decision today.'

'It must be inconvenient for you, having to move in such a hurry,' he said. 'My late wife needed a month before she would even go down to the Midi for the Easter holiday. And then there were the children . . . You have children, Madame Hastings?'

'No,' Elizabeth said. 'Not yet. But we hope to.'

'Ah,' he nodded. 'We have four. All grown up, two married, one son is in the States, another in Cannes, where we have a big office. We do a lot of business there; he's very successful.'

'Do any of them come to Normandy?' He was a widower, and she had the impression that he lived alone in the city and his country home. There was something about him that was sad. The eyes, when they weren't looking at her.

'Not very often,' he answered. 'It's a long way for the married couples to come. A pity, they both have children, but . . .' He shrugged. 'They try to come alternate Christmases. I am quite lucky. They do their best. But children grow up and lead their own lives.'

Elizabeth said, 'How long ago did your wife die?'

'Die? Ah, I'm sorry, my English . . . not late, *former* wife. We are divorced. For five years. She lives in Paris, but we are not friendly. Will you take coffee, or should we go to the rue de la Perle?'

'Perhaps we'd better go,' she agreed. 'It was a lovely lunch. Thank you.'

'It was my pleasure,' Jean Pierre Lasalle said.

He was a charming man, with gracious manners, but she knew he meant it. Rue de la Perle was in the 3rd arrondissement. They entered a courtyard through a heavy oak door. 'It was an *hôtel particulier*,' he explained. 'Converted now into three apartments. It dates from the sixteenth century. Very thick walls. Cool in the summer . . .'

It was indeed cool, shaded by the walls enclosing the old house, and she knew immediately she was going to like it. Inside, she looked round. It was old, and its small windows looked on to a courtyard at the rear, with raised beds full of flowers. There were tapestries in the salon, which was half the size of the grandiose reception room of the other flat, the furniture was elegant but comfortable, the bedroom won her head at once, with a fine half-tester bed and a big open fireplace filled with artificial flowers.

'I think this is the one,' she said, turning to Lasalle. 'But I'd better look at the dining-room again, and the kitchen. We have to entertain a lot of people while we're here. Unfortunately.'

He stood with her in the oak-panelled dining-room. A narrow walnut table, ten chairs with little elbow room . . . Elizabeth hesitated. She liked it, she liked the intimacy and the age and the sense of home; she could imagine spending evenings there with James, playing their noisy games of backgammon, waking in the handsome old bed.

'Madame Hastings,' his voice said gently, 'if your husband has to entertain on a large scale . . . then this is not for you. Forgive me, but I know Parisians. Some would find this place an enchantment. But for a London director of Diamond Enterprises, it is not important enough.'

Elizabeth looked at him in surprise. 'How do you know?'

'Because my wife was very much part of that world. She was extremely rich. Her grandmother was South African; of Huguenot extraction. We went to all the smart parties. I met Julius Heyderman and his wife several times. So I know a little about Diamond Enterprises. I sold Karakov his house. You know him?

'No,' Elizabeth said. Karakov. James had talked at length about him. He was the reason for the move to Paris. To get on terms with Ivan Karakov, bring him into D.E.'s fold. That was what James had said. 'No, I don't. What's he like?'

Again that Gallic shrug. 'A genius. A brilliant salesman. A wonderful judge of stones. A terrible snob, and not at all nice.' He actually laughed. 'It's so pleasant to be able to say that. I couldn't before, because my wife felt it was criticism. Forgive me, I shouldn't be so indiscreet. But . . . I would advise you that rue Constantine is more appropriate. And only for three months. If you were making a home here for longer . . . a year, say, then you would be happier here. It is up to you, of course.'

Elizabeth sighed. 'The Place de la Concorde? It's smaller?'

'It has only one bedroom, but two very large reception rooms and it is very chic. Decorator chic, if you see what I mean.'

'Tablescapes,' she said wearily. 'All that clutter . . . I'd go mad. I'm untidy, anyway. I couldn't bear it. No, I won't bother, thank you. Maybe I should look at rue Constantine again. We've got time, haven't we?'

'Oh yes. I think that's a good idea.'

She felt depressed suddenly. In the car she said, 'I really liked that flat, Monsieur Lasalle. It had such charm.'

'See the other again,' he advised. 'Then make a choice. Believe me, I am not thinking of the money. Only what will be best for your purpose here. And what will please your husband.' He smiled brightly. 'That is always important.'

'It's all that matters in this case,' Elizabeth said. 'I mustn't forget that. And I know it's not the money.'

'You can be sure it's not,' he said gently.

Inside the big salon, Elizabeth said, 'Would there be any chance of putting something of our own in here? It's such a formal room. At my expense I'd like to change the ambience, put in a sofa, a big stool and another coffee-table. I *am* an interior decorator – I have a business in London. So I won't do anything outrageous! Would that be all right with your client?'

Lasalle considered. 'I think so,' he said. 'I don't see why he should object. So long as nothing is removed.'

She took a breath. James would love the place. It had been his first choice when he looked at the brochure. 'Then I'll take this,' she said. 'I know it's what my husband would want. And thank you. You've been very kind and helpful. I'd have taken the rue de la Perle, and it wouldn't have been right.'

At the airport she held out her hand. He kissed it very lightly.

'I hope you'll come and see us,' she said. 'My husband would like to meet you. Especially if you know Karakov.'

'I would be delighted,' he answered. 'I will arrange about the extra furniture with my client. And anything else you would like. Leave it to me. And a good journey home.'

'My husband's office will call you tomorrow and we'll get on with the contract. Goodbye, and thank you again. See you when we come over.'

He waited till she had gone through into the airport before he turned away. She was a beautiful woman, and very nice. He attached a lot of importance to niceness in women. He had overlooked that quality when he got married. It was a hard lesson, but he'd learned it.

When Elizabeth got home, James was already there. He got up quickly and came to kiss her. 'Darling . . . how did it go?'

She sank down into the seat beside him, kicking off her shoes. 'I've taken a flat,' she announced. 'It's the one

89

you liked in rue Constantine. It's so grand and stuffy I nearly decided on somewhere else, but it wasn't really big enough, didn't seat more than ten at a pinch . . .'

He handed her a glass of white wine and sat beside her.

'Thanks,' she said. 'I can do with this . . . It was quite a long day.'

'But are you happy with this place? I don't want you to live somewhere you don't like.' James looked at her anxiously.

'Don't be silly,' she smiled at him. 'I can put some things in and make it comfortable. It'll be great for entertaining the beau monde. You'll love it. The agent took me out to lunch. He was really charming. And he knows this jeweller Karakov. Knows him quite well, he said, or rather his wife did. They're divorced now. He was the one who persuaded me to take the "Palace". Said it would suit us better. You'll like him. I said he must come and see us when we move in. Oh . . .' she sighed. 'It's so nice to be home though. How was your day?'

'Hectic,' he admitted. He didn't say anything, but he was irritated by the idea of the charming estate agent she'd invited to visit them. He had never had reason to be jealous, but he was. Other men must feel about Elizabeth the way he did, and he didn't like it. Knew Karakov, did he? He answered her question with a brief résumé. 'Andrews has made contact in Moscow. About bloody time. And that shit Kruger came up and said he didn't mind lending me his secretary. I hate that man. He takes a swing at me every chance he gets.' Maybe he would have the agent over if he was friendly with Karakov. Just for a drink . . . He slipped his arm round Elizabeth and hugged her. 'Thanks, sweetheart. You've been great about the move and the upheaval. Hopefully we won't have to be there for very long. Not wearing your watch?'

The present ordered from Cartier was upstairs in its

red leather case, in the wall safe in their bedroom. It was gold with a diamond-studded face. Beautiful, as all Cartier designs were, but hardly appropriate to wear in the daytime.

She said gently. 'I keep it for the evening, Jamie. You know how much I love it.' Which wasn't absolutely true.

He said, 'I want you to take all your jewellery with you. Pity so much of it is old-fashioned.' He frowned.

Elizabeth's mother had given her a Georgian diamond necklace as a wedding present. An aunt had parted with a heavy Victorian sapphire brooch, dripping pearl drops. Both were family pieces. Elizabeth treasured them, but couldn't think when she'd ever wear them. His remark surprised her.

'I like old-fashioned things,' she said. 'I actually think all that Karakov stuff is very ugly. So hard and vulgar, all you see is some bloody great rock, no setting at all.'

'Just remember not to say that,' he said softly. 'Maybe I can arrange to borrow some pieces for you . . . he's not impressed by heirlooms, darling.'

'You can borrow what you like,' she said sweetly. He knew what that tone of voice meant, and prepared to retreat. 'So long as you wear them, because I won't. Any messages?' She changed the subject because she didn't want to argue with him.

She was tired, she'd had a long day, enjoyed part of it, agreed to live in a flat she thought looked like the Throne Room at Buckingham Palace, and was *not*, she emphasized silently, not going to be dolled up like an English version of Ivana Trump to impress *anybody* . . .

'I wrote them down off the ansaphone,' he said. 'One was a call from Valerie Kruger, of all people. Wants you to go to lunch.' He hesitated; he'd backed off about the jewellery. He didn't want her getting friendly with Kruger's ex. He knew Elizabeth was hostile enough to Ruth Fraser, and, in spite of what he'd promised, there would have to be times in Paris when the two women met.

'I don't think there's much point in you going.' He said it casually. 'We're not likely to see her any more, our paths simply don't cross—'

'I suggested it,' she retorted. 'Certainly I'll go if I'm free. I liked her. I'll call after dinner. Another glass of wine?'

He got up. 'Not still cross about the jewellery?' She shook her head. He knew how to defuse her. He looked like an anxious little boy, not wanting to be out of favour.

'No. I'm just not into being a glitter bag. Sorry I snapped at you.'

He went and poured a glass of wine for her. He should have wiped that message off. He was a fool.

Elizabeth met Valerie Kruger the day she was driving down to Somerset for her father's birthday. They'd agreed to make it early, as it was a long journey. Valerie Kruger chose San Lorenzo in Beauchamp Place. It was the smartest Italian restaurant in London, patronized by the young Royals, celebrities and socialites, and those who hoped to see one or other. Elizabeth knew it well; she liked the food and the easy atmosphere.

Valerie had asked for a corner table. It didn't give them the coveted view of who else was lunching there, but it was secluded. Elizabeth didn't mind. She wasn't a star gazer. She thought Valerie looked tired and rather strained.

'How nice of you to come,' she greeted Elizabeth. There was a half-finished drink on the table.

'So nice of you to ask me,' Elizabeth answered. 'I'd meant to call you first, but life's been one mad rush in the last couple of weeks. How are you?'

'Fine. What will you have to drink? I was early, so I'm ahead by half a gin and tonic.'

'Just a glass of wine. I've got to drive home this afternoon.'

'To your parents? How lovely.' Valerie was signalling the waiter. She seemed very tense. 'Mine are dead, of course, but then . . .' the smile was forced as if it hurt her '. . . I'm so much older than you are.'

Elizabeth smiled her sunny smile. 'Well, you don't look it. I must tell you, we're moving to Paris for the next three months. It's rather exciting. Do you know it well? Got any tips for me?'

Valerie Kruger looked at her. Such a friendly woman, lacking in guile. As straight as she was beautiful, looking forward to going to Paris.

'I haven't been there for some years,' she said. 'But I heard you were going. So I thought I'd better ask you out to lunch before you went. Here's the menu.'

She hid behind it, not feeling hungry, not caring what she chose. She had made up her mind to approach it carefully. Lead into it. Instead she had almost blurted it out. She had decided to contact Elizabeth after thinking carefully about what she was going to say and why. She had been scrupulous about her own motives. She was eaten away with bitterness and hatred, but she convinced herself that neither of these feelings prompted her. They ordered, and Elizabeth told her about the apartment, trying to make it sound amusing. She mentioned the agent's name, Lasalle, and Valerie looked up and said, 'I met him and his wife when we went over on a business trip. Long time ago. She was very attractive, and an absolute bitch. I remember feeling sorry for him. But—' she forked up some food reluctantly '—I expect he married her for her money.'

'Oh, I don't think so; he was really nice. I was sorry for him, he seemed lonely.'

Valerie said slowly, 'I'm afraid I look at men with rather a jaundiced eye these days. You're probably right.'

Elizabeth said simply, 'I don't blame you. When I

heard what had happened I couldn't believe it. I thought at the time your husband was completely crazy, and I think so now. She's a dreadful woman.'

'Thank you,' Valerie said. 'You know it's surprising how many people found something *nice* to say about her . . . But Dick's not mad. He's in love with her just like he's in love with the business, that's all. I always came a poor second to Diamond Enterprises. Really,' she drew in a breath, 'that's why I asked you to have lunch with me. I told you I'd heard about Paris. I have some mutual friends left who know Dick and hear the gossip. They tell me things . . .' She grimaced. 'It's rather like having a bad tooth. It hurts like hell, but you can't resist touching it . . . So I always listen.

'When they said your husband was taking Ruth along as his assistant – well, I felt I must talk to you.'

Elizabeth said, 'He doesn't want to; she was forced on him. He can't stand her.'

No, Valerie thought, not at the moment. But just give it time. Wait till she's at his elbow, putting her scent down for him like a cat on heat, sharing all his business problems . . . Dick hadn't liked her either at first, just admired her efficiency. His previous secretary had been careless and only interested in getting away out of the office on time.

'I hope you won't take this the wrong way,' Valerie said. 'I like you, Elizabeth, I did from the first time we met. Those awful office parties with the wives eyeing each other up and down and the men smarming up to Arthur's wife. You were so nice, you didn't play games. I don't think you knew that games were being played.'

'I didn't,' Elizabeth admitted. 'I was very young and it was all new to me. I was just bored. Till James started explaining things and I could try and take an intelligent interest. Happily he talks to me about everything.'

'You're lucky,' Valerie said. 'Keep it going. I gave up. I gave up and I stepped away. That's why I'm sitting here without my husband. I should have seen the danger, but I didn't. I felt he was entitled to live for his business, because we never managed to have children and I knew he was disappointed. South Africans are very family conscious, especially if they're half Afrikaans like Dick. He would have liked a big houseful, with himself playing the father figure in the middle. But I couldn't. So . . .'

Elizabeth reached out suddenly. She touched the other woman's hand as it lay on the table, slightly clenched. 'I'm so sorry,' she said gently. 'We've been trying for ages. We've been told nothing's wrong, but it just won't happen.'

Valerie didn't say anything for a moment. She moved her hand, searched in her bag and brought out a packet of filter cigarettes. 'I started this when he left,' she said. 'I hope you don't mind.'

'No, no. It doesn't bother me at all.' She watched the other woman light up and then inhale.

'You're in love with your husband, aren't you?'

'Yes.' Elizabeth was surprised. 'Of course I am. We're in love with each other.'

'We weren't,' Valerie said. 'But it still took Ruth Fraser three years to get Dick away from me. I said I asked you out because you were going to Paris. The real reason is to warn you against her. I don't know why she was the one picked for the job. But I do know why she's taken it. She's getting tired of Dick. He's not going to the top like she'd hoped. So she's looking round for someone else. She's risen on her back in every job since she was twenty. I had her checked out by a detective when this started. I tried to show the report to Dick, but he wouldn't look at it. I don't give a shit, that's what he said, and he threw it at me. She's all I want and I don't care who's fucked her before me . . .' She stabbed out the half-smoked cigarette. 'Dick was fifty-two and overweight. Your husband is young and attractive and he's rich. My source says he's destined for big things in

95

D.E. And that's what she's after. She wants to get to the top herself, and she'll take any man who can help her. Don't let her do to you what she did to me. When you get there, make your husband get rid of her.'

The waiter was beside them. He smiled. 'Coffee, ladies?'

'No,' Elizabeth said quickly. 'It's getting late. I've got to go.'

'You're angry,' Valerie Kruger said. 'You don't think I've any right to talk to you like this?'

'I don't think you've any right to talk about James as if he was anything like your husband. I'm sorry about what happened to you. I know you're hurt and bitter, but I trust my husband. I know James and he'd never behave like that. I'm sure you mean well, but I really must go now. Thank you for lunch.'

She stood up. There was a flush of indignation on her face.

'Just get rid of her,' Valerie Kruger said. 'I'm trying to be your friend.'

'That's very kind of you,' Elizabeth said shortly. 'But I know I've nothing to worry about. Goodbye.'

The first meeting at the office of the Ministry for Nuclear Energy had taken place in a room on the first floor overlooking Red Square. It was a big room with a high ceiling; it was spartan, white walls, reproductions of Lenin's portrait common to such offices had been removed, leaving a large rectangle on one wall. The present occupant had made no political statement. He hung modest oils of Russian landscapes and a group of peasant children, and kept his ideology a secret.

A young man had acted as interpreter. D. V. Borisov had risen from his desk, very functional and pre-fabricated, and walked forward to shake hands with Ray Andrews. He was a tall man in his late thirties, not handsome, with rather heavy Slav features and very black eyes. His hair was cut so short his head seemed shaven. There were no concessions to Western imports. His suit was ill-cut serge, his shoes were scuffed leather, and they hadn't been polished for a long time.

Ray Andrews introduced himself via the interpreter. He was surprised that Borisov didn't speak English. The Ambassador had spoken highly of him, almost as if they were on friendly terms. But then the diplomat was fluent in Russian.

'My Chairman, Mr Julius Heyderman, is anxious about rumours circulating in the industry of the activities of a retail jeweller called Ivan Karakov. He asked me to come over and discuss these rumours with you, Mr Borisov, and to clarify the position if that is possible.'

Ray's tone was conciliatory. The translator rattled away in Russian. D. V. Borisov listened. Once he nodded slightly. He considered Ray Andrews and the look was expressionless.

'Mr Borisov says he is not aware of any rumours. His ministry is not interested in anything but facts.'

It was a bald, hostile statement. Andrews didn't rise. He said in the same pleasant tone, 'I used the term rumours deliberately, because although we are convinced that they represent facts, we can't define them as such without the co-operation of your ministry. Perhaps I can give you the details and explain our cause for concern. It's not just concern for our own interests, but for the industry long term.'

The translation seemed shorter this time. 'Please explain whatever you feel is relevant to our situation here in Russia. The interests of other countries and multinational companies don't necessarily coincide with ours.'

Still hostile. Not, Ray suspected, one of President Yeltsin's free-market enthusiasts. But years of negotiating with African politicians had given him an impenetrable skin. He smiled slightly.

'They may coincide more than they used to,' he remarked. 'Let me clarify.'

The interpreter interrupted. 'Would you like tea or vodka, Mr Andrews?'

It was a technique designed to put him off just as he was marshalling his facts. He knew that one too, from past experience in that failed Russian negotiation.

'Neither, thank you. I don't want to delay you or waste your time, Mr Borisov. As we in Diamond Enterprises understand it, your government has been negotiating an exclusive sale and distribution deal with the firm of Karakov International in Paris.' He paused, meeting the Russian's cold stare with a cool look of his own. He didn't wait for the translator. He cut through him. 'If this is the case, then believe me, Russian interests are not only closely associated with ours, but indistinguishable from them. I don't make this assertion lightly, and I am able to prove its validity beyond question.'

The interpreter said smoothly, 'Mr Borisov has fifteen minutes before his next appointment. He can't give you any more time, Mr Andrews.'

'I only need five,' Andrews answered. 'We have a world monopoly in the sale of diamonds. We control them, and we do this by controlling the distribution and keeping the stocks at a level commensurate with the market. We thus maintain prices and secure the future of all the producers who sell to us. Karakov is trying to break that monopoly by dealing direct with you. If he succeeds, in ten years, that mine of yours at Archangel may as well be closed. There won't be a market for your diamonds worth the expense of maintaining it. Now,' he stood up, 'I won't detain you, Mr Borisov. But I sincerely hope you will give some thought to the basic facts I've put in front of you, and agree to a second meeting, with a longer time scale. Thank you for seeing me this morning. I hope to hear from you.'

He went up to the desk and shook hands. Borisov gave

him a look, it wasn't warm, but at least it conveyed that something Ray had said merited his attention.

The interpreter said smoothly, 'Goodbye, Mr Andrews. I can promise nothing but of course I shall make some enquiries. If I find anything of interest to us, and to your company, I shall ask you to meet with me again.'

The interpreter walked to the door and opened it. Ray Andrews went out. He walked down the stairs. Russian lifts were slow and unreliable, even in official buildings. There was a chronic shortage of spares for everything. What there was filtered through to their illegal markets controlled by racketeers. Like food and clothes and luxuries. Even bread in some areas. Freedom had cost the Soviet people dearly. They were hungry, crime ridden and beset by fiscal fluctuations that sent the rouble diving and encouraged corruption. He wasn't surprised that there were people like D. V. Borisov, whose father had been head of the KGB, who would have welcomed a return to the old political structure. He went for a walk, noting the litter in the streets, the sullen crowds hurrying by, the bare shop windows. No queues. They had been a Western media invention, he knew that. No queues because there was nothing that couldn't be got on the illegal markets in large quantities and triple the price.

He thought about Borisov. The Ambassador's description, a remarkable man, didn't quite fit the dour Soviet-type official he'd encountered that morning. Ray was sure he understood some English, most of them did at his level. It had always been a Russian ploy to pretend ignorance of Western languages. He sighed; he didn't want to walk, he was tired. He'd try and ring Susan when he got back to the hotel. He hoped she wouldn't ask him when he was coming back. He didn't know. He didn't know if he would hear from D. V. Borisov again. Or how long Julius Heyderman expected him to sit it out.

And what was happening back in London while he

kicked his heels in Moscow . . . ? He went back to his hotel and put a call through to Arthur Harris.

He tried to think of something encouraging to tell him. There wasn't much.

'How was the birthday party?' James asked her. He thought she looked preoccupied when she came home the following day. Not quite herself. He was concerned. He wanted to come in and find her happy, smiling at him. Everything was ready. They were packed up, she'd done marvels getting organized at such short notice. He had signed the contract for the Paris flat, and had a meeting with Ruth Fraser. He didn't tell Elizabeth about that.

Ruth had been pleasant, slightly deferential. She had behaved like the efficient secretary-cum-personal assistant going over the preliminaries with her new boss. He noticed her clothes. They were appropriate, too. Elegant but very understated, not too much make-up, just the cat's-eyes emphasized so that when he looked at her, they caught his attention.

'I'm so looking forward to going,' she said. 'And to working with you, Mr Hastings.'

He didn't want to say it, but it was office policy to use Christian names. 'Thanks, Ruth. I'm sure we'll be productive. If there's anything you need, just let me know.'

She had smiled at him, very impersonally. 'I will, thank you. Mr Kruger asked me to send his best wishes for success.'

'That's nice of him. I'm sure he'll miss you.' Best wishes from Kruger? Like hell, James said to himself. All he wishes me is a broken neck . . .

He said it again, 'Darling? How was the birthday party?'

Elizabeth looked up. 'Oh, sorry, darling. I was making mental lists . . . I'm sure I've forgotten something vital.

It was fun, great fun. Pop enjoyed it, and he loved his present. I said it was from you, too.'

'Good,' James said, relieved. She looked rather tired round the eyes. Not surprising after a long drive, then coming back to the last vestiges of the packing. He came and slipped his arm round her. 'Sweetheart,' he said, 'why don't we eat out tonight? Get away from all this . . . We moved house so often when I was a kid, and I always hated it. How about that new trattoria in Gloucester Road?'

Elizabeth leaned against him. He didn't talk much about his childhood, but she knew it had been insecure. His father made money and went where the business was. There hadn't been the foundation of a settled home like hers. No wonder he wanted to get out for the evening. She would have preferred an omelette and an early night.

'Of course we'll go, darling,' she said. 'I love pasta.'

Valerie Kruger wouldn't go away. She had hovered in Elizabeth's mind all the way in the car down to Somerset. She drifted through Elizabeth's dreams, sad faced, full of warning. And the same theme ran through it all. No children. Dick was so disappointed. So he turned more and more to the business . . . *Make your husband get rid of her. Don't let her do to you what she did to me* . . . No children. Nothing to bind a family-minded man to a barren marriage. And a woman who could share the other side of his life had prised him away. The same woman who was going to Paris and would be working with James every day. They were sitting at the restaurant table, drinking Chianti, and suddenly she couldn't help herself.

'Jamie . . .'

He looked up at her. He'd been studying the menu for their main course. 'Made up your mind yet?'

She said, 'No. Jamie, I want to ask you something. Put that down, will you . . .'

He did. 'What is it?'

'If we never have children, will you still love me?'

He actually burst out laughing. 'God you are a nutter! What do you mean, will I still love you? Now listen to me. Just listen. I didn't marry you for children. I'd like them, but not as much as you would. I'm being honest. If we never have any, so what? We'll adopt if you want to. And anyway, there's no reason to talk like that. You'll get pregnant – there's no hurry, and if you'd only stop worrying about it, everyone's told you . . . Sweetheart, I'm not going to sit here and spoil a nice dinner by talking a lot of balls about whether I'm going to stop loving you. Because I'm not. Never. Now make up your mind what you're going to eat. OK?'

She smiled back at him. 'OK.'

That night he made love to her. She knew it was more to reassure her than because he felt like it; he was a very active lover, but she could tell the difference. She didn't feel like it, either. It was less a passionate coupling than a comforting embrace. It should have reassured her, but it didn't.

'I've booked in at the Lancaster,' Dick Kruger said.

They were in bed watching TV. Or rather Ruth was watching the programme and Dick was fretting about losing her the next morning. She was flying in a day ahead of the Hastings to set up his office and her own. The office had rented a small apartment for her near the Invalides on the Left Bank. Two rooms and a single bed. Kruger insisted that she change that. In the interval he would stay weekends at a hotel.

'That's great,' she said. She wished he wouldn't harp on their separation. He needed constant assurance that her reason for taking the offer was to help him and Arthur Harris and sabotage James Hastings. She had said it over and over and it was getting on her nerves. She wanted to watch *Newsnight*.

'I'll come over on Friday evening. Can you meet me?'

'I may be working late. I don't know.' She made a decision. She turned to him. She slipped her hand up and tweaked his ear. His ears were very sensitive. 'Darling,' she murmured, giving up *Newsnight*, 'why don't you wait till the weekend after to come over? I'll have fixed the flat by then. I don't know how it's going to work out . . . I might be busy on Friday until late, even have to work Saturday . . . it depends on Hastings. What will you do, sitting all alone in some hotel? Wait till the weekend after.'

She snapped the TV off, and set about him, her hands wandering, touching him.

He protested. 'Why? Why don't you want me to come? What the fuck am I supposed to do all weekend without you?'

'Play golf,' she murmured, nuzzling his neck. 'And think about what I'll do when you come the next weekend. Call Tony and fix a game for Saturday. Go down to the club for the weekend. I don't want you staying in London getting up to mischief.'

He groaned, clawing at her as she moved on top of him. He'd argue about it afterwards, but now . . . Oh Jesus . . . now . . .

He fell asleep, and she eased out of bed. She showered, dried herself and slipped on a nightdress. They always went to bed naked. She liked the feel of silk after she'd made love. He was a good lover; she'd taught him how to please her and, my God, she knew how to please him . . . She'd shut his mouth that night, and she could relax and think of the future. She wasn't sure what it held. It was all in the balance. The coming fight to a finish between Heyderman and Arthur Harris, Andrews' attempt to scuttle the Russian deal with Karakov, and James Hastings taking the battle to the enemy's heart in Paris. It was so exciting. The thrills of sex were mind blowing, but they didn't last. Pleasure was transient. Power was there the next morning. She liked that phrase.

It pleased her. She didn't love Dick Kruger. Ruth had always been truthful with herself. She might lie to the world, but never to Ruth Fraser, who had been born Ruth Felderman and brought up in a dingy East End two-roomed flat where she and her brother slept on a put-u-up in the sitting-room, and her parents occupied the only bedroom.

She had learned very early in life that you had to work to get what you wanted. Her mother worked; she took in sewing and she kept her family clean and fed. She was a good mother but a hard one. If Ruth came home late from school she was hit. If she didn't finish her home-work on time she was hit. If she talked back to her mother, her father hit her instead. They worshipped the boy. He could do no wrong. She couldn't do right. Her father was a tailor; it wasn't his business. He never got into working for himself. That's why they were poor. Her mother was always reproaching him because he was salaried and other people took the profit home. One night, when Ruth was asleep, she felt her brother's hand on her. He was younger than she was, but much stronger. He held her down, the pillow rammed over her face till she nearly suffocated. He raped her. Then he said simply he would deny it and tell her parents she'd been with another boy and was blaming him. They'd believe him and beat the shit out of her. He'd liked it and he'd do it whenever he wanted. He turned over and went to sleep. When he came at her the next night, and all the nights afterwards, he didn't have to stop her mouth. She let him do it. And when she was sixteen, six months after it first happened, she missed two periods and knew she was pregnant. She didn't tell him. She didn't tell anyone. She packed her few clothes in a cheap holdall, robbed her mother's purse of the week's housekeeping money, and walked out. She went to a Salvation Army hostel, gave her name as Fraser because she didn't know if they would take in a Jewish girl, and got herself a job waitressing.

She slept with the café owner, who was a Greek Cypriot, and saved enough money to have an abortion. It had been done by an old Cypriot woman who serviced the neighbourhood. It was quick and uncomplicated. Luckily the old woman was clean. She boiled her instruments and used clean sheets. Ruth walked away and spent three days in her room. Then she went back to the café. It could have been a downward slide, but Ruth was not going down. She was going up. By any means on offer. She avoided the criminal element. There were petty crooks and pimps on the lookout for a pretty girl, and Ruth was very pretty. She left the café and got herself a job in a supermarket. She waitressed at a wine bar in the evenings and she saved. She slept with the manager of the supermarket, and he made her a supervisor. She went to secretarial classes at night school. At nineteen she got her first office job. It had taken off from there. She lay beside Dick Kruger. He was snoring. She rubbed the silk nightdress, stroking herself like a cat.

Dick had been generous to her. Most men had rewarded her for the way she made them feel; only one had tried to knock her about and bully her, and Ruth had left the job and moved to Central London where she worked at an agency for a while, making a lot of money, buying clothes and shaping herself for a suitable interview with a brokerage firm where a secretary was needed on a permanent basis. She got the job, and she found her true *métier*. She had a talent for business. It fascinated her. The industry and intelligence stemming from her Jewish heritage blossomed in the environment of trading. She was home and she knew it. But she was a woman, and women didn't infiltrate the man's financial world, except through the back entrance.

Dick Kruger, lying on his back with his mouth ajar, was the last of a succession of lovers who had helped to advance Ruth's career. She had been offered marriage by one or two and refused. She was not interested in domestic life. She didn't want children. Never, after that one experience. She didn't want to belong to anyone or own anyone herself . . . Marriage was not for her. Unless it was to the boss. And even then, she wasn't sure she'd settle for it.

Dick wanted to marry her. She'd said yes, for the same reason she'd heated him up that night when all she wanted was to watch her programme on TV and go to sleep. To keep him quiet. She had managed to put marriage on the back burner. Paris came first. The prospect excited her. She relished the challenge. Her own role was not yet clear. She might do exactly what she'd promised Kruger: wreck Hastings' project if she got the chance. Or she might not. It would depend on which side looked like winning. If Andrews succeeded in Russia, then Hastings' role wouldn't be so vital. Arthur Harris might come out vindicated, and Kruger with him. She might need to strike at Hastings if that happened, just to clear him out of Kruger's way. There was everything to play for, and she felt lucky. Her instinct had never failed. There had never been a woman on the Board of Diamond Enterprises. She fell asleep on that beguiling thought.

Arthur Harris took Andrews' telephone call. They had spoken two days before, and Ray had nothing to report but the sterile interview at the Nuclear Energy Ministry. D. V. Borisov sounded like the kind of Soviet bureaucrat that had successfully stifled the Russian economy in the days before Gorbachov. Arthur sighed.

'Well,' he had said, 'there's nothing you can do but wait and then prod them through the Embassy if you haven't had a response by the end of the week. They're as bad as the bloody Africans. Keep me in close touch, won't you . . . I have faxes from Julius twice a day demanding progress reports.' He had taken his mind off his troubles by rereading the brochure on his new racing yacht.

Andrews was put through immediately when he made the unexpected call.

'I've been sent for,' he explained. 'Given a day's notice this time, and a longer interview. I don't want to read too much into this, but I think he's interested. I talked to Sir Peter and he thinks so too. He says this guy doesn't waste time talking unless he means business. Now . . . if he comes up with some concrete proposal, how wide is my brief, moneywise?'

Arthur didn't hesitate. 'No limit,' he said smoothly. 'Whatever he wants, promise it. Whatever it takes, get them to cut off Karakov's supplies. And don't worry. I'll back you.'

'Thanks,' Andrews said. 'Can I call you at home?'

'Call me anywhere, any time,' Arthur said. 'Don't hesitate. Good luck.'

Andrews had rung off. *Whatever he wants, promise it.* He had never gone into any negotiation with such an open-ended brief. It gave him a surge of enthusiasm which had been missing before. He had loved his job, squaring it with his domestic pressures as fairly as he could, but he had begun to lose impetus in the last two years. Begun to drift along, his ambitions on hold, losing sight of the mountain peak. Suddenly they had come into view again. He was ready to do battle with D. V. Borisov.

Dimitri Valerian Borisov was thirty-seven years old. He was very young by Russian standards to hold such a senior position. He owed his advancement to his top scientific qualifications and to his equally distinguished engineering and geological achievements.

He had two brothers and a sister. The Borisovs had been a very close family. As the children of the most powerful man in the old Soviet Union after the Secretary General himself, they were privileged. All doors opened for them academically, or in whatever branch of State

Service they chose. His sister was a paediatrician, his elder brother went into the Army. He had been killed in Afghanistan. Dimitri Valerian knew that he had been tortured to death by mujahideen fighters, a fate so horrible that it had brought about his father's incapacitating stroke. His mother never knew the truth. His younger brother was the exception. He chose no career, settled to nothing, and joined a rock band, playing in Moscow discos. Dimitri Valerian was his father's son. Dedicated, unscrupulous about methods, concerned only with two things: his own promotion up his career scale, and the best interests of his country. Russia had suffered, and still suffered, the birth pains of her new freedom. A freedom which men like his father had supressed with bloody efficiency for seventy years. He loved his father, and he believed that what he had done was necessary at the time, but that time had passed and Russia's greatness lay in a future adapted to Western economic values. Industrial power was the key, now that war had become a form of mutual genocide. Russia must grow economically, her reserves were so vast, her labour potential so immense, if only her structure could be reformed and system made to work . . . He dreamed of Russia's greatness as an older generation dreamed of world domination by a universal creed.

The Englishman was coming for a second interview. He had sensed a very deep anxiety in the man. He was a senior and practised negotiator. Dimitri had researched him long before their first meeting. He knew every detail of that disastrous encounter five years earlier, and his near expulsion from the country. Ray Andrews had no reason to think of the Russians as easy targets for a capitalist giant like Diamond Enterprises.

He had shown no evidence of a grudge. He was composed, outwardly confident in the preliminary stage, and Borisov had been as coldly non-committal as possible, without being openly hostile. He was setting

108

the scene for what might be a very tough round of negotiations. And he had already determined the final price. It would be high indeed.

Ray Andrews was shown in at exactly four-thirty. Borisov was a punctual man who never forgave it if he was kept waiting. His interpreter was beside him.

They shook hands, and the Englishman said, 'Thank you for bringing our meeting about so quickly.'

The interpreter translated. Borisov smiled. It changed his expression dramatically. Some men smiled and it meant nothing but a grimace. Andrews saw a man of humour and even warmth for that brief moment. The translator said, 'Would you like a glass of tea? Or some coffee?'

'A glass of tea, please,' Ray said. 'I got a taste for it when I was here last.'

Borisov spoke. The translator said, 'That can't have been a happy experience for you.'

'No,' Andrews admitted. 'But, under the circumstances, your reaction was quite understandable. It did make my position rather difficult in London.'

'I am sure it did.' He was startled by the voice. Dimitri Valerian Borisov had spoken in English. He said a few words to the interpreter, who said to Andrews, 'Tea will be brought to you, Mr Andrews. My services aren't needed.'

'I wondered,' Ray said, 'whether they were really needed the first time we met.'

Borisov shrugged. 'I learned English at university.' He offered no explanation. 'It's a difficult language for us. I'm told Russian is also difficult for you.'

'I don't speak it, I'm afraid. I have fluent French, because it's a second language in some parts of Africa, where I've spent a lot of time over the years. But for some reason, the English have never bothered to learn other languages. I think it's a great mistake.'

'Why should they, when half the world spoke theirs?'

'I suppose so. Your English is extremely good. You've never been to England?'

'No. One day perhaps.'

Andrews said pleasantly, 'We'd be glad to invite you.'

'I'd be glad to come. One day, when I have a little time for a holiday. I can't think when that might be. We have so much to do, Mr Andrews, to reshape our country. Our problems are enormous. Our economy has been mismanaged and allowed to drift into chaos. Slowly and painfully, we are trying to get it right. Here is our tea.'

A blonde girl in a white shirt and black skirt brought them two steaming glasses, topped with lemon slices. Andrews noticed that she had fat legs.

Borisov sipped. 'I have made enquiries into the . . . er . . . rumours you mentioned,' he said. 'First, I will explain our position. Our previous dealings with Diamond Enterprises . . . your trip here five years ago to negotiate a concession for the mine at Archangel – they did not leave a good impression, Mr Andrews. The man who was prepared to sign away our rights to manage our own diamond mines was a criminal; he had accepted large sums of money for other deals connected with mineral rights. We have no doubt that a bribe was going to be paid to him when he went to London to sign that agreement with you. He is still serving a long prison sentence. Since then we have developed our own resources without Western help. And very successfully, as Archangel proves. We faced great difficulties. To say it was an environmental nightmare was no exaggeration. And a mining nightmare, which was even worse. We had to exploit a 700-metre mud pile of water-saturated unconsolidated Cambrian sediments. That water had to be pumped out, using the open pit method, from an excavation of a final diameter of 9 kilometres. This outflow would have contaminated the local fish spawning grounds. Also dust and leached material would cause widespread pollution. Our local population, educated in the dangers of destroying the environment, were much opposed to any mining operation in the area, where swamps and huge forests would suffer as a result.'

He paused.

Andrews said, 'Nightmare is the only word.'

'We solved our problems,' Borisov said. 'We found our own solutions. We didn't need Diamond Enterprises or any other Western expertise to bring that mine and other smaller mines, into production. We chose to use wider-diameter bore holes in a grid of 4.6 metres or 6.2 metres into the diamond bearing pipes, and removed the debris in solution for treatments. There has been no ecological disaster at Archangel, and we have one of the biggest mines, yielding some of the rarest diamonds in the world.' He smiled. It was triumphant. 'How appropriate that those diamonds should be red.' There was a pause, and then he said, 'I went to the area three months ago. I saw the diamonds in the rough. And some polished stones. Have you seen a sample?'

Andrews nodded. 'Yes. A five-carat flawless red stone. It was breathtaking. Unique. I must say how much I admire your achievements in bringing that mine into production in spite of such horrendous problems. I take your point about doing it without Western technology. Now, I'd like to make a few points explaining our position, and why we wanted the concession in the first place. Will you give me a fair hearing?'

'Why would you expect otherwise, Mr Andrews?'

'Because . . .' Ray had decided to gamble with this man. Gamble on honesty against his suspicion of Diamond Enterprises, and of Western motives towards Russia. 'Because I get the impression you don't like us. Or trust us.'

There was a flicker of surprise. 'That won't influence my judgement. I told you the first time we met, I am only concerned with what benefits my country. If you can show me a benefit, I will listen to anything.'

'Thank you,' Ray said. 'I came out here five years ago to get the concession to develop and run what our geologists believed was a mine to rival the biggest diamond fields in the world. Our motive wasn't to own a diamond mine, however important. Diamond Enterprises isn't a greedy little firm, fighting over a mine concession. What we're protecting is the diamond industry as a whole. We control the distribution and sale of diamonds throughout the world; we keep the prices pegged at the right rate – not too high, not too low. There was a time when the price of diamonds fell to next to nothing in the early Thirties, because the industry was killing itself by price cutting and infighting for power. Jan Heyderman stopped all that. All the wealth that comes from mining diamonds is concentrated and safeguarded by the organizational methods we've built up over the past fifty years. Now Karakov wants to go outside it. He wants to market his goods direct. If this mine is big enough, that could and will undermine our authority. The system will begin to break down. In the end everyone will be the losers, including your country, Mr Borisov. Nobody benefits in these wars. I'm not a mining engineer, and I know damn little about diamonds, but I do know something about economics, and if we can't stop Karakov, then the red diamond that I saw in London means one thing: the death of the diamond industry. That's the truth. That's why I'm here.'

There was a silence. He had spoken with fierce conviction. He had been honest and because of it he had shown that Diamond Enterprises was vulnerable.

'The stability of the market in diamonds is just as much in Russia's interest as it is in ours.' Ray Andrews spoke more calmly. 'You have a vast natural resource which is only just becoming near its potential. Gemstones aside, the demand for industrials is enormous with the opening up of Eastern Europe and the need for advanced technology in countries wanting to compete economically with us and the world as a whole.

'You would have a bottomless source of foreign currency which your country needs. You need foreign investment and favourable foreign loans. I am authorized to recommend both from our Chairman and Board of Directors. If the vanity and short-sighted policy of Ivan Karakov is allowed to disturb the fine balance of our hold on the price and distribution of diamonds, then everything goes down the bloody drain.'

He searched in his pocket and brought out a packet of filter cigarettes.

'Do you mind if I smoke?'

'I'll join you, Mr Andrews. We're not so paranoid about tobacco as you are. We have too many other things killing us to worry about cigarettes. When I went to Archangel, I met Ivan Karakov. He came up on a very private visit. He presented me with one of the red stones he had cut in Paris as a sampler for our government. He suggested I give it to my wife.'

He smiled slightly, mocking the old man's attempts at a bribe.

'I don't have a wife. I presented it to our Gemology Institute. You know he has offered us a guaranteed outlet to the Middle East market? Exclusive rights in those red stones, making their value incalculable since we will be the only source and he the only agent. And for the other coloured stones – fancies, you say in the trade. Green sapphire, blue . . . very clear deep cinnamons. And, of course, the quality of the blue whites, the normal stuff of the diamond trade . . . they seem to be exceptional, too. We have an agreement between Russians, Mr Andrews. We are partners and brothers in this enterprise.'

There was something about him that tempted Ray to take a greater risk.

'With all due respect to you, Mr Borisov, that's

bullshit.' He looked Borisov in the eye, and he grinned. 'I can't claim to know you, but I've still made a judgement. I think you're a patriot. You'd drop Ivan Karakov right in the middle of that pit if I offered you a better deal. And I can offer you whatever you want. So long as it isn't the Chairmanship of Diamond Enterprises!'

Dimitri Valerian Borisov laughed.

'A pity. I might have asked for that. I have been thinking. There are some options I might recommend. For your Board's consideration.'

Andrews controlled his excitement. Negotiations had begun.

'Try them on me,' he said.

'I love this apartment. It's great!'

'I'm so glad you like it,' Elizabeth said. The move was over. Their personal luggage had been unpacked, and the sofa and armchairs she'd ordered were delivered and in place. She and James had shifted furniture, trying to make the salon more informal, and to some extent they had succeeded. He had praised everything, been full of enthusiasm for the apartment, and christened the bed by making love to Elizabeth the night they arrived and bringing her breakfast on a tray the next morning.

'I love you,' he said. 'We're going to enjoy all this and I know I'm going to bring it off!'

Elizabeth had convinced herself that the apartment was less impersonal than she imagined and they would make their mark on it. She was deliberately untidy for a start. James didn't comment, but simply picked the magazines off the floor and arranged them neatly on the marble-topped coffee-table. He knew his wife liked to kick off her shoes and curl up in comfort.

He said they needed a maid. She stared at him. 'Don't be silly, I've got a cleaning lady. Your office fixed her up for me. I don't want a maid.'

'We're going to have a lot of parties,' he explained.

'She'll open the door, take the coats, pass the drinks round when we have just a few people. Caterers can cope with the big flat warming. Darling,' he said patiently, as she started to argue, 'I know you think it's a load of crap, but the French are the biggest snobs on earth and Karakov married his daughter to a Romanian prince just so he could tell people she was a princess. He's been keeping the husband ever since. Ring the agency this morning and get someone. And I've asked the Wassermans round for a drink this evening. They're staying at the Crillon. He's going to make the introduction. Be very nice to them, sweetheart. They're only here to help me.'

'Of course I'll be nice,' she promised. She was surprised that he asked her specially. She was always nice to guests in her own home. Even if it did look like a Hollywood stage set for *Marie Antoinette, the movie.*

'What a nice apartment,' David Wasserman said. He paused and looked round, noting the furniture, appraising the value and authenticity of the pieces. He was quite an expert on French eighteenth-century furniture and porcelain. He loved porcelain and had a small but rare collection.

'It's a bit stiff,' Elizabeth apologized. 'Not really a place to put your feet up, but we'll manage.'

She had shaken hands with them, and done her best to be friendly. She couldn't explain it, but she had got no response from the old man and positively bad vibes from his wife. Now, Clara Wasserman followed her husband in gazing round the room.

'Pity about the soft furnishings,' she remarked. 'They spoil it. Couldn't you get rid of them?' she asked Elizabeth. 'They don't go with the feel of the room at all.'

It was a chance shot, because she saw the sofa and chairs were brand new and felt sure the Hastings girl had ordered them. She stared at Elizabeth with dark eyes, bright with dislike. She didn't like the English, and she especially disliked that type of English woman with her plummy accent, giving off charm and being gracious.

'Not really,' Elizabeth said. 'I bought them. I can't bear sitting on hard-arsed chairs.' Irritation made her spit out her father's description of what he dismissed as bloody awful spindly French rubbish. 'Anyway, do let's sit down, and James'll get us all a drink. What would you like, Mrs Wasserman?'

'Martini,' Clara said. 'No olive, just a twist of lemon. David'll have the same.'

'I'll get them,' James said, trying to be flip, 'I mix a mean Martini, or so I'm told.'

'Don't make it too mean,' Clara said, misunderstanding on purpose. 'We like ours strong.'

For a moment Elizabeth and James looked at each other. He gave a little smile, and David Wasserman saw it.

'I'll take care of that,' he promised. 'White wine for you, darling?' to Elizabeth. She nodded. Before he went to mix the drinks, he said to Clara, 'Liz picked this apartment; the agent who showed it to her said he knew Karakov. Small world, isn't it?'

'Very small,' Clara said. 'Was he in the business? Connected through family maybe?'

'His wife was,' Elizabeth volunteered. 'They're divorced now. He was a very nice man. Jean Pierre Lasalle.'

Wasserman shook his head. 'Don't know the name. Put him on your visiting list, Mrs Hastings. Ivan likes seeing people he knows.'

'I already have,' she answered. 'For himself, really. He was such a sweet man. I must admit, the more I hear about this Ivan Karakov the more curious I am.'

'He's a megalomaniac,' David said, as he always did when the name was mentioned.

'He's a genius,' Clara interposed. 'Haven't you seen his designs?' She took the icy glass of dry Martini and sipped it. She glanced coolly up at James. 'This is good.'

It sounded so ungracious that Elizabeth stiffened. Bloody woman. First the sofa and chairs and then talking to James as if he was a bloody waiter in a cocktail bar. She said in a raised voice that James recognized betokened temper, 'Yes, I have seen them, and I don't like them at all, I'm afraid.'

'Darling,' he was beside her very quickly. 'Here's your wine.'

The atmosphere had chilled and it stayed at the same temperature. Clara didn't talk much. She sipped her drink and listened to the men, ignoring Elizabeth, who had decided that in the cause of peace and to avoid upsetting James, she wouldn't take any notice.

Clara Wasserman disliked her and she also disliked James. For no reason that Elizabeth could see. She sat back, feet curled up underneath her, heels digging into the upholstery because she couldn't take them off in front of the Wassermans, and kept a smile on her face. She was quite innocent of the fact that, to Clara, she appeared supercilious and rather bored by what was a fascinating conversation between her husband and Hastings.

'Now we've got the details worked out, we'd better get down to the business,' David Wassserman said. 'You've been here a week; you haven't been knocking on Ivan's door. So nobody thinks we're anxious. Nobody thinks we're taking them seriously. You're a young boy, James, that's your advantage. When you get to Ivan's age, you think all the young people are fools. I know; I think the same.' He laughed. He had got over his disappointment at not being given the assignment with Karakov. He could see the cunning behind Heyderman's choice, and now that he was committed, he was going to help all he could. Clara had taken it badly, and hadn't been able to cool off. She didn't like Hastings, and she was working off her resentment against the wife. She was a nice enough girl, as English girls went, and they didn't go with David Wasserman at all. Even when he was a young man he had never liked that cool Nordic type, with their long legs and small busts. He liked his own women; they had the kind of bodies women ought to have, round and warm, and the right sort of eyes, dark and full of brightness. Clara had been a beauty when he married her, soft as a ripe fig. He was pleasant to Elizabeth Hastings, because he belonged to a courteous race, but he didn't warm to English aristocrats. He had seen his wife bristle in the first five minutes.

'Now I think the time has come for you to pay our friend a visit. Ring up and ask for an appointment, and don't get mad if he says he can't see you for a week. Ivan likes to play the king; just humour him and play along. Meantime I'll go see him and tell him he ought to see you. Then you'll get a call to come round right away.'

'Why should I be available?' James asked.

'You must be,' Wasserman said. 'Drop everything. You're a young boy, all eager to do business with the great man. Flatter his ego, that's lesson number one.' He turned to Elizabeth, because the idea had suddenly struck him. 'And he'll love you, my dear. He's got a great affection for the aristocracy. Half those god-damned jewels he keeps for show are only there because he bought them from some duchess.'

'He's not that stupid,' Clara Wasserman said. 'Ivan isn't the kind to fall for that kind of crap.' She said the word deliberately. Crap to duchesses. They cut no ice with her. In Clara's world you were what you made yourself; nobody gave a god-damn where you came from or who you were so long as you made the grade. The Blue Book clique didn't count; they were all millionaires, anyway, and most of them had made it out of canned meats and breakfast cereals. She didn't like Hastings, either, and she didn't trust him. He was a phoney, trying to be what he wasn't; she knew the kind. He couldn't deceive her with his English airs and his titled wife.

'I'll call Karakov tomorrow,' James said. He looked over at Elizabeth and smiled, making reparation for Clara Wasserman's remark. She didn't smile back. He got up. 'I think that's all for today then, David. Thanks very much for all your help. We'll put the plan into operation tomorrow. Tonight, Liz and I are going out on the town.' He put his arm round his wife and squeezed her. He was furious with Clara Wasserman.

When they had gone he turned to Elizabeth. 'Darling,' he said, 'I'm sorry; take no notice of the old cow.'

'I'm not having them here again,' Elizabeth said. 'She said that deliberately. Just being bloody rude!'

James knew she was very angry, and he didn't blame her. 'Forget about it, darling. It's only an inferiority complex, that's all. Anyway, we're stuck with them for a bit.'

'You may be,' Elizabeth said. 'I'm not.'

'Come on, sweetheart,' he begged. 'Don't be angry with me. Let's have a nice evening together.'

'Oh,' she said, 'I'm sorry. I didn't mean to take it out on you. It's just that . . .'

'What is it? What's getting to you? Tell me. I know something is.' He sat beside her. 'Ever since you went home for that birthday party you've been on edge.'

'I know,' Elizabeth admitted. 'But it wasn't that. I had lunch with Valerie Kruger and she went on and on about the mistakes she'd made in her marriage and telling me not to let the same thing happen to us.' She looked at him, and he was horrified to see tears in her eyes.

'That fucking woman,' he exploded. 'I'll ring her up and put her straight . . . how dare she talk to you like that!'

'I'm sure she wasn't being bitchy; she really believed I might end up losing you. Dick was obsessed by his business, she seemed to think you were the same. And she was paranoid about Ruth Fraser. She actually told me to make you send her back to London!'

James was white with rage. 'Did she? Did she say that? Inferring I was going to screw around like Kruger! I'm not letting her get away with this, Liz. Why the hell didn't you tell me before, instead of keeping it bottled up and worrying?' His eyes slitted. 'She didn't mention about not having children, by any chance? I bet she did. That's what made you ask that bloody silly question the other night, isn't it?'

He was so angry Elizabeth wished she hadn't said anything about Valerie. She didn't want him blasting on the telephone. She had heard him when his temper was up, and it wasn't pleasant. She said quickly, 'Jamie, listen. Don't get all worked up. I probably took her too seriously, and blew it out of proportion to myself. And you're not to ring her and say anything. No, darling, you're not to . . . I felt so sorry for her, she was pathetic. Now, please let's forget about it. It was my fault for being so stupid.'

He turned to look at her. 'And that balls about Ruth, you're surely not worried about that?'

Elizabeth said gently, 'No, I wouldn't listen to that, and I said so. It was more the idea of not sharing your interests enough that bothered me. And, of course, the baby thing . . . I know it's silly and maddening, but I promise . . . no more of it. If you'll promise me something. Two things.'

'What?' he asked her. He felt so protective towards her; his rage against Kruger's ex-wife still seethed inside him.

'Promise me you won't do anything about Valerie.'

She waited until, reluctantly, he said, 'All right. Just this once. If she tries anything like this again—'

Elizabeth said quickly, 'She won't. I shan't see her again. And the second promise is to tell me more about what's going on . . . I really want to be involved. I want to help while we're over here, not just give parties and faff around being nice to people . . . anyone can do that. I know how much this means to you and I want you to succeed.'

James held her closer. He didn't answer at once. He usually told her the broad outline, but always kept something in reserve. He didn't want to involve her in the fighting and the deals that had to be done for the greater good. He didn't want Elizabeth to know or to be part of something she would see as blatantly dishonest, immoral or underhand. She would view his part in it as a permanent stain on his integrity. She had no real knowledge of the jungle ethics of the business world. She wouldn't understand and she wouldn't condone. But she was right; he was going to need her help. Clara Wasserman was the tip of the iceberg. She had yet to meet Laura Karakov . . . He hadn't met her either, but already he'd heard about her.

'Well,' he began, 'I told you about Karakov doing a deal with the Russians. And Andrews going to Moscow to try and talk them out of it.'

'Yes, I know all that,' she said. 'I know you're supposed to make peace with Karakov and get him back into line. But the way that old man was talking it didn't sound like that. It sounded as if you were setting Karakov up in some way . . .' She frowned. 'Are you?'

He laughed, dismissing it. 'It's just the way David talks. He's a great old ham actor, always has been . . . No, I've got to pander to the bloody man because he thinks he's Jesus Christ in the diamond world. I've got to flatter him, let him patronize me, that sort of approach. That's what David meant. And I'll do it. I'll do whatever is necessary because if I can bring this off, I'll be in line for Managing Director of the London company. I'm going to the top in this industry, Liz, or I'm not going to stay in it at all. I've seen enough has-beens to know that second best isn't for me.'

'I know it isn't,' Elizabeth said. 'And I wouldn't want anything like that for you. I didn't mean that about the Wassermans. I can bite my tongue if I have to. If it's that important. Just let's try and mix them in with some other people next time.'

'We'll do that,' James agreed. He kissed her. 'I love you. Now go and get ready. I'm taking you to Maxims tonight.' She didn't realize till next day that he hadn't told her anything she didn't already know.

6

Ruth Fraser loved Paris. She liked the smell of the city, the opulent shops and wide tree-lined boulevards. She liked the neat little bistros where you could eat the best food in the world for the price of a steak and chips in London. It was so clean, the Parisians were proud of their city, confident in their own image. There was no visible sign of squalor apart from the homeless in doorways and crouched begging in the streets. Ruth passed them as she passed their kin in London. It was an endemic problem without a solution. She didn't feel sorry for them. She could have begged or gone on the game when she was sixteen and pregnant by her own brother. She hadn't. She'd worked. She walked past the losers in her smart clothes and kept her purse tight shut. She liked her apartment, but out of necessity she stored the single bed and crammed a double into the room to accommodate Dick Kruger. The first week she was so busy getting into James Hastings' routine and finding her way round that she didn't think of Dick except when he called. Which he did every night, rambling on about how he missed her, pumping her for information which she didn't have. She countered with questions about the London office. Arthur was in close contact with Ray Andrews. Negotiations were just beginning, but they were tough. Andrews was being asked to give away more than he wanted, but then promises were only a part of the game. Arthur was in good spirits. He'd asked Kruger to go down for the weekend and look at the design for his new boat. She had flared at him when he refused the invitation because he wanted to fly over and see her. Get your priorities right, she told him. Are you crazy? You're Arthur's man, he needs you.

Put your dick on ice, she'd snapped, and say you've cancelled your arrangements and you're coming. No, I won't see you . . . You go down to Arthur.

In the end he'd given way, because she was out of reach and he was too insecure to quarrel with her from a distance. What a fool, she thought, and was aware that her respect for him was shrinking. What a fool to put a fuck in front of an invitation from his boss, the one man who might still see him as a successor, especially if Ray Andrews blew it in Moscow. Then she relented and called him back, not wanting to quarrel with him either. He was her man, at the moment anyway, and they were meant to be working together.

She was sweet to him, and dripped sex down the telephone till he was mollified. The weekend after. That was a promise. And call as soon as he got back on Sunday night and tell her all about it.

She was very careful with James Hastings. She was wary, trying to get the measure of him. She was quick at judging a man's moods and she learned his method of working after a few days. He didn't waste time. He didn't like a lot of detail; he skipped the irrelevancies and honed in on the priorities. She couldn't help admiring his abilities and responding to them. By contrast, Dick Kruger was ponderous and too inclined to meddle. Hastings was polite to her, but cold. She met his attitude with brisk efficiency and unwavering good temper. She smoothed his path, from turning down unsuitable callers in the trade, hoping to get a foot in the door because he had recently arrived, to making appointments for the ones she knew he'd need to see. She had a smart outer office, adjoining his, in the big modern complex off rue de Rivoli. When he came in that morning, she was at her desk early as usual, and he was early enough. He said a brief good-morning.

'I've opened your mail and sorted through it. There are two overnight faxes, one from New York and another from Reece in Johannesburg. Everything's on your desk. Oh, and some bills have been sent on from Thurloe Square. Would you like to see them, or shall I just take care of them and let you have a note later?'

'Take care of them,' he said. 'And get me Ivan Karakov. He's in his office around ten.'

She watched him walk into his office and close the door. She would take dictation when he'd read his mail, probably put calls through for him to London and arrange appointments for the afternoon. A lot of French companies were eager to make contact with him, and the company brokers wanted a meeting. At ten o'clock exactly she called Ivan Karakov's office in rue St Honore.

Then she went into James's office. 'Karakov couldn't take your call,' she said. 'His secretary said he was in a meeting.'

He said, 'Did she say when he'd be free?'

'She couldn't give a time,' Ruth answered. She decided to drop the barrier a little. 'I didn't believe a word of it,' she said.

'I don't either,' James found himself dropping the barrier too. 'Old bastard.'

'Mr Hastings?'

'Yes?'

'Could I suggest something? Don't call him back. He's snubbed you. Leave it for a day or so.'

James said slowly, 'I may just do that, Ruth. Personalities aren't important. But my position as D.E.'s representative is. Call again on Wednesday. He should have talked with David Wasserman by then.'

Ivan Leonid Karakov had been born in a dingy New York tenement seventy-one years ago; his grandfather was a diamond merchant who had hawked his stones round the houses of the rich bourgeoisie in Smolensk and made an occasional sale to the gentry. He sold gold and silver trinkets, boxes and curios, and he had travelled constantly, buying and selling from other merchants. He was a middle-aged man when the last pogrom began, and he had gathered his family together and gone into hiding once too often, while his house was pillaged and his friends whipped through the streets. He made a decision then which was being made by other minority groups all over the world. He left Russia and settled in the United States. Ivan's father was his eldest son, and he was twenty when the family came to New York. None of them could speak a word of English, or had any relatives to go to, but their own community took them in and helped them, and Ivan's father began to ply their trade, and taught the rudiments of it to his own son as he grew up. Their name was not Karakov; Ivan had chosen that for himself when he left home. He had seen it on a shop front downtown selling high-quality leather goods; it had a dramatic sound that appealed to him. He was twenty-five then, and full of electricity; ideas foamed out of him, and all of them were big, bold, impossible schemes which made his conservative father wince. But Ivan knew where he was going, and that was as far away from the family jewellery business as he could get. His father was a good man, and he loved him, but he was small and he thought small. He had a good little business and he didn't want to make it bigger. He wouldn't let Ivan make it bigger, either, and so Ivan decided to go out on his own. He had raised loans and invested the money in diamonds, most of them loose stones. He rented rooms in a good downtown district and had business cards printed: *Ivan Karakov. Fine Diamonds.* Then he went into business. He had a natural genius for business and the same kind of genius for diamonds. His father had trained him well; he knew a lot about stones and he learned more. He had a sixth sense for what was good and what would sell.

And he had a way with people. Even his enemies said he could sell a diamond to the Oppenheimers if he made up his mind.

The bank's money was repaid, and there was a balance of a hundred thousand dollars in the Karakov account. By this time Ivan was thirty-two. He had an office at a smart address up in the East fifties, and he was shrewd enough not to settle in the diamond belt around 46th where there was a jeweller every five yards and the tourists walked down just to look. He didn't identify with the rest. That way people remembered him. He was an easy man to remember and an easy man to like, especially if he was trying to sell to you. He was tall and plump, going very bald, with a neat moustache and small, sharp features; he wore glasses, but his eyes were always bright, too bright to stay on any one object for long, unless it was a diamond, and then they searched as if they were drawing the colours of the spectrum out of the stone itself, searching for flaws, for irregularity, for possibilities of re-cutting. He had a fantastic artistic sense and took risks. His favourite anecdote about himself was the story of a visit he paid to a rich socialite on Long Island after he'd been established for a few years, and his name was filtering through to the big spenders. This woman was well known for her jewels. As soon as Ivan opened his case to show her a few top-grade pieces, he knew she wasn't going to buy anything and had never meant to; she wanted to show him what she had and get his opinion for nothing. It was a trick people often played, and it lost the dealer valuable time and seldom ended in a sale.

But Ivan played it, as he said, right off the cuff. He put his own goods back and settled down to a long session with the client about the quality of her jewels. He admired everything; when she mentioned prices he never indicated that he thought she'd paid too much. He paid her compliments and talked and told her stories and every so often he picked up a diamond solitaire set as a pendant and looked at it again and again. It wasn't for sale, she said. It made Ivan laugh to recall how much she was enjoying herself. He protested that he didn't think it was; it was one of the finest diamonds he'd seen in his life. If she offered it he couldn't give her what the stone was worth. But it was such a pity that the cutting wasn't right. He had explained to her that in his opinion the refractions could be improved by cutting down the sides and eliminating a flaw near the outer edge of the table. If this was done, he said, she'd have a unique diamond, worth three times its present value. By the end of the afternoon, he left the house with the stone and a commission to re-cut and reset it. He took the train back to New York and went to the best cutter in the business. He had known the stone should be re-cut, but there was only one person he knew who could do the cutting. The cutter had his own factory and his three sons were top craftsmen. They sat round the stone with Ivan for three weeks, measuring and making designs. They agreed with him: it should be re-cut; the diamond was a little over 45 carats and blue-white, but poorly cut. The result could be superb. But Ivan knew his client; the stone had to be re-cut so that the weight loss wouldn't matter, and the design must enhance the importance as well as the colour. At the end of three weeks they had agreed on a design, and the famous Karakov cut was born. The diamond was delivered as a unique baton-shaped stone of 29.8 carats. He had set it in a ring and it was revealed in breathtaking purity and fire. Ivan charged the owner more for that re-cut than he could have done for anything in his entire stock, and it made him. He was flooded with orders for baton-shaped solitaires. The cutter came under contract to him, and one of his sons was made permanent consultant in the New York office. A new way had been found to cut fine diamonds, and it was the rage in the trade. It was copied, and the way Ivan confounded his imitators was to buy the biggest and finest stones, and charge staggering prices.

He enjoyed doing business more than just making money, though the profits were enormous. He employed the best men in the trade and he paid them the top wages. By the time he was thirty-seven he was a millionaire and he had married Laura Hancock. Until then he'd been too busy to marry; his father had died grieving because his clever son hadn't taken time off to found a family, and his younger brother was not interested. He had the old man's business and he was content. Ivan liked women; they relaxed him, they enjoyed his stories, and they slept with him readily in the hope that he would give them a diamond, which he did. Most of them liked him; he was a virile man and he gave as much as he got out of his sexual encounters. He had always taken up with blondes; he liked them tall, because it made him feel important, and he liked them to be easy-going and dumb, but not so dumb they didn't know how to behave. He was very conscious of the refinements of life. He had met Laura Hancock at a dinner party given by one of his clients. She was much smaller than he was, pale-skinned and golden blonde. She looked like a pretty, clever doll. Her father was a rich East Coast psychiatrist, and she was his only child. She was intelligent, a graduate of Vassar, which really impressed him, and very sure of herself. He found her fascinating.

He invited her out. He didn't try to sleep with her; he knew from the look in those bright eyes that she wouldn't let him. At the end of six months he asked her to marry him. They both had the feeling they were founding a dynasty, and they went to bed like royalty, determined to procreate. In bed the doll turned out to be a real enthusiast. Ivan had got himself the perfect combination; he had a mistress, a wife who ran his home like a super machine, a mother to his two children, and a business partner who ran rings round everyone else in the office.

Their great disappointment was having no son, but she couldn't be blamed for that. He had been married to her for a number of years before he stopped to think of her as a person, and he was surprised when he realized that she wasn't a nice woman. She was clever; she was efficient; she never nagged him, except when she thought he had made a bad deal; she got on well with everybody it was wise to get on with. She was good to their daughters; she watched over their education and their health and kept him informed about them without worrying him if he had something important on his mind. She amassed treasures with him so that their last apartment was a showplace, and in spite of the gold plate and the bed which had belonged to the Empress Josephine, there wasn't a vulgar touch in anything she did. But she just wasn't nice; he couldn't identify a soft spot for anyone in her character, except where her children were concerned. She didn't love him, he realized that. To Laura, love meant sex, and when she talked about love that was what she meant.

He realized all of this when he could have done with a little love outside of bed. He reached a crisis in his business life during the Sixties when a new and dazzling salesman gained the ascendancy in the US Market with a revolutionary cut and designs of his own. Harry Winston was a phenomenon and Ivan knew his own position at the top was threatened. Americans loved the newcomer; there was no loyalty in the very rich, they followed the fashion, and Winston was the newest and most dynamic in the world of super retail jewellery. Ivan could see his business waning and it brought him close to a clinical depression.

Laura was typically cool and pragmatic. 'You Russians,' she said to him. 'You love to sit around wringing your hands. You can't compete with Harry, so why try?' It had been her idea to move the headquarters of the business to Paris, leaving an office and showroom on Park Avenue to fly the flag. It was something he would never have thought of doing. He regarded himself as bound by the American market. As investigations showed, Europe was booming. Germany had accomplished a miracle in spite of being cut in half by the East–West divide, France was on the economic bandwagon after the end of the Algerian war and stable Government under de Gaulle, and Japan and the oil-rich Middle East was a bottomless well with mega rich vying with each other to spend the most.

The move to Paris fired him with a new enthusiasm. He rediscovered his European roots. He talked of himself, in a thick New York accent, as a Russian refugee. About the same time he discovered that Laura had been sleeping with one of his young salesmen. It was a terrible shock to him. He had thought that, in spite of the blondes, he had managed to keep her reasonably happy. He fired the salesman. When he reproached her angrily, she had only looked at him and shrugged. 'Why get so mad about it? It meant nothing; you're always tired and busy with the move these days. Pay more attention to me, honey, and I won't do it.' He hadn't caught her out again for five years and by that time it was too late; their daughters were growing up and he didn't care enough about her to threaten. He just told her to be careful and they never mentioned it again. She made amends in her own way by dismissing the man herself. It was a French salesman, even younger than her lover in America. He knew what to expect by then, and he had consoled himself with a nice-natured Swedish girl who worked in the Paris office. He visited her off and on for a year, and at the end of it, just because she'd been kind and mothered him a little, he gave her a valuable diamond as a goodbye present. It was 8.6 carats and a fine colour. He had set it at the end of a platinum chain. He wished he'd had a camera to get a shot of the girl's face when she saw it. It would have made the diamond advertisement of the year. Two days later Laura came into the office and picked out a 20-carat blue-white stone, which was priced at $250,000, and said she'd like it as a ring – diamonds on chains didn't suit her. He always reckoned that the Swede was the most expensive piece of tail he'd ever had. That was just like Ivan; he was a character. He was getting to the age when he liked to be talked about in that way. He began to tell some of his clients how he started his business, and the details got a little exaggerated until he wasn't sure of the truth himself. He collected cuttings through an agency, so he could read everything that was written about him or his business. He began buying famous jewels, not only to reset and resell them at three times their original cost, but to get publicity for himself. And he loved the stones. He had agents everywhere who went to auction sales in London, Paris, Amsterdam, Rome, and who got the first offer from the big Antwerp dealers if a really good stone came on the market. He had one man he considered the finest judge of diamonds in the world, even better than D.E.'s David Wasserman, and that was Ernst Richter. He liked and trusted Ernst. Ernst travelled all over the world to buy diamonds for him. He could leave it to Ernst to choose the best; indeed, it was Ernst's repeated complaints that started the war with Diamond Enterprises. Ivan was old now and he liked to make a play on his age; he liked to pity himself loudly because he worked so hard and never went on a vacation, but he was as strong as an ox and as alert as he had ever been. If he had flagged at all in the past year or two, this battle with D.E. was like a new campaign to an old conqueror. He was the biggest man in the diamond business, because Winston was dead, and he knew it. He lived the part and he believed it; he knew what his power meant in terms of money and prestige. He sold the élite of the world their jewels and he bought the priceless and put a price on it that someone somewhere in the world was rich enough to pay. Like the red diamonds. They were his secret weapon in the war he had declared against the whole power structure of Diamond Enterprises. With these priceless jewels, he could break their monopoly, and hold the industry to ransom if he felt like it. And he did feel like it. He felt a sense of mission, which was to open up the restricted diamond markets of the world to the newly liberated Russia with which he firmly identified himself. He had forgotten his grandfather and the pogroms, buried his own cultural heritage, and presented himself as a patriot returning to his roots in the Ukraine. He had given his diamonds a spurious name and invented an Imperial Russian provenance that pandered to his love of royalty. The Romanov Diamonds. Property of the doomed dynasty of the Tsars . . . They were in the mighty steel safe in his office, enclosed in an inner safe, and nobody but Ernst Richter and his team of cutters had ever seen them. Not even Laura. However, he allowed the rumours about them to seep through the trade, confident that after a time the big fish would begin to bite. One of them had. The biggest. His richest and most discerning client, a man who would be negotiating hard if he had been approached directly.

But Ivan was too clever for that. He knew his Arabs. They were born into the market-place like Ivan's Jewish forebears. They loved to bargain more than to sell or to buy. It was the European mistress who was fed the bait. All Ivan had to do was wait, patiently, impassively, for the lady to work on her besotted prince. There were other targets, and Ivan kept them in view. A retired movie actress married to a Brazilian millionaire; one of the great chainstore moguls who had a new young wife who liked presents – in the six months they had been married she had collected a yacht, one of Ivan's $300,000 16-carat diamonds as an engagement ring, and a house in Jamaica. There was also a little-known Italian motor-car manufacturer, who had been a regular customer since he moved to Paris. His wife had an unrivalled collection of fancy diamonds which Ivan had personally built up for her. She never wore them; Ivan had stayed in Milan one year and been furious to find that they kept his beautiful stones in a specially built display case in a steel safe. They took them out to look at and to show to favoured visitors.

The Italians had been brought into Ivan's circle of exclusive private clients by his son-in-law, Prince Eugene Titulescu. Fifteen generations of Romanian aristocrats had produced the beautifully mannered, impeccably dressed tout, who lived in style and moved among the rich and famous by courtesy of the father-in-law who paid him. He was stupid, but not vicious, and he made the best use of his only two assets: his charm and his great name. He was also operating in the most socially conscious community in the world. The Parisian hostesses considered the prince a great asset, and he was particularly successful in introducing the top class of rich client to Karakov because he never attempted to sell them anything.

He liked women very much, but it was a sexless admiration; he hadn't been very happy with his first wife, whom he had married when both were very young. She was a turbulent, passionate creature, whom he had never satisfied; they had no children. She died in a car crash and he had felt both guilty and relieved. The Great War had made inroads into the Titulescu fortune and economic necessity had eaten into their lands, but the prince's family had managed to live in very much their old style: hunting and shooting and spending part of the year in Bucharest. The prince had fought in the last war, and seen some action on the Russian front; the experience had been enough to give him a profound distaste for all forms of physical discomfort and danger.

He had been one of the first to escape when the Russians established their puppet government, and he had taken a few jewels and one small painting, rolled up and hidden in his suitcase, and made his way to France, where he had friends. The jewels brought a good price, and he sold his small Vermeer at Sotheby's in London. He had then sufficient capital to buy a decent apartment and contact his friends. These friends were his introduction to Ivan Karakov. Ivan had seen his possibilities at once, but it was Laura who approached the prince after a three-month campaign in which he was wined and dined and invited to the Karakovs' Normandy château for the weekend. Ivan was a little in awe of him to begin with; he wore an eyeglass on a black ribbon and his manner was so very aristocratic, but once he began drawing his cheque, Ivan felt better. The prince, on the other hand, had been delighted. He had waited hopefully during those three months when nothing else had been found for him to do, worrying that his money was dwindling away and wishing that he had the courage to ask the Karakovs for a job.

He had been working for them for two years when he met their second daughter, Natasha, who had just come back from Mexico after divorcing an international sponger with a German title. The prince had been very charming to her because it was not in his nature to be anything else to a woman, and it came as a genuine surprise when she asked him to marry her. The reversal of the roles took him so much off guard that he couldn't think of a suitable excuse to say no; his mind was made up for him in a short interview with Ivan, who indicated that he was a very lucky guy, so long as he didn't expect to live off Natasha's money or get any special privileges. He had liked his wife in a passive way; she found him kind and restful after her experience with the baron, who had been greedy, unfaithful and blacked her eye when she complained. She was very happy with her prince and very fond of him. They had even gladdened her parents by producing a grandson.

Titulescu was surprised and delighted. Also relieved

that now he was sure of not being discarded like the baron.

The postwar world was a difficult place for a gentleman to make a living. Most people wouldn't employ you, in spite of your title, unless you had something to offer like degrees or specialist knowledge, and all the prince knew was how to live in style. He knew about food and he was an expert on wines. When Laura wanted to dine an important client she often consulted him as if he were a kind of butler, and he advised her tactfully on what to serve with what. She never treated him differently, even when he became her son-in-law. He bore the Karakovs no resentment for the little humiliations they inflicted on him; he understood that they felt it was necessary to assert themselves by reminding him he was on their payroll, and he forgave them. He even managed to ignore it when Ivan called one of his suggestions 'a load of crap' during a meeting in his private office. The prince had shed his pride long ago; if he was proud of anything it was of how well he had survived the loss of his estates and money, when so many of his old friends were bankrupt or dead. If he could initiate the sale of the Romanov Diamonds – the name made him wince – his personal commission would be enormous.

That morning, Karakov's secretary had buzzed through, asking if he could see Mr Hastings from Diamond Enterprises, who was on a visit to Paris.

'No,' Ivan barked back. 'Tell him I'm tied up in a meeting. Tell him to call again. Next week maybe.' He flicked the switch down. 'Who does the bum think he is?' He said it aloud. 'Who does Heyderman think he is, sending some office boy out here to see me? He wants anything out of me, he can make the trip himself. Or send Harris . . . God-damned office boy.'

Ivan had hated Heyderman on sight, and Julius hadn't troubled to be charming. He was irritated with Karakov for making all this trouble, complaining about the quality of his diamonds. He was especially irritated to find Ernst Richter in the office to back up Ivan. He was brusque with both of them, and he completely ignored the prince, who happened to be there. He had made Ivan a lot of promises in a high-handed way and gone back and given instructions to give the Karakov organization a couple of really bad parcels next time they bought anything and then one good one at a 5 per cent increase. He had imagined that would teach him. But it hadn't. It might well have succeeded, because Karakov was no fool and he had made enough compromises in his life to make one more, however much it stuck in his craw. But along came Mirkovitch with the Archangel mine as a proposition that changed everything. The Russian's proposition suddenly gave Ivan Karakov a hand to play in the power game with Diamond Enterprises. A potentially winning hand.

Mirkovitch was a quiet man, around thirty-three. He had a straight deal to put forward, and Ivan was just in the right mood to listen to it. He'd had a report from Ernst Richter on the last Antwerp sale and it was so bad he hadn't bought anything. Ivan got the message and he was seething.

The Russians had a top-class mine which was coming into full production. He backed his statement with samples. Karakov had examined the rough stones himself and passed them to his head valuer. 'These are good stuff.' The valuer took the loupe out of his eye. 'Very good. High quality.'

Two were over 80 carats in weight and very clean. Karakov said nothing. Good, but he sensed that there was more to come.

'We have cut some of the fancies,' Mirkovitch announced. 'Our facilities are not as expert as yours, but these were cut and polished in Smolensk . . .'

'My home town,' Ivan muttered.

'And these at Irkutsk. Blue stones, some green, not

quite clean, cinnamon, deep colour – and these.' He had produced them in a box, not much bigger than a cigarette packet.

Suddenly crimson fire blazed up at Ivan. The valuer gasped out loud. Ivan turned and told him to leave them. He wouldn't even let the expert handle these. Later, he'd have a warning word with him about mentioning what he'd seen.

He'd taken them out one by one, examined them with his own loupe, held them to the light, caressed them between his thumb and forefinger. And then he had looked at Mirkovitch. 'You're mining these?'

'Yes,' the Russian said calmly. 'In large quantities. Some are very big in the rough. Too big for us to cut without the risk of damage. These are just a sample.'

Ivan thought he was going to have a heart attack. His chest felt banded in steel, he couldn't control his pulse or his breathing. He said to Laura afterwards that it was the most exciting moment of his whole life. After a long pause, 'It would be best if I come out to Moscow and negotiate direct. But first I would like to visit the mine.'

When they shook hands, Ivan told his wife, his own was trembling. Mirkovitch had looked at him and smiled. 'I am sure we will work out a deal that will benefit us both.'

Ivan remembered it well and sneered. Waste time on some messenger boy from Diamond Enterprises? With what he had in his safe and the deal with Moscow that would be ratified and signed in the next three months, Diamond Enterprises could stuff themselves.

Dick Kruger had gone over the plans of Arthur Harris's new yacht, looked at the specifications, admired the design, and said all the expected things, knowing that Arthur only wanted his own enthusiasm confirmed. He knew that what Dick didn't know about racing yachts would have filled a blockbuster-sized book.

He sensed that Dick was restless; being a shrewd judge he guessed that it was Ruth's absence in Paris that was making him so edgy. And, of course, his wife Christa didn't help. She wasn't unfriendly to Kruger. On the contrary, she was charming to him; it enabled her to be nasty to Arthur by contrast. She interrupted his explanation of his new toy's potential by coming in and saying in a pained voice, 'Now, darling, haven't you bored poor Dick for long enough?' Then, turning to Dick with a radiant smile, she said, 'Arthur's such an enthusiast, he thinks everyone else is as obsessed about winning as he is. The trouble is, we haven't had all that many successes, have we? We haven't *actually* won a major class for the last four years . . . but Arthur'll go on trying, won't you? Now, it's time for a drink before dinner. Dick, we've got some old friends coming – Sonia and Ralph Mathews. Nothing to do with yachts, I promise you . . .'

Dick Kruger knew the form. He had stayed with the Harrises before, and spent the whole visit squirming on Arthur's behalf. Last time, he had Valerie with him, and Arthur's loutish son had joined his mother in baiting him. Looking at that boy, Kruger thanked God that Valerie hadn't been able to have children. Not that he'd have allowed any son to grow up like Martin Harris. Valerie hadn't been sympathetic. He remembered how her attitude had grated on him. 'Why does he put up with it? He doesn't have to stay with her . . . Some men like being humiliated. I think he gets turned on by the way she treats him . . .' Dick had lost his temper with her. He was loyal to the bone to Arthur, who had always supported and promoted him. The wife was an unmitigated bitch, and he was just too nice to cope with her and the son . . . The sexual innuendo made him furious. Valerie was almost siding with Christa Harris. But then she would. She was always harping on how she valued her female friends and the special intimacy women shared. As if men were some kind of enemy. He felt her attitude was some kind of reproach to him, but he couldn't see that he deserved it. Ruth had never shown any interest in other women. She didn't go to lunch parties, or spend time shopping in little groups with girl friends. She was bored by feminine interests and pursuits.

She boasted about it. 'I like what's going on in the real world,' she said to him. 'Our world. Where the action is.'

It had given him a deep sense of companionship. During that weekend, he thought about her with mixed jealousy and loneliness. The Mathews, Christa's much-hyped friends, turned out to be a stuffy English county couple of stupefying dullness, who made him feel very South African. There was a large lunch party on Sunday where he felt equally bored and ill at ease. They were part of the Solent set, as he described them sourly to himself. They talked to each other about mutual friends in high-pitched voices, and once Dick exchanged a miserable glance with Arthur who seemed to understand. When the party started to break up, Dick found Arthur beside him. He was rehearsing his goodbye speech to Christa, his excuse for leaving immediately already worked out. Arthur touched him lightly on the arm. 'I want you to stay on, Dick. I want to discuss something with you. When everyone's gone, we'll go into my study.'

It was a very masculine room, with a handsome oil of Arthur's winning yacht, *Diamond Lady*, over the fireplace, photographs and trophies everywhere.

'Sit down, Dick,' Arthur said. 'I'm very grateful to you for coming this weekend. I'm sure you were going to pop over to Paris?'

Dick didn't like to admit that Ruth had dissuaded him. He shrugged slightly, and said, 'No problem. I've had a great time.' Arthur's rather sad smile acknowledged the lie. He opened a box of Monte Christo cigars. Kruger took one.

'Christa hates the smell, so I only smoke them in here,'

he explained. 'I've had a confidential fax from Reece,' he said quietly. 'I've got it here. I'd like you to read it, Dick. No-one else has had sight of it. Tell me what you think.'

Kruger read it through, then reread it. He looked up at Arthur Harris. 'Christ,' he muttered. 'Where did Reece get hold of this?'

'He has his sources,' was the answer. 'I never ask what they are. Somebody's been bribed. Or blackmailed,' he added.

'A suite of red diamonds,' Kruger read from the fax. 'Over two hundred and twenty carats in weight. They must be bloody enormous!'

'And of top colour and purity. Worth millions,' Arthur said in his quiet voice. 'Karakov's selling them for the Russians, on commission. They'll be his show pieces for the rest of the goods. And, according to Reece, he's got a client in view. Abdullah Bin Saladin.'

'Their target is his French girlfriend, the actress Madeline Luchaire!' Kruger said. 'That's what it says. Just think of the impact, Arthur, think of the publicity . . . He'll be top of the heap. With a sale like that and the Russians supplying more of the same, he can stick two fingers at us and get away with it.'

Arthur puffed on his cigar. The study was sweet with the aromatic scent of the tobacco. 'Julius wants this information passed to Hastings and Wasserman. He sent it direct to me because he didn't feel the Paris office was secure enough yet. That's the only reason, of course. Another week or so when Ruth had got everything properly set up, we wouldn't have known anything about this.'

Kruger waited. He wasn't sure where Arthur was leading; his expression was mild, as if he were just smoking a good cigar with an old colleague. Then suddenly, he saw the drift.

'If Hastings gets this information,' he said, 'it gives him a prime target – Madeline Luchaire. He'll know exactly how to strike at Karakov, by somehow stopping the sale of this jewellery. He's smart enough to figure out how to do it once he knows she's the client and the prince is the buyer . . .'

'Yes,' Arthur agreed. 'If he knows.' There was a silence then. *If.* Kruger tasted that little word. *If.* He cleared his throat.

'How's Andrews doing in Moscow? Any further developments?'

'He's having meetings with this man Borisov. He seems to have struck up some kind of rapport with him. So he says. They're driving a stiff bargain, as I told you, Dick. Very stiff. Very expensive and with long-term commitments that I'm finding . . . well, quite difficult. But I've told Ray to go ahead. Say yes in general and try to whittle the terms down in detail. He's a very able chap; I'm sure he'll get a deal together. But, of course, he needs time. Russians make a virtue out of dragging on negotiations. They know how it frustrates us. It can tempt us into blunders just to get a resolution. He does need time. I'm confident that he'll bring it off. Then our ambitious friend in Paris can do what he likes with this information. If Ray detaches the Russians from their agreement with Karakov, it won't matter.'

'No,' Dick Kruger said, and smiled, 'it won't. So you think we should sit on this for a while?'

'I think it needs consideration,' Arthur said. 'I don't feel there's any hurry to inform Hastings. He's only just arrived in Paris, he hasn't even met Karakov yet . . . After all, he should be given the chance to persuade him without resorting to interfering with a sale of this importance. Even if he found a way to do so . . . I think we should keep this under wraps for the time being . . . Julius has passed the initiative to us. Would you agree?'

Kruger's eyes gleamed. 'I would. Ray Andrews deserves to bring it off. Why the hell should we hand that shit Hastings something on a plate?'

'We have this information in reserve,' Arthur remarked, 'if all else fails in Moscow. When are you going to Paris, Dick?'

'On Friday night,' Kruger answered. 'For the weekend. Private visit.'

'Give my best to Ruth,' Arthur said. He rubbed out his stub of cigar. Dick Kruger stood up. They walked out of the house and to Kruger's car, and shook hands.

'Thanks for a great weekend,' Dick said. 'Say goodbye to Christa for me. I'll be sending her some flowers.'

She had gone off with some of the guests to look at a local art exhibition in aid of charity. Arthur knew she would come back with a picture destined for the attic. She was generous to good causes. He went back to his study and put Reece's fax in a drawer of his desk and locked it. He could trust Dick Kruger. Their interests were identical.

Elizabeth slept in late that morning. She and James had been out to dinner at the Tour d'Argent with some clients. They were already in demand, and her own background had opened the stuffier French circles to them. She found the parties and dinners an effort; typically, she had been educated to a simple standard in foreign languages and her French lapsed very quickly when the conversation got under way. Fortunately, most people they met spoke excellent English. She found the men flirtatious and inquisitive, and the women guarded because she was so attractive. It was all very smart and amusing and superficial, and eating out so much she was putting on weight.

She had just woken when the telephone rang. She levered herself up on the pillows. James had left hours earlier. He was always in his office by eight-thirty. And they had a dinner party planned for that evening . . . it was time she got up and stopped being dozy.

'This is Jean Pierre Lasalle,' the voice said in her ear. 'Madame Hastings?' The charming estate agent. She had been meaning to invite him round, but somehow she hadn't got round to doing it. James had long lists of people he wanted to entertain.

'Oh yes . . . How nice to hear from you. How are you?'

'Well, thank you. I thought I would call and ask how you are enjoying your apartment. Is everything all right?'

'Perfect,' Elizabeth said. 'I meant to call you, but it's been so hectic ever since we arrived. I'd no idea Parisians were so hospitable.'

'I'm glad to hear it,' Lasalle said. 'They don't have that reputation normally. I was wondering whether you might like to have lunch with me today, and see the exhibition of Impressionists at the Musée d'Orsay. I have tickets for the private view this afternoon. You are probably too busy . . .'

'No I'm not,' she said. 'It sounds a lovely idea. How sweet of you.'

'I will come to the apartment at one o'clock. I've discovered a new restaurant. I hope you like fish.'

'Love it,' she said. 'One o'clock. See you then. Goodbye.'

She set the telephone down. What a nice surprise. James never had time to go to exhibitions or sightsee. Jean Pierre was a nice man, lunch and then the Musée d'Orsay would be something to look forward to. She had heard people talking about the brilliant transformation of a disused railway terminal into one of the finest exhibition centres in Europe. The French had such style and flair; they loved their city in a way that Londoners had forgotten. No Parisians would have dropped litter in the street.

Jean Pierre was very punctual. He walked into the salon and looked round. 'You've made it charming,' he said. 'Much less formal. Are you really happy here?'

Elizabeth smiled at him. 'Yes, I am; I'd rather have been in the rue de la Perle, but then I've always had rather a womb complex. I'm glad you like what I've done. My husband is thrilled, it's just what he wanted. Would you like a drink before we go?'

'No, I think we'd better not risk losing our table. I'm not the only person to discover this restaurant.'

They had a leisurely lunch; Elizabeth found herself relaxing completely, talking about her family and her home, about James and how important it was for him to meet Ivan Karakov. Jean Pierre was a very good listener. When they paid the bill and set off for the Musée d'Orsay, she realized she had monopolized the conversation. He had said nothing about himself. In the car she apologized.

'I'm so sorry, what a bore I've been, talking about myself all the time. I'm afraid it's because you're so easy to talk to; I haven't made any friends here yet, just acquaintances.'

He turned to her and said simply, 'I have been enchanted by it. You are a wonderful companion, Madame Hastings. I've been thinking, perhaps I can help with your husband's problem – meeting Ivan Karakov.'

'Could you? That would be wonderful . . . How?'

'After we've looked at the pictures,' he said gently. 'When you look at Impressionists you can't think about anything else.'

Elizabeth lost track of time. Jean Pierre was knowledgeable and enthusiastic. Listening to him, she began to see the pictures in depth and significance. For the first time the vibrant colours of Van Gogh appealed to her more than the rain-washed colouring of Monet, because he had explained them in terms of the artist's insanity and pain.

When they came outside he took her arm lightly, guiding her across the street towards the car.

'Now *I* must apologize. I do hope I haven't bored you . . . but that period of painting is my obsession. My wife had a Degas, an exquisite painting of two ballet dancers practising at the bar. It broke my heart when she took it with her. I minded much more about losing that picture than losing my wife.'

Elizabeth was surprised by the bitterness in the remark. 'Did you really, or did you come to that conclusion afterwards?'

He looked at her, switched on the engine, and then said, '*Touché!* I minded very much about losing them both at the same time. That was a stupid remark, please don't judge me by it. I would hate you to think I was a cynic.'

Elizabeth said simply, 'It didn't sound cynical, just as if you were still hurt. May I ask you something?' She saw him smile.

'Isn't there someone else in my life? No. There have been women now and again, but no-one serious. Was that your question?'

'Yes. Perhaps you should find someone. I'm sure it wouldn't be difficult.'

'I'm flattered,' he said gently. 'And I think perhaps you're right. I should put myself on the market. Like one of my own apartments. Divorcé, fifty-two years old, centrally situated, with château only eighty kilometres from Paris for weekends. Vacant possession.' He laughed. 'You are sweet, Madame Hastings; you do not think it's funny and you can't hide your feelings. I'm only joking about making an advertisement for myself. But you're right. I think I should find a wonderful woman and settle down with her. Here we are, the palace at rue Constantine.'

He got out and opened the car door for her.

'Thank you for lunch and a wonderful afternoon,' Elizabeth said. 'I've enjoyed myself so much. And learned so much, too. I'll try and persuade James to come with me . . . He really ought to see it.'

Jean Pierre had taken her hand. He paused. 'I said I could help him to meet Karakov. I didn't forget. I will invite them to dinner. I know his wife Laura; she was a friend of my wife's, and she didn't strike me off her list when we parted. I have rented flats to her friends, and if I ask her to dinner, she'll come and so will he. You and your husband will happen to be there.'

'That would be wonderful,' Elizabeth said. 'I'll tell James; he'll be so grateful.'

'I will telephone you with the date,' he said. 'Thank you for sharing the paintings with me. If you enjoy exhibitions, there are several in Paris you might like to see . . .'

'I'd love to,' she said. 'Any time. Just ask me.'

He kissed her hand. 'Oh, I will,' he said.

7

Dimitri Borisov walked from his office to the restaurant. He liked walking; the sky was still light and the air balmy. He loved Moscow at that time of year, before the first bite of frost in the air. People were strolling along, girls and young men hand in hand, elderly people, the inevitable babushkas in their shawls and stout shoes, laden down with plastic bags, *en route* for home. A group of young soldiers, caps slightly rakish on the side of their cropped heads, laughed and ogled two girls across the broad street.

Life had settled into a routine. There was no major conflict, only sporadic outbreaks in the far regions of the old Soviet Empire. They burst like boils, were lanced, erupted briefly somewhere else. It would take more than a mere decade to stabilize the great Russian state. That was Borisov's dream. Stability, wealth, economic power. A return to world status. That was what he worked for, and that was why he was on his way to eat dinner with the representative of the arch capitalist, Diamond Enterprises. He had grown to respect Andrews and then, unwillingly, to trust him. Liking had followed. Dimitri Borisov was his father's son. He had an instinct for people. He sensed weakness and he recognized integrity. His father maintained he could distinguish the sweat smell when someone was lying. Dimitri claimed the same gift.

Negotiations were slow because Borisov dictated the pace. Time was not on Andrews' side; he believed, because Borisov had told him so, that the details of the agreement with Karakov were being finalized at a higher level. They were, in fact, on hold in his department. That very morning he had received a spate of cables from Karakov in Paris asking if there was any reason for the delay. The terms were agreed in broad outline. He wanted to expand the deal and fill in more of the financial details.

The restaurant was privately run, and only patronized by Muscovites. It was small and cramped, there were no concessions to Western style. Bare tables, a hot smoky atmosphere and the best Russian food in the city. And wines unobtainable anywhere else. The cellar had been stocked in the Eighties from the massive wine store taken from Livadia and hidden during the Great Patriotic War. The sweet wines and the oldest vintages, uncertain to have survived for close on seventy years, were shipped to the West for sale, where the tsar's insignia on the bottles attracted speculators.

Dimitri was shown to a table. It was the one he kept reserved. He took his current mistress there. She would have preferred to go to the Hotel Muscova; appearances impressed her more than food and drink. He was very fond of her, but she irritated him.

He had been briefly married to a social psychologist. Her job took her to the Institute of Social Studies at Kharkhov; his was in Moscow. They commuted for a year and then divorced. There were no children. He wasn't about to get married to anyone else.

He sat at his table, ordered a glass of pepper vodka and waited for Andrews. He wasn't late, Dimitri Borisov was early on purpose. He liked the Englishman but he wanted him at a disadvantage. Ray came in, looking round anxiously; the surroundings unfamiliar, the atmosphere thick with smoke and kitchen smells. Borisov rose and the two men shook hands.

'Sorry,' Ray said. 'Have you been waiting long?'

'No, I ordered a drink. Sit down, let us order our

dinner and then we can talk in peace. Will you trust me to choose for you?'

Ray Andrews grinned at him. 'There's no way I can choose for myself. You go ahead. But easy on the vodka. I haven't got a Russian head.'

It was his suggestion that they used Christian names; he had explained that it was a Western practice, designed to democratize business negotiations. For a moment he had expected Borisov to refuse. He had a way of doing the unexpected. He had smiled at Ray and said, 'Democracy is the fashion now. So I am Dimitri and you are Ray. Very good.'

He said to Andrews, 'I hope you like this place. This is where *we* go when we want to eat well and enjoy ourselves. Around midnight they have some music.'

'Gypsy music?' Andrews asked.

Borisov shook his head. 'No. That is for tourists. A balalaika and a singer. He has a fine tenor voice. The musician is usually drunk, but he·plays all the better for that.'

It was, as Ray Andrews wrote to his wife next day, the most extraordinary evening. The food gave him indigestion, but it was delicious and kept coming, one dish after another. The wine sat on his tongue like a kiss. And they talked business while they ate and drank, and then philosophy and politics, and then more business. He didn't bother describing the negotiations to her; she wouldn't have understood and only skipped to something more interesting. He wrote about Dimitri Borisov in terms that would surprise her. A new Russian, the heir of the Soviet system, born into the élite circle that ruled from the Politburo. A man who had adapted to change that had become anarchy in the view of men like his father. But the son had kept his ideals and his patriotism, and abandoned the political stance which was no longer relevant to the future of Russia. That night, with yet another bottle open on the table, Ray Andrews felt a sense of privilege. The Russian was opening his heart and his mind to him. Perhaps they were both a little drunk. It didn't matter. It didn't alter what was being said between them.

'The difference is,' Dimitri said to him, 'I am negotiating for my country. You are negotiating for a foreign-based company that exists through a monopoly. That's why I must drive the hardest bargain I can get from you. Because it's not for myself.' He filled up Ray's glass.

Ray said to him, 'I know that. I appreciate it. But I'm not just a company man. My job is on the line; I've worked all my life for D.E. and it hasn't been easy, with a wife and kids always having to take second place. If I fail on this, my friend, I'm on the bloody rubbish tip. So that's why I'm going to drive as hard a bargain as you are. And no hard feelings!'

Borisov had laughed. 'We understand each other. In a way we have much in common. That's why this business has got as far as it has. I can deal with you, Ray. I can tell you now that I don't like or trust Ivan Karakov, because he is only interested in profits and gorging himself and his business on our diamonds. He pretends to be a Russian. He was born in New York; he talks and thinks like an American. He likes to play-act, but he's as greedy as your people in London and Johannesburg. So I am going to choose between you. And that means I will sign with the partner that gives most to my country. Immediate financial loans without interest and without set repayment, to industrialize the area around Sytykanskaya, so we can bring a new mine into production in two years. Assistance with cleaning and de-polluting the Baikal Lake – it's been poisoned for years, flooded with chemical waste, the fumes alone are causing sickness and death in the surrounding populations. We have to address that problem. We need money, Ray, and expertise. You can give us that.'

Ray had said slowly, 'You've never mentioned Baikal before. You're asking the moon, Dimitri. I can't promise you anything as big as this. Why pick this moment to spring it on me?'

Borisov looked at him. He filled up his glass. Andrews covered his own with a hand, shaking his head. 'Because,' the Russian said, 'it's our price. I didn't know that till last night. I invited you to eat with me so that we could both get drunk and talk more easily.'

'I'm not drunk,' Ray answered. 'And I don't think you are either. I'm not that easy to soften up.' It was said without rancour.

Borisov noted that. 'I didn't think you were,' he admitted. 'But you haven't walked out on me, have you? In my office, I think you might have done . . . So we can still talk. Negotiations are still open. Now have some more wine. It's time for the music.'

An extraordinary experience, Ray Andrews wrote in his letter. But how difficult to describe the singer and his mixture of melancholy and exuberance, the balalaika player lurching at his side, playing his solo to rapturous applause. Impossible to convey the sense of manly comradeship that developed between Ray Andrews and Dimitri Borisov as they ended the evening on their feet, glasses raised in a mutual toast. He had been to Russia five years before and spent nearly six weeks there on this trip. Until that evening, he had known nothing of the city or its people. And, as Borisov told him, Moscow is Russia. What you see and feel here is the heartbeat of Russia. It sounded dramatic and theatrical when he wrote it down in the impersonal hotel room, penned to a woman thousands of miles away, who only wanted to know when he'd be coming home. Ray Andrews read the letter through, and tore it up. It wasn't really written for his wife. He had written it for himself.

He checked the time and put in a call to Susan instead. He said the negotiations were going well, he was missing them all, but didn't know exactly how much longer he would have to stay out there. He listened absently while she talked about the call she'd had from the son at university . . . he was finding the curriculum very hard and wanted to drop a subject. 'Lazy little bugger,' Andrews muttered to himself, suddenly infuriated by the self-indulgence of youth. That, he admitted, was because he had a hangover, and wasn't fair. He recalled his thoughts from other things and concentrated on what had been happening at home.

And, promising to call again in the next day or two, he hung up with a feeling of guilty relief. Then he settled down to draft a long confidential fax to Harris in London setting out the terms put forward for a deal that would break Karakov and give Diamond Enterprises virtual control of the Russian diamond production.

James had come home early and silenced Elizabeth's description of her day by taking her to bed.

And there they lay in a happy doze, until he looked at his watch and said, 'Sweetheart . . . we'll have to make a move soon. So what were you saying you did today?'

Elizabeth sighed in contentment. There was no dimming of romance in that marriage, no danger of their relationship becoming stale.

'I was trying to tell you I had lunch with Jean Pierre and went to the Impressionist exhibition at the Musée d'Orsay . . . Darling, it was simply marvellous. You must come with me.'

He said gently, 'I'm flat to the floor at the moment, maybe later on . . . When's Lasalle going to arrange this party with Karakov?' He wasn't interested in his wife enthusing about Impressionist pictures and how charming her new friend had been. All he could think of was meeting Karakov.

Elizabeth said, 'He didn't say; he's got to fix it with them first. I said we'd be available, no matter what.'

'Clever girl,' he said. 'It'll put that cow Clara Wasserman in her place if you've managed to get us together and David couldn't.' He stretched, arms above his head. 'If I brought this off,' he said, 'we'd have a wonderful life. We'd travel all over the world; we'd have a hell of a lot more money, too.'

'I don't care about money,' she protested. 'We've got plenty.'

'Oh we're all right,' he agreed, 'but we don't know what money means compared to people like Harris and Heyderman. I'd get share options, that would go with the job . . . They could buy and sell both of us and our families and never notice the difference. You know how much Arthur paid for that yacht he raced in the Fasnet – a million! That's what I mean by real money.'

He was staring at the ceiling, lost in a dream where he sat at Julius Heyderman's elbow, and helped to rule his empire.

Elizabeth got up. 'I don't want a yacht,' she said. 'I want a bath and time to get organized. Or your smart French business people won't get any dinner.'

She hated him talking about money like that; it seemed to matter more to him since they started this phase in their lives. He had never drooled over sheer wealth like that before, and it disturbed her. James heard the bathroom door close. He knew his wife. She didn't care about material things. Always having what she needed induced superiority. And moral attitudes. He was surprised by the angry criticism in his own mind. He would have hated a money grubber, and he'd known plenty before he met Liz. It was the criticism of him, implicit in her dismissal, that angered him. Whatever he gained would benefit her even if she didn't want a yacht. She wouldn't say no to a villa at Cap d'Antibes . . . She'd go for that, he thought, becoming really angry. He checked himself, shaken by the intensity of his resentment, as if something had come flooding out that had been penned up, unadmitted for a long time. He was being a bastard, he decided. He was edgy, working flat out, and still hitting the wall because he couldn't get to Karakov.

And that afternoon Ruth Fraser had brought him a fax from London indicating that Ray Andrews was making significant progress. He'd made Elizabeth the scapegoat for his own frustration. He went to the bathroom door, opened it and said, 'Sorry, sweetheart. No yachts. I'd forgotten what a pain you are when you're seasick.' He ducked as she threw the sponge at him, but he heard her laugh.

'God,' Julius Heyderman sighed. 'Oh God, what am I going to do about her?'

Sylvia Heyderman said gently, 'There's nothing more you can do, darling, except keep an eye on her and bail her out when you can. You've tried everything.'

'Bail her out – too bloody right. Arrested for being drunk and disorderly . . . Thank God she was charged in her married name; but one day, one day, Sylvie, the whole mess will come out.'

She slipped her hand in his. He'd thrown down the confidential report faxed in from the firm of solicitors in London who looked after Stella's welfare. It was the third offence in a year; the number of times they had paid off bad debts and got unsuitable tenants evicted from her house in Camden were a mere detail.

'I don't know what to do,' he repeated. 'If she'd only see me, or see you . . . she used to trust you.'

'That was a long time ago,' his wife pointed out. She was so sorry for him; for such a strong man, his anguish over his daughter was pitiful to see. She loved him in her calm way, and she had long since lost patience and sympathy with Stella. Privately, she believed she was tainted with the same instability as her mother. Sylvia was not a woman who found mental illness easy to understand. She had suffered the loss of her first husband at an early age, and reared her three children on her own, running a design business at the same time. Her reward had been to marry one of the richest and most attractive men in South Africa. It hadn't happened because she had wimped out. 'Ever since Jacob was murdered, she's gone out to destroy herself. You can't stop her, nobody can.'

'That bastard,' Julius muttered. 'Once she got involved with that lot, it was bound to end in disaster. I told him not to come back . . . He wouldn't listen.'

'He'd been out of the country too long,' she said. 'He thought he could come back and jump on Mandela's bandwaggon and get away with it. They never learn, that's what's so worrying. Listen, darling, I hate to see you upset like this, with all the other problems at the moment. Would you like me to go over and see if I can get through to her? I don't think it'll work, but I'd be very happy to try if you'd like me to.'

He slipped his arm round her for a moment. 'Thanks,' he said simply. 'I wouldn't let you put yourself in that position. Not after last time.' He frowned. 'I'm sending Reece back to London. I want him to keep a watching brief on that little sod Arthur. He can also make contact with Stella. She's agreed to see him before. He might be able to put pressure on her. And I don't give a damn what kind of pressure it is . . . If we don't get her home here and in somewhere for treatment, she'll end up dead in the gutter. I owe it to Eileen to have one more try.'

Sylvia didn't argue with that. He had never once reminded her that it was her idea to send Stella to Witwatersrand, to involve herself in higher studies and student life. It had worked out only too well. In her first year she had discovered the extreme Left Wing of the anti-apartheid movement and thrown herself, heart and soul, into working for it.

The exhibitionist in her thrived on protest marches, on sit-ins and subversive meetings. She was arrested, released without charge because of her father's influence, endlessly warned and cautioned that one day even Stella Heyderman could go too far. Julius was furious with her, but he couldn't help a stab of pride in her courage and tenacity. His reckless, self-indulgent child had found a cause and she was brave enough to fight for it and dare the oppressive political system to treat her as it treated her black comrades in arms. There were no more defiant drunken escapades. A mature and politically committed young woman embraced the rights of black South Africans to equal rights under the law in their own country; she earned a lot of hatred and abuse, but also a grudging respect. Being a Heyderman didn't help when the police dogs were unleashed on a crowd of demonstrators, and Stella was always in the front rank. Julius's great fear was that she would break the savage miscegenation laws. Nothing could save her from a prison sentence if she were caught in a sexual liaison with a black man. She had affairs with her white counterparts in the movement, but never stepped over the barrier between the races. He knew, because he had access to the police reports on her. And friends in the hierarchy.

'She's your girl, Mr Heyderman, and for that we'll turn a blind eye when we can, but if she cohabits with a black . . .' The lifted eyebrow of the Chief Police Commissioner, the slight shake of the head. 'Six months in the Fort . . .'

It was Reece who told him that a young Marxist agitator had been seen visiting her flat and that the police were about to move in.

Jacob Yakumi had studied law in England and returned to South Africa to act as lawyer for activists accused of political crimes. He was a marked man by the authorities as soon as he set foot in Johannesburg. Julius had acted instantly. He had driven to Stella's address and slapped an air ticket down in front of her. Father and daughter seldom met; she rejected the values and capitalist enterprise which was personified in

Heyderman himself and Diamond Enterprises. She also said, quite genuinely, that however powerful he was in public life, it must harm his reputation to be seen with her. He had always refused to repudiate her publicly, although he had often been pressured to do so.

She was his daughter, and if she wanted to make a fool of herself and had the guts to do so under the circumstances, he wasn't going to interfere. She had loved him in silent gratitude for that endorsement.

'I've come to take you to the airport,' he had said, 'before you are arrested. I don't want to know if you are sleeping with this black – I don't want to think you'd sink so low – but the police have decided he's going inside and so are you. Put some things in a bag and hurry up!'

To his amazement she had laughed at him. He often thought of that scene in mingled pain and disgust. 'I would be, but he won't sleep with me, Dad – he says it's too dangerous for me! I'm not running off and leaving him. They'll take him in and kick his balls to pulp. If you want me to get out, then he goes with me. Two tickets, not one.'

And she meant it. For a moment they had faced each other, locked in a conflict of wills that Julius knew he wasn't going to win. He hadn't tried to argue. 'All right, get packed. Tell me where to find him. You mustn't telephone, his line is bugged. Like yours.'

Reece had gone to Yakumi's office, leased from an Indian in the poor quarter of the city. Reece had simply explained that Stella wouldn't leave without him and would be arrested and jailed. He had a straight choice: walk out of the door and into Reece's car and go to the airport, or commit her to prison. Jacob Yakumi had made that choice. Julius had said goodbye to his daughter in the limousine, shielded by the glass partition.

'I'll make all necessary arrangements for money in London. When the fuss has died down, I'll let you know and you can come home. Now go on, Stella, or you'll miss your flight.'

She'd looked at him for a moment, and then swung the door open. As she turned to go, she paused a moment. 'Thanks,' she said. 'But if it's not safe for Jacob, it won't be safe for me.'

A month later he got a letter to say that she had married Jacob Yakumi, and would not return home until the antiapartheid and miscegenation laws were repealed.

Married. Heyderman had stared down at the letter, and felt an urge to be physically sick. Coloured children. His bloodline tainted for ever, his daughter the wife of a black from the Soweto township. He had given a great shout of outrage and smashed the nearest thing to hand: a clock that Sylvia treasured. Then he got so drunk that the servants had to support him up to bed. She had betrayed him and degraded herself. His only recourse was to ensure that nobody knew what she had done. Except Reece. Reece was the only one he could trust with his humiliation because Reece loved him with the devotion of a dog for its master. Unquestioning, with utter loyalty. And because he rewarded him with his secrets, as much as with money and position in the business, Reece would do anything for Julius. Setting up a trust fund for his daughter on condition that the marriage was never made public was a simple task. He had gone to London to arrange it.

Now he would go to London again for Julius. This time to spy on Arthur, and to see if he could salvage something from the terrible wreck of Stella Heyderman Yakumi's life.

Karakov checked his watch again. Madeline Luchaire, minor movie actress and mistress of one of the world's richest men, had made an appointment for three o'clock that afternoon. She was twenty minutes late. Eugene Titulescu had arranged it, and he waited in the office with his father-in-law, poised to hurry down and meet her at the entrance as soon as her car drove up. Nerves made Ivan snarl at him, 'For Christ's sake, stop walking up and down like a cat on a fucking hot brick!'

The prince didn't answer. He was so used to Ivan's outbursts that he didn't react at all. 'She has to make an entrance,' he ventured after a pause. 'Actresses are like that.'

'Actress, my ass,' the old man said. 'She's just a—'

At that moment the phone rang from reception.

'She's here,' he swung on Titulescu. 'What are you waiting for? Get down there!'

Karakov had met Madeline Luchaire once or twice at starry media receptions. She was a very beautiful woman by any criteria, and all her endowments were natural, from the softly curving body to the lustrous golden blond hair. She was witty, too, if her much reported comment about herself was original, 'Silicone, like soap, never touches my skin.'

She spoke with a Midi accent which encouraged her enemies to spread the rumour that she came from the slums of Marseilles and began her career in a brothel at fifteen. She held out her hand and Karakov bowed low and kissed it.

It was the first time she had come to his headquarters. When Abdullah Bin Saladin bought her jewels, they were taken round to his suite at the Ritz by Eugene Titulescu and left there until he made a choice. He had never received Ivan Karakov. He never dealt direct with trades-men, however prominent. He accepted Prince Titulescu because he bore a title that resembled his own. He was unaware that princes in Hungary and Romania were almost as commonplace as counts in France.

'The prince has told me so much about you, Monsieur Karakov,' she said. 'I'm glad to meet you at last after wearing so many of your lovely jewels. As you see . . .' Her throat was circled by two strands of enormous South

Sea pearls, matching stones gleamed in her small ears, ringed by perfect blue-white diamonds.

'It gives me pleasure to think of you wearing them, Madame,' Ivan said. He knew how to flatter and when he wanted to, he could be very charming. 'Beauty belongs to beauty.' He smiled at her wickedly, sensing a gleam of humour in the violet blue eyes. 'With some of my clients, Madame, I have to shut my eyes and think of the money.'

She laughed out loud. It was a full, throaty sound; old and calculating as he was, Ivan found himself responding. She was incredibly, vibrantly sexy.

'I love jewels,' Madeline Luchaire said, and he could see how she had acquired so many. 'And I've been hearing whispers about some very fine things you've got hidden away. So,' the gorgeous smile beamed at him, 'what have you got to show me?'

He had the plan all worked out. His son-in-law knew what to do; he saw a signal from Karakov and stepped forward, the epitome of old-fashioned elegance. 'Some champagne first for Madame?' he suggested. Madeline liked him. She wasn't fooled by the façade. He was the old man's lackey, just as she was an Arab's sexual plaything. They were both in it for the money.

'That would be nice,' she agreed. 'Fortunately His Highness doesn't object to alcohol, as long as it's in private.' Eugene Titulescu had seen the Highness in question making serious inroads into a decanter of whisky in the privacy of his suite.

'Prince,' Karakov always used the title in front of clients of importance, 'ring down and tell them to bring up the keys.' He turned to her. 'I shall open my private safe for you, Madame. I hope to find something that will interest you.'

He knew exactly why she had come and what she was waiting to see, but he knew that the art of making a super sale was to keep the client in suspense, and then pretend you wanted them to buy something else. Fifteen minutes later, the Dom Pérignon was open and a space had been cleared on Ivan's desk, spread with a black velvet cloth. He had personally chosen every item. There were emeralds from Imperial Russia, originally sold by desperate *émigrés* for a fraction of their value seventy years ago; he had reset them in modern designs because there was no market among the super-rich for old-fashioned jewellery, whatever its provenance. Some, like a brooch that had belonged to the Empress Farah of Iran, were contemporary. Its central stone was a ruby as big as a pullet's egg, surrounded by diamonds of eight carats each, blue-white. It was worth a fortune and he had paid a fair price for it, but it was not for sale and never would be. It was part of the Karakov legend that he owned the Shah's ruby and no amount of money could get him to part with it. Laura wore the brooch on important occasions, but he had never let her keep it. Madeline picked it up, admiring it, touching the big stone with a finger, caressing it.

'No, Madame,' Karakov said softly. 'That is for show but not for sale. Let me show you this.'

He gave her his magnificent oval stone, blue-white and burning with thousands of tiny lights; it was a master-piece of fine cutting. It weighed 120 carats in the rough and Ernst Richter had bought it from a big dealer in Antwerp for 10,000 dollars. It now weighed just over 38 carats and it was perfect. The price was 400,000 dollars. She was gazing at it a little too intently. He didn't want her to get too interested; the big diamond was just to whet her appetite.

'Isn't it beautiful?' Ivan said, taking it from her. 'Prince, more champagne for Madame. You know, there's nothing in the world like a diamond; not even rubies, and they're wonderful stones, not even the best ruby can compare with something like this.'

He moved the stone in his thumb and forefinger; it

flashed every colour in the spectrum. 'Look at that,' he said. 'That's what you get with a diamond – purity and brilliance. You don't get that with any other stone in the world. It's what makes the diamond unique.'

'Yes,' Madeline Luchaire said. 'It's a magnificent jewel – truly magnificent.'

It was time for the real sale to open . . . 'If you like that stone, Madame, then I'm going to show you something really special. Something I don't show to everybody. But I know you'll appreciate them.'

He looked up and his hard old eyes flashed a message at Titulescu. He wanted no interruptions. The prince poured another glass of champagne, and began picking up the jewels and putting them back in the outer safe. Ivan picked up the phone.

'I'm sending Prince Titulescu down to the vaults. Tell them to have the Romanovs ready for him.'

'I won't be long, Madame.' The prince bent over her chair. 'But this is really worth seeing.' He let himself out of the office; he moved very quietly, though he was a big man.

'You mustn't mind me,' Ivan said, 'if I get excited. But these stones are the love of my life. That's why I will only show them to someone who I think loves diamonds like I do. I'm damned if I'll let just anyone see them.'

He scowled, as if he had some unappreciative people in mind. He opened the gold cigarette box on his table. His manners were perfect to his clients, but they were a little artificial, like his eating habits. He had once sat through a formal dinner in Washington where a senator's wife was entertaining them and gone through the tortures of the damned because he couldn't pick his teeth. 'You don't smoke, Madame?'

'No.' She shook her head. 'His Highness doesn't approve of smoking.'

The prince was back in less than five minutes. Normally it took half an hour to get through the vaults

163

and clear a valuable piece before it was taken upstairs, but the Romanov Diamonds had been waiting for him. He had given orders that no calls were to be put through to Mr Karakov's private office, he was not to be disturbed for any reason.

'Ah.' Ivan got up. 'Here they are. Now, Madame, you're going to see one of the wonders of the world.'

He opened the biggest box first, and laid the pieces out on the black cloth. Huge pools of crimson blazed up at them, flashing with incredible brilliance. For a moment the woman said nothing; she didn't even put out her hand to touch them.

'My God,' she said. 'What are these?'

'Diamonds, Madame,' Ivan said. 'Red diamonds from a secret mine in Russia. The rarest stones in the world.'

He took the necklace and held it out between his fingers. It swung in the light, flashing red fire. It was exquisitely mounted in platinum, set so that the stones seemed joined invisibly. They had an unearthly colour and brilliance.

'Take it, Madame,' Ivan said quietly. 'Look at it.'

She held the necklace in her hands and looked into the heart of the central stone.

'They're the colour of rubies,' she said. 'And the fire in them . . . it's incredible.'

'They have an interesting history. Here are the companion pieces to the necklace.' He laid out the ear-rings, the ring and the brooch. She put the necklace down and slipped the ring on her finger. Karakov paused. It was time for the fairy story he had invented to embellish his sales pitch. He spoke slowly, dramatically.

'These stones were mined in Russia in the seventeenth century.' Ivan sat back in his chair; the lady was examining the ear-rings, turning the stones round as if she were hypnotized. 'The location of the mine was kept secret. Legend says that when these stones were found, the slaves working there were killed so nobody would ever discover where they came from.'

He paused for dramatic effect. Madeline Luchaire was still looking at the ring.

'There was no means of cutting them properly, so they never revealed their true magnificence and fire. But they were so unique that only the emperors of Russia could possess them and they were part of the State Treasury. Until Catherine the Great gave them to her lover Potemkin.' Ivan spread his hands, acting the part, revelling in the art of selling. 'He was always short of money and he sold the red diamonds to an Indian princely family to pay his debts. They were not seen again until the early nineteen hundreds, when the raja of the day wore them to the King of England's coronation.

'They were admired by the Grand Duke Michael of Russia, who persuaded the raja to sell them. He presented them to the Tsarina, the last poor lady who was murdered by the Bolsheviks. So they came home to Russia. Now, Madame, because the country has opened up to the West and all the barriers are down, they approached me to re-cut them and set them, because I am the only jeweller in the world who could do it. And to sell them, because I am the only jeweller who has clients wealthy enough to own them. Come over here, come and look at that necklace.'

He led Madeline to the big mirror on the opposite wall. There was a bright ceiling spot placed at an angle just above the glass so as to catch every reflection from diamonds and increase their brilliance.

'Let me put them on for you,' he said.

She lifted the thick curtain of blond hair and he fastened the necklace at the back.

'Ah,' Ivan Karakov said, and this time it was genuine. 'Ah, look at that. Prince, come and look at this necklace.'

They blazed against her skin, great pools of crimson fire that seemed as if they must burn, so intense was the brilliance reflected by the mirror and the light.

She said in a voice husky as if from sexual excitement, 'I must have them . . . When His Highness sees these, I know he'll give them to me.' She turned to Karakov. 'He's not coming to Paris till next month. What can I do? Has anyone else seen them?'

Karakov didn't remove the necklace. He pulled out her chair and Titulescu filled her glass with more champagne. 'No,' Ivan said. 'You are the only one so far. But there is interest. Word has got out and I've had enquiries from Japan.'

'Don't sell them,' Madeline Luchaire said. 'Promise me! Wait till I talk to His Highness. Wait till he comes over. I know I can persuade him.' Karakov pretended to consider. Her hand came out and gripped his arm. 'Please,' she insisted. 'You know how much he's bought from you. Hold them till he comes.'

Ivan said, 'If they were mine I wouldn't hesitate. But I am selling for the Russian government. I'm their agent. If I owned the diamonds it would be easy, but they are pressing me to find a buyer. They need foreign currency . . . If you can persuade His Highness to come sooner, I can delay showing them to the Japanese. But not for two whole months, Madame.'

She drained her glass and set it down. Her expression was determined. 'I'll see what I can arrange,' she said. Her tone was suddenly businesslike. 'On condition that you show them to nobody else, and hold them for his approval. If he thought you were auctioning them, believe me, you'd never make another sale to him. I'd see to it. I want those red diamonds, Monsieur Karakov. I must have them. When he sees them, whatever the price, I know His Highness will buy.'

'I'll bend the rules,' Karakov conceded, 'for you, Madame. But no more than a month. Until then they are reserved for the prince.' He came and unfastened the necklace. She slipped off the ring.

'Thank you,' she said. 'I'll let Prince Eugene know as soon as His Highness arrives.'

Karakov kissed her hand. 'No man could refuse you anything,' he said. 'I'm sure I couldn't.'

He and Titulescu escorted her to her chauffeur-driven Rolls; then he hurried upstairs to call Laura. 'Luchaire's just left, she's crazy for them! She's getting the prince over to see them. We've made the sale; I know it!'

Laura cooed down the line. 'Good, good. We'll celebrate tonight. I always said you'd sell ice to the Eskimos . . .'

She loved success and money; she would flatter him and fuss over him and tell him how wonderful he was when he got home. And expect a big present when he made the sale and collected his commission.

'Tell me, I want to hear everything.'

'I showed her the new Richter stone . . . she started getting interested, but I knew I couldn't sell her that and the Romanovs, so I went into the big sales pitch right away. Eugene did his stuff, pouring the champagne, ass kissing, you know how it is—'

'I know,' Laura interrupted. 'So? Go on, tell me.'

'I got her to try the necklace. She damned near orgasmed with excitement when she looked in the mirror. "I've got to have them, I must have them . . ." I knew I was on the home run. So we agreed on one month. I guess she's calling Riyadh right now . . . He'll come – he won't want to lose out to the Japs, and when he does she'll fuck him blind till he buys them for her. Honey,' he said, 'when I sell these for Moscow, I've got the red diamond concession in my pocket. The deal's as good as signed!'

'You're a genius,' she said, echoing David Wasserman. 'A real genius. Oh . . .' she wasn't a woman to get carried away even at such a moment of excitement, 'while we're

talking, I got a call today from Jean Pierre, you remember
. . . Jennie's ex? He wants us for dinner Tuesday the
twenty-eighth. I have to call him back today. Is that OK?'

Karakov laughed. 'The way I feel, I'd eat with Yasser
Arafat! Sure we can go . . . you like him, he has interesting
parties . . . Say yes. And I'll be home early tonight.'

'I'll make it special for you,' Laura promised. 'For my
clever husband. Love you.'

'Love you too,' Ivan said, and hung up. He was to
remember that dinner party, accepted in a mood of
euphoria, as one of the turning points of his life.

Elizabeth heard her father's voice on the line. It was
unusual for him to answer the telephone at that hour.
He was usually out on council business or sitting in the
Magistrate's Court.

'Dad? Hello, it's me . . . How are you?'

'I'm fine, Lizzie. How nice to hear you. How're you
getting on?' He saw his wife passing the door of the
study, covered the mouthpiece with his hand and called
to her. 'Jill? Lizzie's on the phone . . . Oh yes, darling.
I'm glad you're enjoying yourself. And how's James?' He
asked the question dutifully.

'He's fine, terribly busy,' Elizabeth answered. 'Dad,
listen I've got some news . . .'

'What news – nothing wrong, is there?'

She could never understand why they were so anxious
for her, forgetting that it had been a telephone call that
told them of their son's death in the Falklands.

'Wrong? Dad, it's the best possible news! I've missed!
Nearly three weeks!'

'Missed? Missed what?' Her father belonged to a
generation when monthly periods weren't mentioned, let
alone the subject of advertising on TV.

His wife took the telephone out of his hand. 'Liz . . .
darling . . .'

'I was overdue and did a test,' Elizabeth told her. 'Do

it yourself, I got the kit and followed the instructions and it's positive! Oh Mum, I'm so thrilled, I just had to ring you and tell you!'

Her mother turned quickly and said, 'She's pregnant, isn't that wonderful?'

Then to her daughter, 'Darling, that's great news. Just wonderful. But you must go to a doctor and get it confirmed. Have you told James?'

'No. I've got an appointment this afternoon. I'll tell him tonight. He'll be over the moon. I know he wants a baby as much as I do. Oh, I just wish I was near you instead of over here.'

Jill Fairfax's eyes filled and she blinked the silly tears away. 'So do we, darling. But it's not that far. You mustn't start charging about on aeroplanes, not at this early stage. You *must* be careful for the first three months, but we could fly over and see you. No reason why not . . . Now, Philip, don't start mumbling, we've got nothing so important that we can't take a few days to go to Paris and see Liz . . .'

When she hung up, Elizabeth longed to pre-empt her visit to the doctor and ring James and tell him. But once before she had been late and mistaken the cause. The disappointment had been so great she wasn't going to risk it. No, she decided, I'll wait. I'll tell him tonight when I'm certain.

They'd been so busy entertaining and being entertained, going to the opera and ballet, meeting new people all the time, that the due date came and went without Elizabeth noticing until the day after she visited the Musée d'Orsay with Jean Pierre Lasalle. Four days late. Then a whole week. A wretched false alarm when she thought abdominal twinges were going to bring her hopes to nothing. But false it was, engendered by her own anxiety. Two weeks. She had to confide in someone. She called Jean Pierre and asked him round for lunch. He was so easy to talk to that she found herself admitting her frustration at being childless and how anxiety prevented her from telling James in case she was mistaken.

'He's been so good about it,' she had told Jean Pierre. 'He'd love a family. I just couldn't bear to raise his hopes and then for everything to go wrong again.'

She hadn't noticed his expression, she was too absorbed in her own excitement. When he answered, the meaning passed her by.

'If you were my wife,' he said gently, 'I would want to share that with you. Not have you turn to someone else because you were afraid of disappointing me. Surely he must feel the same?'

Elizabeth had asked him quickly, 'You don't mind, do you, Jean Pierre? You're such a sweet friend and you've been so kind . . . I really appreciate it, you know.'

'There's nothing to appreciate,' he answered. 'It's a very happy friendship for me, too.'

He had given her the name and address of his own doctor and offered to take her for the appointment. Even warned her gently at being over optimistic. His daughter-in-law had been misled by a home pregnancy kit into thinking she wasn't pregnant, when properly supervised tests showed that she was.

Getting ready for the visit to the French doctor, Elizabeth had felt nauseated with nerves. It must be right. Oh please God, she almost prayed aloud, as she had done so often before without consciously addressing any higher Power. Please let it be right this time. Jean Pierre got up and came towards her when she came out of the surgery.

'I don't have to ask what the verdict is,' he said. 'I can see it on your face.'

She caught hold of his hand. The doctor's receptionist stared at them and drew the wrong conclusion. She had known Monsieur Lasalle and his former wife for years. Whatever the situation, the English girl was pregnant and delighted at the news. Ah well, she said to herself, young women were so independent these days. A married woman too.

'He says I'm about two months.' They were in the car on the way back to rue Constantine. 'I must have started before we left London. Oh, it's just so marvellous. I can hardly believe it!'

'And there are no problems?' he enquired. 'You're in good health?'

'Blooming,' she laughed. 'Strong as an ox. He just said not to do too much for the next three or four weeks since it's a first baby. Jean Pierre . . .' She turned to him, her smile so radiant that he forced himself to say it.

'You're so happy,' he said. 'I am happy for you. And for your husband. I envy him coming home to you tonight.'

As they stood on the pavement before the entrance to the apartment, she reached up and kissed him on the cheek.

'Thank you,' she said. 'Thank you for the doctor, for taking me . . . for everything. I'm going to tell James I want you to be godfather.'

He paused for a moment to watch her run up the few steps and open the front door. He was happy for her, he admitted. And very sad for himself. He had been in love with her since their first meeting. He could identify the very moment when it happened to him, as she stood in the flat in rue de la Perle, and he divined immediately that it wouldn't suit her husband's purpose and persuaded her against it. Not, as he told her later, because the rue Constantine was more expensive and he would reap more commission, but because he wanted the right decision for her. That was when he had fallen in love. And kept a little hope and determination to himself. He didn't know James Hastings and it wouldn't have stopped him if he had. A Frenchman doesn't balk at husbands. That's why he had offered to help them meet

Ivan Karakov: to keep the contact going, to make a corner for himself in her life closer than trips to art exhibitions and afternoons spent wandering round Malmaison or Versailles. Now, he would never be more than what she had fondly called him – a good friend. In ten days' time he would meet James Hastings when he came to dinner at his house on avenue Montaigne.

It might help him to accept defeat – he doubted it – if the man was worthy of the wife. He doubted that, too.

David Wasserman was sitting in Karakov's office. He had called in for a friendly meeting, and Karakov had greeted him warmly. They had known each other for years, and they were as near friends as it was possible to be in such a competitive business. David had great respect for Ivan and admired his achievements; the posturing and play-acting amused him because there was a love of the dramatic in him. The man was a giant, why shouldn't he take centre stage? Karakov considered Wasserman the greatest expert on diamonds in the world after himself, and he respected his wife Clara too; there was a woman with a business brain, such a help to her husband . . . she even got on with Laura, who disliked most women on principle.

'Have a cigar?' Karakov offered. He had never smoked; he didn't drink much either and he watched his weight. He and Laura were very health conscious. David pierced a big Punch and lit it, drawing with satisfaction. The rich tobacco scent wafted above them.

'Clara would kill me if she saw me doing this,' he said, and laughed. 'She watches me like a baby.'

'And why shouldn't she? You're a good man, who'd look after her without you?'

'That worries me,' David Wasserman agreed. 'No children, and no relatives.' He didn't need to elaborate. Ivan knew that she had lost many members of her family in the Holocaust. Even now, she woke up some nights crying. For Clara, as for so many Jewish people, that terrible wound would never heal.

They had travelled all over the world together, but nothing would induce her to step on German soil. For years Clara had devoted time and money working for the Jewish women's charity, Wizzo, helping the less fortunate. Together, David and she had worked in the cause of Israel. They were too old to emigrate themselves but their people had a homeland now; they were no longer the wandering race of the world. He had given enormous sums of money for charitable foundations in Israel and persuaded a lot of his influential friends, Ivan Karakov among them, to do the same. He was a Fellow of the prestigious Weizmann Institute, and he and Clara visited twice a year. They had bought a small apartment in Tel Aviv, more as a statement of their faith in the country's future, than because they intended to live there. As David liked saying, it was a young country for young people, with hope and life ahead of them.

He said, 'How's business?'

The same question would be asked all over the world, in Amsterdam and Antwerp, in Hatton Garden and Kimberley, in Paris and New York, wherever diamonds were bought and sold the phraseology was the same. So was the answer.

Karakov shrugged. 'Not bad. Could be better.'

Wasserman smiled and shook his head at him. 'How many million dollars did you make last year, and you say, not bad, could be better?'

'And you, eh? What about you? I thought you were retiring, so what brings you and Clara all the way to London for a Board meeting? And what makes you decide suddenly to come over here?'

It was a direct attack but David Wasserman parried it.

'I was seeing Julius about you. You should be flattered;

173

he only comes to England for the really big problems. And you're a problem!'

'I'm no problem,' Ivan said. 'I'm just unhappy. I don't like the way D.E. does business. OK, they screw the little guys, but not me, not Karakov. I'm not taking any more of his goddamned parcels and you can tell Heyderman. The last was a bastard. I won't buy from them on their terms any more!'

'All right, all right.' Wasserman held up his hand; Ivan was scowling like a dragon across the desk from him. He was getting impossibly autocratic these days. If anyone disagreed with him, he blew up, shouting and ordering them out. David Wassserman wasn't frightened; he had dealt with the late Jan Heyderman in Johannesburg when he was in his eighties, and he hadn't met the man to equal him. That kind of megalomania came in economy packets; Karakov was still only the large size.

'All right,' he said again, 'we know you're unhappy. And we want to straighten our problems out. We don't want you going round telling the world you don't get a fair deal from D.E. It's bad for us, and in the end if it hurts us, it'll hurt you. You know what we've done for the industry—'

'Sure, sure,' Karakov interrupted. 'Jan Heyderman and Pat Harris created the biggest god-damned monopoly there's ever been, and it's still operating. I know all that.'

'What could have happened to the industry without the monopoly?' Wasserman countered. He was very serious on this subject. 'When all the big companies were fighting each other, the price of diamonds fell to a dollar forty per carat. That's what happened before Heyderman and Harris took over. It could happen again.'

'Balls,' Karakov said. 'Don't give me that kind of balls, David; I'm an old guy. I know the fairy stories. What do you want from me today, eh? This isn't a social call. You're busy, I'm busy – what is it?'

'I want you to go easy,' David Wasserman said. 'We don't want a fight with you. Even though we'll win,' he added. His dark eyes were like stones. 'Harris has sent one of his best men to see you. He's young, all right, but he's good, and Julius thinks a lot of him. His name is Hastings. He tried to call you the other day, but you couldn't give him an appointment.'

'Hastings,' Karakov said; for a moment his mind was blank. 'Ah, I know, some guy calls up my secretary and says he's from Diamond Enterprises, and can he come and see me. I remember now. Hastings, that's the name.'

'Why not see him?' Wasserman said. 'I told you, he's young, he's enthusiastic. Julius has given him some points to put forward to you; why the hell can't you be a big man and listen to him? He's all keyed up to meet you. Your name means something in the industry, you know. What have you got to lose?'

'Why don't you put forward the points?' Karakov asked. 'Why send this new guy out here?'

'They want him to cut his teeth,' Wasserman explained. 'I told you, he's young, he thinks he knows everything.' He chuckled and drew hard on the cigar. 'He'd learn from you, Ivan . . . See Hastings, just as a favour to me.'

'Why the hell should I do you any favour?' Karakov countered.

'Because we understand each other. Hastings is a nice guy; you'll like him. He's brought his wife over, she's got some kind of title.' He threw in the sop to snobbery as an aside. 'Think about it, Ivan. Just as a favour. What do you lose?'

'My time,' Karakov retorted. 'And that's worth money. If he's waiting around to see me, don't let him hold his breath. You going now?' David had stubbed out the cigar and stood up. He sighed. 'OK. I got to get back. I'm taking Clara out for lunch.'

Karakov came and embraced him. Business was

business, but they were still friends. 'We should get together for dinner soon. I'll have Laura call Clara and fix a date.'

'You do that,' Wasserman said. He went down in the lift and stood for a moment on the crowded pavement, looking for a taxi. As he drove back to his hotel, he stared out of the window, frowning. He had failed to soften up Ivan Karakov. He had flattered and even obliquely threatened, but nothing had shaken that steely confidence. It wasn't just Ivan's usual mega ego displaying itself. There was something more. Some thing Karakov had in reserve beyond the deal with Moscow which wasn't even signed, that made him so cocksure. He wasn't going to meet James Hastings. He didn't give a damn that he was Heyderman's personal envoy. David Wasserman felt a sharp twinge of indigestion, a sure barometer of his anxiety.

He hurried up to his suite to talk it through with Clara.

Dick Kruger kissed her.

'Ruth,' he said, 'It's been great being together. I wish you'd let me come next weekend. I'm lonely as hell without you.'

'I'm lonely too,' she told him. 'But I've got to take a trip to Antwerp and we won't get back till Saturday evening. We wouldn't have any time. I'm sorry, darling, but I can't get out of it. Hastings wants to go and he wants me with him.'

They were at the airport and his flight to London had been called. She urged him gently towards the departure lounge. It had been a great weekend, just as he'd said. They'd made love, gone out to restaurants, come home and made love again, and driven out for a long Sunday-morning walk through the Bois de Boulogne, Dick holding hands with her like a boy in love for the first time. It was touching and she went out of her way to be fond and reassuring in the only mode she knew. She suggested they went back and spent the afternoon in bed. He'd asked her to marry him again; he even had the special licence with him and he showed it to her. That was touching, too, except that Ruth thought she had managed to put him off before she went to Paris, she didn't want to marry him. He would possess her; he was demanding enough when she was still independent. The more she considered it, the more convinced Ruth had become that marriage wouldn't work. Since she'd been separated from him and out of their office routine, she'd been less clear about their future as a couple. She found the European end of the business even more fascinating than the familiar guidelines of Blackfriars Road. Hastings was going to Antwerp to see a consortium of top diamond dealers, but they would fly back on Friday afternoon. Ruth didn't want Kruger coming for the weekend. She wanted time to herself, and there was now another reason for widening the gap between them.

He wasn't a man to keep business secrets from her. They'd been in tandem for too long. He trusted her and shared everything with her, valuing her judgement.

He had told her about the vital information Arthur was holding back about Karakov's sale of the suite of red diamonds. Having dinner together at the Tour d'Argent, made expansive by wonderful food and very good claret, Dick had leaned towards her and elaborated.

'Andrews is making bloody good headway in Moscow, so why give that shit an advantage when we don't have to? Why hand him anything on a plate?'

Ruth's cat's eyes had gleamed at him; he knew that look of concentration, feline in its stalking intensity.

'He's selling them on commission for the Russians,' Kruger went on. 'We've found that out too.'

'How?' she asked him.

He pulled a face. 'Don't ask me. Reece has some contact inside the Karakov set-up. He's over in London.

He told Arthur, he wanted to know what Hastings was doing about it.'

'And what did Arthur say?' Her voice was very smooth.

'What do you think?' He grinned. 'He said Hastings hadn't made any use of the information so far, but in view of how far Andrews is into negotiations in Moscow, it mightn't matter in the end. Reece'll pass that back to Heyderman. It won't do "wonder boy" any good.'

He signalled the waiter to pour more wine. Ruth refused.

'You have some. I'm not good on too much alcohol. If Karakov manages to sell these diamonds, that should clinch his claim to be a big enough outlet, shouldn't it? Wouldn't that bring the Russians to the table?'

'Clever girl, you always get to the crux, don't you?' He was proud of her acumen. 'Of course it would. They're worth millions from what we hear. Karakov's given them some phoney provenance, but they've been mined in the last two years and he had to re-cut them properly. The Russians didn't have the skills. They made a poor job of it and a lot of the caratage has been wasted, but Jesus, they're still enormous. And unique.'

She said again, 'How do you know all this? Who's Reece's contact? He must be right on the inside and high up.'

'And very well paid,' he countered. 'Reece says he's never been wrong yet. If Andrews does a deal with the Russians and Karakov still hasn't found a buyer, we'll take the jewellery over. We can afford to *buy* them, for Christ's sake, if it's going to clinch the agreement.'

'Yes,' she agreed. 'I can see how that works. But isn't it a risk? Holding out on Hastings . . . supposing Heyderman finds out?'

'Who's going to tell him? Not Arthur, not me. And if something goes wrong for Andrews, then we'll have to pass it on, we won't have any option. But we're gambling that it won't. I've seen the draft agreement with Moscow and, believe me, it's such a good deal they'd be crazy not to take it. Millions in interest-free loans, money for development, even a commitment to fund the de-pollution of the lake at Baikal! You any idea how big that is? Fifty square miles, one of the biggest inland water masses in the world. They'll sign up with us, don't worry.'

Ruth said slowly, 'And does Arthur really mean to give them all that? Will Heyderman agree to it?'

He drained his glass of wine. He looked at her. He said, 'Our company lawyers are drafting it. They know about agreements between us and foreign governments. Arthur's not worried. Now, let's have some of those desserts I see over there. God, isn't the food good?' He had a very sweet tooth; Ruth was always telling him to watch his weight. They hadn't talked about it again and now they were saying goodbye at Charles de Gaulle Airport. He paused for a last embrace. 'I do love you so, Ruthie,' he said. 'I'll call you later.'

He looked so forlorn that she said quickly, 'No, darling, I'll call you.'

As soon as he had gone through into the departure lounge, she ran down to her car and hurried to the office.

Elizabeth had been waiting for him to come home. She had a bottle of champagne in the refrigerator and she had called and cancelled dinner with the Wassermans that evening. Even speaking to Clara didn't bother her; she told the lie and rather enjoyed hearing the old woman's spiteful response.

'You're sick? Oh, that's too bad. Maybe your husband will come anyway. I guess it's nothing serious . . .' She had sounded contemptuous, as if she had never cancelled an engagement because of some minor upset stomach. Elizabeth had put the phone down and laughed. She had something in her stomach, if the old bitch only knew it, and it wasn't over-rich food.

She stayed by the window, waiting for his arrival. He used the office car and driver, and when it finally drew up outside, she was in the hallway with the door open.

James came hurrying in, looking anxious. 'Darling . . . What's the matter? David was in my office when his wife called. She said you were sick – what is it?'

Elizabeth came and put her arms round his neck and smiled into his face. 'I am sick,' she said. 'Especially in the mornings. And I'm going to be, for the next seven months.'

He was so happy there were tears in his eyes. He couldn't take it in. He wanted to hear the details over and over again, holding her close, even placing a proprietary hand on her flat belly as if to convince himself that it was true.

'Oh Liz, my darling . . . This is so wonderful.' She had to keep telling him there wasn't any doubt. The doctor had confirmed it, taken a second test for routine confirmation, but only because she had insisted.

'And you never said a word,' he reproached her. 'Why didn't you tell me?'

'Because,' she said, 'I didn't want you to be disappointed. It has happened so often before, me thinking I felt different and then the bloody monthly coming right on time. Or a few days late. Darling Jamie, I'm just as thrilled for you as I am for myself. And the good news is, I'm healthy and fine; he checked everything. They're amazingly thorough these French doctors, not like at home, where nobody makes a great thing about having a baby. Blood tests, blood pressure, the lot. He did say I shouldn't do too much for the next few weeks as it's a first pregnancy. But that was all. So I rang that old bat and put off dinner tonight. I thought we'd celebrate on our own. The drink's in the fridge. So why don't we start? I'll get the bottle.'

'Oh no you won't.' He sprang up. 'You stay there. You're not bending down and lugging bottles . . .' She laughed at him. He laughed back. It was pure happiness between them. 'Aren't I the lucky man?' he said softly to her. 'You just stay put till I come back. I'm going to bully you so you might as well get used to it.'

They finished the champagne over dinner, and settled for the evening into the big comfortable sofa Elizabeth had bought. He held her in the crook of his arm and she nestled close to him.

'I had the laugh on David Wasserman,' he said. 'I wish you'd seen his face when I told him we were meeting Ivan Karakov. He'd spent half an hour telling me how hard he'd tried to persuade the bugger to give me an interview, and how impossible he'd been. So I just said, I wish I'd known because you'd already arranged it. Through a mutual friend. He was really rather pissed off.'

'Not as pissed off as Clara,' she giggled. 'I get up her nose . . . you ought to have heard her when I telephoned. Taking it for granted that you'd come and leave me all alone on my bed of pain.' She smiled up at him. 'I'd forgotten about Jean Pierre's dinner party. He was so kind today, I asked him to be godfather.'

'Jumping the gun, aren't you, darling? We'll be home when it's born. I wonder what it is?'

'I'm not going to find out,' she said firmly. 'They can scan all they want, but they're not going to tell me. You don't want to know, do you? It would spoil it.'

'Whatever you say,' he agreed. 'And now, Lady Liz, I think it's time you went to bed. Come on.'

'Life,' Elizabeth said happily, 'is going to be a nightmare, I can see.'

8

'How much longer do you think we'll have to stay here?'

Reece looked at her anxiously. She was frowning and she hadn't spoken much since he came back. The light shone on her brown hair from behind; he wished she wouldn't go to the hairdresser. He hated it cut short and crimped into curls. He liked it as it used to be when they were young, long and dark, hanging in waves past her shoulders.

'I don't know; not too long.'

'I hate London,' she said. 'I want to go home.'

Home was their flat in Johannesburg. When their parents died they had sold the house on the Cape where they were born and moved to the great gold capital, where Reece got his first job and she began taking a secretarial course. They had a little money, but not enough to manage without both working, though he hadn't liked the idea at first. She was so precious to him and not strong; she had never been strong. He was afraid something might happen to her. He could remember one night when she had a fever – he was about twelve and she was ten – and he had sat outside her door all night, crying because he thought she was going to die. Nothing had happened between them then. Nothing would ever have happened if she hadn't started it. Their father kept a general store in a small town on the Cape. He had come out from England as a young man, and married an Afrikaans girl.

They had been a dour couple, wrapped up in their business and the minutiae of their daily life; the brother and sister grew up within certain set limits. If they did wrong they got a hiding; if they were good they didn't get one. The first time his father took the stick to his sister nearly drove Reece mad. He was a sallow, puny boy, and when he flew at his father, kicking and punching out, the old man sent him flat on his face with one push. Reece had realized then how much he hated his father, how much he hated everyone except Joy. They were alone in the world, the small world of the shop, with its stuffy smell of soap and paraffin and stale food, and the hard, dry, sun-scoured world outside, where the dust rose from the streets and nothing ever happened.

'The moment I can, I'll take you back,' he said. 'I promise.'

'You're always promising. Last time you said it wouldn't be more than six months. It was a whole year. Now we're back, and you still don't know how much longer we'll have to be here. I miss the sun. I'm always getting colds. You went on ahead and I had to come over by myself. I was frightened sick in the plane. You know how I hate flying. I thought you might have waited for me.'

Reece put down the book he was reading. He knew the signs. She was discontented and spoiling for a row; he dreaded those rows; they made him sick inside. They upset her, too, in spite of the fact that she provoked them. She looked pinched and red-eyed for days after they'd had a quarrel, and he couldn't help making it up. He'd had a hard day and he wasn't going to fight that night. He wanted to sit quietly at home with her and read, or listen to music.

He said patiently, trying to explain, to placate her, 'I couldn't help it. Mr Julius wanted me to go immediately. I've been trying to see that daughter, and she won't even answer and let me in. He's so worried about her. Be reasonable, Joy. She's like a gun at his head. I feel so sorry for him.'

'Well, I don't,' she said angrily. 'She's filthy, marrying a dirty Kaffir! Why should he care what happens to her? He should let her die in the gutter. That's where she belongs.'

Reece didn't answer. He knew his sister in this mood. She looked up at him, her eyes bright with malice.

'Don't forget what he owes you,' she said. 'One day someone should tell him . . .'

'Don't talk like that, Joy.' For a moment his voice was quite sharp and his face was the face the outside world knew; he seldom spoke or looked like that at his sister, but when he did she lost her ascendancy over him. She had once or twice suggested he should blackmail Julius Heyderman, and she still couldn't realize that he would never do it. 'Anything I've done for Mr Julius he's more than paid back. I've told you not to mention that business! It's all over. He knew nothing about it.'

'He didn't have to,' she said, 'it's a great thing to be a Heyderman. You can do what you like and someone like you bails him out. And that daughter.'

'She doesn't matter,' Reece said. They had forgotten about their disagreement because the Heydermans and the Harrises were their favourite topic. They roused a mixture of jealousy and interest in his sister, who plied him with questions about them all. She took a malicious delight in the rivalry between the two men, but she couldn't quite make up her mind who she wanted to win. Julius would, of course; her brother would see to that. She'd read a book once about the Chinese tongs and thought how well the description of the hatchet men fitted her brother. Everyone was uneasy with him, except her. She could twist him round her finger. And nobody knew; nobody had any idea. 'The only thing that matters is to keep Mr Julius away from scandal. And anxiety. A man with his responsibilities can't be worried about family matters all the time. He'd never be able to run the business.'

He spoke about his employer as if the dictator tycoon were a kind of benevolent English head of department being protected by a devoted spinster secretary. He had brought that attitude with him to Diamond Enterprises when he was still a minor employee; his readiness to tackle difficult problems caught his senior's eye. Somehow the word had got round: if there's some dirty work you want done, someone threatening a lawsuit against the company, someone who is making a noise about the price they got for their diamonds, put Reece on to it; he'll sort them out. And he did. He was said to know people in the Joburg underworld, one of the toughest crime capitals in the world. Once or twice he had been seen going down streets at night where no respectable person was safe. And everything that was said about him was true.

It began when he was sixteen and his sister came into his bed, whispering and pleading and guiding his hands to her. He hadn't known until then what he wanted, or that he had been wanting it from his first signs of puberty, but it happened between them, and they had shared their secret and their guilt. There was no cause for jealousy between them, because she never encouraged men and he wasn't aware of other women. They drew closer and closer; by the time their parents died they had been lovers for nearly ten years, and they felt and spoke and behaved alone as if they were married. But it was a lie, and it took its toll; it had made an outcast of Reece before he ever went out into the world, and he behaved like an outcast. He hated and despised people because he knew how they would hound him and his sister down in horror. He had no pity and no scruples because he felt instinctively that he had forfeited the right to both himself. The world and all the smug, respectable people in it would think that what he and Joy felt for each other was dirty. So he looked on the world with the same eye. When he became personal assistant to Julius Heyderman, for the first time in his life he worked for a man he could admire, a giant among pygmies.

Heyderman bound Reece to him with confidences, and he gave the insignificant, dull-seeming man a sense of importance and self-respect because a man like Julius Heyderman held him in regard. Reece hero-worshipped him, and would do anything for Julius Heyderman because he had given him the means to protect Joy.

They had a fine collection of classical records, and a superb hi-fi player. They had been to several concerts at the Festival Hall, and sat holding hands in the deepest enjoyment. They hadn't made friends in London any more than in Johannesburg. They had agreed to that long ago. They had their world and it didn't admit attachments.

She wasn't as dark as he was, nor as thin. She had a round, petulant face and hazel eyes. She was thirty-eight, but she looked much younger, as if her maturity had stopped in the very early twenties. She was the type of woman who would look young for years, and then crumple like a paper bag.

Reece couldn't understand why she was so irritable and snappish at times. He did everything for her, spoiled her and paid her more attention sexually than most men were said to do with their wives.

But she wasn't always like that; she made it up to him after she'd been quarrelsome. Really, they were very happy, perfectly suited.

'Joy, I tell you what we'll do. I'll get seats for that new production at the Old Vic tomorrow, and we'll have a night out. We'll go to the theatre, and have a nice supper afterward. How would you like that?'

'That'd be lovely,' she smiled. 'I'd like to do that.'

They settled down in contentment with their books for the rest of the evening.

*　　*　　*

186

'Mummy?'

'Yes, darling.'

'When's Daddy coming back?'

Susan Andrews put down her darning. Their daughter was doing some homework at the desk by the window in their sitting-room. Susan was glad of her company. Ray had been away for over a month, and she was very lonely.

'I don't know, darling. He said in his last letter he hoped to be back soon, but I don't think he will be, or we'd have heard.'

'He's a long time,' the child said. 'What's he doing out there, Mum?'

'Trying to make a business agreement, darling. But it's slow going.'

Susan had tried to take it all in from his calls and letters, but it was difficult; it was especially difficult to visualize Ray building a relationship with an ex-Communist Russian. To her, all Russians were Communists and not to be trusted. She tried to write back intelligently, but her letters always ran away with her and she ended by sending him pages about Frances's skating lessons or Peter's last letter from Canada. The refrigerator had gone wrong, and there was a sudden warm spell; everything was off when they went to make breakfast in the morning and the repair people hadn't come for two days. Their friends the Simpsons had been round and they'd had a very pleasant evening; it had cheered her up. She'd had an invitation from Mrs Arthur Harris for a company dinner at the Dorchester for one of the South African gold mines directors. She was terrified having to go without Ray, but she supposed she'd have to; she thought it advisable to get a new dress, but couldn't make up her mind whether to buy something locally or go to town for it. She missed him dreadfully, and when did he think he'd be getting back? Would he cable her the very minute he knew?

That dinner invitation was hanging over her like the sword of Damocles. When she first opened it, she decided not to go; to accept and then be ill. Then she worried in case somebody knew she was only making an excuse, and of course it would reflect on Ray. All these things had a bearing on a man's career, and it was getting worse. Big industries felt they had a stake in their executives' private lives; the wrong wife can ruin the most promising man. She had heard that said several times, and wondered miserably whether it applied to her. They were so happy, she and Ray and the children. Ray was brilliant, at the top of his profession. Why couldn't they be content with that and leave her out of it? She had nothing to contribute, and she admitted that humbly. She wasn't a great wit or good at making conversation, and she wasn't a beauty and a socialite like James Hastings' wife, or sophisticated like Valerie Kruger. Why couldn't Mrs Arthur Harris let her stay quietly at home waiting for her husband and not put her through this ordeal? It was a compliment, of course, to be asked. She said that loyally to herself. It showed that Ray was much closer to Arthur than anyone else for him to ask her when her husband was away. She had written her note of acceptance and stuck the engraved card on the mantelpiece in the mirror frame. It watched her like a threat, and there were only five days left. She had been hoping and praying that Ray would be back in time; then it wouldn't be so bad. He knew she was nervous and he always stayed close and looked after her. It wasn't so bad when Valerie Kruger was there because she used to come to Susan's rescue and keep her out of Christa Harris's way. Mrs Harris was a woman that Susan found it impossible to like, loyal as she was to Arthur personally. There was something about the way the other woman shook hands and said hello that made Susan instinctively look down to see if she'd spilled something on her dress before she left home. One went to these awful formal parties and had one drink before dinner and talked about nothing to people who kept looking round while you were speaking in search of someone more amusing or important. And you ate the dinners, often listening politely to the conversation going on between your neighbour on the right and his neighbour, and sipped at the wine, and longed to go home. The coffee stage was the worst, because Arthur was very expansive after brandy, and he kept his guests sitting on, talking about the business, until his wife gave the peremptory signal and got everybody up. Susan had seen her do that once when her husband was in the middle of a sentence. She had felt terribly embarrassed for him and thought it the most ill-bred thing she had seen in her life. There wasn't much choice in her wardrobe. She had worn everything before, and she knew she wouldn't look right in any of them. Short or long. The wretched card didn't say. Just black tie. If only Ray were here he could have made enquiries, or asked Kruger's mistress Ruth Fraser what she was wearing. The recognition given to that relationship had shocked Susan. None of the other wives liked Ruth; what wife would, with that background – confidential secretary, mistress? She stood her ground at all the parties, Dick's big diamond blazing on her engagement finger. She had always been friendly to Susan, and Susan was too self-effacing to realize that it was because she had been nice to Ruth when they met. There was a long red silk jersey dress that Ray liked very much, but it was three years old and she decided definitely against it. She had a black silk cocktail dress which was quite nice, but she'd worn that last time she was invited to a theatre party, and her best, the short green faille, which Ray had paid for as a present, was too summery for autumn.

'I'll have to get something new.' She said it aloud. 'But it does seem a shame, just for one evening.'

'What are you going to buy, Mum?'

'A new dress, darling. I'm going out to a dinner, for

Daddy's office. Get on with your homework. Supper's in half an hour.'

'Lucky thing,' the child sighed. 'I wish I was going to a party.'

Susan put away the darning in her workbox, and went out to the kitchen to prepare the supper.

The kitchen was the joy of Susan's life. She and Ray had planned it together; it was state of the art labour saving, brightly decorated, a joy to work in. Ray had insisted on spending more money on the kitchen than anywhere else in the house.

'You spend so much time in it, looking after us all, it's going to be just what you want. No expense spared . . .' Susan loved him for appreciating what so many people think mundane and belittling. Her job, as he emphasized, was as important to the general welfare as his own. She chided herself for complaining about the wretched party, when Ray was struggling with his business problems in Moscow.

She decided to go shopping the next morning. She'd need shoes and a bag to go with the new dress. Spending money on herself still worried her, a legacy of the early days when both were working to pay off the mortgage on their small flat, and money was in very short supply. Together they had made the upward climb. Now they had a nice house, two cars, expensive holidays and supported their children in education. She owed it to Ray to put on a brave face and go to the party looking nice. But if only, she sighed, thinking of that dreadful entrance on her own, if only by some miracle, Ray got home in time . . .

Dimitri Borisov shook hands with Ray Andrews as usual, but there was a sharp look in his eye that Ray hadn't seen in their meetings for some time. He had left the final draft of an agreement with the Russian almost ten days ago and heard nothing until the peremptory summons to come round to his office that afternoon.

'Sit down,' Borisov said. 'I've sent for some tea. Now . . . I've had this agreement looked at in detail by our contract department and there is one area I am not satisfied with . . . a very important paragraph dealing with your company's commitment to the Baikal project. That seems to us ambivalent. I've marked the relevant paragraphs. Here.'

He handed the document to Andrews. Andrews read it, looking for flaws. He knew it had been carefully drafted in London, and, on first reading, couldn't see anything that might cause Borisov a problem.

'It looks all right to me,' he said. 'And remember, it's only a final draft; if it's a question of re-wording the de-pollution project more strongly, then that's easily dealt with.'

Borisov shook his head. 'No,' he said slowly. 'Re-wording isn't enough. You're not a lawyer and neither am I. Ray, we've come very far in our negotiations. I'm optimistic that we'll have something to sign soon enough. I have been to see the President with this document. He and our contract experts are agreed on one point. It is not strong enough on our problem with Baikal. Everything else, the loans, the concession to sell our diamonds, in principle the output from Archangel, everything is acceptable. But not this.' He tapped his finger on the marked page in front of him.

'Right,' Andrews nodded. 'I take the point, Dimitri. Let me get this clear. Baikal is the linchpin, and our commitment to it has to be straight down to the bottom line?'

'That's the President's instructions to me,' Borisov answered. 'Without that he won't ratify any agreement with Diamond Enterprises. The document with Karakov is ready for signature. That is not a bluff, it's the truth. And the President doesn't want any delay. You have no time to manoeuvre.'

'No,' Ray Andrews agreed. 'I accept that. Look,' he had made a judgement and decided to act on his own initiative, 'I haven't the personal authority to guarantee this. If I send it back to London, the bloody lawyers will drag it out for weeks. It's taken long enough to get this through on both sides. If my Chairman gives you a personal authorization and guarantee of our commitment, will that do for you? Will that satisfy the President's requirement and give us time to get the actual documentation prepared for signature? In other words, lift the deadline and give us a guarantee that you won't sign with Karakov?'

D. V. Borisov looked down at the draft and then up at Ray Andrews. 'I will recommend it,' he said. 'When will this personal letter from your Chairman be sent? I'll need to take it to the President, and he'll want to know when to expect it.'

Ray stood up. 'The quickest way is for me to go back to London and get it for you. One to one, I can explain the situation to him better than faxing or telephoning. He trusts my judgement, and he'll do what I suggest.'

Borisov stood up and came round the desk. He placed a hand on Andrews' shoulder. 'Do this,' he said, 'and we will sign within three weeks. That is my guarantee to you. By Russian standards, that is very fast – when will you leave for London?'

Ray said, 'I'll leave Saturday night. I should be back by the middle of next week.'

'Good,' Borisov said. 'I will take you to the Bolshoi to celebrate. If you bring me the letter.'

'I'll bring it,' Ray Andrews promised. 'I promise you.'

Arthur Harris had left his wife in the hallway. The party at the Dorchester had finished early because several of their employees had trains to catch, or a wife driving home so her husband could have a few drinks. It had been a good evening, as far as he could judge. The food and service were excellent, the atmosphere convivial, induced by pre-dinner drinks and plenty of wine afterwards.

The South African guest of honour had been effusive in thanks and seemed to have enjoyed himself sitting next to Christa. Arthur had watched her being charmed, and marvelled at her capacity to act a part when she wanted to: the perfect boss's wife. But for how long? They hadn't talked much on the way home.

'It went well, I think,' she had volunteered.

He had waited for some scathing comment to follow, but she had said nothing more till they were inside the hallway.

'I'm going to bed, are you coming?'

'Later,' Arthur answered. 'I have some work to do.'

He wondered why she'd asked him. They hadn't shared a room for years. He went into his study, poured himself a mild whisky and soda and sat down to think. Andrews had flown in the day before, bringing the Russian conditions with him. The same terms of agreement that Arthur already knew, and which his lawyers had drafted so carefully. The huge loans, interest free, the development and financing of the mines in the Archangel area and the project to de-pollute the biggest water mass in Eastern Europe: Baikal. With his personal written guarantee that Diamond Enterprises would provide the technical means and the full funding.

It was impossible. He couldn't do it. He couldn't promise something that Julius Heyderman would reject out of hand as an open-ended commitment that could drain their resources for years to come with no return in sight. Arthur couldn't put his name to that guarantee, and without it, the Russians would go ahead and sign with Karakov. Ray Andrews would have failed, and Arthur's head would be on the chopping block. He sipped his whisky slowly. He was going to lose, and he had accepted that at some point during the evening, when he looked across and saw Ray with his wife Susan. He had registered rather numbly that she looked quite well dressed for once. They were a nice couple; good family people. Ray was loyal and gifted, and he would be ruined, too. A sense of sadness had come over Arthur. He had lived for his business for so long, because it was his only source of happiness, besides his sailing and his yachts. What else did he have? A miserable marriage, poisoned by the sense of failure which Christa embodied sitting there, looking attractive and desirable; a son who despised him because his mother set him the example; Julius, longing to get rid of him, and now being given the opportunity. He had lost everything.

He heard the door open and he looked up. His wife stood there.

'Aren't you coming up? It's after one . . .'

She wore a lace-trimmed négligé and her face was still made up. He stared at her.

'I won't be long. I'm just going through some papers.'

She advanced towards him. She sat down facing him. 'What kind of papers?'

Arthur braced himself for the inevitable attack. Whenever she mentioned the business she did so in a way that undermined him. It was his most sensitive spot. She took a cigarette out of his silver box.

'You're not smoking,' he protested. 'You never smoke. You hate it!'

She lit it, and said, 'I smoke sometimes. I feel like one now. What are you working on?'

I smoke sometimes. He had been banished to his study if he wanted a cigar . . .

'Nothing much,' he said. 'Just routine stuff.'

'You don't bring back routine stuff and sit over it till one in the morning,' his wife said. 'Why don't you tell me?'

'Because I'm tired, and it's complicated. You wouldn't be interested.'

She blew out a cloud of cigarette smoke; it rose and drifted over the circle of light from the desk lamp. He waved it away, and put his papers back in the drawer.

'You're in trouble, aren't you? Why can't you be honest with me? I'm your wife.'

Arthur shut the drawer and locked it.

'I find that difficult to believe at times. Why this sudden interest in my welfare? It's not like you.'

'You're very quarrelsome,' she said coolly. 'You must be upset about something. I'm not just thinking of your welfare, my dear Arthur. I'm thinking of our son as well. I've known things weren't going well ever since Julius came over. It's perfectly obvious the London office is on the mat with my brother. Now tell me what it's all about. I've got a right to know.'

He had begun by confiding in her when they were first married; they hadn't been so unhappy then because they didn't know the ill adjustment between them was going to be permanent, and she seemed to be in love with him and anxious to make the marriage a success. It had been a great relief to talk to her, and to feel that she was his ally and sympathetic. But the atmosphere between them had begun to change; she showed her sexual disappointment in flashes of spite which wounded him deeply, more so because he was fully aware of the cause. And then their son was born and she turned away from him completely, and all those early confidences became weapons with which she taunted him. He had not discussed anything with her for years, and at this crisis in his life, he couldn't bring himself to risk it.

'We're having some trouble,' he admitted, 'but it'll pass off. It's only to do with this new Russian mine, and Andrews will sort it out.'

'You've a lot of confidence in him, haven't you?' she said. She leaned forward and the gold lights in her hair glowed under the lamp. 'Arthur, let's stop fighting just for a moment. We've been fighting each other for years, but this isn't the time to do it. Julius is really after your head, isn't he?'

'He's been after it for thirty years,' he said. 'You've always known that and it never stopped you taking his side against me.'

The sad eyes were bitter as they looked at her. He had loved her so much and wanted her, and there had been so many moments over the years when he felt that love again and fought it down because the pain of her refusal would be so great.

'He's my brother,' she said. 'And I love him. But that doesn't mean to say I'd like him to kick you off the Board. We've got Martin to think of; he ought to take over from you in due course.'

Their son was another nail in the marital coffin, indeed the final one that closed the lid. They had been in league together, mother and son, since he was a tiny child; she gave him everything he wanted, partly in protest against Arthur's realistic attitude to showering money on the young before they'd learned how hard it was to earn it – she called him mean, and bought the boy a Porsche for his twenty-first birthday, and if ever Arthur criticized his son, she took sides with Martin.

'If Martin's going to succeed me, he'll have to do better than he's done so far,' Arthur said. 'When I was at Magdalen I left with a first in PPE. He'll be lucky at this rate if he gets a third. He won't work.'

'He will,' she said. 'You're always trying to force him. He won't let you; he's too like me.'

He looked at her and he smiled suddenly. 'If he had a tenth of your determination, my dear Christa, he'd amount to something. I know it annoys you, but I'm afraid he's a bit of a weakling like his father.'

She didn't answer him at once. She still wasn't sure why she had come down to his study. She didn't understand her own motive in seeking him out to try and establish some communication after all these years. It was instinctive. He was in trouble, and it was too serious for her to sit back and enjoy it, as she had done before. Her son's future might be threatened. She knew Julius disliked him. Fear for Martin brought her closer to the stranger she had been married to for nearly thirty years. He and he alone could turn the threat aside.

'What are you going to do?' she said. 'How are you going to fight Julius?'

'It will depend on Moscow,' Arthur said. 'And on Andrews. If his head rolls, then your brother will be in a position to take a cut at mine.'

'You mustn't let him,' she said. 'You mustn't let him win. It doesn't matter what you do, you've got to beat him.'

He smiled again. 'I'll try, my dear. I haven't run this business for all these years to let Julius lever me out on a pretext and put his own lackey in. That's what he's been after for years, of course. But he couldn't do it, because there just wasn't anyone of my stature to take over. No, I'm not being conceited, it's the truth. You may think I'm a fool, Christa, but I've run the London operation for all these years. And made a success of it.'

She went straight to the point in the disconcerting way that women have when important issues are at stake.

'Who's the lackey?'

'James Hastings. He's been given the easy option in Paris. Andrews was sent out to do the impossible.'

'My God,' she said. 'Hastings – I never liked him. So that's why he's in Paris – why on earth didn't you tell me all this before?'

'There was no point in worrying you. Really, my dear, it all boils down to this. We made a mistake, just pure bad luck, that's all, and we missed the mine in Moscow. That's what Julius is holding against me. Another complication has arisen which makes this Russian mine extremely dangerous to us. Put simply – if Andrews fails, it's going to be very awkward for me. If he fails and

Hastings' operation succeeds, I shall be finished. Now, have I explained it?'

'Yes,' she said. 'Yes, you have.'

He looked very grey and tired; his gentleness had been the first thing that attracted her. She had been madly in love with him. But he had been too gentle, that was the trouble. He had tried so hard to please her and failed so often that she had ended up by hating him. Suddenly she felt afraid. Things were going wrong with him. It had never occurred to her that the *status quo* might change. She got up and shook out the skirts of the négligé; it was white and transparent like the nightdress underneath it.

'Arthur,' she said. 'We should be together in this. Come to bed now.'

At the tone in her voice, he looked up and saw her standing there, her body showing through the white folds. She reached up and undid the satin ribbons holding the négligé at the neck and it opened, showing her skin and the rise of her breasts. He felt the colour coming into his neck and creeping up, but there was no heat anywhere else in his body, no stirring at all. Suddenly, unbelievably, he felt nothing for her, neither desire nor hurt. At last, after all these years, he was free of her.

He gave his gentle, sad smile and shook his head.

'Not just for the moment, Christa. You go back to bed. I'll come up later.'

She looked at him without answering, and slowly she fastened the négligé ribbons into a tight bow.

Her eyes filled up with tears. 'You'll never get the chance to say no to me again.'

Arthur said gently, 'I'm sorry, but it was never much of a success with us, anyway. I think it's best if we leave things as they are. Good night, my dear.'

He didn't watch her go out. The door didn't bang, which surprised him. She had been crying. He didn't feel anything, not even a sense of satisfaction that for once the roles had been reversed. He was free of her for ever.

It was a strange sensation, as if a weight had been lifted that he didn't realize he carried.

The Russians wanted him to promise the impossible. To write a personal guarantee committing Diamond Enterprises to untold millions of expenditure. He got up, refilled the glass with another modest whisky and sipped it. If he did it he was finished. If he refused, the result was the same. So what had he got to lose? A signature could be repudiated, given the right circumstances . . . He smiled to himself. Always the grey man, the careful, calculating negotiator. Arthur Harris, the high-risk taker? He had defeated his wife after nearly thirty years, and it had been so easy. And so liberating. He would defeat her brother Julius Heyderman; he knew that now with a confidence that was euphoric. He would do whatever had to be done to achieve that.

The telephone was ringing. Stella Heyderman Yakumi sat within easy reach of it and listened. She knew who her caller was; she'd already hung up on him once that day and twice the day before. It was Reece, her father's personal, private creep. Come to sort out her problems. She didn't need him. The London solicitors were paid to do that. She didn't mind calling on them when things got out of control. They were a step removed from her family and her home. Her old life in South Africa. She was cut off from it all, and that was how she managed to survive. The flat was small and untidy, situated in an area of London with a large black population. She and Jacob had chosen it deliberately so that he could live and work among his own people while their exile lasted. They had been very active in local affairs, involved in social projects aimed at bettering the lives of the black community. Self help, Jacob called it, ironically echoing the philosophy of his hated enemy, Margaret Thatcher. The black people might be West Indian through the forced migration of slavery, but they were still Africans like himself; they needed self-respect and self-reliance to give them identity. Jacob believed his mission was to teach them these qualities and how to achieve them.

Then, and only then, did he try to educate them in his own political beliefs.

As the telephone rang, Stella looked at his photograph, a big enlargement specially done after his death. It smiled at her from a table where she could see it from any angle in the room. It was her talisman, as much as any animist sacred tree or rocky outcrop. He had been dead for two years now. She often talked to him aloud. It depended on how much she had had to drink. She was sober that afternoon. The couple she had been persuaded to give temporary accommodation to in the flat below had finally been bought off and gone, leaving a vindictive mess behind them. The solicitors had dealt with that, and they had contacted a cleaning firm to steam clean the basement. Her tenants had smeared their own excrement on the walls as a parting gesture to their benefactress. They were drug addicts, but then that was why Stella had taken them in. She was trying to do what she felt Jacob would have wanted. But the trouble was she wasn't Jacob; she was known to be a rich white woman with a drinking problem that made her a soft touch.

Their friends had rallied to her after Jacob's murder. Friends in the black and white communities who had worked with them and respected them. They had respected Stella, too. Only a very brave woman would have married a black South African and gone with him into exile. They might have reacted differently had they known she was Julius Heyderman's daughter. All that money and influence. No wonder they managed to get out, when others in the ANC went to Robben Island, and their families were put on restriction, renewed year after year. No-one knew who Stella was; that was the deal Reece had negotiated, and she had honoured it because it was their guarantee that one day they would be able

200

to go home and Jacob would be safe. She trusted her father. He had never broken a promise to her. His name must be protected at all costs. No political capital must ever be made by Jacob or his political associates that his wife was born a Heyderman. So far as friends and family in South Africa knew, Stella had gone to South America and was working in a mission school in Peru. Her reputation supported this story, nobody questioned that she would be crazy enough to do such a thing. Jacob's family knew that he had escaped to London and married a white woman. His ANC contacts in England knew her as Suki, which happened to be her childhood nickname.

They had lived on her trust money, and what he earned by giving legal advice and writing articles for ethnic news sheets and magazines. He also gave private tuition to black youths studying for a career in law. They had been ideally happy in their new life.

At last the telephone stopped in mid ring. Stella looked at it. She hadn't eaten since the night before, just washed herself out with cups of strong black coffee. The hours stretched ahead, empty of purpose. She was lonely; the good friends had given her up after a decent interval of trying to help. Many of them despised her for escaping into alcohol abuse. Her husband had been such a fine, strong man. How could she be so weak, so insensitive to his memory? Idealists, as Stella recognized now, were often judgemental and unforgiving. She didn't care. She had never been loved, in her own cognizance, except by Jacob. Her father didn't love her, that's why as a child she had wished her mother's unborn baby dead. And from that sequence came insanity and misery. She knew all the reasons. A series of thoughtful, kindly therapists had explained it to her, and she had nodded, as if the revelation would loose the emotional knots inside. It didn't; she knew rationally that she shouldn't feel guilty or rejected, but the fact was that she did. Only the furies driving her to strike back by being different, by rejecting her father and her background, gave relief. Until she met Jacob.

She had loved the black people suffering under apartheid because they, too, had been rejected. She had hated herself and her own kind. That sense of anger made her bold and committed, ready to risk herself by political protest. But, inside, she knew it was a sham, a weapon used to wound herself and her father. And the stepmother who was trying to please him by winning her confidence. But Jacob Yakumi changed everything. She had suddenly discovered that love was stronger than hate, sweeter than anger. Love was warmth and security and a deep passion for a man who valued her and loved her for herself. A gentle, dedicated man, with unshakeable belief in the basic goodness of humanity.

Incredibly, there was no hate in Jacob Yakumi. He understood his enemies and he pitied them for their ignorance. Fear made them cruel. Stella had sat at his feet and worshipped. She had never expected him to love her. To use her, to accept her resources in the fight against oppression, but never to love her. When she accepted that love, she found a true sense of self-worth for the first time in her life. She must be of value for such a man to love her. He had refused her passionate plea to sleep with her, because he wouldn't put her at risk. And afterwards, when they were married, he had refused to have children. 'One day something may happen to me. You couldn't go home with a coloured child. There's plenty of time. We'll wait and see how the world changes.' The world had changed, faster, more dramatically than they had dared to hope. South Africa changed direction; led by a brave and visionary government, the conflict between the black and white races was in the process of being resolved. Excesses, murderous tribal rivalries, and blood-shed on both sides couldn't halt the move forward to political equality and majority rule. That was when Jacob decided to go home. His place was with his people. With the men and women of Soweto where he was born.

But he wouldn't allow Stella to come with him. It was far too dangerous; it meant breaking their agreement with her father, who would never consent to her return at such a time of racial tension and instability. It wouldn't be a long separation, Jacob had assured her. Stella had wept and pleaded but in the end he had won her over to his way, as he had always done. The murder squads were out, both black and neo-Nazi white.

Soweto was no place for a white woman, even if she was married to an ANC activist. And Soweto was where he must go.

Less than a month later he was dead.

Stella still woke, drenched in sweat, and crying out at the vision of him lying hacked to death outside his home. Her life, her future and her hope had been murdered with him. There was not enough pure idealism to sustain her; that was what their friends couldn't understand or forgive. It was the man, not his mission, that had held her together. Without Jacob, she had nothing to survive for, and she'd gone back to the drinking habits of her youth when it was the panacea for her pain. Her father had come over to see her. She didn't want to see him. He represented what had killed Jacob; it was irrational and unjust but she couldn't bear his sympathy because she didn't believe for a moment it was genuine. He wouldn't be sorry Jacob was dead. He'd be relieved. He'd want her to come home, to shed her past and Jacob's name and pretend to the world she'd been in South America. She refused to speak to him. She had opened the door to her stepmother Sylvia by mistake.

She thought of Sylvia then, in the silence of the room when the telephone stopped its insistent ringing. So elegant, so out of place in that environment, with her chauffeur-driven car parked outside. The expression of concern on her handsome face.

'Oh, my poor Stella.'

She had pushed in before the door could be slammed on her and tried to embrace her. Stella held her off. She actually pushed her. But she knew Sylvia had got the pungent whiff of stale alcohol. In self-defence, in semi-drunken fury, she had screamed abuse at her. She had accused, without reason or thought, her father of not protecting Jacob . . . shrieking that he had friends, political influence . . . he could have done something . . . And then the final cry that sent Sylvia turning on her, all patience lost. 'You're glad he's dead . . . You didn't want him home . . . you didn't want anyone to find out about us . . .' She liked to tell herself that the mask dropped then, that Sylvia Heyderman gave up pretending. It was much easier to ignore her stepmother's tears and to dwell on her reproach.

'How could you, Stella . . . ? How could you say such a wicked, filthy thing about your father? He saved Jacob from prison, he supported you both for years . . . How could you? But you're drunk. That's all you can do, that's all you're made of – that boy was worth ten of you!'

She had slammed the door after her. It was beyond Stella to rationalize why she would talk to Reece and reject her own father. Reece represented everything she hated in her father's world. The fixer for the big capitalist enterprise, the paid lackey. She fell into the out-dated Marxist terminology because she could hide behind it.

Hide from her own heartbreak and her self-destructive flight into alcohol abuse. She could despise Reece, while taking what was on offer. She couldn't have despised her father. She knew that as her genuine friends gave up, the parasites moved in, playing on her sympathy and her need for justification in her grief. She believed she was carrying on Jacob's noble work for the oppressed when she allowed herself to be exploited by people he would have dismissed with contempt. Then the lawyers had to be brought in, to pay off, threaten, sort out the problems she had brought on herself. Anything rather than the police or publicity. Reece had written to her asking for an interview. She'd torn the letter up. She put the phone down whenever she heard his voice. But she was going to see him, and she knew it. She was trying to be strong and resist as long as she could. She had gone through a lot of money, paying off debts for sponging friends, buying off a malicious couple who insisted she had promised them a loan. She couldn't deny it, because she couldn't remember, but they frightened her, so she wrote out the cheque. Her quarterly allowance was spent, and she needed money.

She would see Reece. But he would have to sweat for a few days longer.

'You know, I feel rather nervous,' Elizabeth admitted.

James stared at her for a moment. 'Nervous? Why?'

'Supposing the Karakovs don't like me? Clara Wasserman didn't . . . I know how important this dinner is for you, darling. I hope I make the right impression.'

He said fondly, 'Don't be silly; these people are not like the Wassermans – they're big time, they're international. You'll be my greatest asset, don't you see? They'll love you. All you have to do is be yourself.'

He came and squeezed her gently to him. It was rather touching; normally so confident and out-going, so certain of being liked wherever she went. He had suffered social nerves, never Elizabeth. But pregnancy did funny things, no question . . .

'We're going there with all flags flying. I want you to look especially beautiful, and put on all the family jewels. You'll charm them out of their skins!'

'I'll try,' she promised. 'Do I have to look like the Christmas fairy? You know I hate that sort of thing.'

'I know,' he said. 'But it's what impresses some people. Money, showing off . . . I know how you hate it, but just this once? Please?'

'Oh, all right.' Elizabeth kissed him quickly. 'I'd better get ready then.'

Upstairs he fastened her dress at the back. She was still very slim, but there was a new fullness in her breasts that he found very exciting . . . She stood before the looking-glass, fixing the massive Victorian pearl-and-diamond brooch at the neck of her dress.

'Oh hell, I can't get this thing done up . . .'

He came round and adjusted the brooch for her.

'There,' he said. 'That's fixed and the safety catch is on. Mustn't lose Great Aunt Agatha's brooch, must we?' He ran his fingers down her neck and stroked her shoulder. 'You know, this baby is making you more sexy than ever. What I'd really like to do is stay at home and make love to you.'

Elizabeth leaned against him. 'So would I,' she whispered. 'I won't always be like this. A lot of men get turned off when you get heavy . . .'

He closed both arms around her. 'Well, this one won't,' he said.

When he let her go, he said softly. 'You're wonderful, and don't worry about tonight. You'll have your walker looking out for you.'

'Walker?' she picked up her bag. 'You mean Jean Pierre?'

'Well,' James said lightly. 'That's what he is, isn't he?'

Suddenly she was angry. 'No, he bloody well isn't,' she said. 'He's a good friend and I like him. And he's doing *you* a very big favour by giving this party. So don't be a shit, James.'

James retreated hastily. 'Only joking, don't be so touchy! He's a nice guy and you're right, I owe him. Now stop giving me that laser look or I'll deconstruct before your very eyes!'

He could usually defuse her by making her laugh.

'You're just jealous,' Elizabeth said, 'because he's so cultured and charming . . .'

He draped a wrap over her shoulders. 'And you're crazy about him,' he added. 'Can't have you getting cold. Let's go.'

Lasalle had a house behind avenue Montaigne. It was approached by a small courtyard that reminded Elizabeth of the apartment she had preferred on the rue de la Perle. It was intimate and belonged to an earlier age.

Jean Pierre met them at the door. 'How lovely to see you both,' he said.

He shook hands with James and bent over Elizabeth's hand without actually touching it. He was a very correct man in public.

'You look charming, as always,' he said. 'Do come in and have a drink.'

As she passed close to him, he added, 'How are you feeling?' in a lower voice.

'Sick as a cat,' she murmured back. 'But only in the morning. Oh, Jean Pierre, what a dream of a room this is.'

It was beautifully furnished; one glance told her that James was impressed by the exquisite taste, the clever placing of fine French furniture and lovely objects. They were introduced to four other couples.

'Monsieur and Madame Hastings,' Jean Pierre introduced them.

A waiter offered champagne. Elizabeth opted for mineral water. James drank his champagne rather quickly; she realized how anxious he was feeling, and determined to make amends for being snappy with him. Maybe he had said that about Jean Pierre because he was a little jealous . . . She went across to James.

'Relax, darling. And don't worry. It'll go well.'

At that moment the drawing-room door opened, and their host came in with Ivan and Laura Karakov. Ivan always liked to make an entrance. He had timed his arrival just right. A little late, but not too late. His glance swept round the room; he had met the British diplomat and his wife before, and the distinguished French author whose companion was a *directrice* of the couture house of Saint Laurent. A German industrialist whose wife was one of his biggest clients, and a man who looked rather flamboyant in that company, with a theatrically pretty woman, probably American, he judged, and another younger pair, both obviously English. A good-looking man and a very beautiful blonde girl. Guided by Jean Pierre they acknowledged their acquaintances among the guests, Ivan bowing low over the German lady's hand and beaming at her husband, and then they were face to face with James and Elizabeth.

Before Jean Pierre could introduce them, James stepped forward. 'James Hastings,' he said. 'My wife, Lady Elizabeth.'

Laura Karakov held out a birdlike hand, weighed down by a huge diamond. 'Laura Karakov. My husband, Ivan . . . Oh dear, Jean, we've done it the American way . . . Do forgive us.' She flashed a dazzling smile upon him.

Karakov did not hold out his hand. He gave Elizabeth a polite inclination of the head, and James a look of dark hostility.

Hastings. James Hastings. David Wasserman had mentioned a titled wife. So this was Julius Heyderman's troubleshooter.

Elizabeth smiled at him. 'I've heard such a lot about you, Mr Karakov, I've been looking forward to meeting you. I understand you and Jean Pierre are old friends?'

She had a charming smile, he decided. Beauty appealed to him in women, but then he knew so many beauties, and a lot of them owed their perfection to the surgeon's skill. In their social circle, naturalness and warmth were as rare as his red diamonds.

'We've known each other a while,' he admitted. 'His ex-wife was a friend of ours, but, even though they split up, we're still fond of him. How come you know each other?'

'My husband is over here on business,' Elizabeth said. 'And Jean Pierre found us a furnished apartment.'

'Oh?' Ivan pretended ignorance. 'Will you be in Paris a long time?'

'I don't know,' she said. 'That depends. Oh, no thank you, no champagne, I'll have a glass of mineral water.' She turned to the waiter who had approached them with a tray of drinks.

'You don't drink, then? Wise lady,' Ivan remarked, taking a glass for himself.

'Normally I do,' Elizabeth said. 'And I love champagne. But I'm pregnant, so it's water for me from now on.'

Old instincts stirred in Ivan; he liked the idea of children and big families. He decided that he liked her. No French woman would have been so forthcoming on first acquaintance. He found it refreshing. He smiled at Elizabeth and it was friendly.

'Congratulations, my dear,' he said. 'Is it your first?'

'Yes,' she nodded. 'We've been hoping for a baby for ages. We're terribly excited. Do you have a family?'

'I have two daughters,' he said.

'How lovely. Do tell me about them.'

'Why don't we go over there and sit down,' he suggested. 'I'm an old man, and I don't like standing. And you shouldn't.' He slipped a hand under her elbow and guided her to a sofa.

'Tell me about your daughters,' Elizabeth said. 'Do you have grandchildren?'

Ivan leaned a little towards her. He was beginning to relax and enjoy himself. 'Most women ask me about my jewels,' he said.

Elizabeth laughed. 'I'm sure they do. But I'm more interested in people. I'd love to hear about the jewels later on. Tell me about your family first.'

'My eldest daughter is in the States; she wants to go into business so she's taking a degree in gemology and business studies. She's a very ambitious lady, very bright. Like her mother.' He glanced over at Laura. She was talking to the Americans; he noted how quickly she had abandoned Hastings.

'My second is interested in husbands. She's had two already. The first one was a disaster and he cost a fortune in alimony. Now, she's married to a prince. Prince Eugene Titulescu. I have a little grandson and he's a prince, too. He's two years old, just starting to talk. We're crazy about him.' Which was true in his case; Laura went through the motions, but she wasn't at all patient with small children.

Elizabeth said, 'Titulescu? I'm sure I know the name. Is it Hungarian?'

'Romanian, very old family. Lost everything when the Reds took over after the war. It was terrible what happened to people like Eugene. Thank God it's different now. Russia's becoming a democracy.' Ivan never missed a chance to emphasize that.

Elizabeth said, 'I think my grandfather used to shoot with a Prince Titulescu before the war . . . in the Thirties. I'm sure I've seen photographs of him outside some vast castle with mountains of dead birds, in an album at home. He was mad on killing things. He shot with the Esterházys too, in Hungary.'

Ivan accepted a second glass of champagne. He loved talking about the old aristocracy. He was really enjoying himself. He decided to flirt a little, just to remind himself what it used to be like. She was very sexy in an off-beat way.

'Can't I tempt you? Just a little sip for luck?' He offered her the glass.

Elizabeth decided that she liked him. He had a twinkle in the eye. From James's description she had anticipated meeting a monster.

'How sweet of you – why not?' She drank a little and gave the glass of champagne back to him.

'May I ask your family name, Lady Elizabeth?'

'Only if you promise not to call me that. Liz, please.'

'No,' he corrected gallantly. 'You're too beautiful. Elizabeth.'

When she gave him the surname, he nodded. He hadn't heard of them, but England was full of old blood and little money to go with it. He said, 'I think your aristocracy are wonderful. I admire the way they've coped with a changing world. Is your home open to the public?'

She shook her head. 'No, it's not big or important enough. We're not at all grand, you know. In fact, I never use that title.'

Ivan grunted sympathetically. 'I have English friends who say it puts ten per cent on the bill. But I guess your husband's proud of it.'

'I suppose he is,' she smiled at him. 'But I can't think why. He's romantic about things like that. I often tease him about it. After all, he's the successful one. I'm just my father's daughter.'

'That's what you say, and it's charming to be so modest. But I guess any man would be proud to be married to you.'

'You must feel the same about your wife,' she remarked. 'She's incredibly elegant.'

Ivan laughed. 'She should be, she spends enough money on it! But you're right. She looks good. I'm lucky.'

Elizabeth watched Laura Karakov for a moment. Elegant was right. She was so small and thin, almost Oriental and she had emphasized this by dressing in a slim sheath of vivid green silk, her blond hair drawn down either side of her face like a classical ballerina. The face itself was remarkable. It was old, but there wasn't a line on it. It was smooth and drawn tight like a mask. She had brilliant black eyes, heavily mascaraed, with a mouth painted the same crimson as her nails. Round her neck she wore a twisted rope of multicoloured beads and a bracelet to match. It didn't occur to Elizabeth that what she supposed was costume jewellery were cabochon rubies, emeralds and sapphires. Ivan heaved himself up from the sofa. He held out a hand to help Elizabeth to her feet.

'I think we're going into dinner. I hope we're sitting next to each other.'

'I hope so, too,' she said. 'I haven't asked you about the jewels yet!'

They weren't seated together, but James was beside Laura Karakov.

He had set out to charm and impress, knowing that she would see right through him, but counting on two factors. One, that she was well known for liking handsome young men, very young, in some cases, and two, that she would be curious about him and hope to glean some information. She was Karakov's right hand, a super businesswoman, calculating, reputedly more ruthless than her husband in commercial dealings. She was a good talker, with a sharp spice of American wit, and a tinge of malice that made her amusing. She oozed sexuality in a way that he found embarrassing.

He felt as if he were sitting next to a dangerous snake, that weaved and swayed, and provoked before it struck. And then she did.

'You're over to try and talk my husband round, aren't you? May I call you James?'

'Please . . .' he said quickly. Then, 'He won't see me. I wish you'd try and persuade him.'

He'd not only deflected the bite, he'd bitten back. She acknowledged this with a slight smile. Clever. Fast moving. Like dropping the wife's title in case Jean Pierre didn't use it.

'Why should I?'

'Because I hear you have more influence over him than

anyone else, Mrs Karakov. Or may I call you Laura?'

She didn't respond to him. If he was going to play games, he'd soon learn not to give her an opening. 'He listens to me,' she agreed. 'We talk things over. If you had anything new to tell him it might be different. But you don't, do you? So why should you waste his time?'

James said gently, 'How do you know what I've got to offer? How does he, when he won't give me a chance to explain? I need to talk to him. I think he needs to talk to me, and that's no kind of ego trip on my part. We don't want to quarrel with your husband. He's too important. He's too big a man in the industry.'

She spat the venom with a smile. 'You should have thought of that before you gave him lousy goods at the top price. Tell me,' she changed tack abruptly, 'how come you know Jean Pierre?'

'We rented our apartment from him,' James answered. 'He's been very kind to my wife, taking her to exhibitions, showing her round. I've been so busy setting up our office. I believe his wife was very well connected?'

'Yes, Jennie . . . lovely person, great friend. Such a shame they didn't make out – but then, so few marriages last these days. He's an attractive man, don't you think so? I wouldn't let him take your wife to too many exhibitions. And what a lovely girl she is. Ivan loves blondes. And titles. Our daughter is a princess.'

'How nice,' James had stiffened at the oblique way she talked about Elizabeth. The jibe about Jean Pierre had not escaped him. 'And who is the prince? Is he French?'

The bright dark eyes considered him. 'Romanian,' she said. 'Titulescu. He works for Ivan.'

'That's handy,' he agreed. 'He's your principal salesman, isn't he?'

She laid down her fork. 'He's a fart,' she said calmly. 'But our daughter likes him, and they've got a little boy. So it suits everyone. How long are you staying over?'

James looked across at Karakov, who was talking to

the jolly Embassy wife and looking bored. 'As long as it takes to see your husband.'

Laura Karakov laid her red-nailed hand on his arm for a moment. The big diamond blazed in the candlelight. 'Don't hold your breath, will you?' Then she turned and began to talk to the German industrialist on her left.

'Darling,' James came up to Elizabeth after they left the dining-room. 'You all right? I saw you doing great stuff with him before dinner.'

'He was rather nice,' she said. 'I liked talking to him. You looked pissed off sitting next to the wife.'

'I was,' he agreed. 'But I didn't mean to let it show. She's a real bitch, but never mind. I'll get there. He's coming over to you again. I'm going to have a word later.' He moved off before Ivan reached her.

'Oh good,' Elizabeth said. 'I hoped you'd come and talk to me. I saw Jean Pierre looking purposeful with that American in tow. He's a famous theatrical producer. Max something or other. I saw the last play in London. All about a wife finding out that her husband was gay. I thought it was dreadful.'

Ivan laughed out loud. 'I thought so too. I'd have walked out in the middle but we were taken. No,' he said firmly to their host as he approached them. 'No, you're not stealing this lovely girl away from me. Is he?'

She turned to Jean Pierre, smiling her thanks to him for what he had done. 'No, he's not,' she said. 'I'm very happy where I am. Besides, I want to hear all about Mr Karakov's jewels.'

'Then I won't disturb you,' Jean Pierre said. 'My friend Max will be devastated, he's been longing to talk to you, Elizabeth. But I know my friend Ivan, too. He won't let go of you.'

'Speaking of jewels,' Karakov said, 'that's a very nice piece you're wearing. Lovely quality.' He eyed the brooch. 'Reminds me of something I sold Elizabeth

Taylor. I had to reset it for her, she hated anything old-fashioned . . .'

Laura Karakov was watching him. She heard Elizabeth laughing. She could have repeated every anecdote by heart. Ivan was playing his chosen role, the great character with a weakness for beautiful women. It didn't bother her. He was vain. He loved an audience. The diversion would be good for him. He had left the house that night in a belligerent mood. The reason he gave was an angry telephone exchange with the New York Sales Director. Figures for the half-year had been disappointing. Showing off to a compliant young woman would soothe his feelings. Laura wasn't jealous of Elizabeth, she wasn't petty. She had met and socialized with people of all nationalities and prominence without feeling inferior to any of them. Including the great Hollywood stars in the early years. She knew her own worth. She preyed on them and they let her. That was enough.

James was stuck between the German lady and the producer's wife. He talked diamonds to the German who seemed obsessed by owning jewellery, and theatre to the younger woman who had played in a number of musicals before she married. At one point he excused himself and went over to Jean Pierre.

'Can you try again?' he whispered. 'I must get a chance to talk with him.'

'I'll try,' the Frenchman said. 'But unfortunately Elizabeth is making herself too agreeable to him. He seems to be enchanted, I've never seen him in such a good humour. Come with me.'

Jean Pierre moved towards Karakov and Elizabeth with James following. He had promised to help James make the contact, but he disliked being pressured. What decided him was a brief glimpse of Elizabeth looking tired when Karakov was in full acting mode. He came up and said in a firm but charming voice, 'Now you have had your turn, Ivan; it's time you talked a little to the husband or he will become jealous. Elizabeth?'

She rose at once, giving her place to James. She smiled at Ivan, who had got up. 'I've loved our conversation. Perhaps you and your wife would come and dine with us one evening? It would be great if you would.'

'We'd enjoy that,' Ivan was gallant to the last. 'Please call us.'

Jean Pierre murmured to her, 'I had to break it up or your husband wouldn't have talked with him at all. Come and sit next to Max. He really does want to talk to you. So do I.' For a moment he touched her arm. 'But the host never gets to enjoy his own party. Ah, Max . . . I've brought Lady Elizabeth over. Ivan was monopolizing her.'

'I'm not surprised,' the producer was flagrantly unfaithful to his wife and couldn't resist a pretty new face. His wife watched him set about Elizabeth with her usual resignation. There was nothing to do but pretend not to notice. After all, she had married a genius. All geniuses were flawed. Somebody had told her that and she repeated it daily, like a prayer. Elizabeth asked him quickly what new play he was working on, and he launched into an excited monologue. She listened, smiled vaguely, and tried to rest her back against the unyielding upholstery of a Louis XV chair. Her back was aching, and she felt slightly sick after the rich food.

At the far end of the room, Ivan was also leaning back, a glass of Armagnac in one hand, looking at James with hostile eyes.

'I'm telling you,' he said, 'I think your organization stinks.'

'I think you're being a bit hard, sir,' James replied coolly. He had called Ivan sir because he knew the old man expected deference and it cost James nothing to say it. 'I know we've had our misunderstandings . . . that's why Julius sent me over to try and sort them out. He's very anxious to get the relationship back on its old friendly footing.'

'Friendly footing!' Ivan jerked forward aggressively, eyes flashing. It was part of his technique to show bursts of anger. It put his opponents off stroke. 'Listen to me,' he said. 'I'm an old guy, and I was top of this business when you were crapping in your diapers! I've dealt with you people since I started. The only footing anybody gets on with you is, take our terms or we'll break you. No goods, no supplies. I've known respected men in the trade who were ruined because they wouldn't pay top prices for lousy goods. Well, I'm not one of them!'

He set his glass down and glared at James. 'You've run this industry too long. You think you can play God. Well, not with me. I'm too big for you, son.'

'Nobody is denying that,' James answered. 'You're the best in the world. I said before, we can't afford to fight you. And no disrespect, you can't afford to fight with us.'

'You want to bet?' Ivan grinned at him. 'Just talking about your organization gets my stomach acids working. Have a brandy.'

It was a sudden peace offering, and James acknowledged it by saying quietly, 'I'm going to make peace between you and Diamond Enterprises, and nothing's going to stop me. If we've been wrong in the past, then I've got Julius's brief to put it right. So long as we don't break up the family. Now, sir, if you'll excuse me, I think my wife's a little tired, so I'll take her home. It's been a wonderful evening. Thank you. And I meant what I said.'

Karakov looked at him. 'Good night, Mr Hastings. And you take care of that girl. She's more precious than a diamond.'

Jean Pierre came to the door with them. 'I hope it's been helpful,' he said to James. 'How did you get on with him?'

'Better, right at the end,' James said. 'But Liz was the star. He was eating out of her hand.'

Jean Pierre said, 'How could he help it?'

He smiled at Elizabeth, and James said quickly, 'I can't thank you enough. It was a great evening, anyway, and very good of you to set it up. I'm sure he'll agree the business meeting. Now, darling,' the grip was very proprietorial and he moved her firmly through the front door, 'time you got your feet up. Good night, and thanks again.'

He settled Elizabeth in the car, got into the back beside her, and told the driver to take them home. He pulled her into the crook of his arm. 'Thank you, sweetheart,' he said. 'I saw the effort you made tonight. I know how you hate this kind of lousy artificial set-up, and I'm sorry about the Lady Elizabeth bit. I just felt it might help. You were great with the old man. Thank you.' He kissed her and held her close.

'I wanted to help,' she said softly.

She was so sweet and loving, he thought, holding her close. He said, 'And you did, darling. Now we'll see what happens. He's right, you know. You're more precious to me than his bloody diamonds are.'

The Karakovs had a post-mortem. Sitting up in bed, while Ivan brushed his teeth and took a last pee, with the bathroom door open, Laura called through to him.

'So, what's his next move?'

The lavatory flushed, and he came out. 'He'll want an appointment. He'll want to give me a lot of crap and promise this and that, and I'm going to play along.'

Laura frowned. Cleaned of make-up, her face was sallow and showed signs of her age. The sleek hair fell to her shoulders, giving her a grotesque illusion of youth till she turned face to face. 'Why?' she said. 'Why waste your time? Everything's set.' Then suddenly. 'Or is it? What haven't you told me?'

'Nothing,' he protested, and then because he had never kept any business secrets from her, 'I got an answer back from Moscow. Mirkovitch says they're still working on the deal. No details, nothing concrete to say what's holding it up. I faxed him yesterday.'

'And that's bad?' Laura questioned. 'You think you should go out there yourself? It worked before. You talked with that guy Borisov . . . Why not miss out on Mirkovitch and go to the top?'

'Because I won't need to,' he retorted. 'And I can't. Luchaire says the Saudi is coming over specially to see the Romanov Diamonds. I can't go to Moscow . . .'

The Romanovs. Laura grimaced. He even called the red diamonds by the spurious attribution when he was talking to her. He had convinced himself of his own deception. Of such are the world's great salesmen made. She cut through the crap, as she put it mentally.

'You're keeping your options open through Hastings in case something gets screwed up with either of the deals,' she stated.

'Why not? I like options. You never know when you might need one. But I'm confident. I'll sell the Saudi my diamonds, and I'll sign with Moscow. Meantime, let that smart ass think he's getting somewhere.'

He heaved himself into bed, reached for the light switch, and rolled over on his side, away from her. They hadn't slept together for the last five years. He was past active sex, and he knew it. He had energy only for his business now.

Ruth came into James's office. 'I've got an appointment for you. That social contact must have worked a miracle. The secretary was all over me like a rash. She's offered an eleven o'clock appointment for next Thursday. Karakov's office. Do I confirm?'

James looked up at her. He had been bent over some faxes on his desk. They had come in with the first batch that morning. Faxes from Johannesburg, mostly routine, faxes from Brussels where he was planning to take a meeting and spend a few days with Elizabeth. And a confidential fax from Arthur Harris in London.

'What?'

She said patiently, 'I have an appointment for you with the great man. Eleven o'clock next Thursday in his office? Do I confirm? I said I'd call back before lunch.'

She noticed that he was very pale. Normally he was rather tanned; it went with his dark hair and eyes. But not then. He wasn't just pale, he was white.

'Mr Hastings? Is anything wrong?'

'Wrong?' he repeated. 'No, nothing. Good news, in fact.' She didn't move. He forced himself to say, 'Andrews has just left London for Moscow. It looks like he's got an agreement with the Russians. Yes, take the appointment for me. It doesn't seem all that relevant, if this is right.'

Ruth said quietly, 'Is it certain? Andrews has done a deal?'

He wished she'd go away. He wanted time to compose himself, to absorb the shock. Andrews had been given the impossible to do, and, according to Arthur's smug communiqué, all very confidential, as he insisted, Andrews had done it.

'As certain as anything can be that isn't signed,' James answered.

'Then something could still go wrong,' Ruth suggested. He looked up at her in some surprise. It wasn't the reaction he had expected. She was Kruger's mistress, she belonged in the other camp. She should have been euphoric.

'Yes,' he said, 'I suppose it could. It seems Arthur Harris has agreed to some very stiff terms. He's just sent the broadest outlines, of course, but the details should be interesting. He could be taking a big risk. Which isn't like him.'

'No,' Ruth agreed. 'It isn't. He's over-cautious, if anything. Funny, Dick never mentioned it. He was on the phone to me last night. Maybe he doesn't know about it. Is there a copy of that fax to Mr Heyderman?'

James glanced down quickly. In his first reaction he hadn't thought to check. 'Yes,' he said. 'But surely they'd get fuller information.'

Ruth came close to the desk. 'You would think so. Maybe nobody's seen the terms except Ray Andrews and Mr Harris. Which could mean that they are *very* steep . . .'

Clever, James thought, his mind racing on the same lines as hers. A very clever lady. Andrews and Harris keeping the small print to themselves until it was all signed up . . . Rushing it through . . . a matter of days, the fax insisted. He'd made minimal progress while Andrews was racing ahead with a deal in Moscow. However expensive, it was still a deal that would kill the Russian alliance with Karakov.

'Well,' he said. 'It's great news for the business. If it goes through, we'll be packing up here.'

'Mr Hastings,' Ruth said. He had told her to use his Christian name because it was company practice. But she never did. 'I'm going to ask you something.'

'What is it?' he said.

Ruth said simply. 'Do you trust me?'

James stared at her. 'What the hell kind of question is that? Of course I trust you. Shouldn't I?'

'No, you shouldn't. I'm Dick's lover, and he hates you. But I'm fair about some things. I've worked for you long enough to admire you. You've got a great business talent. I like that. I identify with it. There's been something worrying me for a while now. Something I'd like to talk over with you. I don't want to discuss it here. Could we meet for a drink this evening?'

James said, 'You don't want to talk about it in the office?'

'I'd rather not,' she answered. 'I've only just come to a decision. This minute. I need to put my thoughts together. Do you mind?'

'No, I don't mind. Where would you suggest we meet?'

'Somewhere discreet,' Ruth said quietly. 'You don't want to be seen drinking with your PA. There's a bar near my apartment. Nobody we know would go there. Bar Germaine, rue d'Hôpital. Around seven-thirty?'

'Seven-thirty,' James agreed. 'Am I going to be glad about this?'

'I don't know,' she said. 'But I know I'll feel a lot better.'

Ruth left the office ahead of him. The day had gone by quickly, with no further mention of the meeting. She didn't need to think her decision through. She realized she had made it a long time earlier. She had been waiting to get the timing right. Hastings was going to lose out; Arthur Harris and Dick, the old men hanging on to power, were going to win. Ruth didn't want that. There was no future in their victory for her, only the impor- tunities of Kruger who wanted to get married and tie her down. His insistence every time they met had made the choice for her. She didn't want marriage and security. She wanted excitement, risk and the ultimate goal. Women were going to the top in other industries – why not Diamond Enterprises? She hurried down to the Bar Germaine to wait for James.

James had called the apartment. 'Darling, everything all right?'

Elizabeth, used to at least one telephone call a day, laughed at him and assured him she was fine.

'I'll be late home, maybe not till eight-thirty. I have a meeting.'

'Don't worry,' her voice reassured him. 'Is it im- portant?'

'It might be,' he said. There was no point in mentioning Ruth Fraser. No point at all. He'd tell her about it when he knew what Ruth had to say. If it was helpful. He didn't see how it could be. He couldn't see how anything would help when he was so far behind compared to Ray Andrews. All he could hope for was some last-minute hitch in Moscow. The tone of that confidential fax had been so optimistic, even boastful. It made him sick with envy.

Elizabeth said, 'I had a call from Mum this morning. They're planning to come over early next month.'

'That's great,' James tried to sound enthusiastic. 'Great. I'll be home as soon as I can. Love you, Liz.'

'Love you too,' she responded.

He was going to need that love. He was going to need his wife and the baby and the whole domestic set-up as a compensation for what he was going to lose. He hung up and went outside, dismissing his car and driver. He travelled by metro. It was a furious meanness directed against himself and his failure. If he hadn't been so late he would have punished himself by walking.

Ruth Fraser waved at him from the rear of the bar. She had chosen a secluded table. He came and sat down. She had a glass of wine in front of her.

A waiter appeared, and James said briefly, 'Scotch whisky and Perrier, please. No ice. Sorry I'm late.'

Ruth said, 'I was early. I'm always early when I've something on my mind. And this has been very much of a worry for some time. Before I say anything, I want you to promise me something.'

The green cat's eyes looked at him; he hadn't noticed the intensity of their colour before. 'Promise what?'

'That you won't use this against Dick.'

James leaned towards her. 'Look, I'm not promising anything till I know what this is all about. So let's get on with it, shall we?'

He had been brisk, almost rude. He was tempted to get up and walk out, but he wasn't sure why. The half-lie to Elizabeth nudged his conscience. Ruth didn't waste any more time. He was no fish to be played a little before being hooked.

'You've been trying to solve your problem with one hand tied behind your back,' she said coolly. 'Information was sent to Arthur Harris in London and he deliberately withheld it from you. It came from Johannesburg. It would have given you a head start with Karakov. They didn't want you to have the advantage. They gave Ray Andrews time to get his deal done first.'

'What information?' James asked her. The waiter brought his whisky, folded the bill under the saucer on the table and left them. 'What information?' he repeated.

'Karakov has a suite of diamonds,' her voice was low, urgent. 'They're priceless, and he's been commissioned to sell them by the Russians. He stands to make a fortune from the sale, but more than that, it'll clinch the deal for him. It'll prove he has the outlet for their stones, and he can market them anywhere in the world. I should have told you before. But he made me promise.'

'Jesus,' James said slowly. 'The bastards. Has he made the sale?'

'No, not yet. I'd have heard. But I know who the client is. The Saudi prince. His girlfriend wants them. The actress Madeline Luchaire. She's got him by the short hairs. He's given her millions in jewellery already. My guess is, he'll buy the red diamonds. It won't matter if Andrews signs the agreement in Moscow first. But either way, you're dead.'

James leaned back slowly. 'Yes,' he said. 'If that's the scenario, I'm dead. Why have you decided to tell me this now?' He tried to keep the rage out of his voice; he was careful not to look at her.

'Because I don't want you to lose,' Ruth said. 'I want you to win. I've made my choice. I'm on your side. If you'll have me. I know you're very angry, and you've every right to be. It was a dirty dishonest trick Arthur played on you, and Dick went along with it because he's

224

jealous of you. I'm not trying to excuse him, I'm just saying how it is.'

'Yes,' James said. 'Yes, I see. And Heyderman thinks I have this information and I've made no use of it?' A suite of priceless diamonds, a sale that would prove Karakov's boast that he could sell anything as well as Diamond Enterprises and break their stranglehold on the world market. And he had done nothing to frustrate it.

'Reece faxed it to London weeks ago. You were supposed to be told by Arthur. So you could find some way of screwing up the sale. It looks like you've done nothing about it.'

'Oh my God,' James muttered. 'All this time wasted, trying to talk to that old bastard, when I should have been following this up!'

She leaned towards him. 'So that's why I have to make it up to you. I told you, Mr Hastings, I'm on your side. I love this business; I don't want to see that old fart doing us damage. I can help if you'll let me. And trust me, in spite of what's happened. Will you?'

'I don't know,' he said. His anger was ebbing away. All he could think of was the million-to-one chance still on offer. The chance to somehow, by whatever means and at whatever cost, ruin Karakov's deal and cut the ground from under Arthur Harris before an agreement was signed with Moscow. Trust this woman, who was his enemy Kruger's lover, who'd gone along with the deception until the last minute . . . ? Trust her and believe that she had changed sides? He had no option, and he knew it. She was his inner line to London through Kruger. She had abandoned Kruger, he realized that. She had made herself his ally because her betrayal of Arthur's confidence would cost her her job if it was found out. All he had to do was tell them.

'It looks like I've no option,' he said at last. 'We need to plan this. We need every bit of information we can get . . . How far the sale is advanced, when is it likely to be concluded . . . anything. But where do we get it?'

'I've been thinking,' Ruth admitted. 'I think there's only one source. Reece found out about the diamonds and the deal with the Russians. He must have a spy right inside Karakov's office. Someone really close to him.'

'Then that's where we start,' James said. 'If Harris thinks he can fuck me up and get away with it, I'm going to show him just how wrong he is . . . I'm going to London to see Reece myself.'

'If you do that,' she said quietly, 'they'll know you're on to it. If I go, nobody will suspect anything. I'll see Reece. I'll tell him what's happened. He'll come up with an angle. He wants you to win, too. Shouldn't you be going home? It's nearly nine o'clock.'

James had forgotten about time, about Elizabeth, about everything.

'Nine – hell. I said I'd be back at eight-thirty. Look, we can't stop here. I'll call my wife. You order something to eat, anything.'

He hurried off, asking for a telephone. Ruth watched him go. There was nothing better than a crisis for bringing people together.

Susan Andrews kissed her husband goodbye for the second time. She couldn't help clinging a little, she hated him going, and again there was no set date when he would be coming home.

'It's going to be all right, isn't it?' she insisted. 'Now you've got that guarantee?'

He'd explained it as simply as possible, to reassure her. And to reassure himself, too. Arthur Harris had signed his life away, and he hadn't even argued. That made Ray uneasy; it was so out of character. There was an air of recklessness about Arthur that disturbed him. He had read and reread the guarantee he was taking back to Borisov, and he couldn't fault it from the Russian viewpoint. Arthur had given them an open-ended deal

226

on Baikal, underwritten by himself. When the agreement was signed in Moscow, he couldn't see a way out of it. Which meant that Arthur risked business suicide by not consulting Julius Heyderman or the Board.

'You look worried, darling,' his wife said. 'Are you sure everything's going to be all right? Oh, your flight's being called again. Ring me, won't you?'

'Tomorrow night,' he promised. 'And everything's fine. I'll be home as soon as I've tied things up out there. I'll get you a mink hat!'

He embraced her, and hurried through. He settled down on the flight with a large vodka. He was getting quite a taste for it. He'd done the impossible. Whatever happened afterwards, he had negotiated a deal with Moscow that would cut the ground from under Ivan Karakov, and leave Diamond Enterprises with their monopoly unchallenged. The consequences long term of what Arthur had agreed were not his responsibility. He just wished he wasn't so uneasy when he should have been triumphant.

9

'Darling,' James asked her. 'Any calls for me?'

Elizabeth said, 'No. Are you expecting something special?'

He frowned. He'd poured himself a whisky as soon as he came home from work, which was unusual. He'd kissed her, asked after her day without waiting for an answer and gone to the drinks table.

'Yes, from London. They should have called by now . . . We've got to go out, and I'll miss it.'

'James, what's happening in London? I've never seen you so uptight. Can't you tell me?'

He was instantly contrite and concerned for her. He came and hugged her gently, and apologized.

'I'm sorry, sweetheart; I've been like a bloody cat on a hot brick these last few days. I don't mean to take it out on you. Kiss me?'

It was warm and loving, even passionate. She held tightly to him.

'Tell me about London,' she said.

He released her. 'It'd take too long to explain,' he said. 'And we've got to get ready. I just wish we could cancel the bloody dinner.'

'We can't,' Elizabeth pointed out. They couldn't get out of dinner at the British Embassy. The ambassador had been at school with her father, they'd served in the same regiment.

Elizabeth went upstairs leaving James finishing his drink and hoping that Ruth would call. She was seeing Reece that afternoon. He hadn't been able to concentrate on anything else that day in the office. He had been irritable and snappish; he couldn't have sat down and talked through the details of Arthur's attempts to wreck his chances because he was too involved to deal with his wife's questions and her inevitable moral judgements on Ruth's decision to change sides. She would see dumping Dick Kruger and allying herself with his enemy as evidence of cold-blooded ambition. He could imagine every word she'd say, and he couldn't have argued against any of it. Ruth Fraser was a lethal specimen, a deadly operator for her own ends to the detriment of anything and anyone who barred her way. But he needed her. He couldn't afford to worry about motives or ethics. His career, his future were on the line and he'd have teamed up with the worst denizen of hell if it meant winning.

He thought tenderly of Elizabeth. She'd been feeling sick and wretched, and he hadn't made enough fuss of her lately. She was everything good in his life, the better half of himself. She and the baby were his lifeline if everything else went wrong. He must never forget that. He tore his mind away from the silent telephone and hurried upstairs.

As they dressed, James tried to make amends. 'What did you do today? Did you rest in the afternoon?'

'I went round the Louvre with Jean Pierre this morning.'

He smiled at her. 'I think old Jean Pierre fancies you,' he said. 'Not that I blame him.'

At that moment the telephone rang. He swung away from her, moving at speed across the room. 'Hello? Ruth? Yes . . . how did it go?'

Elizabeth stood very still. *Ruth*. 'I'll wait for you downstairs,' she said.

He nodded, frowning. While she waited, Elizabeth poured herself a glass of Perrier. Was she just imagining an unwillingness to talk about his business problems with her? That had been the start of the Krugers' marriage break-up. She remembered Valerie's warning. *She wants to get to the top herself and she'll take any man who can help her . . .*

The door opened and James came into the room. He was smiling. It was a look she recognized, almost predatory, full of the energy she once found so exciting. Now, for the first time, it made her uneasy. She said quickly, 'Is Ruth in London? Why didn't you tell me?'

'It was good news,' he said. 'I'm going to enjoy our evening now. I'll tell you about it later, sweetheart.'

Ruth was back in her old office next door to Kruger; her replacement had been shunted to another room to make space for her. Dick was like a schoolboy, fussing over her, telling her everything. And talking wedding plans till Ruth could have screamed at him to stop. But she gave nothing away. She played the role he expected, made love to him at night as if their relationship was as strong as ever. Also she reckoned she was paying off a little of what she owed him, even if he didn't know about the debt. She had her own standards, and she dealt fairly with a man who had been good to her. Kruger had been very good, very committed and helpful. And generous. She repaid in the only coin she knew, because in the last analysis she was incapable of love. She listened to everything, storing information to feed back to James, and told Dick Kruger nothing of importance.

'How's that shit doing?' he asked her in their private moments; they always discussed business after making love.

'Doing the high society circuit,' she reassured him. 'And busy seeing people in the trade. He's had a run-in with Karakov . . . well, I told you, they met at some party, and he's going to see him next week, but nothing came out of it. Karakov's treating him like an office boy.'

That had delighted Kruger. 'When this deal's signed

up in Moscow,' he exulted, 'that's about all he'll be round here! Arthur's getting cables from Julius asking what the hell is happening in Paris . . .'

Casually, Ruth had asked him, 'Is it a good deal? We must have given a lot away for them to come round so quickly.'

Kruger had parried the question. Not, she realized, because he wouldn't tell her, but because he wouldn't admit he didn't know. He was proud of his relationship with Arthur. But this time Arthur hadn't shown him the small print.

'It's tough,' he admitted. 'But then nothing's for nothing.'

Her excuse for coming over was to co-ordinate and update the information on Andrews' progress. She boosted Kruger's ego by saying that Hastings was worried about how well the London office was doing, and hoped to sharpen up his end by poaching some ideas. It surprised her that Kruger was so easy to convince. But then he loved and trusted her. She was his ally, soon to be his wife. So he believed what he wanted to believe and passed his confident assessment on to Arthur Harris.

'Hastings is running scared,' he told him. 'He's sent Ruth over to spy on what's happening over here.' He laughed at the way Hastings was being duped. 'If only he knew,' he exulted.

Arthur said simply, 'She's very loyal to you, isn't she, Dick?'

Kruger didn't even notice the element of question in the remark. 'She's going to marry me, as soon as the Paris operation is wound up.'

'She'll make you an excellent wife,' Arthur remarked. 'You're lucky, Dick.'

'Second time round, I certainly am.'

Arthur changed the subject. He didn't have any belief in women's loyalty. 'I'm seeing Hugh Fuller today,' he said. 'He's got the final document ready to send on to

231

Moscow. Then it's up to Andrews to get it through and signed. We'll have a big celebration, my dear Dick. And I want you to know I'm so grateful for all your support. It won't go unrewarded.'

Ruth had been in London for three days when she met Reece at the Regent Palace Hotel. The choice of meeting place seemed an odd one; the place was full of tourists, impersonal and bustling. It was like taking tea at Victoria Station. Tea was what Reece had suggested.

She hadn't been diffident. But not abrasive, either. Reece wouldn't have forgiven any sign of aggression in a woman, Ruth sensed that. She had told him quite coolly that Arthur Harris had withheld his information about Karakov and the sale of the red diamonds to give his own man, Andrews, an unfair advantage. Reece hadn't said a word. He had merely put down his teacup, carefully without making a clink of china against itself, and then said, 'How do you know this?'

And she had answered, 'Because Dick told me. I felt I owed it to James Hastings to tell him the truth. I felt it wasn't fair to him or to the business to restrict information between colleagues.'

Reece had said in his South African voice, 'It's certainly unethical. Mr Julius wouldn't like it at all. So what is Hastings going to do?'

'Make up for lost time,' Ruth said. 'Find some way of screwing up the sale.'

He looked disapproving of the vulgarity. He hated loose talk or bad language in women.

'Which is why I've come over to see you. You found out about the diamonds and the Saudi's girlfriend. Can you find out some more details, something for us to work on? Could you help get an introduction, say, to this woman Luchaire? That was James's idea. If he could somehow make contact with her . . .'

Reece finished his tea; he spooned a residue of sugar

out of the cup, then wiped his mouth with a spotless white handkerchief. His sister did all his ironing, shirts, underclothes, pocket handkerchiefs. She liked him to look impeccable, and he always wore white shirts and a plain tie with his dark suits. Ruth waited. She had an impulse to scream at him to stop wiping his mouth like some old woman, and get on with answering. But nothing of her feelings showed.

'I don't think I should mention this to Mr Julius,' he remarked. 'I know he'll feel very badly about it. And Mr Arthur is his brother-in-law. If Hastings can make use of the information even at this late date, no real harm has been done. Even if it was intended.'

Ruth was reminded of the reptile that spat venom at its enemies when Reece said that.

'So, can you help?' she asked him.

'I think so,' he said after another long pause, when he lifted the teapot and decided there wasn't enough left for another cup. She hadn't touched hers, and by then it was cold. 'I'll see what can be arranged. On one condition.' He looked at her.

'Whatever you say,' Ruth agreed.

'This meeting and our conversation are confidential. No memos, no written communication, even between you and Hastings. Absolutely off the record. The consequences would be very serious if there was any breach of confidentiality.'

He didn't say for whom, he didn't need to.

Ruth understood. She said, 'Nothing will be on record, we're discussing this outside the office. We'll keep it that way.'

'That's wise,' he remarked. 'Leave it with me. And I need a note of your private number. I'll communicate there.'

She said quickly, 'Not at weekends, Dick comes over Friday night till Sundays. I will try to stop him but I can't guarantee it.'

'I'm aware of his trips,' Reece said. 'As he's party to this misuse of my information, I think you should reconsider your relationship, if you want to stay in the business. Unless you mean to marry him and resign.' He glanced down at Kruger's diamond ring on her finger.

Ruth stood up. 'Marriage is not on my agenda,' she said. 'I have other interests. In due time I shall give this back to him. Now I'd better go. Thank you for the tea. And thank you for any help you can give us. I know James will be very grateful.'

'I'm sure he will,' he said. He didn't get up or even look after her as she left. Joy would be entranced when he told her what had happened. He couldn't wait to get home. And from home he would make the relevant telephone call.

Prince Eugene Titulescu went twice a week to Le Club Gymnastique to have a massage and a sauna. It helped to keep his weight down, and there were signs of portliness around his middle. His wife was proud of his figure and she had complained that he was getting heavy. He hated the club. Given a choice, he would never have gone there, but he had no choice. It was the story of his life. He had been moved like a pawn on the chessboard by forces beyond his control. He had made the best of his circumstances, and took comfort in that.

He went to the sauna room first, and sat on the bench with a towel round his middle while the steam rose and he began to sweat. He waited, glancing up as the door opened and a new client came in. It wasn't long before he saw him. He made his way to the bench and sat down near Titulescu.

'Hotter this time,' he remarked.

'Yes, it seems so.'

There was a strained silence for a few minutes. The man was a little younger than the prince; he had a plump, soft body and a sad expression. He kept pushing his

234

sweat-soaked grey-blond hair off his forehead. He was a French politician on the former President Giscard d'Estaing's political staff, and now moving quietly up his Party's hierarchy. He was constantly tipped for high office, but still waiting.

'I'm sorry about this,' he murmured to Titulescu. 'I got the call yesterday. You must know how difficult this is for me?' He looked appealingly at him.

'I do,' the prince said. 'It's worse for you, perhaps. What do they want this time?'

His companion shifted a little on the bench; he was miserable in the heat. But it was the only safe place where they could communicate. The club was the smartest venue in Paris, where the élite went to work out and relax.

That was where he and Eugene Titulescu had first met, by chance, three years ago. Both were happily married; the politician had three children, the new Princess Titulescu was already six month's pregnant. It had been innocent enough. A simple friendship had brought them to a brief homosexual affair. Both were surprised by what had happened; neither were driven by the powerful urges common to so many men of similar bent. Their friendship had gone too far; that was acknowledged between them. Neither could afford too much self-examination. Neither wanted to; they retreated from an episode both felt was best forgotten. And then the blackmail started. The politician had been shown photographs and told to contact his former friend. He wasn't asked for money. He was asked to pressure Eugene Titulescu for information. Refusal meant exposure for them both. He would be destroyed politically, the prince would lose his wife and his job. Neither of them knew who wanted the information or what use they made of it, but at regular intervals, Ivan Karakov's son-in-law would supply answers to questions. Once, he had been forced to reveal figures. He repeated in a mumble, dashing sweat out of his eyes, 'What is it this time?'

'I got the message yesterday. That's why I made the appointment for you.'

The club had called Eugene's home to say he had a massage fixed for that afternoon, and, knowing what it meant, he had taken the appointment.

'They want you to fix an invitation for a diamond executive called Hastings. Do you know him?'

'Yes, I know of him,' Eugene said. 'What sort of invitation?'

'With the actress Madeline Luchaire. Preferably when her lover is in France. It's very urgent. Very important you succeed. That's all they said. I'm so sorry, Eugene. They sounded quite threatening. I suppose you can make sense of it?'

After a pause, the prince said slowly, 'Yes. Yes, and I think I can make sense of who's been persecuting us for all this time.'

'They're calling back this evening,' his companion said. 'What shall I tell them?'

Titulescu got up, pulling the towel modestly around him. 'That I'll do what I can. I've no choice, anyway.'

'Neither of us have,' was the answer.

For a moment Eugene looked at the Frenchman and shook his head. Then he made his way to the door out of the steam room to take his shower and go up for his massage. He didn't fall asleep. While the man worked his muscles and pummelled his body, Eugene lay prone, and tried to work out how to get Karakov's biggest client and the representative of his greatest enemy to meet each other without his own part being found out.

'Hugh,' Arthur said, 'you know how I hate having my hands tied.'

Hugh Fuller nodded. He was the senior partner in Fuller, Haines & Gibson, and he had been Arthur's solicitor and personal friend for twenty years. His business earned a huge retainer fee from D.E., and they dealt with all their legal problems from the London end. They were sitting together in Arthur's club in St James; they had dined very well, and drunk a bottle of Mouton Rothschild followed by some Dow '66, which had launched Fuller into a long dissertation on the merits of various shippers. Arthur and he had a lot in common. Both were sailing men in their spare time, and Fuller was very rich. They were much the same age, although the solicitor had a thick head of white hair and white moustaches which made him look like a retired general.

'Moscow's demanding more and more from us,' Arthur went on. 'They're making us pay through the nose for this agreement. You know I had to give a personal guarantee – I showed it to you. It's unheard of – it's practically blackmail!'

'More or less,' Fuller agreed.

'But Julius is insisting I go ahead. He doesn't care that I've had to put my reputation and my position on the line.'

Arthur knew that Hugh Fuller didn't like Julius Heyderman. He looked on him as a bumptious South African. The lie he had just told would enlist his sympathy.

'He's landed me with an impossible situation because he knows that if the whole thing turns out to be a financial disaster, I shall be held responsible!'

'Well, my dear chap, you tell me how I can help and I'll do my best.'

'I've had to tie myself hand and foot to the de-pollution of this Baikal lake area. That means spending millions over an unspecified time – an open-ended drain on our resources! And Julius insisted that I accept this ultimatum. So I had no alternative to writing that letter and sending it back to Russia with Ray Andrews. Bring us two brandies, will you, George, and some cigars?'

'Certainly, sir.'

Hugh said, 'You should never have agreed to it without talking to me first. Tell me, apart from your guarantee, how firm must this new agreement be?'

He turned to the boxes of cigars the club servant had brought them and began opening the boxes and feeling a cigar here and there between his fingers; he held one or two to his ear to test them for dryness and finally settled on a large Ramon Allone.

Arthur said, 'I'll have one, too, please, George. Thank you. The agreement? Well, it's got to satisfy the Russian government that we can't get out of it.'

'I see.' Fuller lit his cigar and drew hard to get it going. 'Now, Arthur, we've been friends for a hell of a long time. Tell me what you want me to do.'

'I want an agreement that lets me out of that commitment to Baikal. That's the bottom line. The rest can be as watertight as you like. It may not prove to be the problem I anticipate. Then there won't be any need to take advantage of any loophole. Quite the reverse. But I must have an escape route. Otherwise I could be ruined. What can you do about it, Hugh?'

'I don't know yet; that letter you wrote is not binding on D.E. It *is* a test of your credibility and good faith. I'll have to look into the actual contract. It'll take me a few days. But I'll try to think of some way round it.'

'It's got to look all right to them,' Arthur said. 'And their lawyers are not fools.'

'No,' Fuller agreed. 'I don't suppose they are. But then by the time our department has drawn up the full commercial agreement with some new clauses . . . which I shall suggest – I think you can trust me to look after your interests. How urgent is it?'

'Andrews is pressing for the final document to be ready for signature within a week,' Arthur said, 'if you can manage that?'

Fuller coughed for a moment on his cigar. 'It's pushing it, but I'll get it done. Even if I have to draw it up myself, don't worry.'

'I'm very grateful to you,' Arthur said. 'I've taken the blame for a lot of bad debts in this business, and I don't want to be shipwrecked by this one. All Julius takes into account is success.'

'I know,' Fuller said. 'He's too ruthless for my taste. You've got to have some ethics – even in business. Forcing you like this isn't fair. You leave this to me. I'll find a way out! Now tell me, how's Christa?'

An hour later they left the club, or rather Fuller left it and went home in a taxi. He had a firm conviction that running a car in London was a waste of time and money; he had a large, sedate Daimler, which was ten years old, and when he and his wife went down to the country at the weekend, they drove that.

Arthur had arranged to stay the night in his club; it was well past twelve and he was tired. Also he felt disinclined to go back to the house and put up with Christa demanding to know where he had been and what he was doing. It was ironical and annoying that after all these years she should suddenly become jealous and accuse him of having a mistress. When he thought about it in cold blood, it amused him. She was quite powerless to hurt him now, and the knowledge drove her to absurd lengths in spite and undignified outbursts. She had rationalized his rejection of her that night by assuming that he was involved with another woman.

He hadn't had a mistress for a very long time, and the more she accused him, the more the idea appealed to him. He felt like a nice woman, not a girl, he hadn't that kind of taste at all, but a woman, somewhere in her thirties, with a good figure and a pleasant disposition who would go to bed with him and be a companion to him as well. He thought once or twice of some of their friends, and then decided against looking near home. Besides, he was too busy to take on a woman at the moment. Afterwards, when this Russian business was all tied up, he would take a good look round and find himself somebody nice. After years of living with his wife, nice was the adjective that appealed to him most when he thought of a woman. He felt confident with the way the evening had gone. Hugh was a good friend; Arthur had enlisted his sympathy, he knew what was needed. He looked and sounded like a blimpish old fool, but he was one of the sharpest solicitors in practice.

Reece brushed the chair seat before he sat down. He looked across at Stella Heyderman and said, 'Miss Heyderman, why don't you get this place cleaned up? What would your father say if he could see this?'

He gestured primly at the mess surrounding them. There were old newspapers on the floor, dirty glasses, dust thick enough to write on, some of Stella's clothes flung on a chair with a pair of shoes kicked off and left lying. The room smelt. Of stale alcohol and cigarette smoke. She looked a wreck. Drunk for days, he suspected, but finally sober and willing to see him. The money had run out. He knew the scenario. He thought she was the most dreadful, disgusting woman, sitting there, red eyed and sluttish, glaring at him. She was always rude to him. He didn't mind; he despised her, so nothing she could say or do to insult him made any difference. Poor Mr Julius, he thought. To be cursed with a degenerate daughter. But then the mother was mad. It obviously ran in the family. Such a pity she hadn't gone back to Soweto with her black husband. They might have been rid of both of them.

'I've told you,' Stella shouted at him. 'I'm Mrs Yakumi. You call me by my name or you can get out of here!'

Reece shrugged. 'And then what would you do for money?'

She had kept him hanging around, refusing to speak

to him, or answer his calls. He felt she deserved to be humiliated.

'I've spoken to the solicitors,' he said, 'and they won't release your allowance until they have my authority. You might as well know that your father has given me the power to cut off all funds.'

Stella looked at him with loathing. Her credit was gone; she owed money for everything. Desperation had made her agree to see him. Her father couldn't have given him power over her. He'd never treated her like that before.

'I don't believe you,' she said. 'He wouldn't. He wouldn't let a little creep like you tell me what to do.'

She drew her knees up and wrapped her arms around them defensively. It was a childish posture that made her look vulnerable. Jacob used to tease her. 'You're such a little girl, Suki . . . you're like my little child . . .' He had comforted and reassured her as if, as well as her lover, he was the father she had never known in that mode.

Reece answered coldly, 'I have the paperwork with me if you want to see it.'

He reached into his briefcase and brought the power of attorney out.

'He's not trying to be unkind,' he insisted. 'All he wants is what's best for you. He wants you to stop playing this stupid game and come back to the real world. He wants you to come home.'

'Then he should have protected Jacob! He knew he was going back, I wrote and told him . . . I asked him to get police protection . . .'

The tears were overflowing now. Reece listened unmoved. He had heard it all before. The bitter reproaches against someone he knew was blameless, the self-pity, the tears. He waited till she paused.

'He was murdered by his own kind,' he said. He had never discussed it with her on previous encounters. Just sat till she'd exhausted herself and spewed out her spite against her long-suffering father. This time he changed tactics. He had Julius's authority behind him, and the last-resort instructions. *Whatever has to be done to make her come home. Whatever it takes . . .*

'The ANC murdered him,' he went on, raising his voice as she began to interrupt. 'Savages,' Reece said. 'Dirty savages. They cut him to pieces. And these are the people you want to see running our country. Just think what they did to Yakumi . . . one of their own. It was all good fun to march and demonstrate when it was a way of getting under your father's skin and upsetting him going off with a black – but this is for real now. You've got your way, you and all the rest of the Commie Liberals . . . I hope you like it.'

Stella took a deep breath. She was trembling. How dare he! How dare the white-livered little rat talk to her, Stella Heyderman, like that!

'By Christ!' she spat at him. 'Wait till I tell my father what you've said. I'll have you fired!'

Reece smiled at her. 'That's better,' he said. 'You sound like a Heyderman for a change. It's only skin deep, isn't it, all this posing about equal rights for black and white? You were just play-acting, getting attention; well,' he drew out the word, 'the act's over, Miss Stella. There's no Yakumi here to keep up the pretence for you. Just a lot of freeloaders and bums taking Heyderman money. Mr Julius sent me over to tell you, it's got to stop. Your debts will be paid off – and I mean the legal ones, bills, rent arrears, nothing else. And I'm instructing the solicitors to give notice that your lease here won't be renewed next January. You know I mean it, don't you?'

Stella got up. 'You shouldn't threaten me, Reece. Maybe I am my father's daughter. You'll be sorry for this.'

Reece got up slowly, unhurried. He wasn't going to be dismissed. Instinct detected fear in her, in spite of the attempts at bluster.

'No I won't,' he said. 'All I want is your father to have some peace of mind. He's a great man and he doesn't deserve what you've done to him. I'm going back home before Christmas. Either you fly back with me, or you'll be out on the street. I don't think Yakumi's friends will pay your booze bills for long. Please think about it. I'll let myself out.'

Stella said loudly, 'I'll never go back. Jacob's friends will take me in. I'll tell them the truth. I'll tell them who I really am!'

He paused and shook his head as if he pitied her. 'If they knew that,' he said, 'they'd spit on you for not going with him. They'd say, she could have protected him, with all that money and power. Just like you say about your father. But nobody could stop what happened. He was a marked man. I'll be in touch in a few days. Think about Christmas in the sun, instead of in this dump!'

Stella looked round wildly for something to throw at the closed door. Her shoe thudded against the panel and then rolled across the floor. The trembling had become a violent shivering fit. She didn't bother going to the back of the sofa where she kept a bottle, just for emergencies, because she'd already looked and it was empty. As empty as her purse.

'Jacob!' She cried his name out loud. 'Oh Jacob . . . why did you do it? Why did you go and leave me?' The cry of self-pity and despair became a burst of hysterical weeping. *Nobody could stop what happened. He was a marked man.*

She had fought her family off since his death. She'd abused and insulted her stepmother Sylvia and as good as accused her father of complicity in Jacob's murder. It had seemed as if she could go on striking out at them to relieve her own agony indefinitely. But it was the end, and she knew it. Never, ever, would that despicable little shit have dared to trash her like that, unless he had her father's blessing. Come home or sink into the gutter.

Slowly Stella wiped her wet face with a grubby tissue found in her sleeve. Christmas in the sun! Did they really think that mattered to her now? Was it their idea of a bribe? She laughed in fury at the idea. Didn't they know that when Jacob Yakumi fell under the machete blows of his killers, the sun went down on her for the rest of her life . . . ? Better the gutter. Better to die and shame them one last time. She had so often thought of it. But Jacob wouldn't let her. He was in her mind, in her heart, refusing to let her take the coward's option. He was very strong in his insistence; his voice reproached her in her head when she gave way to weakness like thoughts of suicide. He would want her to fight back. Never to surrender, either, and go tamely back to the environment that was responsible for his death. She remembered Paul Mkoza, his great friend, a fellow lawyer and activist in the black community in London. A scholarly, serious man who had left South Africa long before she and Jacob fled to England. He had been the first to come and break the news of his death. And the last to abandon her when she abandoned herself to days of alcohol abuse. It had taken a long time, but in the end he had given up because he realized there was nothing he could do. It was more than a year since she had spoken to him. He had a dedicated young wife; Stella had felt she disapproved and influenced him. Sober as she was, Stella didn't blame her.

She knew the number so well. She dialled. He was her last hope. He might be able to advise her. At least she could assure him she was sober.

When he answered, she spoke quickly, stumbling over the words, assuring him that she hadn't been drinking, that she needed his help. Just one more time for Jacob's sake.

He was a patient, courteous man. He let her speak, and then he said, 'My dear Suki, I'm so glad to talk with you. You've been on my mind for some days. I was going to call you . . . ask you to come and see Rose and me.

And we have a friend staying. Someone I think you should meet. But only if you're well and strong enough.'

'I'm not drunk,' she said simply. 'Paul, I want a friend to advise me. I know how much you loved Jacob. I can't turn to anyone else. When can I come round and see you?'

Paul Mkoza was consulting his wife; Stella knew by the pause that followed. Then he said, 'This evening? For supper? But Rose says I have to explain about our friend first. In case you don't feel you can bear it. He was in Soweto when Jacob was murdered. He has things to tell you about what happened. Do you want to hear them?'

Stella said slowly, 'He was there?'

'Yes.'

'I want to hear them,' she said. 'I'll come right away.'

10

'Elizabeth, are you preoccupied today? Are you not feeling well?'

Jean Pierre had suggested lunch; Elizabeth had a clear day and she always enjoyed his company. He had sounded so eager to see her, she didn't want to disappoint him.

The intermittent back pain had stopped and she felt less sick in the mornings. Her doctor said she would soon start feeling more energetic and the nausea might stop altogether. But otherwise he was satisfied with everything. She had gone away reassured and told herself not to be a wimp about a bit of backache.

Jean Pierre had chosen the same restaurant where they had lunched on her first visit to Paris. She looked at him and said simply, 'I'm fine; you're nearly as bad as James. He never stops fussing. I've stopped telling him anything because he thinks every twinge needs urgent medical attention.'

She hesitated. 'But,' she said, 'there is something I'd like to talk to you about. You're such a friend and I don't think you'll laugh at me.'

'Never,' he said. 'I knew there was something. You see how well I know you? Tell me.'

'Oh . . .' She started breaking up a bread roll, crumbling it to pieces. 'Oh, it's just me being stupid . . . James has a secretary, PA.'

He looked up sharply. 'A woman?'

'Yes. She's generally bad news. She broke up another director's marriage and went off with him. In fact his ex-wife took me out to lunch to warn me about her. I didn't take any notice. I even told James, and he was spitting over it.'

He said, 'But you are taking notice now? Why?'

'Because there's something going on in the business and she's very much part of it. And James didn't say anything to me. Apparently that's her technique. She makes herself indispensable to the boss and he starts confiding in her and cutting out his wife. Jean Pierre, I have no reason to be worried, but I am. Maybe I'm failing James by not understanding what he's up against . . . maybe I make too many moral judgements.'

'Maybe,' he said gently, 'you are just pregnant and feeling insecure?'

'I've no other excuse,' Elizabeth said. 'James seems to be more in love with me, more caring, more committed than ever. So why am I worried?'

'Because what that poor jealous woman said has stayed like a poison in your mind. And there is only one way to get rid of it. You must talk to your husband. Tell him what you feel. You must trust him. When trust is gone, there is no hope for a marriage. I know, because it happened to me. My wife started suspecting me, perhaps because we weren't happy anyway, but I wasn't unfaithful. She still suspected me, so in the end I was. Talk to James; whatever you do, don't brood. Especially at this time.'

'I will,' she said. 'Thank you so much, Jean Pierre.' She reached out and touched his hand. 'You're such a friend,' she said.

He placed his hand over hers. 'No,' he said. 'I'm not a friend. I'm a fool. I've just given you good advice. I'm a fool because I am in love with you. I have always been in love, from the first day we met. So I'm not just a friend. Didn't you have any idea?'

'No,' Elizabeth felt the colour rushing into her face. 'No, truly I didn't. I'm so sorry, Jean Pierre. I wouldn't have encouraged it. I feel so awful. And you've been so sweet to me, and so helpful to James, too . . .'

He said sadly, 'What an idiot I must seem to you. A middle-aged fool loving another man's pregnant wife, without any hope . . . But I had to tell you. Really because I was tempted to add a little poison of my own just now. But then I thought of what's best for you, and not myself. That's love, I suppose.'

'That's real love,' Elizabeth agreed. Her eyes filled with tears. 'I'm so terribly sorry.'

'Please don't regret anything. I've been happier than for years. Now I want to say something else. If ever he fails you, or you need me, I will be there for you.'

'He won't,' Elizabeth said quietly. 'Jean Pierre, I think I ought to go home.'

'Of course,' he agreed. 'But I promise, I will never mention anything like this again. Can I go back to being your good friend?'

She hadn't the heart to say anything but, 'Yes, of course you can.'

Outside her apartment he took hold of both her hands and kissed them. 'Another piece of advice,' he said gently. 'Don't tell your husband. I don't think he'd believe in friendship.'

Then, abruptly, he let go of her and turned away.

'Why don't we go home?' Clara Wasserman demanded. She was tired and irritable and missing her own environment. 'We're doing nothing here.'

David understood his wife. She was still fired up because he had failed to get a meeting for James Hastings with Ivan, and Hastings' wife had succeeded. He thought her dislike of Elizabeth was exaggerated, but he didn't say so.

'Nothing is happening,' she repeated. 'Hastings hasn't made any impact; Laura just laughed about it the other night. You've got better things to do than sit around here.'

'Such as what?' he challenged. 'I'm doing this for Julius, and for myself because I love the game.'

'You're not carrying the ball,' she countered sharply. 'Since when have you watched from the sidelines?'

'Clara, Clara,' he reproached her. 'Stop fighting my battles for me . . . I'm too old to run. I'm watching and I know something's going to break. I feel it here.' He touched his middle. 'In my gut, like always. Never wrong. You know that—'

'All I know,' she said sharply, 'is that Andrews is pulling off a deal in Moscow – you saw the fax, you told me. When it's signed up, Ivan'll have to make peace and we go home. So why wait?'

'I saw the fax, and it looks good. But I still say something's moving right here. I don't know how or where, Clara, I just know it. When it does, I'm going to be here. I could end up being the referee when that ball gets dropped. Trust me.'

'You and your gut,' she grumbled. But she couldn't argue with conviction. David had an instinct, and it had never been wrong. She said, 'You think Hastings is going to pull something? How, what's he got?'

Wasserman shrugged. 'I don't know, Clara. But tell me one thing . . . why's Ivan changed his mind? Why a meeting suddenly? When I talked to him he wouldn't even think about it.'

'He bullshits,' Clara retorted.

'No, I can tell the difference. He wasn't bullshitting. He wouldn't let Hastings get near enough to spit on him. So I think he's worried; maybe he's heard some rumour from Russia . . . Don't forget one thing: Hastings is bright and he's hungry. He's on the line to do something on his own account, no matter what Andrews negotiates. And he's not the kind that gives in. So stop packing suitcases and watch the game with me. Now I'll order us both a drink. Dry Martini?'

'After all these years you have to ask?' She looked up

at him and smiled. 'Hastings may be smart but I tell you – at his age you were ready to bite the ass off a bear! Make that a large Martini.'

'He's going to help; look, it's only a week!'

James banged his fist on the desk.

'But time is what we haven't got! I get another fax saying Andrews expects the final documentation to arrive in Moscow by the end of this week and they'll sign up. For Christ's sake, Ruth, go and call in on your ansaphone and see if there's a message.'

She said calmly, 'I already have, just an hour ago. Nothing. Getting worked up won't help. I have confidence in Reece. He said he'd arrange something and he will. Why don't I ask for some coffee?'

James looked at her. So cool. So burnished. From the sleek dark hair to the gleaming shoes on her small feet. Not a sign of the tension that was tearing him apart as the days went by and they heard nothing from Reece.

'What have you got in your veins,' he said irritably, 'ice water?'

Ruth smiled. 'When it comes to business, anti-freeze. I'll get the coffee.'

He had cancelled his trip to Brussels to meet the dealers. He couldn't bear being out of Paris till he knew something was moving. And he was worried about taking Elizabeth in case she got over-tired. So he sat and waited, with that nerveless woman at his side. The meeting with Ivan had led to a second one, and a surprising invitation to join him for lunch. All good signs, except that there was no real progress made; just an endless repetition of the old man's grievances and vain outpourings, but they hadn't even begun to negotiate, and they both knew it. Meantime, Ray Andrews was working miracles in Moscow.

Ruth brought him a cup of coffee. She placed it on the

desk and said, 'If you don't need me, I have some work to do.'

'No problem,' James answered. He was glad to get rid of her. Now that he was seeing her as a person, he found her a disturbing woman. She radiated sexuality, not of the greedy lust of Laura Karakov, but something cold and infinitely calculated. He felt she could climax physically, while she was mentally running through a balance sheet.

She had an exceptionally acute business brain, untouched by any emotional hang-up. Her response to a problem was purely cerebral and practical. He could see what had snared Dick Kruger: the combination of a man's intellectual approach and a powerful sex attraction. She never put a foot wrong with Hastings himself, nothing in their relationship had changed fundamentally except the conspiracy to defeat Karakov and frustrate Harris.

But the cat's eyes had the yellow tinge of the tiger; she was his ally, but she wouldn't hesitate to bite his head off if it brought her what she wanted. He would always bear that in mind, whatever the outcome of their partnership. In her own office Ruth paused from working. She had forgotten her coffee and it was tepid. She sent one of the secretaries out for a refill. He wasn't the cool type she had expected. Hastings was a prey to nerves; tension showed in his irritable response, in the restless harping on the time factor. Waiting got to him. But that was true of most men. Kruger was just as uneasy on the knife's edge. Maybe this stoic patience was a woman's trait, she thought. They'd learned patience the hard way. How to plan and manipulate to make up for their physical weakness and inequality in the accepted order. How to strike from behind, because they couldn't deliver a frontal blow and hope to survive. But things were changing now, the balance was shifting. She had gone to see Reece for her own purposes, not just to help Hastings. She wanted to bring herself to his notice, to impress him. He was the key to Julius Heyderman. He would report back. If Hastings succeeded, it would reflect on her. Failure would only damage him. She would gain credit for having tried to help.

She had taken note of Reece's advice about Dick Kruger. *I think you should reconsider your relationship, if you want to stay in the business . . .*

Dick was planning a trip over that weekend. It would soon be time to cut the lover's knot.

Stella closed the front door of her flat. She removed the key and switched on the lights. She was very calm. So calm she couldn't feel anything. She went into the kitchen and made herself tea. She drank it slowly, tasting nothing, staring ahead and seeing nothing.

They had been very kind to her, even Rose Mkoza, masking her disapproval of Yakumi's useless white wife. They had listened gravely while Stella explained that she wanted to stay in London, and not go home to South Africa.

She was finding it impossible to resist her family's pressure. They had no idea who that family was. To them, the parents of Suki Yakumi were just another example of white racists, prepared to accept their daughter now that her black husband was dead.

There was no sign of the friend, the reason why she had hurried to get there, driven by the demon of needing to hear what happened at first hand. She went through the motions of discussing her problem when she wanted to leap up and scream at them. Where was he, this witness who had been in Soweto and had things to tell her? It was like torture, sitting there.

Then Paul Mkoza said, 'I think it might be better if you did go back.'

He looked at his wife Rose, and she nodded.

Then he said, 'You could carry on his work. England

is a bad place for you. I asked our friend to wait while we talked in private. I needed to know what your problem was. Now, if you are ready, he would like to talk to you.'

Sitting in the silent kitchen, Stella went through it all again. Moment by moment, word for word, as if she were replaying a film in her mind. The young man with a black skin and Chinese features, legacy of a mating between a black woman and one of the coolies brought in as slave labour in the early part of the century. He was a student, visiting his family on the night Jacob Yakumi was lured out of his house and hacked to death. An intelligent, politically active young man, who favoured the left of the ANC party. And a man impelled by a sense of justice to make enquiries into the murder.

'I'm not important, you see,' he had explained. 'People weren't afraid to talk to me. I was just visiting my family. So I heard things that the officials and the police wouldn't be told. We're not a people who like secrets. Only fear makes us hide things. And there was a lot of fear in Soweto. But not of our activists, or the Inkatha killers. They were not responsible. Yakumi was not killed by either of them. That was the convenient theory, put out by both sides, trying to blame each other. The police didn't believe it, either, but it suited them to have the parties accusing each other at that time.'

Stella had felt her throat tightening so that she could hardly swallow. It was a terrible effort to speak. 'If Jacob wasn't murdered by political opponents, then who did kill him?'

'Gangsters,' he said it simply. 'There are plenty of them in the Township. They sell drugs and alcohol and stolen goods. They kill for money. Someone paid one of their gangs to murder your husband, Mrs Yakumi. And to use machetes so it would look like a political killing.'

She felt Paul Mkoza's arm come round her and

supposed she looked as if she might collapse. She remembered moving away, freeing herself.

'Who paid them?' She heard herself repeating it. 'Who paid them? Tell me . . .'

Then his answer. 'I don't know the name; it could have been a personal enemy, perhaps. But then people said he had no enemies. He'd been in exile. A white racist fanatic, maybe. But you weren't with him. There was talk of a white man with a lot of money, asking for a job to be done . . . only whispers through the Township. A rumour coming from Johannesburg. The gangs operate there, too. Just talk and nothing more. But I believed it – there was truth in it. I believe someone had him murdered and it wasn't anyone in ANC or Inkatha. It was a private killing.'

A private killing. She had conquered the panic rising in her. She mustn't lose control or she might scare the young man off. She saw the Mkozas watching her intently.

'Nobody knew this white man . . . knew what he looked like?'

He had hesitated for a moment. 'I have tried to find that out, too,' he said. 'Now we are in government the police have to listen. I felt very deeply about this murder. I said, it's not too late for justice. Now . . . we can get justice for our people. There are informers in Soweto. In every township. It's a legacy of the past; soon,' he said confidently, 'they'll be stamped out. But I gave one of them some money to ask in the criminal element. All he could tell me was the white man was small and thin like a snake. And not Afrikaans. But he had power. Power and much money from a great business in our country. That is what the informer was told. That's all. It was a business killing, that was all he could find out. Business makes no sense to me, Mrs Yakumi. Your husband had no links with any business.'

'No,' Stella heard herself agreeing. 'No. He was a civil

rights barrister. All he ever did was try to help his people.'

'It was one of so many deaths at that time,' he said quietly. 'Whoever is responsible will not be punished now. I tried, but I couldn't find out any more. He was a great man, your husband. He won't be forgotten.'

He had spoken Jacob's valedictory. Paul and Rose Mkoza nodded in agreement. 'A great African taken too soon. He would have been in our government if he had lived.' Then Paul came close to her again, comforting her. 'You must be proud of him, Suki. And glad that it wasn't treachery that killed him. It was a terrible burden for us, thinking that fellow Africans would kill such a good man. We were afraid ANC members were jealous of him coming home, that one of our people was to blame. That gave us a lot of grief. Inkatha kills for the love of it, it's in the Zulu blood. But now we know it was a white crime, bought with white money. It's easier for us all to bear.'

Stella had looked at him, so serious, so sure that he spoke for her, too. She got up slowly. 'I'm so glad,' she had said, 'that makes it easier for you.'

She had walked out, leaving them staring, puzzled, after her.

'If you want to go to Brussels, I'm perfectly all right to come. Jamie, I don't want to feel a burden to you. I want to be part of what you're doing.'

They had driven out of Paris that Sunday, and lunched in a pretty restaurant near Fontainebleau. It was a cold day with rain clouds gathering outside.

James said, 'What's all this about, darling? I don't want to go to Brussels at this time, anyway. As for being a burden . . . come on, what's bugging you? Something is.'

Elizabeth took a breath, *Talk to your husband. Tell him what you feel.* Advice from a man whose own marriage had failed. Given because he loved her.

'I feel there's a lot going on and you're not involving me at all. It worries me, because I know how much the business matters to you and I don't believe in compartments in a marriage. You're going to freak when I say this, but I can't help it. I don't like the idea of Ruth Fraser being in on everything and me being left out.'

James stared at her.

'I knew you'd be furious, but that's how I feel,' Elizabeth said. She began to destroy the bread roll, exactly as she had done with Jean Pierre. He didn't say anything, he watched her pulling it to pieces.

'I see,' he said. 'What you're really saying is you're frightened I'll sleep with her because that's how Kruger ended up? You think I'd cheat on you?'

'No,' she said in distress. 'No, of course I don't think anything like that. It's just that she's got such a reputation as a man eater and Valerie didn't realize what was happening until it was too late. And I'm having this baby and I can't go on trips with you . . .' She fumbled in her handbag for a handkerchief. 'I'm sorry, darling,' she said. 'But it's been preying on my mind.'

'If you cry,' James said softly, 'I'm going to be really angry. You are the biggest bloody fool – bottling all this up and getting yourself upset till you have to sit here and talk a load of balls about me going off and fancying Ruth Fraser! It's just as well we're in a public place, or I might thump you! Baby or no baby! Now, just listen to me. And for Christ's sake stop taking it out on the bread roll.'

He leaned across the table and pulled her hand away, holding it firmly.

'Let's start with the business then. You want to know what's happening? All right, I'll tell you. Harris is trying to screw me up; Ruth told me, because Kruger, who sees her every weekend incidentally, told *her*. Karakov has some fantastic red diamond jewellery that he's going to sell on commission for the Russians. I'm not supposed to know about it, but now I do, and I'm working out how to wreck the sale. And Ruth is helping me. That's what's going on. Now why is she doing it? Because she hopes to swap Kruger for me? I can see you thinking it.'

Elizabeth said, 'Well, she is, isn't she?'

He shook his head at her. 'For an intelligent girl you're pretty stupid sometimes, darling. No, she isn't. She knows she'd be out on her little arse if she even batted an eyelid at me. She's not interested in men; all she wants is to get on in the organization. Knocking up Kruger was one step up the ladder for her; coming down on my side so I win is another. That's how she operates. And I'll tell you one thing: if I do screw up this deal of Karakov's, I'll be the blue-eyed boy with Heyderman. And that'll rub off on her, too. So I go up the ladder and I take her with me. Only I'm not going to, you sweet silly thing, because I know she'd knife me one day like she knifed Kruger. But at the moment I need her. She's vital to me till this is over. Now,' he demanded, 'are you satisfied? Have I explained it to you?'

'Oh,' Elizabeth sighed. 'Yes, you have. I feel such a fool, as if I didn't trust you . . . I wish I'd never mentioned any of it.'

'It's that bloody woman Valerie,' he said, echoing Jean Pierre. 'She put the poison in. Now you promise me you're not going to think about it again?'

'I promise,' she said.

'And I promise something, too,' James told her. 'I was wrong; I didn't tell you what was happening. Maybe I thought you'd say how rotten it all was, and I don't much like it when you do. You are a bit heavy on the moral aspect, you know—'

'I know,' she said. 'But you know what I think so you don't have to keep saying it. That's my mistake. I won't make judgements any more.'

'You don't have to,' he smiled. 'I can read you like a book, my darling. You know, I was thinking the other

257

day, you're the best part of me? I'd be a total bastard without you to put me straight. So go ahead and make your judgements. They're good for my soul. I do love you so much.'

'I love you too,' she said gently. 'I'm so glad we talked this through. I feel closer to you now than ever. To hell with Ruth Fraser. *I* want you to win!'

James signalled the waitress. He said gently, 'Madame would like some more bread.'

Andrews put the call through from his hotel. 'Dimitri? Ray here. I have the letter you wanted with me.'

Borisov laughed. He sounded happy. 'Bring it over. As soon as you like. You are a man of your word, aren't you!'

Ray laughed, too. 'You know the old saying, "The word of an Englishman". No, maybe you don't. People don't operate like that any more. I'll see you soon then. And don't forget, you said we'd celebrate!'

'I haven't,' Borisov answered. 'I have the Bolshoi tickets in my desk drawer.'

Later Ray sat reading Arthur's letter. The niggling feeling of doubt had returned as he waited. It prompted him to say, 'You know that's not binding on Diamond Enterprises? It's only an expression of his good faith. It binds him morally, but it would not commit us without Board approval. That will come with the finalized documentation. And that,' he added as Borisov laid down the letter, 'should be with you in about ten days. But my boss has put himself on the line by what he's written. It's his reputation he's pledging there.'

'I know,' the Russian said. 'That's why I asked for it. Because a man in his position couldn't make that commitment unless he was genuine. My friend, I congratulate you. You must have great powers of persuasion.'

Andrews grinned. He needn't have worried. Borisov was convinced, so he should be.

'I'll take you to dinner tonight,' he said. 'After the ballet. And you're invited to London when we sign up, as D.E.'s guest. I'll make sure you have a great time.'

'I look forward to it. I shall see that the President has sight of this as soon as possible. We'll meet at seven. The performance starts at eight.'

He came and shook hands with Ray Andrews. Then suddenly he embraced him in the Russian way. 'My friend,' he said. 'I mean that.'

'Darling,' Sylvia Heyderman shouted. 'It's Stella! She wants to talk to you.'

She had been swimming when the poolside telephone rang. Julius was swimming at the far end. He swam powerfully for exercise every morning and evening.

He called out to her, 'Stella? Hold on, tell her I'm coming . . .'

After months and months of silence, suddenly his daughter was making contact. He climbed out and ran to the pool house, dripping water. Sylvia handed him the phone. She said quietly, 'She sounded all right, not unfriendly.'

On the line in London, Stella heard the whispered words. *All right, not unfriendly.* Not drunk or abusive. She could visualize the scene. The huge luxury pool, gleaming blue in the sunshine, her father, swimming like an athlete to keep in good shape, Sylvia tanning her neat body with a heap of glossy magazines to hand.

She said, 'Hello, Dad. How are you?'

'Fine, fine,' he sounded a little breathless. 'How are you? It's good to hear your voice, Stella. Really good.'

'Good to hear you, too,' she said. 'It's been such a long time and I realize how unfair I've been. So, can we talk a bit?'

'As long as you like.'

Sylvia draped a towel over him. He shrugged it off impatiently.

'Reece came to see me,' Stella said. She was amazed at her own calmness. 'He suggested I came home. I told him to piss off because I didn't like his manners. But I've been thinking about it, and that's why I called. I don't want to deal with him again, Dad. You wouldn't believe the way he talked to me.'

Julius said, 'Don't worry. He won't do it again. I'll sort him out if he thinks he can take liberties with you. You just tell me what you want.' And then, because he couldn't help himself, 'Oh God, Suki, it's such a relief to speak with you and know we can still continue.'

Suki. Stella winced. A business killing, the student had said. A thin white man with the power of a snake. The money and the backing to contract on Jacob's life.

'It's a relief for me too,' she said. There was a pause and then, 'Dad, I've decided to come home. Living here like this won't bring Jacob back. I'm sorry I've been so bloody to you, but I just had to take it out on someone.'

'Of course,' he agreed. 'I understand that. The one you've really been punishing is yourself. And from what I know about Jacob, it's the last thing he'd want. Everything he fought for has come true now. So at least he didn't die for nothing. If you can think of it like that, it'll help.'

I hear you, Stella said to herself. I hear what you're saying and I believe you, because you've never lied to me or pretended. You've cut my heart out with the things you've said, with your lack of love and your priorities for everything else but me. But you never lied. So how can you speak about Jacob like that when you paid to have him murdered . . . ?

'I'm trying to,' she made herself answer him. 'That's why I want to come home. He wouldn't see it as a betrayal now that things have changed.'

'They certainly have,' her father said. 'And so far, it's working out for all of us. But you'll see for yourself when you get here.'

'I have a problem,' Stella sounded hesitant. 'I don't want you to take this wrong, Dad, but I've no money and Reece won't authorize my next allowance. I'm skint. I need new clothes and I want to move out of here; I hate it. I'd like to stay in a decent hotel and get myself back on track. I look like a bloody bagwoman at the moment.'

Julius hesitated. She was asking for money. Money to rehabilitate herself, to leave the miserable environment with all it represented. Or to escape and take off, having made a fool of him.

But, even before he could answer, Stella said, 'I know what you're thinking. I'm not lying to you. I've had enough of living in shit. If you don't trust me I can't blame you. Tie it up as tight as you like, but don't leave me dependent on Reece. I won't come back if he's involved in anything to do with me.'

A thin white man with the power of a snake.

'I'll cable the London office,' Julius said. 'They'll open credit accounts for you. Right away. You move out and take a suite at the Dorchester. We use it a lot. Just book yourself in. And buy whatever you need, don't worry about money. When will you come back?'

She said, 'Are you planning to come over? We could fly home together.'

'I wasn't,' he answered. 'But I will. I can tie it in with business. Go to the Dorchester. I'll call you there this time tomorrow. And don't worry about Reece. I'll kick his backside. You won't hear from him again.'

'Thanks, Dad,' she couldn't keep a slight break out of her voice. She hated showing the emotion. He would kick Reece's backside. She could just imagine how brutal he would be. Even though he had sent Reece to hire Jacob's killers . . .

'Stella,' Julius said. 'Sylvia sends her love . . . I'll talk to you tomorrow. Just take care, will you?'

'I will,' she promised. 'I'll take care of everything from now on.'

When she put the phone down, she burst into tears. It was the first time she had cried since she heard how Jacob Yakumi died. In spite of it all, kindness from her father could still make her cry like a child.

Ray Andrews was asleep; he was lying in the double bed with his head back and his mouth open, and Susan came in very quietly to see if he was awake and wanted anything. That wasn't the real reason; she came because she was hoping that she might accidentally wake him up, and she wanted to talk to him, sit on the edge of the bed and drink cups of tea and ask him all about everything. And tell him all about what had happened while he was away. She stood looking at him for a moment; he looked like a schoolboy, with his rumpled hair and the old-fashioned striped pyjamas. His arms were crossed above his head and he was snoring. He had come back exhausted after two hectic days of eating, drinking and going to the Bolshoi Theatre, meeting more and more Russians. His breath smelt of brandy, and she had stopped herself from mentioning it just in time. He had kissed her and their daughter, and then he'd gone upstairs and had a bath and fallen into bed.

'That you, darling?'

'Oh, darling, did I wake you? I just popped in to see if you were awake and wanted anything.'

'I'd like a cup of tea,' he said. He struggled up on the pillow and yawned. 'And a boiled egg, no, two boiled eggs, and some toast and marmalade. Darling, I'm starving. Come and say good-morning to me.'

'God, I missed you,' he said after a minute; they were still embracing, and she was pressing her face against his cheek. She had soft skin and smelt sweet. He loved her so much that it hurt, and he turned her head round and kissed her hard.

'I'll get your breakfast,' she said. She drew away from

him, flushed and smiling, trying to tidy her hair with one hand while he held on to the other.

'All right,' he said. 'I'll get up and wash and shave.'

He hummed to himself as he scraped at his beard; he had given up using an electric razor, it never felt as clean as the old-fashioned shave. He was still tired, but it was a triumphant tiredness. He had brought the deal off; he had gone out to fail, with everybody feeling sorry for him, and come back with the thing in the bag.

He ate his breakfast while she watched him and drank tea, and in between he told her what had happened in Moscow.

'Darling, you're marvellous. Nobody could have done it except you!'

'No, I don't think they could. I can't think of anyone who'd have dealt as well with Dimitri as I did. And I'm not boasting, Sue, I promise you.'

'I know you're not,' she countered. 'You must have got on well if you were on Christian-name terms. That's unusual, isn't it?'

Ray grinned at her. 'Yes, very unusual. They're pretty formal; not like the West, where everyone's cosy and calls the Prime Minister John . . . But there's always an element of luck. We related very quickly. That didn't make it easy, he was as shrewd and ruthless as you can find anywhere. But I understand him.'

'Why?' Susan protested. 'You're not ruthless.'

'Oh no? I was there trying to ruin Ivan Karakov, sweetheart. And I was doing it for business. Borisov is a genuine patriot. He really wants to put his country on its feet. I respected him a lot. And I liked him. I tell you something,' he went on. 'I trust that man, and I know he trusts me. I'd stake my life he won't go back on anything he promised. That's why I decided not to hang around in Moscow. He's got all the documents, and he'll be coming over to London to sign up with us.'

'Oh darling,' Susan stared at him in horror. 'You know what happened before!'

'Forget that,' he said. 'Nothing will go wrong this time . . . Borisov will keep his word to me, and I'm going to make sure we keep ours to him. We're going to bloody well clean up Baikal and help the Russian environment. And exploit the Russian diamond potential to boost their foreign currency. It won't just be profits for us and nothing for anyone else. We're going to show the world that we can keep a promise, too!'

'My dear Françoise,' Eugene Titulescu bent over her hand and kissed it lightly. 'How elegant you look, as always.'

The woman smiled up at him and preened at the compliment. She was very elegant; her taste and flair for clothes compensated for her remarkable ugliness. Combined with wit and charm, and a large inheritance from her American grandmother, these qualities had netted her three husbands, all well connected and poor, but with the social entrée she craved. Françoise had married a Spanish count whose names and titles were as long as his bank balance was short. He had died of a heart attack before Françoise had time to get bored with paying his bills and look for someone else.

She was an old friend of the prince and his wife; she loved Eugene and was sorry that Karakov's predatory daughter had grabbed him first. She was a very good client of his father-in-law. She was famous for her collection of jewels and her voracious pursuit of celebrities and the socially prominent. She didn't know it, but she was Eugene's last hope when he invited her to lunch. He chose the Ritz, because it was a fraction more exclusive than the Crillon, attracting old money, as he put it, rather than new media names. He gave her champagne in the bar, delighted her with items of gossip about mutual friends, and waited until they were having coffee after a superb lunch before he asked her for a favour. It always amazed him that such a thin woman could eat so much and drink such quantities without either putting on weight or getting drunk. He smiled at her.

'I hear,' he said gently, 'that you are entertaining royalty next weekend at Roc d'Or.'

She beamed back at him. 'How did you know?'

'Because I hear everything of importance, my dear. And nothing you do escapes attention, you must know that . . . It's a great honour, I believe. They seldom accept private invitations.'

'Yes, but then darling Madeline is such a dear friend of mine,' she retorted. All her friends were dear and darling, even those she rather disliked. 'She's persuaded him to spend two nights with me before they go on to Paris.' She giggled maliciously. 'She wants him suitably enchanted before she asks for an especially big gift. But then you know all that, don't you?'

'I do,' he responded. 'But I never discuss a client's business. Except perhaps with a very special friend.' He gave her a warm smile. 'I have my favourites, my dear Françoise, as you know.'

She said sweetly, 'I do, my dear Eugene.' She believed him when he said he had persuaded Ivan to reduce the price of a rope of pink pearls, which, in fact, he had been unable to sell to anyone else. She never forgot a favour; it was one of her many good points.

Impulsively she said, 'Why don't you join us,' then regretted it because he would have to come with his wife. As she was Karakov's daughter, it wouldn't be at all suitable. The Arabian prince might think it was an attempt to influence him. Eugene saw the impossibility turn into a God-sent opportunity. He could think quite quickly when he was under pressure.

'Oh sweet of you, of course, but, no, it wouldn't be proper. In view of the gift you mentioned . . . which, of course, we mustn't talk about. But I could suggest another couple.'

Countess Françoise's bright eyes hardened. She chose her own guest list and didn't like being importuned on behalf of anyone else. Even by such a dear darling friend as Prince Eugene.

'Not if I don't already know them,' she said firmly. 'I have my houseparty made up. I was making an exception for you.'

'And I'm very touched,' he countered smoothly. 'But these are very special. English, just arrived to live in Paris. He is rich, handsome and distinguished . . . he works in the City . . .' He glossed over James Hastings' career very quickly, and went on to the real bait on the hook. 'His wife is the daughter of the Earl of . . .' He saw the eyes soften at the name and title. 'A very beautiful and charming girl, typical of the family. They were constant guests of my grandfather in the shooting season. I know she would be a great asset. Your VIP is a lover of the English aristocracy.'

Françoise looked at him. She smiled. 'Darling Eugene,' she said lightly, 'are you doing me a favour or asking me to do one for you?'

'Both,' he said simply. 'I would be very, very grateful if you invited them, just for one night. It would be a personal favour to me, and it would introduce a charming young couple into your circle. I'm so glad to see that you are wearing your pearls.'

It was a risk, but he took it. She had a sporting instinct and a robust sense of humour that went back to her Arkansas ancestors. She laughed.

'Point taken, Eugene. You saved me a lot of money. I never forget a good turn. Let my secretary know their full names and addresses and I'll invite them. If they're your protégés, I know I'll like them.'

He saw her to her car, kissed her hand and thanked her gravely. 'Any time I can be of help to you again, my dear Françoise, you only have to give me a call.'

Then he went back into the hotel and made a telephone call.

The following morning, at seven a.m., Ruth Fraser answered the phone in her apartment. It was Reece on the line.

'You'll be getting the invitation some time today,' Ruth said. James had got up from his desk; he was walking up and down in excitement. Reece had come through for him, just as Ruth insisted he would. They would be invited to fly down to Cap d'Antibes to stay at the same houseparty as Madeline Luchaire and the Arab prince.

He had asked for the opportunity and it had been arranged for him. Everything would depend on what use he made of it.

'How the hell did he fix it?' he said, more to himself than to her.

'Better not ask,' Ruth answered.

James said, 'He's twisted somebody's arm . . .'

'Dick says we've got a contact in Karakov's office, and they're pretty high up . . . We've had confidential information passed to us before.'

The figures, James remembered. Details of Karakov's sales worldwide. Someone very close to the top must be in D.E.'s pay. Someone important enough to get an invitation for two strangers from one of Paris's most socially ambitious hostesses.

'Ruth,' he said, 'get David Wasserman on the line for me. I want a meeting with him. Just say it's urgent.'

She smiled at him. 'Exciting, isn't it? How I'd love to be a fly on the wall down there. Can I ask you what you're going to do?'

He could feel her excitement; she was high on it, eyes shining, radiating a fierce tension. This, he realized, was what turned her on. This was Ruth Fraser's fix. Not sex, that was her weapon, not the diamond-hard efficiency, the cold pursuit of a man like Kruger for her own aims, but the sheer thrill of power and intrigue.

'I haven't worked it out,' he said. 'That's why I need to see Wasserman. He may come up with something I'd miss.' And because he owed it all to her, he said, 'I'll tell you the details as soon as I've got something lined up. And I won't forget how much you've helped to bring this off, Ruth. You'll find me very grateful. If I shaft Karakov, you can pick your own job.'

She turned at the door of his office. 'I can't think of anything I'd rather do than work with you. I'll get Mr Wasserman for you now.'

'And to think,' David Wasserman said, 'Clara wanted to pack up and go back home! Wait till I tell her what we'd have missed. You know, James, if you bring this off, you'll break Ivan's heart!'

He laughed.

'Just a hint will be enough – they're the most suspicious goddamned race in the world. Except for us.' He chuckled like a mischievous old gnome. 'You'll do it, James my boy. And I'll be right here watching.'

'I'm going to do more than hint,' James said. 'I'm going to fix that old bastard if it's the last thing I do.'

'Now, now,' David advised. 'Don't get involved in a personal fight. Take my advice. Always keep business separate. It's got nothing to do with feelings. Ivan's not a bad guy. He gave you a hard time, but so what? He's done it to me, too. I've known him for years, and we've had our disagreements. In the end he'll deal.'

'In the end,' James said flatly, 'he won't have any bloody option.'

When David was telling Clara word for word about their meeting and the plan they had evolved, he said, 'He's a tough guy, and vindictive. He hasn't forgiven Ivan for balling him out in the beginning. That's a bad characteristic if he wants to be the top man. I tried to tell him, don't get involved. Leave feelings out of it. It's the only way.'

'And you're not surprised?' his wife asked him. 'You like him, I don't. He won't listen to you. He won't even be grateful for what you've done to help. And without you, and your idea, he wouldn't have a card to play. You should have been the one to do the business here, not him.'

David didn't argue. He loved her loyalty. It was so blinkered and uncompromising. In her eyes he was the best and there was nobody to match him. But in this instance, Clara was wrong.

He said gently, 'Sweetheart, would we be going for a weekend with a jet-set countess? No, we wouldn't. So be realistic. Hastings has something to offer which we don't. He's young, he's smart, and he's got a wife people like to invite.'

Clara actually snorted with indignation.

'Don't talk to me! All that social crap! So what the hell's special about her? She's just another blonde with a smell under her nose.'

That wasn't right, either, but he didn't argue. Being a woman of strong gut feelings, Clara let her emotions get in the way of her judgement sometimes. Elizabeth Hastings had really riled her.

He said gently, 'Aren't you glad we stayed now?'

'Oh yes, sure I'm glad. You look ten years younger already. Excitement is good for you. And I like it, too.' She smiled fondly at him. 'When is this weekend?'

'In ten days' time,' he said. 'The invitation came by special messenger when I was with him in the office—'

'Then why don't we invite Ivan and Laura for dinner?' she made the suggestion slyly. 'On the Saturday night?'

They looked at each other with the malice of old age. 'We can have a little fun of our own.'

*   *   *

Stella had been at the Dorchester for a week. The office had pre-empted her and booked a suite on Julius's instructions. She wanted a simple double room, but she decided not to change it. After so long the luxury felt alien, and she herself was so ill at ease that she almost walked out and went back to the dingy flat. But that meant defeat, that meant she was retreating and, if she did, then Reece would win. She had to keep her father's confidence and trust. She dared not lose the independence he had given her. Otherwise she would never be able to prove that Jacob's death had been orchestrated by her own family in order to conceal her marriage. It all made sense to her. She could and did build on the disconnected facts set out by Mkoza's student friend.

When Jacob went back, it was inevitable she would follow, and the truth would come out. Julius Heyderman's daughter had married an ANC activist and had been living in exile with him in London. That couldn't be allowed to happen. Why, she demanded over and over, didn't she realize it before? And then savagely she blamed herself for wallowing in drink and self-pity, letting the truth die till it was almost too late . . . Months had passed while she sank lower, lost her few contacts and became a name in a solicitor's file, paid to cover up and keep her out of public disgrace.

And there, smirking like a death's head, was Reece; threatening her, withholding money, manipulating her to please her father and get her back to South Africa, cowed and discredited. She didn't touch a drink. She set about herself with a degree of self-hatred that bordered on cruelty. She went to the beauty salons; she had facials, manicures, hair treatments. She ordered expensive clothes and hired a car and driver. She became Stella Heyderman, rich, pampered, able to buy anything she wanted. And she talked regularly to her father and Sylvia on the telephone, assuring them she was well, happy to be back in her own environment, and ready to come home with them in time for Christmas. Julius had kept his word. But then he always did, as she admitted. Reece didn't contact her. His role was assumed by someone from the accounts department in Blackfriars Road, who called to see her once and gave her details of the funds and credits available. He was very deferential. She felt like yelling at him to stop crawling, that she was just another human being, for Christ's sake. But she didn't. She played the part expected of her.

Then she ordered the car to take her to an address in the Strand. She had found it by looking through the *Yellow Pages* under 'Detective Agencies'.

'A. G. Miller,' it said. 'Private Detective Agency. Divorce Enquiries a speciality.'

The idea had come to her that morning; it seemed to be fixed in her mind as soon as she woke up, as if someone had put it there in the night. Find out about Reece, get something on him first. Then decide what you are going to do.

The office of A. G. Miller was on the third floor, and she climbed the steps, passing the shabby landings with a glass-fronted door on each, and then she came to Miller's door, which was just like the rest. She went in and she was in a small outer office, where one girl was typing. The inside of the place was clean, and when she went in to Mr Miller's office, it was a well-carpeted, functional room, and Mr Miller himself looked like a middle-grade civil servant. He was a tall man; he wore a dark suit and a plain tie, and he wore glasses. He carried himself as if he had been in the Army, but he was in fact a former Metropolitan police officer.

She sat down and took a cigarette, offering him one. She had given the name of Phipps, which was one of her mother's family names.

'No, thank you, Miss Phipps. I don't smoke.'

It was all so ridiculous, she felt as if she had got into the wrong office. It wasn't in the least like the place

Raymond Chandler described in his books, and there was not the slightest connection between Mr A. G. Miller and Philip Marlowe. Even the secretary outside was as plain as a pikestaff.

'I want someone investigated,' she said. 'Do you do that?'

'It depends on the type of investigation. Is this a family matter, or is it a possible divorce case?'

'It's a man I know,' she said. 'I've reason to think he's undesirable, and I have a sister who wants to marry him. I want you to find out everything you can about him.'

'I see.'

Mr Miller didn't believe a word of it, but then most of his clients told lies to start with. Even the wives who wanted their husbands watched always had some cock-and-bull story about really trusting them, and only wanting to be sure. Some of them were exceptions, some of them were businesslike about it, because they wanted to be free, and these were the easiest to deal with. They paid up and they didn't argue, and they weren't always ringing up to find out what he had found out. One or two of the people who asked him to take cases were just plain nuts. This girl wasn't one of those; everything about her showed that she was rich, and he had already fixed on twice his usual fee plus expenses. He didn't swallow that one about her sister. She wanted to get a line on the man herself.

'This sort of thing can take some time,' he said. 'And it'll be expensive. I must warn you about that, Miss Phipps.'

'I don't mind,' she said. 'I don't mind what it costs. Don't let that worry you, Mr Miller.'

'Very well then, give me the details, please.'

'The name is Reece. He's working in the London office of Diamond Enterprises at Blackfriars at the moment. He's a South African who's over here probably till

Christmas. That's as much as I can tell you, but it should be enough.'

'You want him investigated for this past year, is that right?'

'No,' she said. 'I want everything about him; birth records, parentage, every damned detail. I want to know what he eats for breakfast and whether he wears pyjama trousers in bed. You'll have to send someone out to the Union to do it, but it doesn't matter.'

'We have an association with a firm in Cape Town and another in Johannesburg; we can come to an arrangement with them to do the South African end of it.'

He coughed and wiped his mouth with a coloured handkerchief; it was the only discordant thing about his whole appearance. It was bright yellow and red.

'You realize that a complete investigation of this kind could take anything up to a year or more?'

'I know,' Stella said. 'I've got plenty of time. Rome wasn't built in a day. What retainer do you want?'

'Five thousand pounds,' Mr Miller said. 'And expenses. The full fee will be near twenty thousand, when we give a complete report to you. Is that agreeable?'

'Perfectly.'

She opened her bag and took out her new chequebook. She wrote out a cheque and handed it to him. He gave a quick look and saw that she had signed herself 'Heyderman'. He knew at once who she was because of the South African connection. He folded the cheque and put it away.

'Leave your address and telephone number with my secretary, Miss Phipps, and I'll contact you in a week's time and tell you what arrangements I've made and what the preliminary results are. Would you like a monthly report?'

'Weekly,' she said. 'If you don't mind.'

He did mind, but he couldn't afford to for that kind of money.

'As you like. You'll be hearing from me. Good-morning, Miss Phipps.'

She turned at the door. 'The name's Heyderman,' she said. 'But you saw that on the cheque. We won't monkey about with each other, Mr Miller. Goodbye.'

'But why should this woman ask us when she's never even met us?' Elizabeth had the letter in her hand. It was crested and embossed, heavy as vellum.

'Because,' James explained, 'it's been set up so we can meet Madeline Luchaire and her Arab. And stick one on Karakov. Darling, this is the break I've been waiting for. My one chance to get my blow in before bloody Andrews brings in the Russian deal. And looking at the time scale, the luck's running my way.'

There had been another cable from London that afternoon. The agreement had reached Moscow and was being considered. They expected agreement in principle and a representative to come to London before the end of the month to sign. Time, he repeated to Elizabeth, would win it for him. In ten days they would fly down to Cap d'Antibes, guests of this obliging countess with a Spanish name like a mouthful of marbles, and get to the Arab prince before he went to Paris and bought Karakov's red diamonds.

Elizabeth looked up at him. She was sitting, feet curled under her on the sofa, and she shifted slightly to ease the niggle in her back.

'How are you going to stop him? How can you?'

He hugged her gently. 'I have a lovely, neat little ploy, but I'm not going to tell you, darling, till we get there. David dreamed it up with me this morning. All I have to do is make the opportunity. And I will. And when it's all over, we can go home and get the house ready for the baby. We'll be on top of the world.' He kissed her.

She was rereading the letter. 'She's so anxious to meet us . . . says that she met my father in London. Dad hardly ever goes to London,' Elizabeth said. 'I bet he's never met her in his life—'

James said, 'Anyway, what the hell does it matter? I told you, it's been set up for me. That's what counts. Why are you moving about . . . uncomfortable? Here, I'll shift.'

'No,' she said quickly. 'No, don't. I like you close to me. It's just this silly backache again. I think I'll go and see the doctor next week. Maybe he can recommend a masseuse or something.'

'I'll take you,' he said. 'And this evening you're going to have a nice quiet evening. Feet up and do nothing.'

'I gave Louise the night off,' Elizabeth reminded him. 'I thought I'd make dinner for us.'

'*I* am making dinner,' James announced. 'And you are going to do as I say and take it easy. You've probably pulled a muscle, you're always doing too much. First we'll have a glass of champagne to celebrate. Or I will. Perrier for you.'

'Perrier,' she sighed, smiling at him. 'You really are hopeless, the way you spoil me. I spoke to Mum today. They should be over soon. After we get back from this great weekend.'

'Good,' he said happily, and meant it. 'We'll give them a great time. And you'll enjoy having them, won't you? If it wasn't for old Jean Pierre, you'd have been lonely. He hasn't been around for a while, has he?'

'No,' Elizabeth said. 'He's rung once or twice, but I've been busy. We'll have him to lunch or dinner with my parents.'

'Good idea,' James said firmly. 'He's nearly the same age . . .'

Joy Reece had never seen her brother so upset. When he came home from the office, he had slumped in a chair and hardly spoken to her. He looked very sallow and sunken eyed. She came over to him.

'What's wrong? What's the matter, darling?' She never called him that except when they were making love.

He looked up at her miserably. 'Stella,' he said. 'She called Mr Julius and complained about me. She told him a pack of bloody lies. He was furious with me. He yelled at me, Joy, and the way he talked you'd think I was some kind of servant . . . He said if I upset her again, I'd be out on my ass. Those very words.'

Her face flushed. She put her arm round him protectively. 'That little bitch,' she spat out. 'And how dare he turn on you! How dare he, after all you've done for him. I'd like to give him a piece of my mind . . . I'd tell him about his daughter. Dirty little drunken bitch,' she said, hissing with rage.

'It's not his fault,' Reece protested. 'She worked him up . . . I don't blame him when I think about it, she's been such a worry to him, he'd believe anything she said. I was just hurt, that's all. I'm glad not to have the responsibility any more. You know where she is? The Dorchester! She's got money available, credit through the office . . . It'll end in disaster, you'll see. Thank God I won't have to pick up the pieces when she goes out and gets drunk and disgraces herself.'

'Never mind,' his sister comforted. 'Never mind, he'll find out what a mistake he made, treating you like that. And I hope she gets herself splashed all over the tabloids! That'll serve him right!'

She rocked him a little, it was an old childhood habit. When either one had been given the stick by their father, the other used to cradle them in their arms. She let the subject go, because she knew he didn't want to blame Julius Heyderman. He would let Heyderman kick him, and lick his hand like a beaten dog afterwards. It made her seethe with fury, but she couldn't do anything about it. For some reason beyond her understanding, her brother needed that relationship. He needed his hero to worship. Joy didn't suffer from a dependence on anyone but him. And her mother's Afrikaans blood made her a good hater. She would hold the grudge for a lifetime. One day, she muttered to herself, one day I'll pay them out, those bloody Heydermans . . . one day. She cooked him a special supper that evening and fussed over him till he cheered up. In bed together he drew her close to him.

'Joy,' he whispered. 'What would I do without you?'

'We've got each other,' she said. 'That's all that matters . . .'

Elizabeth had dressed after the examination. Now she sat facing the doctor in his consulting room.

'Madame Hastings, the backache is the first sign of uterine contractions. It means the uterus is irritable and may try and reject the foetus. It is close to the menstrual cycle, and that is always a dangerous time.'

He saw her lose colour. She had been a good patient, sensible and unfussing and he liked her.

'You should go into a clinic for the next few days. With complete rest and treatment, we should be able to prevent a miscarriage.'

She didn't answer; she sat looking at him.

He said kindly, 'It is a sensible precaution. I will make arrangements for you to be admitted this afternoon.'

Elizabeth found her voice. She tried to keep it steady.

'Am I going to lose my baby? You must tell me.'

He shook his head. 'No, as I said, this is only a precaution . . . It is quite common for a first pregnancy to have little grumbles. You are healthy, your child is healthy; all you must do is rest and you may not even need any medical treatment. Above all, Madame, you must stay calm and not worry. Stress causes more miscarriages than many people realize. I am very confident everything will be all right after a few days.'

She opened her purse, took out a handkerchief, put it back unused. She felt too shocked to cry. They were due to leave for Cap d'Antibes that day. The niggling discomfort had died down over the last weeks and she'd seen no reason to consult the doctor. But that morning it had returned, and the niggle was now a definite pain. To lose the child, after so long, so many disappointments. To call James and tell him . . .

She said it aloud. 'I can't bear it. It's too much.'

The doctor said, 'I'll telephone the clinic now. I'll tell them to expect you by midday. Go home now, and don't worry. Will your husband be with you? Would you like me to telephone and reassure him?'

'No,' Elizabeth said quickly. 'No thank you. I'll tell him myself. But I can't go in until this afternoon. Not before three o'clock. Will it make all that much difference?'

He came and helped her into her coat. 'No no, I told you, it's a precaution.' She looked so stricken that he decided not to argue. An hour or two would be less harmful than any added emotional trauma. 'But you are to go straight home and rest. No engagements, no exertions. I'll call in to the clinic to see you this evening.'

She had a taxi waiting. Three o'clock. By then James would be on his way to Cap d'Antibes. He had to go. She reasoned with herself during the drive back to the apartment. The weekend was vital. If he missed this opportunity, his career prospects were ruined. He had made that clear often enough. The chance to meet Karakov's client was vital to him. If he knew she was in danger, that there was any threat of a miscarriage, he wouldn't go . . . It was only a precaution, the doctor said. She kept repeating this, insisting on it. Going into a clinic was just being sensible because of the little pains. Grumbles, he had called them. A few days and she would be home and her pregnancy would be on course. If she let James know anything, he would sacrifice his one chance for nothing. They had arranged to meet at Charles de Gaulle and catch the two o'clock flight to Nice. He had taken his cases to the office, hers were already packed. Casual clothes, evening dress for the inevitable dinner party.

She paid off the taxi and went slowly up the steps to the front door. Her legs felt as if they might buckle under her. Inside she broke the rules and poured herself a small glass of brandy. It made her feel sick. She rushed to the bathroom and threw up into the basin. She was shaking all over, and the pain had moved from back to front. She washed her face and went back to her bedroom and lay down. Keep calm, don't worry, rest, wait till he was at the airport and call him there. Convince him it was a muscle, a disc . . . It wouldn't be long. If I can sleep a bit, she thought, just doze and try to relax. She took deep breaths as recommended by the antenatal teacher, and folded her hands across the little swelling in her belly, as if she could still the ache in her treacherous womb.

Poor Liz, James kept thinking. The aircraft rose steeply through a thick bank of clouds and juddered with turbulence. Poor kid, putting her back out. Stuck in bed over the weekend. His first reaction had been to turn round and go home. He could go to the bloody villa on Saturday in time for the dinner party. She had been very firm when he had suggested it. Even angry, saying he was fussing about nothing, reminding him how important it was to meet the Arab and his girlfriend, and all she had was a twisted muscle needing a couple of days' bed rest.

The flight to Nice was being called as they argued . . . He gave way because she convinced him it would worry her more if he cancelled. He'd call this evening, he promised. And if luck was on his side, he might be able to get back on Sunday morning. He'd do his damndest. She had the maid Louise sleeping in; she even teased him by saying she could call Jean Pierre to come round and keep her company. They were laughing as he rang off and went through to catch his plane.

The sister in charge came up to him. 'Monsieur Hastings?'

'No.' Jean Pierre got up. 'No, I'm not the husband. I'm a friend. How is she?'

'She's quite well,' the answer was brisk. 'But I'm afraid she miscarried. There are no complications. It was quite straightforward. She's sedated and sleeping now. She asked for her husband. Can you contact him? I understand he's away for the weekend.'

She wasn't hiding her disapproval when she said it. She had a very cold eye.

'I haven't an address or telephone number. I went round when she telephoned. She was too distressed to tell me anything. I'll call his office. They'll know where to find him.'

He had been on his way out when the telephone rang. He had been tempted to leave it, he was already late for an appointment. Then he realized he must have forgotten to switch the ansaphone on, and with some irritation he turned back and took the call. It was Elizabeth.

'Jean Pierre . . . Jean Pierre . . . Can you come round? The maid's out, and I'm bleeding . . . I'm having a miscarriage.'

He heard her sobbing. He jumped lights and nearly collided with a lorry on his way to rue Constantine. The door was open; she must have dragged herself to open it before she collapsed in the hall. It was a blur after that. The call for an ambulance, the rush to the clinic. The long wait for news. He would never forget the agony on her face as he held her hand in the speeding ambulance.

'Poor little thing,' she kept saying. 'Poor little thing . . .'

He bowed his head and shed tears as if the child was his own.

He got through to the Diamond Enterprises office. He

asked for James Hastings' secretary. There was a buzz
and then a woman answered.

'Mr Hastings' office.'

'I need to contact Mr Hastings. My name is Lasalle. I
understand he's away for the weekend.'

'Can you tell me what it's about?' She sounded
pleasant but firm. 'Perhaps I can help? We're not supposed to give out private numbers. I'm sorry.'

'Yes,' he nearly shouted at her. 'Yes. Tell him his wife's
had a miscarriage and she's asking for him. She's in the
Marthier Clinic.'

There was a pause, then he heard the cool voice say.
'I'm so sorry to hear that. Is she in any danger?'

'No, she's not,' he answered. 'But she's very traumatized. She needs him. Now can you give me the number?'

'That won't be necessary. I'll speak to him myself and
give him the message. Please tell his wife how sorry I am
and wish her better soon.'

Then she hung up.

A car sent from the Villa Roc d'Or met James at Nice
Airport. It arrived in Cap d'Antibes and took a long
private road behind electronically controlled gates out
onto a rocky promontory overlooking the sea. James's
case was taken by a uniformed flunkey and he was
greeted in the hall by his hostess.

'Monsieur Hastings? I am Françoise de Reayles de
Zulueta. How nice of you to come. Where is your wife?'

She was so ugly he was taken by surprise, until she
smiled. The charm of her personality made up for
everything.

'Oh, I am so sorry, Countess,' he explained. 'She was
taken ill at the last minute. She hurt her back and she
only called me at the airport. Her doctor insisted
she stays in bed. She's expecting a baby, you see. She
was so upset about it, and I feel terrible arriving without
her, but I had no way of letting you know.'

'What a disappointment,' Françoise said graciously. 'And how miserable for her. Backs are such a nuisance and so painful. I shall look forward to meeting her another time . . . Now, Paco will show you your room, and then please join us through here,' she gestured to an archway on the left of the hall, 'for a drink before we change for dinner. All our other guests are here.'

James didn't waste time in the bedroom. He could see that money and taste were evident down to the smallest detail. He could unpack later. All he wanted to do was get down and meet Luchaire and the Arab. He had everything planned. Word perfect, like an actor knowing his lines. Thank God for old Wasserman. Only a real diamond man would have thought of it.

Privately, Françoise was irritated that the wife had backed out at the last minute. She didn't believe in sudden slipped discs. Nothing so trivial would have made her cancel an important engagement. She was annoyed because the missing girl was a social asset, and because it left her with odd numbers at too short notice to get someone else. Eugene might have got the price of her pearls reduced, but he had upset the balance of her houseparty by asking her to invite the English couple. She would be very sharp with him next time.

As they sipped champagne in the big vaulted room with its magnificent view over the sea, she was mollified by James's good looks and charming manners. He paid her a lot of attention, and was making a good impression on her other guests, the Wildensteins, France's richest and most prestigious racehorse owners. The Saudi prince was passionate about horses, and was the most successful racehorse owner in his own country. His ambition was to rival the Mahktouns, but so far his father had forbidden him to own and race horses in Europe. Madeline Luchaire and her prince were the last to come down before dinner. Being an actress she had to make an entrance. James was talking to Wildenstein's elegant wife with one eye on the archway. He saw the countess move forward. They had been absent from the brief drinks before he went upstairs to bathe and change. Madeline came in on the prince's arm. She was a lovely woman, James admitted, sheathed in a special glamour, and she had a radiant smile that encompassed them all. Her lover was in Western evening dress. A white tuxedo showed off a tall, athletic figure. He had a classical Arab face, strong features, acquiline nose and a rather cruel mouth. He was as impressive in his own right as any European royal. James was the last to be introduced. He kissed Luchaire's hand, brushing an egg-sized sapphire ring as he did so, and bowed when he shook hands with the prince.

'Unfortunately,' Françoise was saying, 'Lady Elizabeth had to cancel at the last minute. She isn't well. Such a pity.'

'I'm sorry to hear that,' the Prince said. 'It's not serious?'

His English was impeccable, with a faint American accent. He had been educated in the States.

'She's pregnant,' James explained, judging that a bad back wouldn't be considered reason enough to opt out.

The prince smiled. 'Ah, then she is right not to take risks. Travelling by air is bad for women when they are expecting children.'

He passed on, leaving Madeline with James. 'She's lucky,' she said. 'I would love to have a child, but my career makes it impossible. It's so demanding.'

By the look of her, James thought, she'd been getting sore heels upstairs for most of the afternoon. He had tried to phone Elizabeth from his room, but the number was engaged.

'My wife was dying to meet you,' he said. 'She's a tremendous fan. We both loved you in *Twilight World*.'

He'd done his homework. He'd memorized the names of recent plays. If he couldn't get an opportunity with the prince, she would have to be the target. It was important to make friends with her.

Dinner was a long and formal ritual. The prince only drank fruit juice, but for everyone else the wines were as superb as the food. The conversation didn't spark; rich and cultivated though he was, he lacked humour and lightness. He had a brooding personality that only warmed when he looked at Madeline Luchaire. She gave a great performance. James watched the clever nuances of a competent actress with a small talent in a one-woman part. A woman hopelessly in love and lost in admiration for her noble lover. She gazed at him, she deferred, and she flirted in a language that excluded other people. She earns her loot, James decided. She's got that bloody great hawk of a man on a silk rope, but I bet she never puts a foot wrong. She wouldn't dare. And she'll get her red diamonds out of him unless I pull this off. He realized there wouldn't be a chance that night. It was too soon to manoeuvre himself into a private conversation with the prince. Even with Luchaire herself. Above all, it had to be done in seeming innocence, almost a throw-away remark . . .

He fretted at the length of time they stayed in the dining-room, and then he was free at last, the countess didn't follow the English custom, and they all left the table together.

He came up and said, 'Would you mind if I slipped away and telephoned my wife? I tried before dinner, but it was engaged. I want to make sure she's all right.'

'Of course,' Françoise agreed. 'There's a telephone through there.'

He dialled. This time a high-pitched buzz greeted him. Out of order. It couldn't be. He went through to the operator who was surly and obstructive. James snapped back furiously and was finally told that there was a fault on the line. It should be in order by the morning. He hung up, worried and fuming. Liz would be expecting a call from him. He wanted to talk to her, tell her how it was going, say how much he missed her and hoped to get back the next day, if it was possible.

He was alive with excitement. The challenge was there, waiting to be met. His chance to throw the shit back in Arthur Harris's face. He'd cheated him, holding back so his ally Ray Andrews got the glory, and James came back a failure. Sad-eyed, over-cautious Arthur, pushing through an open-ended commitment with the Russians to save his own skin, and destroying James's career in the process. He'd see. He'd learn that Hastings knew how to play outside the rules, too.

The prince went upstairs early. Looks between him and Madeline could have bent spoons. The Wildensteins were elderly and followed suit. The evening was over, and Françoise said they would meet for breakfast beside the pool. If he hadn't brought a costume, she said, he could borrow one. She kept a selection for her guests. The pool was covered and heated at this time of year. She wished him good night, and remembered to ask if he had got through to his wife. He knew she wasn't really interested, so he said simply, 'Yes. Thank you. She sent her regrets.'

Upstairs, on an impulse, he tried the number once more. The maddening whine buzzed in his ear. He banged the phone down and prepared to sleep . . . By the pool in the morning. Informal, casual, a perfect opportunity.

He drifted off very quickly.

Ruth Fraser tidied her desk. She checked that there was enough water in the vase she kept filled with flowers. She liked flowers on her desk. It was an individual touch. Kruger always bought them for her in London. Out-of-season roses, all the year round. They were delivered every week by special order. He was arriving from London at seven. Depending upon what happened at Antibes, it would be their last weekend together. She hadn't made the call to James. She had hardly considered it, even while she listened to Lasalle and registered the name of the clinic. So the wife had miscarried. A dim memory of her own wretched abortion surfaced for a few minutes and was quickly suppressed. There was nothing to be gained by upsetting Hastings. He might even abandon the weekend and rush back to Paris. He couldn't change anything by wrecking his career and putting *her* future in jeopardy. She decided quite calmly that she wasn't going to say anything. It was a chance she had to take. She left the office early, and went back to change before driving to Charles de Gaulle to meet Kruger. She was determined to give him a good time. She owed him that. And she might still need him if James Hastings didn't bring it off.

Elizabeth looked white and drawn; her eyes seemed too big for the gaunt face. She was sitting up and he saw the hopeful look change as she saw him. No word from the husband. Not a call, not a message. Jean Pierre came and sat beside her. He took her hand. It felt cold.

'Don't worry, he's probably flying back right now. How are you feeling?'

'Gutted,' she said. 'Absolutely gutted.' A tear seeped down her cheek. 'Poor little thing,' she repeated.

He took the limp hands in his and held them. 'There are no complications. You're healthy and there's no reason why you can't have another child. You must think of it like that . . . This can happen. My wife lost her first and then went on to have two sons. Please, Elizabeth.'

She wasn't listening. 'The doctor says I can go home tomorrow,' she said. 'Maybe James will be back by then.'

For a moment her mouth twisted as if she was in pain. 'I suppose he couldn't just walk out because of the business. But he could have called me.'

'He will,' Jean Pierre tried to reassure her. 'It may be

difficult to get through. Our telephones are not as reliable as in England.'

'Don't lie to me, Jean Pierre,' she said. 'They're better. He just hasn't got through because he doesn't want to come back. That's what I think. He's disappointed and upset, so he's decided to stay till he's done what he went for. I know him; I know how much his career means to him. And this is so important . . . and you did say I wasn't in danger? After all, looking at it sensibly, there's nothing he could do for me, is there?'

She had stopped crying. She looked dead eyed suddenly, and he had never imagined her being bitter.

'And what will you say if that door opens and he walks in?'

He was doing his best, pleading for James against his own conviction that Elizabeth was right. He had stayed on in the South of France to finish his business commitment. His sense of rage was growing as he sat with her, waiting for the message or the man himself, until it was too late and the nurses told him to go home. They would give Elizabeth a sedative and she could be discharged tomorrow.

Outside her room, Jean Pierre said, 'I will take Madame Hastings home with me. Unless her husband comes back in time.'

In his own apartment he poured a whisky and sat thinking about what to do. Elizabeth had told him the name and address. He had offered to telephone, but she wouldn't let him.

'He knows,' was what she had said. 'It's up to him.'

He sipped his whisky and decided that she was right.

And then he let his imagination run ahead to what the scenario might be in the end.

If he ever fails you, or you need me, he'd said the day he'd told Elizabeth he was in love with her.

He won't, was her reply.

But he had. At a moment of real crisis in her life, at a

287

woman's lowest ebb after the loss of a baby, James Hastings had opted for the business interest and left her vulnerable to another man. If he called, he might shame the bastard into coming back. It might save the marriage. It might leave Elizabeth with a man who didn't know how to cherish her in the real sense of that old-fashioned word. But he did. He loved her and he had been with her when she needed him, just as he promised. Hastings was going to lose her, and he was going to make sure he did. He finished his whisky and went to bed.

'It's so peaceful here,' Madeline Luchaire remarked. She sat close to the edge of the big blue pool, the steam rising from it under a glass roof. Françoise was swimming with Madame Wildenstein. Out of deference to her lover, Luchaire was wearing a long robe. Arabs didn't approve of women exposing their bodies. She had the prince beside her, and James had come to join them after they had eaten breakfast. He had called home as soon as he woke, but the line was still out of order.

'It's lovely, especially the weather. Paris is wet and cold,' James agreed.

'Like London,' the prince remarked. 'You work there, Mr Hastings?'

'Yes,' James answered. 'I'm a director of Diamond Enterprises. We're expanding our Paris office, that's why I'm here for a few months.'

He realized he had the prince's attention.

'Diamonds? That's very interesting. You are the biggest in the industry, aren't you?'

'We are, and I know people call us a monopoly, but we're the best safeguard the trade has, *and* the public. Before we took control of distribution and set up our Central Selling Organization, diamond dealing and retailing was the most unscrupulous and dishonest business in the world. Every man for himself, no stability in prices or quality control.'

'I can see that,' the prince nodded. 'We had the same problems with oil. You have to bring any industry of that importance under responsible control.'

James knew this was his opportunity. He had the complete attention of the prince.

Madeline stood up. Business discussion bored her. 'I think I'll swim.'

The Arab nodded. 'Yes, you swim. I will talk to Mr Hastings. My friend likes to wear diamonds, but she is not interested in the technicalities.' He smiled after her indulgently.

James watched her slip off her robe and slide gracefully into the pool. He leaned forward in the chair.

'You're so right about being a responsible monopoly,' he said. 'And I can tell you, Highness, that, though I'm in it, diamonds are the crookedest commodity in the world; you've no idea the tricks some of the most reputable dealers get up to.'

'I can imagine,' the prince said. 'But not the big men, surely? They have too much to lose by being dishonest.'

'Depends on how much they stand to gain,' James said. 'Do you know there's a set of diamonds which are being offered for sale in Paris at the moment at an astronomical price, and part of them are said to be fakes? I won't tell you the name of the jeweller, but the whole trade knows there's something wrong with these stones, that's why nobody'll touch them. But he'll sell them to a private client.'

The prince's face was quite impassive.

'That's very interesting,' he said. 'What sort of diamonds are these? I thought you couldn't fake diamonds?'

'Normally you can't,' James said. 'But these are fancies – coloured diamonds. They're red. And that's where the faking comes in.'

'Go on,' the prince said. He glanced at the pool for a moment. Luchaire was swimming with the countess and Wildenstein's wife. They were laughing. 'Go on, Mr

Hastings. This is fascinating. How do you mean, that's where the faking comes in?'

'Radiation,' James said. 'This man bought a few genuine red diamonds from the Russians. They're producing one or two now, said to be a fine deep colour. But there weren't enough of them to make into the kind of jewellery that sells for millions of dollars. I think I heard that there were about five red stones in the original lot, two or three of them were quite big, and he re-cut those. So he's made up the rest with ordinary diamonds which have been irradiated to change their colour, and given them a phoney provenance that they belonged to the Tsars. It's a really clever fraud.'

'It is,' the prince agreed. 'I didn't know you could change diamonds by radiation.'

'You can; it was only done as an experiment to see what it would do to a diamond to be put into an atomic reactor. It will turn a yellow stone brown and a bluish or steel-coloured red. The colour's not permanent, though; if you re-cut the stone it comes out to its original colour. Anyway, that's what this man is supposed to have done with these diamonds; taken some of his best ordinary goods and had them irradiated to match the genuine stones.'

There was a long pause.

'He is taking a risk,' the prince said at last. 'Tell me, Mr Hastings, do you think the story is true?'

'I don't know,' James answered. 'I couldn't tell even if I'd seen the diamonds; I'm not an expert in that field. But I take notice of what other dealers say. I should think there's something fishy about them; after all, you just don't find that many red stones all together.'

'No,' the prince said, 'I suppose you don't.' He looked at James. 'I will let you into a secret. I was going to buy those red diamonds. I was going to give them to my friend. They're the Romanovs, aren't they?'

'Yes,' James admitted; he had hesitated for a second.

'Yes, they're the Romanovs. Look, Highness, I had no idea you knew anything about it, or I wouldn't have told you.'

'You mean you would rather I paid millions of dollars for something which was not genuine?'

'No, I mean I wouldn't have repeated what may be a rumour,' James said. 'There's no proof of this.'

'I don't think proof is necessary.' the Arab shrugged. 'What you have said makes sense to me. I'll put it this way to you, Mr Hastings. Would you advise me to buy them?'

'No,' James said, 'I would not.'

'Then I am in your debt. You needn't be embarrassed. When I explain to Madeline she will understand. I'll have to think of something else to give her to make up for the disappointment, but I know she would hate to look a fool; as much as I would hate to be taken for one. Thank you very much. You've saved me a lot of money.'

He stood up. He held out his hand to James. 'I am grateful to you. I'm glad we met. Are you going to swim?'

'I don't think so. I think I'll go and phone my wife again and see how she is.'

James went into the house, into the big, arched room and shut the door. It was all over; he'd done it. The prince wouldn't buy the diamonds now. Breaking faith was an unforgivable sin in Arab ethics. James knew enough about them to know that. The prince would revenge himself on Karakov as a matter of honour. So would Madeline Luchaire. If he'd been tricked into buying the red diamonds, her lover wouldn't have forgiven her either. She'd take care to spread the word round the millionaire jet set, so nobody else would touch them, at any price. He had done it, he said it aloud. He'd got Karakov in the jugular. Whatever Andrews achieved in Moscow, it would cost Diamond Enterprises millions and James himself had disabled their competitor and damaged his reputation for the cost of the air fare to

Nice. He actually laughed at the idea. The world, as he had told Elizabeth, was now their oyster and the pearl inside was the biggest. He reached for the telephone. It was nearly lunchtime. They must have mended the fault by now. He could make an excuse and go home. He couldn't wait to tell her. And then to go and open up the office and fax Julius Heyderman direct in Johannesburg. Arthur Harris could get stuffed. He was now openly Julius's man. When he dialled, the number rang. He could have shouted with relief and exhilaration. He didn't wait when it was answered. He said, 'Liz? Liz darling.'

'No, Monsieur, it's Louise.'

It was the maid.

'Louise? The phone's been out since yesterday. I want to speak to Madame.' He was smiling, brimming over.

'I'm sorry, Monsieur, but she's not here. There was an emergency . . . we must have left the receiver off . . . She was taken to hospital.'

'Hospital? What hospital? What's happened to her?'

He heard himself yelling; he didn't realize he was shouting in English. He had begun to shake. Emergency. Elizabeth and the baby . . . With a great effort he calmed down and spoke French.

'Tell me, Louise. Just tell me, where is she, and is she all right?'

'I don't know, Monsieur. Monsieur Lasalle took her to the hospital in an ambulance. I've heard nothing since I put the telephone back this morning. The doctor will know. I'm so sorry.'

'Yes,' James said. 'Yes, I'll call him. Christ, I can't remember the number . . . Louise, look it up for me, will you. Dr Gaston Fabre, rue de Courcelle . . .'

He kept muttering, come on, come . . . until she found the name and address and the telephone number and repeated it. He hung up and began to dial so frantically, that it was a misdial and he had to start again.

'Monsieur Hastings?' The voice was cold. 'Ah, yes. I'm sorry to say your wife miscarried but she is perfectly well, and has left the clinic this morning. I saw her and said she was fit to go home. She left with Monsieur Lasalle, since you had not returned in time.'

'Returned?' James couldn't believe it. 'How the hell could I return when I didn't know anything about it? Surely to God you or Lasalle could have contacted me?'

'I understood your office was informed,' the tone was openly hostile now. 'Your wife was haemorrhaging and too distressed to give details of where you were staying. I must point out that I am not responsible for anyone but my patient. I do know that she was very traumatized, and your support at this time would have helped her. But if you didn't get the message, then that explains it.'

He didn't actually call James a liar, but the voice conveyed it.

'Just tell me,' James said. 'Just tell me – is she all right?'

'I wouldn't have let her leave if she wasn't. Monsieur Lasalle is looking after her. Goodbye, Monsieur.'

The line cleared. James slammed the receiver down. Lasalle. The good friend and admirer that instinctively he had never trusted. He hadn't taken her back to their own apartment. He had taken her away from James.

When Françoise saw him come out, she smiled and said, 'Lunch is in half an hour. This afternoon I hope you can amuse yourselves for a little while. We're going to great friends of mine for drinks and then a few more friends are coming to dinner . . . My dear James, you don't look well . . . Is anything the matter?'

He was grey faced, his expression was simply distraught. She was shocked and came close to him. She was a kind-hearted woman and she rather liked him.

'What is it?'

'My wife,' he managed to say it calmly. 'My wife is in hospital. I must get back to Paris. I must call the airport—'

'Leave it to me,' she said firmly. 'You get ready and Paco will drive you to Nice. I am so very sorry. I do hope she will be all right. And the baby.'

'That's gone,' he said, and his voice cracked. 'She lost it.'

He turned and sped up the stairs to throw his clothes into the case.

There was no flight for three hours, Françoise told him.

'I'll charter,' he said. 'I must get home. Say goodbye to everyone, will you. Sorry, but I'll just go right to the airport and fix something.'

The cost of a small private jet was mind bending. James didn't even hesitate. The doctor's chill approach screamed at him during the flight. *She was very traumatized . . . your support would have helped . . .* But he hadn't known, he cried out. No-one had contacted him. His office had been told . . . Who had told them . . . or said they had?

Elizabeth had called Lasalle for help. While he was in the villa, trying to ring through, the phone was off, unadjusted in the panic that must have taken place.

Haemorrhaging, the doctor said. He felt sick at the picture in his imagination. Why had nobody called him that morning, at the villa? She must have recovered by then, or she couldn't have been discharged. She knew where he was. Why didn't she contact him? He knew the answer. Because he knew Elizabeth. She thought he had been told and was ignoring it because he wanted to get his business deal done first. He knew her pride and her priorities.

And that bastard had taken advantage of the situation to move in on her, take over what was James's role, and move her out of James's reach. He probably never called the office; nobody would have dared withhold such a message from him. No, Lasalle must have lied, hoping to turn his wife against him. To get her for himself.

And she had gone with him. She wasn't to blame. He

thought of her in misery and realized how hurt, how abandoned she must have felt. And be feeling still. No word, nothing. Just silence while she suffered and their child died. But not for long. He would land in twenty minutes. He knew where Jean Pierre Lasalle lived. That night he would have Elizabeth back and safe with him. With all the terrible misunderstandings cleared away.

The door was opened by Lasalle's housekeeper. He pushed his way past her into the hall. He stopped. The place had an empty feel to it.

'Where are they?' James demanded. 'Where's my wife?'

'Monsieur has gone to Normandy. He told me he would be away for some time. I know nothing about any lady, Monsieur.'

James said slowly, 'Where in Normandy?'

'He has a château outside Caen. I can write down the address and telephone if it's urgent.'

'Thank you,' James said. 'It is urgent.'

'Elizabeth,' Jean Pierre said gently. 'He's on the telephone. Do you want to talk to him?'

'No,' she said. 'I don't.'

'He says he is coming down tonight . . . he is being very abusive, I don't think you should see him, but I will do what you want.'

'I don't want to talk to him or see him,' she said slowly. 'I want some time and some space. Tell him to leave me alone, Jean Pierre. Don't let him come down here. I won't see him if he does. Make sure he understands that.'

'I'll tell him,' he promised.

'Elizabeth won't talk to you and she doesn't want to see you,' he said. 'She says to leave her alone. If you have any decency, you'll do what she asks. If you abuse me like that I shall hang up on you. I suppose you brought off your big business *coup*, so you thought you could come home and talk her round? You shit, Hastings. You've lost her, and you deserve to; you try coming here and upsetting her, I'll call the police. Go back to your business.'

He banged down on James. He went back to Elizabeth. She was crying. He put his arms round her.

'My darling,' he said softly. 'Don't, don't cry like that. He isn't worth it. You're safe here with me. I'm going to look after you. I love you. I'll do anything to make up to you for all this.'

She let him hold her. It was as if the tears were shed by someone else. She felt so dead, so wounded inside. He was kind and he was trying so hard to help her and protect her. He talked about loving her and she hadn't the heart or energy to stop him. James had come back. He wanted to see her, to talk her round, to exploit her love for him so she would forgive him for putting her last in the order of his life. She knew how convincing he would be. How he'd plead, and argue and coax till she ended up by being sorry for him instead of angry. But she wouldn't let him. She thought while Jean Pierre's arms were holding her, I want time to mourn my baby. At this moment I don't think I can ever forgive him for not being with me. Whatever the reason, whatever the excuse, I don't care. I can't cope with James as of now. I may never be able to; I don't know.

She said, 'I don't know what I would have done without you. I'd better call my parents tomorrow. They're planning to come over. I can't face it tonight.'

'You don't have to face anything,' he answered. 'I will take care of everything. I will speak to your parents if you like. Just leave it to me. And now I think you should take your sleeping pill and get a good night's rest. Tomorrow you'll begin to heal. The Normandy air is famous. You'll sleep well.'

*　　*　　*

The phone was ringing. There was a glass of neat brandy beside his chair. In his eagerness to get to the phone, James knocked it over.

'Liz?'

It was David Wasserman. 'I couldn't wait. I've been sitting here hoping you'd call . . . How'd it go? James?'

'Fine,' James said. 'I screwed up the sale . . . My wife lost the baby while I was away, and I think she's left me. Otherwise, it was a big success.'

'I don't believe it,' Wasserman said; he hissed at Clara to be quiet. She was by his elbow, trying to listen in. 'I don't believe it. What can I say? Are you alone there? You want me to come over?'

'No thanks. Don't worry about me.'

'Listen,' Wasserman was concerned, 'you don't sound too good. You need a friend. I'm on my way.'

'No,' James repeated. 'I'm pissed and I'm going to bed. I'll be in the office around eight Monday morning. I have to check on something. If you want details, come there. And thanks for offering, but don't worry about me.' He repeated himself. 'I'll get her back.'

'Well?' Clara demanded. 'So, what happened? What went wrong?'

'With the business? Nothing. Between us, we've shafted Ivan. But he says his wife had a miscarriage and she's left him. He sounded stewed to the eyeballs.'

'Oh,' Clara said. 'Well, if she has left him, it's no bad thing . . . So she loses a baby. These things happen. Does she have to make a drama out of it? He needs a wife that understands him, someone to be there for him. Don't ask me to be sorry about it.'

'I'm not,' her husband said curtly. 'I'll go and see him at the office on Monday morning. Maybe there's something I can do to help . . .'

James finished the brandy. He poured another and sat close to the telephone. She must be asleep by now, he decided. Asleep in Lasalle's house in Normandy. She wouldn't call him now. He didn't go to bed, he dozed in the chair and woke bug eyed with a hangover just after six o'clock. He showered and swallowed some pain-killers. He forced himself to eat breakfast and drink coffee. He watched the dawn come up over the rooftops of the city, and opened the balcony windows for fresh air. The dome of Les Invalides, Napoleon's massive tomb, was briefly touched with red and gold as the sun came up.

Your office was informed. The doctor's words beat in his head like a metronome. *Your office was informed.* And Lasalle's bitter accusation followed on. *I suppose you brought off your big business* coup *so you thought you could come home and talk her round . . .*

Standing on the narrow ledge in the chill wind coming off the Seine below, James realized that losing control was not the way to reach Elizabeth. She believed he had abandoned her, that at the crisis point he had put his career before his responsibility to her. However mistaken and unfair, he had to accept that and prove to her that she was wrong. There had never been such a need for self-control and cool thinking in his life, if he wasn't going to lose everything that really mattered.

The office was open by seven-thirty. He walked through, nodded to the two secretaries in the outer complex and went into his private office. Ruth Fraser didn't get in till after eight. He buzzed through to the switchboard. 'I want a record of any calls that came through for me after midday on Friday.'

'There's a note of them on your desk,' he was told. 'I put them there myself.'

He looked. There was a list. Half a dozen calls, all listed with time and reference. All business. No record of anything else. Nothing.

The door opened and David Wasserman said, 'James,

my boy – how are you? We've been worried sick, you sounded so bad last night.'

'Hello, David. Yes, I was,' he admitted. 'But I'm in control now. Thanks for your concern. Sit down.'

He could imagine how sympathetic Clara had been towards Elizabeth. Wasserman thought he looked dreadful, as if he hadn't slept at all. But he said he was in control, and he was. Almost dangerously pent up.

'First things first,' James said. 'The Saudi swallowed our story. He'll never buy anything from Karakov again. And he won't be able to sell those red diamonds anywhere in the world after they've finished bad mouthing him. You don't cross an Arab and get away with it. Luchaire will be so disappointed she'll spread the word everywhere. So we have the old bastard by the short and curlies. That was a great idea of yours.'

He didn't sound enthusiastic.

'But you made it work,' Wasserman pointed out. 'Congratulations. It was a lovely piece of business. You should fax Heyderman right away. And London. This gives them more muscle in the Moscow negotiations.'

James said coldly, 'I'm not giving them anything. I'll help Harris as much as he helped me. I've already drafted a fax for Heyderman. Here, read it.'

After he'd looked through it, Wasserman said, 'You've given me a lot of credit, James. Very generous of you. But you must let London know. I admit Arthur tried to piss on you, but he's still the boss.'

'He won't be for long if I can help it,' James said. 'Why don't *you* fax him, or call him? I've got other things to do as soon as I send this to Johannesburg.' He paused. 'Better still, have a private word with Reece as well. If I've blown your trumpet, you can blow mine.'

Wasserman nodded . . . Dangerous was the word. Whatever had happened in his personal life, Hastings was out for blood. 'Sure,' he said. 'Everything gets to Julius through that little creep. You have him on your side, you're on your way. I'm so sorry about your wife and child. You want to talk about it? Is there anything I can do to help?'

'Nothing,' James answered.

'You want to tell me why she left? James, listen. I'm old enough to be your father. We never had a family, Clara and me, so I feel for you. I really do. You can talk to me.'

James shook his head. 'It won't help, David. She thinks I stayed to get my business finished and left her to go through it on her own. It's that simple. Someone was supposed to call here and leave a message, but they never did. There's no record, just business calls.'

David Wasserman pulled a wry face. 'So you'll have to convince her,' he said. 'She'll listen. Give her time to get over it. It's a big shock, losing a child. Just give her time.'

'Time is what scares me,' he said slowly. 'You don't really know my wife. There are some things she'd never forgive. But thanks anyway.'

'Well,' Wasserman heaved himself slowly out of the chair. He was getting stiff. His age was showing. 'Well, I'm sure it'll work out. Now why don't you come and have dinner with us tonight? And we won't talk about it. Clara wants a blow-by-blow account of the weekend, she lives for the business. Eight o'clock at the hotel?'

'I'll let you know,' James promised.

When Wasserman was gone he buzzed Ruth's office. 'I'm back,' he said. 'Come in, will you?'

She was so quick, she must have been poised, waiting. 'What happened? Did you get what you wanted?'

She hadn't remembered to say good-morning, or observe the ritual between boss and secretary. She hadn't been told the details. Just that he and Wasserman had an idea that could wreck the sale of the red diamonds. She looked at him, bright eyed with anticipation. The predator about to leap on its prey.

He said, 'Don't worry. You picked the winning side.'

'Oh.' She sounded breathless. 'Oh, congratulations. Can you tell me about it?'

'No,' he said. 'Better not. But that old sod won't be selling any diamonds on commission for the Russians. He won't be selling much for quite a spell. Ruth, did you get a message about my wife on Friday?'

She had been preparing herself for this. Lasalle's call had come through to her from the switchboard. She hadn't noted it.

'No,' she said. 'Why? I thought she was with you. Is something wrong?'

He wasn't going to discuss it with her. He didn't answer; he picked up the fax and said, 'Get this faxed through to Heyderman, will you please. Wasserman's handling London.'

'Yes,' she was reading it at speed. 'My God, you must feel like celebrating. I know I do.'

She flashed the white sexy smile at him. He remembered what he owed her.

'Wouldn't be possible without you. I haven't forgotten. I'm going out for the rest of the day. I'll call in sometime to check on my calls, you deal with everything till I get back tomorrow.'

'Can I reach you if I need to?'

'No. I'll be moving around. See you tomorrow, Ruth.'

She came a little closer to him. Her cheeks were glowing as if she had just made love. 'I'll bring the champagne for us tomorrow. If you don't mind?'

He didn't answer. He just walked out of the office.

He was upset, she had expected that. But, so upset that he didn't seem to care about what he'd achieved? That surprised her. There was no sense of triumph, no euphoria. Just a grim detachment. He hadn't smiled or responded to her enthusiasm. He almost seemed to resent it. Her offer of champagne to celebrate had been rebuffed by silence. To hell with him, she thought. So he was moping about the miscarriage. That wasn't going to spoil it for her. She'd send the fax to Johannesburg immediately, ignoring the time difference. Wasserman might be handling London for him, but she was going to put in a personal call to Reece and give him the news. What better way to remind him of her part in it? She moved behind James's desk and perched in his chair. It felt comfortable. She made the call to London on his telephone.

11

'I told you not to come here,' Jean Pierre said. 'I warned you, Hastings.'

They were standing in the hall of the château. Lasalle stood squared up to him, glaring.

James said, 'I know, and I'm not here to upset anyone. I just want to see my wife. If she says no, I'll go. Will you tell her I'm here?'

They were of a height and a weight, but not an age. If Lasalle lost his temper, and it looked as if he might, James didn't want to hit him. He turned away, avoiding a physical confrontation.

'She has a right to know I'm here,' he stated.

'She has a right to get well without you causing any more trauma,' Lasalle snapped back at him. 'Haven't you hurt her enough?'

'I'm not going to argue with you,' James said. He had made up his mind to be calm on the way down. 'You've been very good to her, and I'm grateful.'

'I love her,' Jean Pierre said. 'When she's got rid of you, I want to marry her.'

It took the last of James's self-control, but he managed to say, 'Just let her know that I'm here. That's all.'

There was a moment's hesitation, and then Jean Pierre swung away from him with an exclamation and went through a door leading off the hall.

It seemed a long wait. There was an old French Cartel clock on the wall above his head, and it ticked like a bird scarer, minute after minute. The hall was cold. Stone floors, not much central heating. He made observations just to occupy his mind and stop himself jumping up and bursting through that closed door. It opened on a last explosive tick of that damned clock, and James was on his feet.

Lasalle came out and said, 'Elizabeth will see you. But only for a few minutes and with the door open. If I hear any raised voices—'

'You won't,' James said curtly, and walked past him.

He was shocked when he saw her, she looked so thin and drawn. The bloom and beauty had gone. She was sitting on a sofa by a big log fire and the room was as warm as the hall had been cold.

'Liz,' he said, and came to her. 'Oh Liz, darling . . .'

He sank down beside her and burst into tears. In all the years Elizabeth had never seen him cry. She said in a low voice, 'Don't do that, James, please. Otherwise I'll start. I promised Jean Pierre I'd be calm.'

'Yes,' he said. 'Yes of course. I'm sorry. I won't make a scene. I won't say anything to upset you. But please, can we just talk for a minute?'

'I don't know what there is to say,' she said. 'Everything's gone wrong for us, that's all. The trouble is, I can't really feel anything. I'm numb. How did your weekend go?'

'Oh don't,' he begged. 'Don't say that. Liz, I didn't know. I never got a message about anything. I couldn't even get through to the flat because someone left the phone off the hook!'

'There was a bit of a panic,' she admitted. 'I asked you about the weekend because I know how important it was to you . . . I wasn't trying to score a point. I lied about putting my back out. I was due to go to the clinic, anyway, but I thought you'd cancel everything and come home, and it was probably a false alarm. I did know how much it mattered to you.'

He looked at her. He reached over, surprised at his own tentativeness, and took her hand. It was limp, returning no pressure. 'This isn't you,' he said, 'looking at me like that and talking like this. You should have told me. Of *course* I'd have chucked the bloody weekend.' And then, because he couldn't help himself, 'It was my child, too.'

'Yes,' Elizabeth said. 'I know you wanted it, I'm so sorry.'

He wasn't getting through, and he knew it. He clutched at her hand in desperation and felt her resistance. 'That doesn't matter. Nothing matters but what's happening to us. Liz, I can't bear this, you're the only thing I care about in the world. If I lose you, I've lost everything. I didn't know – I didn't know anything was wrong! For Christ's sake, what kind of a man do you think I am?'

'I'm not sure,' she said slowly. 'I'd like to believe you, James. But I can't quite. I've been thinking ever since it happened. You know, from the day I married you, I've done what you wanted. I dropped things I liked doing because they didn't interest you. I even stopped seeing so much of my family because I knew it was a strain for you. I mixed with people I didn't like much myself, because they were your friends and useful to you . . . I uprooted and came over here, and gave up my big chance to do the Lord Chancellor's job, just because I put you and your career ahead of anything I wanted—'

'Liz,' he interrupted. 'Liz, what are you talking about? You told me you didn't get it.'

'I lied,' she said quietly. 'I turned the commission down and came here with you instead. Oh, I didn't *mind*, James, it was my choice. I had my priorities right. You needed me here. I let you use me socially because it was all part of your business. You knew how much I hated doing it. How much I've always hated that sort of ghastly snobbery. But I went along with it because I loved you so much and I believed you loved me the same. But you didn't, did you? Not when it came to the bottom line.

That's the trouble. I can't get rid of the doubt.'

He said slowly, 'What can I say to all this? I'm sorry? I didn't know? I thought you were happy, that we had everything going for us. All right, I was selfish, I didn't think enough about you and what you were giving up all the time. I'll change. That's a promise I'm making to you now, this minute. If you give me another chance, and believe me, it'll be what *you* want. We can work it out together. As for not loving you . . . Oh Christ, Liz, what does it look like?'

'It looks like you want me to come back and start again,' she answered. Suddenly she softened, as if she pitied him. 'I don't know if I can do that now. My mother's coming over at the end of the week. I'm going down to Freemantle for a while.'

Freemantle, the big house in its parkland, where he had always felt so ill at ease.

'Don't,' he said, quickly. 'Don't cut yourself off. Go home. I'll be back soon, I'm finished with this bloody place. All right, I won't stay at the house if you don't want me to, but don't go to Freemantle.' He covered his face in his hands. 'We'll never get back together if you do.' She heard him say in a muffled voice, close to breaking again. 'Are you going to leave me for that bastard? He said you were . . .'

He felt Elizabeth touch him on the arm and turned to her. She looked so sad. 'No,' she said. 'He'd like me to, but no. I'm going home, James, to my own home, not London. I need space and time to sort myself out. I won't throw our marriage away, but I can't promise anything. I do want you to leave me alone till I've made up my mind. Will you do that?'

'Yes,' he said. 'If that's what you want. But, Liz, how long?'

'I don't know that either,' she said. 'James, I'm sorry, but would you go now, please? I can't take any more at the moment.'

He stood up. He bent down and kissed her on the forehead.

'I'll wait,' he said. 'However long it takes, I'm going to get you back.'

He walked out into the hall past Lasalle; for a moment their eyes locked in an exchange of cold antagonism. 'I may not win,' James said quietly, 'but you've lost.'

He drove back to Paris and his office. That night he went to dinner with the Wassermans. When they opened champagne he drank it. His life was on hold. There was only Diamond Enterprises left.

Julius Heyderman put down the fax from Paris and laughed out loud. Hastings had done it. He'd cut the legs off Karakov. No sale of the red diamonds, no foreign currency for the Russian government. Proof positive that there was only one reliable outlet for their stones in the world market, and that was Diamond Enterprises. They were on the point of signing up with London, and this would seal the package. He was in such a good mood he called Sylvia and told her to get some cronies round for dinner. And start setting up some dates for them in London. Stella was getting back to normal. The bills for clothes and luxuries and the suite at the Dorchester proved that. He didn't care. They'd go to London and all fly home together. The first family Christmas in God knows how many years. Then, when all the dust had settled, he would set about levering Arthur Harris out at the March Board meeting. He was a truly happy man.

'Ray,' Arthur said warmly, 'come in, come in. What can I do for you?'

When he came back from Moscow Andrews had noticed the change in Arthur Harris. He had lost that air of sadness, that was, in fact, deceptive, because he was as clever and as ruthless in his way as Julius Heyderman. Now he looked confident, almost rosy cheeked. He beamed his smile at Andrews. The documents were ready, the Russian representative was scheduled to fly into London for the signing in less than ten days. The only sour note in the symphony of success was James Hastings' nasty *coup* in Paris. Harris had admired the result. Ethics were one thing and big corporate ethics, with hundreds of millions at risk, had to be something different. But nothing outshone Andrews' achievements.

'I've had a fax from Moscow,' Ray said. He was frowning, looking slightly puzzled. 'Can't make it out. They want me to fly back as soon as possible. No explanation.'

'Get on to your friend Borisov,' Arthur suggested. 'Find out what's the problem. Some little hitch, I expect. You can probably sort it out on the telephone.' He went on smiling confidently at Andrews.

'I tried,' Ray explained. 'He was out of the city till tomorrow. He's expecting to see me there; they gave me an appointment. I think I'd better go.'

'Well,' Arthur said, 'since everything's so close to signature, you might as well. We don't want a last-minute delay on some little detail at this stage.'

'I'm sorry, Sue,' Ray said later as he packed. 'It's just a bloody nuisance having to go off at the last minute. But I shouldn't be away more than a couple of days. We're missing the Morrises' anniversary party, too.'

Susan handed him some clean shirts. 'Can't be helped. I'll go anyway. They are our oldest friends. Ray, why do you think they've asked you to go back?'

'I don't know,' he said, closing the case. 'Just some bureaucratic nit-pick, I expect.' He kissed her. 'Bye, darling, sorry to bugger up tonight. We'll make it up to Jo and Ian when I get back.'

'It's all going so smoothly,' Reece said, 'I've taken a week off. You've had this horrible cold so long a break will do you good. Do us both good. I've booked into the Royal Crescent at Bath. It's a really top hotel, and there's plenty to do and see, and a good playhouse. We won't stint ourselves.'

Joy looked up at him and sniffed. She had a reddened nose and she looked sallow and unwell. He was so good, so thoughtful. She smiled up at him, dabbing at her sore nose with a handkerchief. The waste basket beside her was full of used tissues.

'Lovely,' she said. 'When do we go?'

'Next week,' Reece assured her. 'They can tear each other to pieces while I'm away.'

'What about her?' Joy never used Stella's name if she could help it. She waited, hoping for bad news.

'Still buying up London,' he retorted. 'Looking up friends of Mr Julius. Entertaining them at the hotel. I can't believe it's going to last. But she's not been drunk so far.'

He had a contact at the hotel who reported to him for a consideration. It wasn't financial, that wouldn't be tolerated. But there was a risk of scandal with Miss Heyderman, and he was acting in their best interests as well as hers, by keeping track of her.

Joy said nothing; she was disappointed. They changed the subject and made plans for their stay in Bath.

Stella was reading Miller's report from Johannesburg. It was detailed, and she skipped impatiently through the dates of birth, addresses, education. The image was grindingly dull. A shopkeeper, married to an Afrikaans farmer's daughter, two dreary children brought up over a grocery shop. She had started smoking heavily; she hadn't touched alcohol and cigarettes helped to keep her calm. What interested her was Reece's rise in Diamond Enterprises. From a low-paid position as an accounting clerk, he had been promoted suddenly. Speculation was all they had to go on, but he was supposed to have informed on a colleague who had links with the illicit diamond mining operation that drained millions of dollars in stolen goods. The man had been caught and convicted as a result of Reece's detective work. Julius Heyderman had picked him out and promoted him into the main office. A troubleshooter, a fixer. A spy on his own kind. Heart and soul the Chairman's man. It was Reece who arranged for Jacob Yakumi to get out of South Africa because he had a powerful contact in the police; Reece who dealt with the London solicitors in control of her finances. Reece was reputed to have contacts among the gangs and informers in Johannesburg; he had a big budget and the authority to use it.

Now she was reading very carefully, the cigarette smouldered in the ashtray at her elbow. On Yakumi's return to South Africa, Reece had been in the country. He was often in London for a few months' stint. No doubt keeping tabs on Arthur, she thought, but not then. He wasn't even absent on a short trip from the time her husband went back to Soweto till he was murdered. Black people didn't talk to white investigators, but Miller's associates had blacks and coloureds on their payroll. They talked of rumours of a white man with money being involved in the killing, someone connected with the diamond industry. Yakumi was anti-capitalist and a dangerous new voice in the emerging forum of the country's government. She threw the file aside. Stubbed out the butt of the cigarette and lit another. What none of them knew was the real motive: his marriage to Heyderman's daughter; he had been murdered to stop that ever being made public. She inhaled and then reached for the telephone.

'Mr Miller, please. Miss Heyderman.'

'You got the report,' Miller said. 'I think they did a very good job. He sounds an extremely shady customer. Not that there's any proof of anything.'

'No,' Stella agreed. 'There wouldn't be. He doesn't

operate like that. I think you've probably done as much as you can. Send me a bill, please.'

Miller hesitated. 'Well, I have a man up in Bath at the moment,' he explained. 'Reece is there, staying at the Royal Crescent. He's booked in under the name of Ryan. Do you want me to call my man off the case?'

The Royal Crescent. What was the little swine up to, staying at a place like that?

'There's a woman with him,' Miller added. 'Maybe that's why he's using a phoney name. I sent a man down there when he left London. They travelled together.'

'Let me know what you find out,' Stella said. 'Forget what I said about cancelling. Keep on to him.'

She had always thought of Reece as a sexless creature, like an earthworm, without sexual organs. Living it up with a woman at the grandest hotel in the West Country . . .

'Jacob love,' she said out loud, 'don't you worry. I'll get that bastard if it's the last thing I ever do. And when I do, I'll nail my father, too.'

Later that afternoon she took a call from Julius. He was in good spirits, making plans for the London trip. He asked how she was and she said exactly what he wanted to hear. She was fine, glad to be back in her own environment; she'd gone to lunch with their English friends who wanted to know all about Peru. She made him laugh describing how she'd dodged the questions. 'I told them it was full of Indians and snakes, and that satisfied them.' He was looking forward to the trip, and so was Sylvia. He planned a big party, and, of course, he wanted her to be there. She said she wouldn't miss it for anything. When they rang off, she ran herself a bath and lay in it and cried with hatred for him, and with the need for this love he was showing her for the first time. But that wouldn't protect him when the time came. She would destroy him even though she knew it would destroy herself. She owed it to Jacob.

*   *   *

'I'm not going to lose you,' Jean Pierre said. He put his arms round Elizabeth. 'I shall come to England.' And then, looking down at her he asked the question for the last time. 'Are you sure you want to go, my darling? You don't have to run away from me.'

'I'm not running away,' Elizabeth said. 'I know that's no solution. But I can't think clearly yet, and I need a complete break while I make my mind up what to do.'

'You won't go back to him,' he insisted. 'I swear to you before God, I spoke to his office and told them to get into contact with him. I told the girl what had happened, and she promised to call him immediately. He's lying.'

'Yes,' she said slowly, 'I think he is. It's just whether I can come to terms with it, Jean Pierre. How can I ever thank you for all you've done for me?'

'By keeping in touch,' he said. 'Let me come and see you before long. Remember I am always there for you. I love you, Elizabeth. Will you kiss me goodbye?'

'Yes.' Elizabeth reached up and put her arms round his neck. She blinked back tears. 'I don't deserve you.'

He kissed her like a lover and she let him.

On the way to the airport, Jill Fairfax turned to her. 'You'll be all right when you get home to Freemantle. It's a great place to lick wounds. Your father and I found that after Nick was killed. Just walking round the park and being at peace makes you feel better. You'll get over this, Lizzie, and I promise we won't try to influence you, whatever you decide to do. We just want to look after you till you're fit again.'

Her restraint had surprised Elizabeth. There were no fulminations against James, just a firm approach to bringing her back home. She had been charming and grateful to Jean Pierre, but Elizabeth sensed a reserve. She said, looking out of the car window, 'It was difficult saying goodbye to him, Mum. I was quite upset.'

'That's because you'd cry about anything at the moment,' Jill said. 'And he's been very kind and supportive.'

'He's in love with me,' was the answer.

'Well, that's obvious! Of course he is . . . There'll be plenty of time to see that in proportion after you've come back to normal.' She slowed for a signpost, then took the route to the small airport. In love. She'd realized that as soon as she saw Jean Pierre Lasalle with her daughter. She had imagined an elderly Frenchman, a fatherly friend who had come to Elizabeth's rescue. There was nothing paternal about the very attractive middle-aged man who met her at the door of the château. If she was reserved with him, he was equally distant with her. He didn't want her to take Elizabeth away, and he conveyed that politely enough. His resistance prompted her to book a flight home earlier than planned. Lizzie, she felt, needed a break from the whole set-up, especially from a man smothering her with love and attention after the shock of a miscarriage and the apparently callous behaviour of her husband. The word 'apparent' crept in, and she was surprised at herself. She had never liked or trusted James to make Lizzie happy. If the question had been put to her before it happened – Would he let his wife down at some point? – she would have said most likely, Yes. But she had a doubt about this, and it niggled. She would see the situation in better proportion when she was home and could talk it over with her husband. She said in her brisk way, 'Nearly there now. Pop's meeting us at Heathrow and we'll all drive down together. And I've got a super new Labrador puppy. I can't wait to show her to you.' She put a hand on Elizabeth's knee. 'You've got guts, Lizzie. You're like Nick. I'm not worried about you.'

David Wasserman had invited James to lunch. They went to a brasserie close by James's office; Wasserman couldn't digest a heavy lunch and he found the French food too rich. James had no appetite anyway and didn't want to waste time outside his office. The old man looked very lively as he greeted James. He could hardly wait to tell him the news while they ordered.

'It's all over the trade that Karakov's lost the sale of his diamonds,' he reported. 'There's a rumour he's had a row with Luchaire and he's threatening to sue because he held the jewellery for her on a promise of purchase.'

He grinned like a mischievous old gnome.

'She says, "Go ahead, sue, and she'll expose you as a cheat and a faker!" I tell you, he nearly had a heart attack after that letter from her lawyers. Now he's threatening to claim millions of dollars for defamation and damage to his business reputation . . . My boy, there hasn't been a scandal like this in the trade for years! We're all loving it. Laura's busting a gut to stop him making a fool of himself and going to court. I heard from a very good source that Luchaire's Arab went to Cartier and bought a ruby-and-diamond necklace for two million dollars, and then very expensive pieces from Andrew Grima and Boucheron, just to make it up to her. I passed the information on to Mirkovitch, just as a piece of in-trade gossip. A friendly call to Moscow . . .' He chuckled again. 'I could hear him choking. James, you're a real operator! I guess you're anxious to get back home?'

He knew Elizabeth was in England. When he asked if that meant good news, James had said, 'Not particularly,' and changed the subject. Wasserman was wise and he didn't mention it again. There was a very deep wound there, he judged, and it was filling up with bitterness.

He went on, 'You plan to see Ivan again, or shall I take up the negotiations? That would free you to close up here and go back to London. I'd be glad to do it if you want.'

He was longing for the chance, as James recognized. Nothing would please him more than to sit round and do some hard trading with Ivan Karakov.

'I think I'll tie up the situation personally,' he said. 'And I think I know the way to do it. I'd appreciate your advice, David.'

Wasserman hid his disappointment. 'Just ask,' he said.

He listened and he shook his head in admiration. 'You're a genius. That's going for the jugular. I wish I could be there to see it.'

'You will be,' James promised. 'I'm passing the next stage to you. The most difficult part, but if I'm a genius, you're the master. And, I think you'll enjoy it.'

He smiled at Wasserman. As David told Clara afterwards, it was the first time he'd seen Hastings smile since it all happened. And it wasn't a nice sight.

'Won't you sit down, Mr Hastings. Can I offer you a drink?'

'No thank you, Mrs Karakov.' He chose the upright Louis XV chair opposite her. It was three o'clock in the afternoon and when he telephoned the day before, she'd given him the appointment at once. David was right; she was more than half the business and three-quarters of the brains. Her blond hair was dressed up high, drawn back from her ears, and a row of plump, glistening pearls were round her neck. Her eyes were as hard as two black stones. He wasn't bothered by the stare. Even Clara Wasserman admitted that he had changed very much since he had lost his wife. He was a very hard man now.

'Why do you want to see me particularly, Mr Hastings? I didn't tell my husband because you said you wanted to have a private talk with me, but I must say I've been very curious about it. What do you have in mind?'

'Business,' he said. 'The business between Karakov International and Diamond Enterprises. We've been buggered about long enough, Mrs Karakov. We want this dispute settled, once and for all.'

She didn't flicker an eyelash. She had heard tough talk before and she could give it back; and she would, with pleasure. He had irritated her when they first met: he had such an unconsciously superior air. She said very calmly, 'We've had enough of it too, Mr Hastings. I think Ivan's made our attitude plain to you? We're just not satisfied with the treatment we've been getting from you. If you want to get the thing settled, then give us what we ask. It's quite simple.'

'What makes you think you're in a position to insist on any terms at all?'

She hadn't expected that. She paused and crossed her legs and pulled down the grey Chanel skirt over her knees. They were bony and they showed her age.

'You're being rude, Mr Hastings. Don't you think you should have asked to see my husband if you meant to behave like this?'

'No,' James snapped. 'I don't. At the moment, your husband is in no condition to talk business with anyone. He's suffered a reverse, I hear. I thought that what I had to say was best said to you. You can pass the message on.'

'Let's hear it, then,' she said. Her voice was soft and cooing, and it made the words very insulting. 'I may pass it on, or I may not. It depends on what you have to say.'

'Just this. Your husband was trying to do a deal with the Russians behind our backs. We've known all about it, and we did nothing because these things have happened before, and they usually die out. But unfortunately, the Russians got you really involved. So we had to take measures. Those measures have been effective. We had to teach your husband a lesson. That lesson, Mrs Karakov, was the loss of a ten-million-dollar sale to Prince Abdullah Bin Saladin. I hope you'll take it to heart.'

She got up out of the chair in a single movement. Under

the make-up her face turned white. 'What do you mean, a lesson? What do you know about the sale?'

He looked up at her. He said, 'You've lost ten million dollars and your firm has suffered a loss in reputation that can't be counted. That, Mrs Karakov, is just the beginning if you go on fighting us. We'll break you into very small pieces. Tell your husband that. Tell him to stop arsing around. His agreement with us is due for renewal this month. Tell him to get in touch with David Wasserman and get it fixed up. On the same terms, Mrs Karakov. In the meantime, we shan't supply you or any agent likely to sell to you with a single stone. Remember what we were able to do about those Russian diamonds, if you don't think we can do it.'

He walked out of the room and the apartment without waiting to hear her answer.

'Lizzie, it's the second time he's rung up today. Don't you think you ought to speak to him?' Elizabeth's father looked at her. 'He's back in London, you can't expect to avoid him indefinitely. Flowers, letters, telephone calls. I'm beginning to feel sorry for the poor devil, and I never thought I would.'

'I know you are,' she said. 'Mum is too. I thought you'd both be quite different. It's not as if you ever liked him.'

'That,' her father said, 'has nothing to do with it. What we're concerned about is your happiness. You're fine physically, you're a perfectly healthy girl, but you're utterly miserable and we don't like to see it. You've no energy, no interest in life, and it seems to me you're punishing yourself as much as James. I'm not sure I believe that chap Lasalle. How do you know he ever left such a message?'

'Because he told me and I do believe him,' Elizabeth said. 'Would you lie about something like that, Pop?' she challenged him.

He hesitated. 'I might,' he said. 'When I was in love with your mother I'd have done any dirty trick to get her. All's fair in love and war. I just don't think you should condemn your husband on his say-so. He asked to see me, by the way. I said I'd meet him. I hope you don't mind, Lizzie. I don't want us taking sides. If you go back together, he'd never forgive us, remember that.'

'I don't think it's very likely,' she said slowly. 'I feel very sorry for him, but that's all.'

He looked hard at her. 'Are you saying you don't love him any more? Are you really saying that?'

She shook her head. 'No. I do love him, that's what hurts so much. But I can't trust him, Pop, and I can't live with that. You see him if you want to, but don't raise any hopes. I'm going for a walk.'

When she had gone out, Jill Fairfax came in. 'Well, what did she say?'

'Much the same as she says to you,' he answered. 'I can't help feeling she's going to regret this later. She still loves the bloody man, that's the trouble. And I must say he's taken enough stick about this and still come back for more. I told her I'd meet him, but I'm not sure how much good it'll do.'

'There was a letter from that Frenchman,' his wife said. 'I saw it in the post this morning. Now that would be a disaster. He's years older than Liz, and it'd just be on the rebound. I very nearly tore it up.'

'Next time,' he said, 'put it in the bin. I don't like the sound of him. Never liked the French, anyway. Jill, try not to worry. You said yourself girls get very mixed up emotionally after a miscarriage. I'll see if I can talk James into being patient a bit longer. I'd better be off, we've got a Council meeting at two-thirty.'

Ray Andrews went up in the lift to Borisov's office. He'd had a good flight over and he was quite looking forward to seeing the Russian. A genuine friendship had grown up between them over the long period of negotiations.

He went into the outer office, and the secretary nodded and said to please wait a moment; she would tell Borisov that he was there. He didn't expect to wait, and the delay surprised him. Minutes passed, and he fidgeted on the hard chair. Then the door opened and she came back.

'He'll see you,' she said. 'Please to go in.'

Ray had a smile ready when he walked through the door and his hand was reaching out to shake Borisov's. The Russian was sitting behind his desk and he didn't move.

'Dimitri,' Ray said. 'How are you? It's nice to see you again—'

'Sit down, Mr Andrews.'

Ray stared at him. *Mr Andrews*. Borisov's face was like a mask, no expression, not a glimmer. He might have been looking at a complete stranger. Ray sat down. He said, 'What's the matter? What's wrong?'

Borisov had a glass of tea in one hand. He drank some, and stared at Ray Andrews over the rim of it.

'Why did you try to cheat me?'

Ray Andrews jerked as if he'd been struck. 'What the hell are you talking about? Cheat you – what do you mean?'

Borisov finished his tea and put the glass down.

'You've seen this agreement, haven't you, Mr Andrews?'

'For Christ's sake,' Ray exploded. 'Stop calling me Mr Andrews! Yes of course I've seen it. I've gone through it line by line and clause by clause. It's perfectly in order!'

'I'm glad you're satisfied with it.' He sounded calm, but the pale eyes were bright with anger.

Ray said desperately, 'But what's wrong with it? Tell me!'

Borisov sighed. 'You must think we're very naïve, just ignorant Russians who can be taken in by clever Western lawyers. Well, you've misjudged us, Mr Andrews. We have clever lawyers, too, and our President suggested they should take a closer look at this document you want us to sign. This honourable agreement between our government and your company. With your Chief Executive's personal warranty.'

He hadn't raised his voice once.

Andrews said, 'What's wrong? What did your people find?'

'A loophole,' Borisov answered. 'A clause which amounted to an option, in your company's favour. The agreement states that you undertake to send a team up to Baikal within two calendar months of the date this comes into effect. It also undertakes to keep them there for at least a year and thereafter until such time as the operation shall be concluded. Here it is, clause ten, page three. See for yourself.'

He leaned across the desk and handed the document to Andrews. It was interminably long, involved and printed in small type. The clause and the section Borisov mentioned were scored in red ink. He read it twice and then he looked at the man on the other side of the desk and shook his head.

'I don't see anything wrong with that. The team of environmentalists and experts goes in two months after this is signed, and stays there for a year; that's the minimum time for any operation of this nature. We'll just be getting into our stride at Baikal by then. It can't be done any quicker, it's not a possibility.'

'I know that,' Borisov said. 'We have environmentalists here, you know. They're not completely ignorant of the size and complexity of our problem at Baikal.'

'Stop being insulting, Dimitri,' Ray said. 'You've picked on this clause ten and you've made a dreadful accusation. Please be good enough to explain it.'

'If I have been rude, then I apologize. I shouldn't allow myself to get angry. We have had this sort of experience before, when dealing with business in the West. You don't know what is wrong with your agreement, Mr Andrews? Then I'll explain. It is hidden in these nine words. "Until such time as the operation shall be concluded." There should be "by mutual agreement between the parties". That would have bound you, that would have meant that you couldn't come up to Baikal for a few months, and then abandon the project as uneconomic. That was what I particularly stressed in my talks with you. The need for a commitment to the project without prejudice or time limit. In return we became part of your diamond monopoly. But you send me an agreement worded in such a way that you can walk out of Baikal any time you choose after a year, and we have no way of stopping you. Just by omitting those few little words, "by mutual agreement between the parties".'

'Christ Almighty!'

Ray Andrews got up and handed the agreement back to Borisov. He waved it away.

'Keep it, Mr Andrews. It is of no use to me. I shall have to make a very humble apology to Ivan Karakov for the way we have been delaying.'

'I didn't know about this,' Ray said slowly. 'I can't expect you to believe me, but I went back to London and explained exactly what we had agreed. I got the personal guarantee you asked for, and I accepted this agreement in good faith. My Managing Director, Arthur Harris, was personally responsible for having it drawn up.'

Dimitri Borisov shrugged; he looked at Ray Andrews with indifference. The friendship which had grown up between them might never have existed.

'He promised me,' Ray said. He had begun to sweat. He felt so angry that he shook inside. 'He gave me his word that we were going ahead with this and dealing straight with you. I believed him. You're not the only one that's been cheated. Anyway, they didn't succeed in fooling you. I'm sorry. That's all I can say to you. I'm sorry. But I wasn't a party to it.'

'We will make an agreement with Karakov International,' Borisov remarked.

'Yes,' Ray said. 'I expected that.'

'When are you leaving?'

'I'm booked back on Tuesday.' He felt sick with shame.

'I should go earlier. There's nothing to keep you here.'

On an impulse, Ray Andrews walked to the desk and held out his hand. Dimitri Valerian Borisov ignored it.

'I didn't know about it,' Ray said again. 'It doesn't matter, but I'd like you to believe that. I didn't know about it. They cheated me too.'

Suddenly Borisov stood up, took Ray's hand and shook it. 'I do believe it. I wish you a safe journey home.'

'Goodbye, Dimitri.'

He walked out of the office, and he was in the street when he found he was still holding the useless agreement. He'd keep it. He'd take it back to London, and throw it down in front of Arthur Harris, just as it was. He went back to the hotel, and wrote out an open fax for London. He addressed it to Harris.

AGREEMENT UNACCEPTABLE. DEAL OFF. RETURN-
ING AT ONCE. ANDREWS.

When he got to his room to pack there was a fax waiting for him.

PARIS DEAL SUCCESSFULLY CONCLUDED. HASTINGS
RETURNING. CONCLUDE YOUR END AS SOON AS
POSSIBLE. WE'VE BROUGHT OFF THE DOUBLE.
REGARDS. ARTHUR.

It was the racing term that really made him mad. He lost his temper! He tore the fax in half and threw it across the room. Hastings had done his part. Nobody had buggered him up and let him walk into it. But he had made a success, too, and Arthur had ruined it by a dirty trick; it made him sick to think of it. He had been sent out to lie to a man who had trusted him, and now his career was ruined because Arthur had cheated him as well as the Russians. They had all supported Harris over the years; he had, and Kruger and old Wasserman, who had a soft spot for him, and God knew how many smaller fry. Heyderman treated him as a fool.

'By Christ,' Ray said to himself, 'he's right. There's no fool as dangerous as a dishonest one. But this time, he's going to take the full responsibility. I'm not going to shield the bastard this time. He's screwed the Russian deal, and I'm going to say so.'

He made that decision, and he knew what it would mean, and he wasn't even worried. Something had happened to him in that office, while Dimitri Borisov exposed what he was doing as a dirty, crooked confidence trick. Something had happened to him which might have happened at any time, but which had simply happened now. He had had enough. He caught the plane that evening, and spent part of the long journey drafting a full report on the progress of the Russian operation from start to finish. He was going to give it to Reece.

'Thanks, Joy dear,' Reece shuffled the pages she had typed for him. She was looking better after their holiday in Bath. And he had good news for her. She would soon be back home in the sunshine, in time for Christmas.

'Mr Julius says I'll be going back with him this time. He thinks it'll be tied up by then and we can leave the London end till the Annual General Meeting in March.'

She looked at him. 'Does Arthur Harris know what's going to happen? Are you sure he hasn't any idea?'

'No,' Reece answered. 'I've been compiling my report with Andrews and you're the only one who's seen it. He may think he's in for a fight, but he won't know what's going to hit him till he hears this put to the Board.' He tapped the papers. 'I've put everything Andrews told me into this. It'll finish him.'

'Well,' his sister said, 'Heyderman's wanted to get rid of him for years. That's something else he owes you.' She was knitting him a dark blue pullover and her thin fingers flew in and out with the needles. She was delighted at the prospect of Arthur Harris being thrown out. Other people's misfortunes always cheered her up, and she hated Harris because her brother did. He had humiliated Reece, and now he was going to pay for it.

'He was never much good,' Reece said. 'Nothing like Mr Julius. He's carried him for years. This time he's made his last mistake.'

'What will this new man be like?' she asked. 'Does he know what's going to happen?'

'No,' Reece answered. 'I've kept clear of him. Mr Arthur might draw conclusions. And Kruger's lady friend gave *him* the push. It's all drama at the office these days.'

'Ruth Fraser,' Joy muttered, counting stitches. 'She's a dreadful tart, isn't she?'

'Dreadful,' he agreed. 'She's working for Hastings now. I expect she'll shack up with him now he's separated from his wife.'

'They've no morals,' Joy said primly. 'Like a lot of monkeys. Oh, won't it be nice to get home and away from this awful cold weather?'

Prince Eugene Titulescu was playing with his little son. Ivan's daughter watched them, smiling in contentment. She adored her child and she was very fond of her husband. He wasn't the greatest lover, but she had settled for domestic life without the turbulence of passion. Her German baron had combined sexual virility with demands for money and blows when they weren't met. Eugene was a good husband, a devoted father, and an old-fashioned gentleman who bore her father's temper and tantrums with stoic patience.

He had suffered from both in the last few weeks. She said, 'I talked with Mother today. Thank God she's finally succeeded in calming Daddy down.'

The prince was bouncing the little boy on his knee, making horsey noises. He stopped and said, 'He was in a better mood today.' He smiled at his son. 'He didn't actually shout at me . . . No, sweetheart, that's enough. The poor horse is tired . . .'

He set him down, and the boy toddled over to his mother. 'You've been so good about it,' she said gratefully. 'But it's been a terrible time for him. Thank God he's dropped the idea of suing that actress. Mother talked him out of it. He wouldn't even discuss it with anyone else. I really thought he might give himself a heart attack. He gets so emotional about things.' She took her son's hand. 'Now, darling, I'm going to take you to find Angela, it's almost bath time. We'll come and say good night when you're in bed.'

'And I'll read you a story,' the prince promised.

He sighed when he was alone. The past few weeks had been a nightmare. His father-in-law had vented his rage on him, insulting and abusing him without reason, even blaming him because he had introduced Madeline Luchaire in the first place, and the prince lived in hourly terror of his part in the débâcle being exposed. He had arranged for Hastings to meet Luchaire, as his blackmailer demanded. Now, as the allegations about fraud and faking flew about, he understood why and what had happened. Hastings had planted the lie, and he had helped him do it. If his wife's family found out they would be merciless. Fear haunted him. He lost weight because he was too worried to eat, and he slept so badly that his wife suggested he should see his doctor.

With threatened law suits, publicity, a vindictive woman whose greed had been frustrated and Ivan

Karakov, raging and irrational . . . between them Eugene's future would be blown to dust. He would lose his job, his wife would leave him, he would lose his little son. He suffered in silence, waiting for the worst.

Then suddenly he saw Karakov changing; the tyrant was becoming low spirited, a tired old man who had lost the will to fight. The disaster with the red diamonds had been a mortal blow. He didn't call them the Romanovs any longer. He had lost his own illusion. They were unsaleable and he was muttering about sending them back to Moscow. He was ill tempered with Eugene, because his son-in-law was an easy target, but even that was diminishing. Much as he disliked her, the prince had to admire Laura Karakov for the way she soothed and manipulated the old man into pulling back from a law suit, and, even more surprising, persuaded him to mend his quarrel with Diamond Enterprises. There was no more talk of breaking the cartel and going out into the market alone. David Wasserman was in and out of the office, and slowly Ivan seemed to recover. Business was good, the rumours had become out of date and, because his reputation for straight dealing was so widely known and respected, Luchaire's spiteful campaign was losing impetus. He couldn't sell the red diamonds, but there was a rumour of a big 'sight' of goods coming up in Diamond Enterprises London offices, and he had been promised a particularly fine parcel, as a reward for coming back into the family. He recovered, but his son-in-law judged that underneath the bluster and the posturing, Karakov was a chastened man. Eugene bore him no ill will for his bullying; he was not a man of strong emotions and he wasn't vindictive. He was just grateful that the danger was over, and he had escaped unscathed. He was back in safe harbour, and that was all he asked of life. He went out to read his little son a bed-time story. It was always the same one about a family of mice. The boy never tired of it.

*   *   *

The Wassermans stopped off in London on their way home to the States. They invited James out to dinner to celebrate. They were booked into the Connaught; they loved the elegance of the hotel and they knew the food was the best in London.

'Well,' David said, 'it's all fixed. Ivan signed up like a lamb. Right back where he started. And it's all due to you!'

'And since the Russians threw out Andrews' deal,' Clara reminded them, 'you're the number-one boy . . . You'll go to the top.'

'Maybe,' James answered. 'But I feel sorry for Ray. Arthur cut the ground from under him by slipping an escape clause into that agreement. I have a feeling that he won't get away with it this time. Andrews is out for his blood.' He smiled, it wasn't humorous. 'So Arthur's been making a special effort to be nice to me. I've been lunched and invited down to Hampshire for the weekend . . . He needs an ally and he thinks I'll fall for it.'

'You're not going?' Wasserman enquired.

'No. I haven't forgotten what he did to me. He can sink, I'm not throwing him any bloody lifeline.'

Clara didn't say anything. Hastings looked older, and there was a bitterness about him that was disturbing. She still didn't like him as much as David did, but she had to admire the toughness and resolution that brought a man like Ivan Karakov to his knees. As she said, he would go to the top. What was really disturbing was that he didn't seem to care. She blamed the wife. Running out on him just when he needed her most. If he had a grain of sense he'd file for divorce and go out to have some fun. Only David's stricture prevented her from saying so.

James said, 'You'll be glad to get home. And while we're paying compliments, only you, David, could have negotiated with that old sod and talked him round. Here's to you.' He raised his glass.

'Here's to all of us,' Wasserman responded. 'And to business.'

James said harshly, 'That's for sure.'

Miller had gone down to Bath himself after reading his legman's report. He was shown into the manager's office. He was very pleasant, almost apologetic, about involving him in questions about the hotel's clients, but there could be a criminal offence at issue. The manager had been mollified and alarmed at the same time. Criminal offence could mean scandal for the hotel. He sent for the register as Miller requested. Miller studied it. The entry was clear, written in a copperplate hand. Someone trained in book-keeping, he thought. *Mr & Mrs Ryan*. The home address and the date. *Nationality: South African*. He noted it all down. He wanted as much detail as possible to keep his rich client interested. He didn't want her cancelling the investigation.

He said, 'What room did they occupy?'

'A double bedroom on the first floor, facing south. He asked for that specially. They had tickets for the theatre, and they stayed from Friday to the following Sunday night.'

The manager was a large, imposing man, but this kind of enquiry upset his nerves. The last time a lady had lost two pieces of jewellery out of her room and the police had to be called, he hadn't been able to eat for three days, it upset his stomach so much.

'They seemed a very pleasant couple,' he said. 'Very quiet.'

'Yes,' Miller said. 'They usually do. Is the room vacant? Could I see it?'

'It's occupied,' the manager said. 'But I can tell you anything you want to know about it – I don't see what difference it makes?'

'Has it single beds, or a double?' Miller asked.

The manager coughed. 'A double. He asked for that

when he telephoned to make the booking.'

'Yes,' Miller said. 'I see . . . Tell me, is this the lady who was registered as Mrs Ryan?' He produced a street snap of Reece's secretary leaving the office.

The manager shook his head. 'Oh no,' he said. 'That's not her. This was a smaller woman, dark-haired, not very nice looking. Younger than this one. I heard him call her Joy, if that's any help.'

'Just to make sure,' Miller said. 'Would you mind identifying him? Is that the man who came here? It's only a formality, but we've got to be thorough. Finding the woman is going to be a nuisance, though. I can see that.'

The manager looked at another street snap, this time taken outside Reece's rented flat. Miller had a very good man on street photography. People never knew they were being taken.

'Oh yes,' the manager said. 'That's him. And that's the lady who was with him just behind there! That's her! I'd know her anywhere from that photograph.'

Miller took the print back and looked at it. There were several similar prints in his file at the office, part of a series, and one of them showed this same girl holding Reece's arm. They hadn't bothered to investigate her because the hall porter had told his man that she was his sister. The card in the entrance hall said, *Mr P. and Miss J. Reece. Flat 27.*

'You're sure this was the woman?' he asked. 'You couldn't be mistaken?'

'Definitely,' the manager said; he was feeling pleased with himself for recognizing her. 'That's the one; just as I described her to you. Small and darkish and no oil painting. I told you, he called her Joy.'

'That's right,' Miller said. 'So you did. Well, thanks very much. I'll have to have a record of this entry in your register, but you shouldn't be troubled again. Thanks very much for your help.'

'Not at all,' the manager said. He cleared his throat. 'You mentioned a criminal offence . . .'

'Yes,' Miller said. 'So I did. This looks like being very nasty.'

He went outside and found a pub around the corner and ordered himself a beer. Nasty wasn't the word for it. He wondered what Miss Stella Heyderman would make out of this when she got his report.

'It's not very nice, Miss Heyderman,' Miller shook his head. 'But there it is; you never know what you are going to find when you start looking into people's private lives.'

Stella was still reading it. She had come down to the office when he phoned her, and she had read the report there. 'You're sure this is right? You're absolutely sure it's his sister?'

'No doubt at all,' Miller said. 'I was going to get in touch with you at once, but I thought we'd better make a few more checks just to be sure. I asked a contact in Spain to look up the hotel where they stayed earlier in the year – he asked a few questions and it was the same answer. Mr and Miss Reece. Single rooms this time, because they had to show their passports on registering, but in adjoining rooms. Same identification as the hotel manager in Bath. Brother and sister. Oh, and we uncovered something else. This isn't very nice either, I'm afraid. One of the Spanish maids talked her head off after our contact gave her a couple of hundred pesetas. She said they were always in one room during the afternoon siestas, and she told our chap that one day she was looking through the sister's drawers and she found a cane hidden in the clothes. So it looks as if it was incest with trimmings.'

'Christ,' Stella said slowly. 'They were into that, too . . .'

Miller shrugged. 'I have had cases like this before and you do find that there's an element of perversion in it

330

apart from the incestuous relationship. The point is, what do you want done with this?'

'I've been trying to think of that,' she said. 'I know what I'd do with it if I were in the Union. I'd send it straight to the police, but I don't know whether it's an offence here or not.'

'Oh, it certainly is,' he said. He looked quite pained at the suggestion that there wasn't an English law to provide for all contingencies. 'This is a criminal offence. They'd both go to prison for this. No doubt about it. But is that what you want? I mean you can't just inform on them and then drop out. We'll probably have to give evidence if it comes to court and we can't guarantee to keep your name out of the papers. I don't want to mislead you, you know. You'd better think it out.'

'I have thought it out,' she said. 'I am leaving for Johannesburg on the twenty-second of December. It'll take the police a few days to get their teeth into this, won't it?'

'Oh I should think so. Slow but sure we are. I was in the force for years and I've got a lot of friends still there. They wouldn't rush the thing; they'd have to question the couple and make their own enquiries to corroborate what we've told them, that is if you've decided that you want us to tell them anything.'

'Yes, I have.' Stella stood up. She felt quite different from what she had imagined. She didn't feel vindictive or exultant. She felt rather sick, as if she had stepped in a mess of worms. But she had no hesitation. 'You send your evidence to the police. Fill in a few more details if you like. The expenses will be all right as far as I'm concerned. My father is coming over on business and Reece will be leaving England at the same time as we do, so if they fool about, the police will miss them. You might impress that on them.'

'I will,' he said. He thought she worked things out very quickly; there wasn't any fumbling in her mental processes. 'You want the police to charge Reece and stop him leaving the country,' he said. 'That's what you want, isn't it?'

'Yes,' she looked at him. 'He has friends in the police at home. He won't buy his way out over here. Let me have your account, Mr Miller. And thank you very much. You've done a wonderful job for me. If I know anyone who wants a good detective, I'll send them along to you.'

'Goodbye, Miss Heyderman; thanks very much. I'm glad you're satisfied.'

'Oh, I am,' she said. 'I'm the most satisfied customer you'll ever have.'

'I thought we'd have more privacy here,' Philip Fairfax said. 'And the food and wine are excellent.'

James had never been to Boodles before; he had seen it through the famous bow window and glimpsed a coal fire and men sitting in leather chairs, but nobody stopped and looked in; it was unthinkable. He liked the interior; it was very comfortable, and there was a club smell of leather and cigars and men, the atmosphere of an old house where women weren't allowed. He followed Elizabeth's father into the dining-room, and they were given a corner table. He had been surprised to be invited, although he had requested a meeting with Liz's father. The lunch must have significance. His father-in-law must want something. Probably an uncontested divorce for Elizabeth. That, James decided, was the reason behind the friendliness. They had never liked him, or wanted Elizabeth to marry him. Realizing it was inevitable, the family had put a good face on it, but James hadn't been fooled. Now they had their daughter back, and no doubt they felt he could be got rid of, and she would end up with someone they felt was more suitable.

Philip Fairfax said, 'Let's look at the menu, shall we? And what would you like to drink? I'm sure they'll have the steak-and-kidney pie, it's the best in London, and I can order a decent claret.'

He looked enquiringly at James. Such good manners, such an impenetrable barrier between them. James could never get through to him.

'I don't drink at lunchtimes, thanks. I don't mind what we eat, you order whatever. What I would like to know is why I'm here.'

Elizabeth's father frowned. This was awkward, this head-on approach. Not the way he liked doing things at all.

'To talk about Lizzie,' he said. 'And see what we can do to help you patch it up. You sure you want the steak and kidney?'

James said, 'Yes, yes, anything. You mean you're not against me?' He couldn't believe it. 'After what Liz's told you?'

'Liz told us what that bloody Frenchman told her,' was the answer. 'I don't happen to believe him, and neither does Jill. All I can say is, James, you must have been stone blind not to realize he was in love with her. Stone blind,' he accused.

James said slowly, 'Yes. I must have been. He was so much older, it never occurred to me. Before we say anything else, I promise you I didn't get a message that Liz was in hospital, or losing the baby. I flew straight to Paris after speaking to the doctor, but Liz had left the clinic and gone to the country with that bastard. That's what happened and that's the truth.'

There was a pause. Then Philip Fairfax said, 'I'm sure it is. What we have to do is get Elizabeth to believe it, too. She still loves you, as you obviously love her. But she won't listen to either of us. And that bugger's coming over to see her. He writes and telephones; it's like water dripping, drip, drip, and it's very worrying. I think you should come back with me and talk to her. She'll be furious with me, but that can't be helped. It's going on

333

too long, James. These things can reach a point of no return when it's too late. What do you say? Ah,' he turned to the club servant. 'Morning, Tom. Two steak-and-kidney pies and a half-bottle of the house red. You're sure you won't join me, James? No point ordering a decent bottle just for me.'

James shook his head. Go down to Freemantle and see Elizabeth. Take her by surprise. Try to make her believe him. Hurry, because another man was taking advantage of the situation and was in pursuit. Letters, telephone calls, drip, drip, drip . . . planning a visit to see her. The food arrived; they ate in silence. He hadn't answered Fairfax's invitation. Fairfax didn't press him. He watched his son-in-law in his quiet way, and was pained by what he saw. A bitter man, consumed with hurt. When the coffee came, he repeated the offer.

'Will you come down with me? I'm leaving around five o'clock.'

'No,' James said. 'No, I don't think so. I couldn't take it if Liz sent me packing again. That'd be the end as far as I'm concerned. Funny thing, Philip, you and Jill never really liked me, but you don't believe I could behave like an utter shit. My wife does. That's hurt a lot. *Nothing* in the world meant more to me than her and the baby. She's got to reach that conclusion without any more begging from me. But, thanks anyway. Thanks for being a friend. I didn't expect it.' He got up.

Philip Fairfax said, 'I'm so sorry, James. We're on your side and we'll do what we can. If that bloody fellow comes over, he'll have to see her in London. I'm not having him in the house.'

He shook his head slightly as he watched his son-in-law leave. These things can reach a point of no return . . . it might well be that James was there already.

12

'If you've come to see Mr Hastings, he's out of the office till three this afternoon.'

Ruth Fraser spoke as if Kruger was a stranger. Quite calmly, with that impersonal expression that tore at him with rage and hurt.

'I've come to see you,' he said.

'I've asked you not to do this,' Ruth answered, lowering her voice. 'The office is not the place.'

Kruger came close to her desk. He stared down at her. 'Fuck the office. How could you do this to me, Ruth?'

She smelt sour whisky on his breath. There were rumours that he kept a bottle in his drawer and drank through the day. She decided not to provoke him. She softened her attitude.

'Dick,' she said, 'be reasonable. I didn't want to hurt you, we had wonderful times together. I said all that . . . but while we were apart, I realized I didn't want to marry you. I didn't want that kind of commitment. It was better to end it when I did. Can't you just accept that?'

'No,' he glared at her. 'Because it's not the reason. You left me because you were fucking Hastings behind my back, and now his wife's left him, you think you'll make it up the ladder with him. That's why you left me. Tell the truth for once. That's why!'

Ruth glanced at the door, his voice was raised. People in the outer office could hear.

'Will you shut up and stop yelling at me.' Her control snapped suddenly. She had been sorry for him at first.

Now she was beginning to hate and despise him for being so weak. Pleas and self-abasement had been followed by abuse. Now it was spilling over into her professional life. She couldn't allow that. She got up and came round the desk and faced him.

'Get this straight,' she hissed at him. 'I don't want you any more. I'm not fucking Hastings or any other man. I never was. You just made that up because you can't admit I got bored with you and wanted out. That's the truth. You're too old, and you bored me – in bed and out of it!'

He hit her; the slap caught her on the side of the face and she staggered back. Her hand came up to her cheek.

'Get out,' she said. 'Get out of here before I call security!'

He swayed slightly. 'I'm going,' he said. 'But don't think you and your boyfriend are going to get away with it! There's a fight coming up . . . one bloody fight to the death in this company, and he's going to lose. Goodbye, bitch!' The door slammed shut behind him.

She went through to the private washroom and bathed her face with cold water. She could see signs of swelling. A bruise would follow; it was throbbing painfully. She was shaking with shock and anger. The blow reminded her of other blows; the cuff across the face when she didn't finish her schoolwork, or was slow to wash up after meals. Or, sometimes, for nothing, just because she was at hand and her father was in a bad mood. If any man got rough or hit her, Ruth wanted to kill them, just as she had secretly wanted to kill him.

A fight to the death in the company. He was drunk and boasting, but the undercurrents were all round her. Tension and rumour about what would happen at the Board meeting. An open row between Arthur Harris and Ray Andrews. They had been heard shouting at each other after Andrews came back from Moscow. Julius Heyderman would be on his way over soon, to chair that

Board meeting. With James Hastings poised to strike and take the prize.

Thanks to him, she had been given a bonus and a salary rise. Nothing had changed in their relationship, except that he was even more distant, if that was possible. He had shut himself away and nobody was allowed to get near. Ruth didn't even try. She knew his wife and he were separated; office rumours said she'd gone funny after a miscarriage and walked out. Ruth didn't think about it; she'd seen the Lady Liz once or twice and instinctively disliked the type. Privileged, nose in the air, spoiled rotten . . . And a fool, to let a man like Hastings go just because she'd dropped a baby. Ruth could have given her a few pointers about men . . .

There was a noise behind her and she heard James say, 'Ruth? Sorry – the door was open . . .' Then, as she turned to face him, 'Christ, what's happened to your face?'

'Dick Kruger happened,' she said. 'Excuse me, Mr Hastings.' She passed by him and back into her own office.

He followed her, 'You mean he hit you?'

'He was drunk,' she said. 'He's barged in here once or twice, abusing me, but this time it got out of hand. It's all right, it was only a slap. But he's a big man.'

'He's a bastard,' James exclaimed. 'I'll see he doesn't come in here again! I'll go and have a word—'

'No,' she stopped him. 'Please, it doesn't matter. He won't come back. I don't want any fuss.' She surprised herself by saying, 'My Dad used to belt me . . . it's no big deal.'

James said, 'Ruth sit down. Look, I'll get a car to take you home. Maybe you should see a doctor. That's going to be very painful.'

'How was your lunch?' She was making conversation to get the situation back to normal. She didn't want him making a scene with Kruger, and have Kruger repeat his accusations. Hastings might feel he couldn't keep her on as his assistant.

James sat down on the edge of the desk. She was in a chair, a hand pressed to her throbbing cheek.

'My lunch?' He paused for a moment. Then he said, 'I met my father-in-law. I thought he was going to ask me to give my wife a divorce. I was all ready to fight, all squared up,' he raised both fists in mockery. 'I've come to the conclusion I'm a hopeless judge of people. He never liked me, my mother-in-law didn't either. I thought they'd be on my wife's side. I was wrong. Absolutely dead wrong.'

Ruth stared at him. He wasn't really talking to her, more to himself aloud. 'They want to get us back together. So it shows how wrong I was.'

Ruth waited for a moment, and then said, 'Is there any chance? I mean I've known things were not right, but I don't really know why you separated. Was it losing the baby? Was she depressed or something like that? I never liked to mention it.'

'No,' he answered. 'Not so simple. There's another man involved.' He got off the desk and stretched as if he were stiff and aching. 'He told her a lie and she believes it. She thinks I stayed down at Cap d'Antibes while she was having a miscarriage, and pretended not to know because the business was more important than what was happening to her. This bastard was with her in the clinic, and he pretended to call my office. He never did. So she thinks I'm the kind of shit who'd do a thing like that.'

Ruth felt the other side of her face flame red. There *had* been a message and she'd taken it. And never passed it on. Because she hadn't trusted him to make the right choice and put the business first. She got up and said, 'I am sorry, Mr Hastings. I hope it'll work out. I will go home, if you don't mind. I'm getting a nasty headache. I can drive myself home.'

'Don't come in tomorrow if you don't feel like it,'

James said. He was sickened by the incident. Kruger, all of six foot two and two hundred odd pounds lashing out at a woman like that. He hadn't meant to talk to her or anyone, but he was glad he had. Some kind of burden had been lifted from him. 'Look after yourself,' he said.

'Thanks,' Ruth managed to smile at him. 'You're a very kind man. I appreciate it.'

She didn't bother going to the doctor. She took painkillers and put an ice pack on her cheek. She had never had a conscience; it was kill or be killed in this life, as far as she was concerned. Nothing in her experience from childhood onwards had convinced her otherwise. Hastings had come back from Paris as the hero figure, all the more remarkable because of Andrews' failure with the Russians. Hastings would get to the top and he owed it to her sense of priorities. She hadn't given him the message about his wife. If she had, he would have made the wrong decision. She hadn't even remembered the incident, or connected it with Elizabeth Hastings leaving him. Mentally she shrugged it away, out of her mind. There was a price to pay for everything. Nothing is for nothing, as her mother used to say. He'd get over it. He'd find someone else. She settled down to watch TV and have a quiet night. If her face didn't look too obvious, she'd go into the office tomorrow.

'Dick,' Arthur Harris said, 'you've been drinking. It shows.'

'I know,' Kruger said miserably. 'And I've just made a bloody fool of myself.'

Harris said quietly. 'You were bound to sooner or later. I did warn you. What happened?'

'I went to Ruth's office. We had a row and I hit her.'

'Oh, for God's sake,' Arthur exclaimed. 'Is she hurt? Dick, how could you do such a stupid thing?'

'She goaded me,' he muttered. 'I only slapped her.

You'd have done the same if she'd said those things to you!'

Arthur doubted if Ruth could have matched Christa at her best, but he didn't argue. He came and put a hand on Kruger's shoulder. He looked wretched and ashamed in spite of his bluster. A big man brought to his knees by the bite of a small, deadly asp. That's how he pictured Ruth Fraser. Small and quick, with a lethal strike.

'You're well rid of her,' he said. 'Just be thankful you didn't marry her. That's the mistake that matters. Do you think she'll use it to make trouble? I might have a word with her and defuse the situation.'

'No,' Kruger dismissed that. 'She's got what she wants. I'll bet it's not the first time a man has thumped her. Jesus, to think I left Valerie for her – all that alimony, the house, all the aggro . . .' He rubbed his hands across his face. He looked at Arthur. 'You're a real friend. I won't forget it when we sit down round that table and anyone starts shooting at you. I'll nail Andrews to the bloody wall!'

'Not if you're half-full of Scotch,' Harris said. 'You've got to pull yourself together, Dick. Stop boozing and feeling sorry for yourself. Julius will be here in a week's time, and we'll be fighting for our business lives. Andrews has turned his coat. He's going to speak against me at that Board, and my guess is that when he's done it he'll resign, just to emphasize the point. He was bad enough when he came back, losing control and making wild accusations. When he heard that Russian had been dismissed from his job, he went right over the edge. He's blaming me for that, too. Makes you wonder just how friendly they got . . .'

They glanced at each other, the follow-up unspoken.

Kruger sneered, 'Yes, doesn't it! But if it comes to a vote, you'll win, Arthur. You've got a bomb-proof case. Nobody could expect you to agree to those bloody terms, they were outrageous, open blackmail. Don't worry,

I'm with you. David's loyal, he's coming by Concorde specially, just to support you. Johnson's never taken a stand about anything, he's not interested.'

The distinguished mining engineer was well known for his view that Board meetings and bumf, as he called them collectively, were a waste of time.

'Hastings,' Arthur murmured. 'What about him? I tried to talk him round, but he didn't respond.'

He was relieved to see that Kruger had sobered up. He'd drunk several cups of coffee.

'He'd vote down his own mother if it suited him,' Kruger snarled, the mention of Hastings always enraged him. 'I don't know what he'll do. If he votes against you, and you win, he's in an impossible position. At worst he'll abstain. So, on the face of it, you've got the head count, even without Andrews. I don't know why Julius bothers, he must know he can't vote you off. He likes to bully, that's all.'

'Maybe,' Arthur said. 'We'll see. I have this gut feeling that it won't be resolved without a lot of blood-letting. On all sides.'

'Don't let it worry you,' Kruger insisted. He was feeling very emotional and protective towards Arthur. They had been colleagues and good friends for many years. Arthur gave him his gentle smile.

'Oh it won't,' he said. 'So long as I win.'

Stella couldn't stop shaking. She wanted a drink so badly, she had rushed out of the hotel to stop herself calling room service and ordering a bottle . . . any bottle of anything. She walked at a frantic pace through Hyde Park, fighting the impulse to have just one to steady her nerves before she went to the airport to meet them. A group of joggers looked back at the woman swathed in expensive furs, talking loudly to herself. Quite off her trolley. She was talking to Jacob, trying to persuade him that facing her father was too much to ask, without even a little crutch. Like one stiff vodka. But Jacob wouldn't agree. He argued in her head, calm and persuasive as usual, that she was brave enough to carry it off. Drink had nearly destroyed her. She'd promised him so often that she would never slip downwards again. Then, when justice was done to him, she'd have something to live and work for in her own country. He wouldn't give way, however hard she pleaded. In the end, she slumped down on a seat by the Serpentine and watched a gaggle of au pairs with small children, teaching them to throw bread to the ducks. It was cold, but she was warm, snuggled in the fur. She'd bought it to spite her father, but he'd only said, 'Good, glad you're being sensible. Hope it's a nice coat.' Jacob had convinced her; she wasn't going to have a drink. She was going back to the hotel and get in the chauffered car and drive down to meet her father and stepmother at Heathrow. And, when the moment was right, she'd give them the report on Reece as a Christmas present. She gloated over the scene in her imagination. Julius, incredulous, outraged, and then accused in turn. That was the finale she had planned. Herself centre stage, confronting him with his guilt. Denouncing him for Jacob's murder. She clung to the scenario, she whipped herself up into fury and vengeance. She had to, because she couldn't admit that the unloved child inside was longing to see her father and be in his good grace. She explained that to Jacob, too, and he understood. She left the seat and started back to the Dorchester. Crisis over. Stella still sober and in control. On her way to play the reformed dutiful daughter and give her father a hug and a kiss in the airport after a long, sad separation. She was still talking to herself, and some of the foreign girls with their children looked after her and laughed among themselves.

It wasn't so difficult after all, she thought as she looked back on that meeting. Not nearly so awkward. He had moved with his long stride towards her, and for a moment she felt dizzy. Then he was holding her, kissing her heartily on both cheeks, and saying loudly, 'Suki . . . so very good to see you . . . So good.'

Her cheeks were wet. It was silly not to have expected a little age after so long, but it shocked her to see grey in his hair and lines that hadn't been there last time. He was such a big, overpowering man, he seemed to swallow her into himself while they embraced. Then Sylvia; elegant, handsome, coming to kiss her and say how well she looked. Last time they had seen each other, Stella had screamed abuse and called Julius a murderer. Her stepmother showed no sign that she remembered.

They had driven back to London together, lunched in the restaurant, and then Julius had set off for his office. When he had gone, there was a moment when Sylvia let the pretence drop.

'I'm very glad you're reconciled,' she said. 'I do understand what a terrible time you had after Jacob's death. But it was hard for your father too. He's not a young man any more and he's got a lot of business worries at the moment. So I do hope, Stella, that you won't do anything to upset him.'

A voice like cracked ice. No pleasant smile this time.

'I won't,' Stella answered. 'I've stopped trying to hurt myself and everyone else. You don't have to lecture me.'

'I wasn't,' Sylvia said. 'I just happen to love your father, that's all. And I know he loves you. Now, I'm going upstairs to sort out my luggage and have a rest. He never seems to get jet-lagged; I'm exhausted. We'll see you in the bar around eight o'clock. If being in the bar worries you, we don't have to meet there.'

Stella stood up. 'I always go there in the evening,' she said. 'And I never drink anything but orange juice and Perrier. See you at eight. Sleep well.'

She went up to her own suite, kicked off her shoes and fell onto the bed.

I know he loves you.

She shut her mind to the warm feeling creeping over her. It had been more of an ordeal than she realized. She fell asleep immediately.

When she woke it was late afternoon. The idea was in her head as if someone had put it there while she slept. Punishing Reece isn't enough. You've written the finale, but it's not a curtain call. You've got to have proof, or you'll never be able to do it. And there's only one way to get that.

The next morning she made an excuse to Sylvia who wanted to go shopping for Christmas presents, and took a taxi down to Bickenhall Mansions in Marylebone, Flat 27. The names were on the front door beside the entry phone. *Mr P. and Miss J. Reece.* She pressed the button and waited. A tinny voice answered, 'Yes? Who is it?'

'Stella Heyderman. I'd like to talk to you.'

Joy was tempted to keep the door shut. But if she did, and Heyderman was told, it would react on her brother. Curiosity played a part; she had never seen the woman and she wondered what she would be like. An arrogant bitch, lording it over the employee's sister. She might try, Joy decided, but she wouldn't get away with it. But why had she come there at all? Joy felt suddenly uneasy. It must mean trouble of some kind. Maybe Stella was in trouble and was seeking out Reece behind her father's back . . . That must be it. She opened the flat door. Stella was tall; she wasn't prepared to look up at her. She said in her nasal voice, accentuated by the persistent cold, 'Come inside. I'm Joy Reece, Piet's sister.'

'Piet.'

Stella had never heard a Christian name for him before. It was always Reece, the sexless ambiguity. Sexless. She shuddered, looking at the plain dumpy girl. She was wearing an overall and she'd been cleaning, because there was a duster and a tin of spray polish on the table by the door. She followed her into the sitting-room.

'Sit down, won't you?'

Joy was playing hostess, raking Stella with sharp eyes. Noting the expensive clothes, the scent, the trappings of money. But the face gave her away, she thought spitefully. She looked raddled, much older than her late thirties. The face would never recover from the disgusting life she'd led.

'What can I do for you, Miss Heyderman? My brother's at the office, if you were wanting to see him.'

'No,' Stella said. 'I really came to see you. Do you mind if I have a cigarette?'

Joy grimaced. Filthy habit. Typical.

'I do have a cold,' she said.

'Then I'll try not to blow smoke your way,' Stella said and took out the pack and her lighter. She was quite calm; there were no tremors, no nerves like the day before. Knowledge gave her command of the situation. She saw the woman's hostility and contempt but it couldn't touch her. She knew what she was going to say.

'How did you enjoy Bath?'

The question brought a gasp from Joy Reece. Her mouth fell open and then shut like a trap.

'We had a few day's holiday. It was very nice.'

'I'm sure it was. The Royal Crescent is a lovely hotel. That's where you stayed, isn't it?' Stella inhaled and then turned her head aside, blowing smoke away from her. 'Registered as husband and wife.'

She thought the woman was going to collapse. She turned a ghastly grey colour and caught hold of the back of the sofa to steady herself. She didn't say anything, she just swallowed and stared wildly at Stella.

'I've seen the hotel register,' Stella went on. 'I had you and your brother followed. Very interesting. What a close relationship you have.'

The sound was like an animal. A snarl, choking in her throat.

'That's a filthy lie. We shared a room to save money.'

'You couldn't economize in Spain in the summer, but you managed. Especially in the afternoons. Why don't you sit down, you don't look very well.'

Niggers, Reece called Jacob's people. Kaffirs. Fit only to be servants, the permanent underclass born to submit to the whites. Stella knew the type, she knew how they thought and spoke among themselves. The perverted creature had openly insulted her because she had been married to a black.

She showed no mercy. 'There's no use denying it. And it's a serious offence. You and he would go to prison.'

Joy Reece was not a coward. Cornered, she instinctively fought back.

'You can't do anything to us,' she said at last. 'You try it and I'll drag the Heydermans down with us. Starting with your father.'

She had recovered by now; bright colour burned in her cheeks. It was Stella who turned pale.

'How could you touch my father? You're just bluffing . . . Miss Reece.' She made the term sound like an insult.

Joy was gathering strength. 'You owe my brother everything,' she spat out. 'Covering up for you. All these years – and after what he did for your father!'

'You mean getting my husband murdered?' Stella said it very quietly. 'Isn't that what he did? I know about that, too.'

Joy made a gesture of contempt. 'You can't prove anything . . . Blacks murdered a black. That's what they do all the time.'

'Jacob's murderers were paid.' Stella kept her voice steady but it was becoming an effort. 'Paid by your brother. I have proof. That's why I'm here.' It was a lie but it was her one chance.

Joy uncoiled her body from the sofa and sprang up. 'This is the thanks my brother gets. Trying to protect your rotten family! He's loyal, that's his trouble. He just had to protect the great Mr Julius, his hero. "Think what

the scandal would do to him if that marriage gets out!"
That's what he said. You try to hurt either of us, you
dirty bitch, and I'll say your father *told* him to get rid of
your black. I'll swear it, and I'll make Piet swear it too.
So what are we going to do about that, eh?'

Stella picked up her bag; there was no ashtray. She
stubbed the cigarette out on a plate holding a cactus in
a pot. She felt almost light headed.

'Nobody will believe you,' she said. 'My father had
nothing to do with it.'

'No,' the older woman sneered. 'But it'll be his word
against ours. Just think about that. Now get out. Get out
of my flat! There's nothing you can do to us.'

She rushed to the door and flung it open. 'Out!' she
shouted.

Stella looked at her. 'If you weren't so sick, I'd feel
sorry for you.'

She heard the front door slam like a bomb burst behind
her. In the corridor, waiting for the lift to take her down,
she leant against the wall because her legs were trembling.

My father had nothing to do with it. And the retort,
spat like snake's venom, *No. But it'll be his word against
ours . . .*

The lift stopped, and she stepped inside.

A man said, 'Good-morning. Ground floor?'

'Yes,' Stella nodded. 'Yes, ground floor please.'

Reece had acted on his own initiative. *He just had to
protect the great Mr Julius, his hero . . . I'll say your
father* told *him to get rid of your black* – The vicious
face swam in front of her eyes. *I'll swear it, and I'll make
Piet swear it too.*

She heard the man beside her say again, 'Ground
floor?' and realized he was holding the door open for
her. 'Oh thanks.'

They walked out together through the lobby and on
to the Marylebone Road. The sun was shining. He smiled
at her, and hurried off. She stood by the kerb. Several

347

taxis with their orange lights glowing slowed as they approached but she didn't move. Her father had not been responsible for Jacob's death. She stood breathing in the fumes of London traffic and said out loud in a great sigh, 'Thank God. Oh, thank God.' She wasn't saying it to Jacob.

James woke very early. It was the morning of the Board meeting. He pulled back the curtains and looked out. It was still semi-dark. Street lights were still on, and they showed puddles of rain shining in the gutter and sheening the pavements. It had rained hard during the night. He had moved out of their bedroom, into one of the spare rooms on the floor above. The house had been so full of Elizabeth that he took to spending two or three nights a week at the Lansdowne Club. Kind friends asked him away for weekends. He couldn't bear to sleep in their old bedroom. Her clothes were in the cupboards, some make-up was left in the bathroom cabinet. He imagined her scent lingered in the air. Gradually he had forced himself to behave rationally. He stopped staying in his club, moved everything upstairs and resumed living in their house. He had already decided to sell it after Christmas. The day he called in the estate agents he would have accepted that the marriage was over. He had stopped writing or trying to make contact with Elizabeth after his lunch with her father. Lasalle was coming over from Paris. That had bitten deeply into him. Elizabeth knew the score. If he was what she wanted, so be it.

He remembered that other Board meeting at the end of the summer. Coming home in high excitement because he had been given the assignment in Paris, he'd said to her, 'I could be in line for the top job.' And he knew that now he was. He had his role in the coming fight worked out. He didn't have to get dirty hands or kick his Managing Director when he was down. Others would do it for him. When it was all over, he'd pick up the prize.

He worked through till ten-thirty. Ruth was in and out of the office, trying to conceal her own excitement. Just before he left for the Boardroom on the top floor, she came up and said, 'Good luck, Mr Hastings.'

He said, 'I think it's Mr Harris who's going to need the luck. Thanks anyway.'

He met Kruger in the passage; they shared the lift without speaking. Inside the Boardroom Reece came up to them. He ignored Kruger.

'Can I have a word, Mr Hastings?'

'Yes, of course.' James hadn't expected that. He followed Reece to the far side of the room. He smiled and nodded briefly at David Wassserman who was already sitting down in his place.

'What can I do for you?'

'Mr Julius wants to know where you stand.' The voice was very low.

James stiffened. He had always disliked the man. 'It's a bit late to ask that, isn't it? We start in a few minutes.'

'What do I tell him?' Reece demanded. 'The timing doesn't matter. It's the advantage that counts.'

'Tell him,' James answered, 'that he has my support. Which means I'll abstain. Excuse me.'

He turned away, moving to his place at the table. Ray Andrews came in. He looked grim. Then Arthur Harris, followed by Johnson, the mining engineer, tanned by the West African sunshine. He'd been called back from a site in Angola.

Harris looked round and said with a quiet smile, 'Good-morning.' Then he took his place.

There was a pause. Wasserman sipped water and scribbled something on the pad in front of him.

'It's late,' Harris remarked. 'Julius must have been held up in traffic.'

Reece's chair scraped back. He knew instinctively when

Heyderman arrived. Julius looked as fit and bronzed as always. James watched him, admiring the authority, the power that surrounded him like an aura. Mentally and physically he towered over them all, dominating the room even before he opened the meeting. Then it began.

Routine business, some directors' reports, reference to minutes of the last meeting. Tension was building up; Heyderman was orchestrating it like a showman.

He sat back in his chair, sank his water in a gulp, and then said in a loud clear voice, 'I think I speak on behalf of the whole Board in congratulating James on the way he concluded a very difficult negotiation with Karakov International. We all know Ivan,' he glanced round for confirmation. 'It needed a very skilful touch to make him see reason. He's signed a new agreement with us, on the same terms, and we're all one happy family again. I think it appropriate that we pass a resolution formally congratulating James on his achievement. I propose it, who would like to second?'

Wasserman raised his hand. The move had caught Arthur Harris off guard. Dick Kruger reddened, but said nothing.

'Carried unanimously,' Julius announced. 'Good.'

He poured a whisky from his personal decanter and filled it with water. He put the glass down and stared straight at Arthur Harris.

'It's time now to come to the most important item on the agenda. Ray Andrews' report on the negotiations in Moscow. It's very detailed and long, but I'm sure you've all had time to read your copies. Right. As I see it, there are certain very important points which Ray might like to explain.'

'Yes,' Kruger spoke up. 'I should think so. I read it as containing an oblique attack on Arthur. It needs a hell of a lot of explanation if you ask me.'

Arthur Harris said quietly, 'I don't think we should start by saying damaging things. Ray is quite free to

350

allege what he likes. I've read the report and I'm quite prepared to answer for my decisions. And to ask him a few questions.'

He gave Andrews a hostile stare.

'Ray,' Julius addressed him, 'you say that you carried out the negotiations with the Moscow representative right up until he asked for a specific guarantee from Arthur as Chief Executive?'

'I did,' Ray Andrews answered.

'You also state that, without that guarantee, the Russians wouldn't consider an agreement.'

'They made that plain. They wanted a commitment from us to finance the Baikal de-pollution project. That was the price for agreeing to sell their diamonds exclusively through our organization. They knew they were in a strong position, that we needed them to maintain our monopoly, and they had an outlet big enough through Karakov to do it without us. And even destabilize the whole industry in the long term. That's why they insisted on Arthur's personal guarantee.'

'Even though they knew it was personal, and not binding on the Board?' That was Dick Kruger again. 'Or didn't you think to point that out?' Andrews didn't look near him. He spoke directly to Heyderman. 'I made certain my counterpart, Borisov, knew that. He was looking for integrity, not just legality. I believed he was getting it when I brought back the guarantee and the document for signature which had been drawn up. I believed that it was a valid document backed by the Managing Director's word of honour.'

James fiddled with his pencil and pad. This was becoming lethal.

'This agreement,' Arthur interposed. 'The terms were literally dictated by the Russians, isn't that correct? Interest-free loans, development of the Archangel mines, and, above all, an open-ended commitment to de-pollute the enormous water mass at Baikal. A project in which we had no possible commercial interest and which would have involved us in incalculable cost. If it could even be done. Isn't that what they demanded?'

Slowly Ray turned to face him. 'Those were the terms, yes.'

'They could almost be described as blackmail,' Harris said quietly. 'They held a gun to our head and expected me to pull the trigger.'

'That was not how I understood it,' Andrews said. 'I negotiated in good faith. I put that agreement forward believing it to be an honest document. If I'd known that an escape clause was being inserted, I would have approached the problem quite differently.'

Julius sipped whisky. 'How differently?'

'I wouldn't have presented it,' was the answer. 'I would never have tried to cheat them. I would have gone on trying to find a compromise, keeping the talks going. I don't say I would have succeeded, but the door would have been open. As things are, they see Diamond Enterprises as a company whose word can't be trusted.'

He turned to look at Arthur Harris.

'All you had to do was be honest with me, even if you couldn't be honest with them. I believed then, and I still do, that I could have negotiated a satisfactory deal. All the more so, since Karakov lost credibility They'd have dropped the Baikal commitment without him as a bargaining point.'

'You talk about honesty,' Arthur said angrily. 'You impugn me to justify yourself. You allowed this Russian to drive you into a corner and I was expected to agree to conditions that nobody could justify without some safeguard. If you call that dishonest, then you have no sense of loyalty or responsibility to the company or the colleagues you've worked with all these years.'

Andrews flushed a deep red. He turned right round to face Arthur.

'I've worked for this company for over twenty years.

It's because I have a sense of loyalty and responsibility that I placed this report before the Chairman and the Board. Because you didn't deal honestly with me, as your representative and negotiator, you put me in an impossible position, and seriously damaged the credibility of Diamond Enterprises with the Moscow government. As they see it, we can't be trusted.'

There was a long silence. Arthur had turned a sallow grey. Then Julius spoke.

'It seems to me,' he said, 'that we have reached the heart of the problem. Let me set it out as I see it. Andrews got an agreement on terms that you accepted in principle without detailed reference to the Board. You gave a broad outline, which appeared, on the face of it, to be stiff but acceptable. This was not the true picture of the commitment. That, as you've admitted, was unacceptable commercially, so you inserted a clause that invalidated the investment in Baikal without informing the Board or Andrews. As a result of this deception, the negotiations were broken off, and the logical outcome should have been an alliance between Karakov International and the Russians that could have broken our monopoly and flooded the markets within five years. Just because,' he glared at Arthur, 'Hastings brought off a brilliant *coup* in Paris, that scenario was avoided. But it doesn't excuse you. We will have to re-open negotiations with Moscow, but from a serious disadvantage. Ray, I have to ask you a difficult question. Do you believe that the Russians will invite us back with Arthur as Managing Director of the London office?'

Ray Andrews didn't hesitate.

'No,' he said. 'Our only hope is a fresh start.' He picked up his glass of water and drained it.

James was watching Julius Heyderman; a faint flush had come up under his collar and there was the touch of a smile at each side of his mouth. He's going for the kill, James decided. The room was so quiet you could have heard the dust settle. Heyderman turned to Reece.

'Reece, where's that confidential report we got from our Moscow Embassy this morning? Give it to me, I'll read it out.'

'This is the one, Mr Julius.'

'Thank you.' Julius looked up briefly. 'I made private representations to our Ambassador, who is known to me personally, and, in reply to my letter, he sent the following. I quote.'

He didn't even need glasses to read it.

' "My dear Julius, etc. etc., I have made discreet enquiries as you requested, and I can confirm that, after the dismissal of D. V. Borisov, and the appointment of a new Director of Mineral Development, a Gregor Leontov, the Government is prepared to consider re-opening negotiations to the preliminary stage with your company. Only the chronic shortage of foreign currency and the need to find a profitable outlet for their extensive diamond mining operations have overcome a strong reluctance to deal with Diamond Enterprises under any circumstances. One condition was made very clear. Mr Arthur Harris must not be involved in any part of future negotiations. They were adamant on this point. I hope this is of some help, etc. etc." '

He let the papers fall on the desk.

'This seems to confirm what Ray has just said. Beyond any argument. They won't touch us with a bloody barge pole so long as you, Arthur, remain as Managing Director!'

Slowly, Arthur stood up.

'Are you attacking me directly, Julius? I want to be clear about this. You are supporting Andrews and accusing me of negligence and dishonesty and being a liability to the company?'

'I am not accusing anyone or attacking anyone,' Heyderman said harshly. 'I am putting the facts before the Board.'

Dick Kruger had been gearing up to fight back. Heyderman might overawe the others, but Dick was no coward, and one look at Arthur's stricken face fuelled his notorious temper.

'Well, let's take a close look at the facts then,' he said. 'Arthur was backed into a corner by a clever Russian who seems to have out-negotiated Andrews at every turn. He looked for a way out, and he very sensibly took one, in the company's interests. He's been insulted and abused for doing so, but we'll leave that aside. The facts are, the Russians need us more than we need them. They can't sell their goods at a profit without us, and anyone who deals with them, like the trade in Amsterdam for instance, can be told bloody clearly they won't get any goods from us! So they'll have to come back to the table and talk business. It's just a face-saving bluff. Andrews fucked up and he's trying to put the blame on Arthur. That's the truth of it!'

'Thank you, Dick,' Harris said quietly. 'I think you've made the point.'

For a moment it seemed to James that Kruger had swung the issue in Harris's favour.

Then Heyderman's chair scraped back and he stood up. It was a clever move because he dominated them even more from a height.

'You ask if I'm attacking Arthur. The answer is, Yes, I am. Five years ago we lost the concession on those Russian diamonds because of incompetence here in London. Now we lose it again, thanks to your personal intervention. Hastings saved your ass. But I'm not going to let you hide behind that. Incompetence and dishonesty have caused us a loss of business and reputation that no responsible Board could sustain. I formally propose a vote of no confidence in the Managing Director.'

A brief, shocked pause, and then Andrews said, 'I second the proposal.'

'Right,' Heyderman said briskly. 'Let the vote be taken. Reece, you're taking this down?'

'Yes, Mr Julius. Those in favour.'

He counted the raised hands out loud.

'The Chairman, Andrews, Johnson . . .' There was a hesitation while he looked round again. Another hand went up. 'Wasserman,' he intoned. Arthur put a hand to his face. A nerve under his left eye began to jump. They had known each other for thirty years. He had assumed automatically that David Wasserman would be on his side.

'Those against the resolution.'

It would need a two-thirds majority to carry the vote. There were four committed already. Three remained.

Reece said, 'The Managing Director, Kruger.'

They were all looking at James. His moment had come.

'Are you abstaining, Mr Hastings?'

James spoke quietly. 'I've worked with Arthur for fifteen years. I couldn't in conscience vote for him on this issue, but, equally, I'm reluctant to vote against him. I'm abstaining.'

He didn't look at any of them. Suddenly Ray Andrews got to his feet.

'At this point I'd like to say something,' he said. 'I'm over forty and nobody wants to start looking for a job at that age unless they have no possible alternative. But that is what I feel. I didn't tender my resignation before so I could attend this meeting and register my vote. Chairman and members of the Board, my letter of resignation is already waiting in the Chairman's office. Good-morning to you.'

He walked to the door and closed it firmly. It shut with a click like a revolver shot.

'So,' Julius Heyderman said loudly, turning a blue glare on Arthur Harris, 'we have just lost one of the ablest men in the business. We have, to all intents and purposes, a two-thirds majority in a vote of no confidence in you, Arthur. I shall expect your resignation by tomorrow morning at the latest!'

Arthur had sat absolutely still while the drama with Andrews came and ended. Now he raised his head high and looked directly at Julius. He sounded completely calm.

'I haven't the slightest intention of resigning.' He gave David Wasserman a look of bitter reproach. 'This has been an illuminating experience for me. I've heard myself accused of dishonesty and misconduct in the most outrageous terms by a man I promoted on to this Board. I've seen an old friend vote against me – you could at least have warned me, David – and Jan Heyderman's grandson try to force me, a Harris, off the Board.

'Well, gentlemen, I'm not going to resign. I am going to fight you, Julius. You started this war against me, and I'm going to carry it to the shareholders at the AGM. If you thought you could push me out behind closed doors, you underestimated me. But then you always have. But don't underestimate the extent of my holding and the holdings of members of my family. We will conduct the next stage in the full public domain. Now I have work to do, if you'll excuse me.'

He left the table and Dick Kruger picked up his notes and followed him out of the room.

Heyderman said briskly, 'No further business. Everything will be in the minutes. Let us hope,' he added, 'that when Arthur's had time to cool down, he'll see sense. Good-morning.'

David Wasserman came up to James; they walked out into the corridor together.

'It's a bad business,' he said. 'I didn't like voting Arthur out, but I hadn't any choice. Not just because of the Russian deal, but what he did to you . . .' He shrugged. 'You can't have a business run like that. You were right to abstain.'

James said, 'Do you think he'll back down?'

357

'No,' the old man said slowly. 'No, I don't think so. But Heyderman's never lost out yet. The real loser will be the business in the end. Keep in touch, my boy. And keep your head down till this is over. I'm getting Concorde back this afternoon. I'll be glad to get home.'

He sounded weary and depressed. It had cost him, James realized, to go against someone he had known and worked with for so long.

Sylvia had booked seats for the new Ayckbourn play. She loved the theatre; Julius humoured her by going, and she pretended not to notice if he fell asleep during the performance.

Stella was included in the party, with a couple of friends and their young son and daughter-in-law. So far, Stella hadn't once stepped out of line. She was friendly, amenable to Sylvia's social plans, and seemed so anxious to please her father that it made Sylvia feel nervous. Above all, she was sober.

The crucial Board meeting had taken place that morning. Sylvia didn't attempt to ring up and ask what had happened; Julius hated being disturbed in his office. For the sake of the evening ahead, she only hoped it had gone as he intended. She was neutral about Arthur Harris and positive in her dislike of her sister-in-law, Christa. Christa was acid tongued, jealous of her brother, and a shrew to her self-effacing husband. Sylvia was thankful they were a continent apart and didn't see more of the couple than was the minimum when they came to London.

She came back from a shopping expedition and the hairdresser to find a message from Stella, 'Please let me know when Daddy comes in; I must see him.'

Sylvia frowned. They were all meeting at the Aldwych Theatre. There wouldn't be time to spare.

She called Stella's room. 'I got your message,' she said quickly. 'Are you all right? Nothing wrong, is there?'

Stella's voice sounded thick as if she had a cold. 'No, everything's fine. Is he back?'

'Not yet, I'm expecting him at any minute. We're going to be rushed to get to the theatre by a quarter-past seven . . . Is it so urgent?'

A pause, then the answer, 'Yes. I'm afraid it can't wait. I'll come down. It won't take long. I'll come now.' Then she hung up.

Sylvia opened the door of the suite. To her relief Stella was dressed and ready for the evening. Her eyes looked puffy as if she had been crying.

'Oh God,' her stepmother said, seeing her in the light, 'what's happened?' You look awful. What's the matter?'

'It's all right,' Stella said. 'I haven't been on the booze, don't worry. I've just had a good blub.' She used the childish term without thinking. 'It won't make us late, Sylvia, but I couldn't wait till tomorrow. Here's Dad now.'

Her stepmother noticed a long brown envelope which Stella had left on the table. Julius came in.

'Hi,' he said. 'Sylvia, Suki . . . Sorry I'm a bit late.'

'How was the Board meeting?' his wife asked.

He scowled. 'The little bastard's threatening to fight it out at the AGM. We'll see. Forget it, let's go to the theatre.'

'Daddy,' Stella came towards him, 'I know it's not the right moment, you're rushed and you've had a bad day. But I have to show you this. Please read it.'

His impulse was to refuse. He was in an angry mood. He hadn't expected Arthur to oppose him. He wasn't used to being thwarted. His despised brother-in-law had suddenly turned and shown that, after all these years, he had balls.

Stella picked up the envelope and handed it to him. There had been a call from Miller when she got back to the hotel. She had spent the afternoon agonizing about what to do.

'Before you read it,' she said, 'I have to explain something. I believed Reece was involved in Jacob's murder. I hired a private detective to investigate him. That's what they found out.'

He stared at her. He raised his voice. 'You what? What the hell do you mean?'

Stella interrupted him. 'Read it first, you can yell at me afterwards. I'm trying to protect you, that's why it can't wait.'

He grabbed the envelope from her. Sylvia gave her a look of angry reproach.

Stella said simply, 'Get Dad a drink; I think he's going to need it.' Then she sat down to wait.

At one point her father jerked his head up and stared at her in horror. 'Good Christ!' Then he read on, his face flushed a deep red.

'They're going to be arrested,' Stella said. 'I heard today. You've got to get him off the payroll before it happens. That's why it couldn't wait.'

Sylvia was beside him with a whisky. 'Darling, what is it? What's happened?'

He swallowed hard, and then said, 'Reece. The filthy, bloody little pervert. Incest. Oh good Christ,' he repeated. He held out the report to her. 'Here read it!'

Stella said, 'I went to see the sister. I accused Reece of having Jacob murdered. She admitted it.'

They heard Sylvia exclaim in disgust. 'Oh my God,' she was saying. 'My God, how revolting! Julius, what are you going to do?'

'Fire him,' he answered. 'By special messenger tonight. Before this filthy mess blows up in my face. My personal assistant . . . God Almighty.'

He sprang up. 'I've got to deal with this right away. You go to the play, make my excuses. I'll join you for dinner later. Ring down and ask for secretarial services and lay on a special delivery.'

He swung away from her and back to Stella. 'You're

not going either,' he said. 'When I've dealt with this, we're going to talk, you and I. I want some explanations!'

'Darling,' Susan Andrews said firmly, 'you did the right thing. We talked it over and I'm sure it was right.'

She slipped her arm round Ray's shoulders. He had walked through the front door to find her waiting and told her in one sentence that his career with Diamond Enterprises was over. He had resigned at the Board meeting. He sat down and suddenly he seemed depressed and older. Anger had sustained him up to the last minute. Now it was purged and the reaction had set in. She knew him so well, and she loved him enough to pretend that she wasn't frightened, too.

He'd find another job. Not as well paid, perhaps, or as senior, at his age, but something would come along. She got him a large gin and tonic and said simply, 'I'm glad. And you're not to worry or to have any regrets. The whole thing was disgraceful. Now I've booked a table at Martino's, we're going out to dinner and celebrate a new start. So drink that up, darling, and let's go.'

Ray looked up at her. She wasn't clever, and her early prettiness was fading; grey peppering the brown hair and a few lines under the eyes. But she was loyal and loving and he had never wanted anyone else from the day they married. His mother, a shrewd Scottish lady, had said when they became engaged, 'She's sterling, Ray. You won't regret it.' Sterling she was; not just his lover and wife, but his best friend. He reached out for her hand and held it tightly.

'Thanks, Susie. Thanks for everything.'

Sylvia didn't enjoy the play. She couldn't concentrate; Ayckbourn was difficult enough without her thoughts wandering back to that scene in the hotel. The picture of that horrible little creature in bed with his own sister kept intruding on the theatricals taking place on stage. She felt slightly sick. Julius would cope with it. Nothing was dangerous enough to overwhelm him. That reassured her. But Stella – putting detectives on them – that was a warning sign. Not quite the compliant, rehabilitated daughter, come meekly back into the fold. She sighed inwardly, and joined in the long applause when the play ended. It was a relief to get out of the theatre. She gathered her guests together and set off for the Savoy. They kept two places at the table for Julius and his daughter, but they never came.

'You never loved me,' Stella was pacing up and down as she talked. 'I was in the way.'

Julius was sitting on the sofa, watching this strange creature stripping layers off their relationship. Not in anger, but quietly.

'That's not true,' he said. 'I never understood you. You didn't fit, from the time you were a baby. You weren't like Eileen, or like me . . . you were some throw back. If I tried to hold you, you fought and wriggled to get away. You were difficult and wilful. Your first bloody word was "No"!'

'I wasn't a boy,' Stella retorted. 'You wouldn't have minded then. You wanted someone like mother, all soft and feminine and clinging. I wasn't made like that. I wanted both of you to love me, and when you didn't, I hit back.'

'You certainly did,' he agreed. 'From the moment your mother broke down you made everyone's life hell. And you went on doing it.'

'Because I felt what happened was my fault,' she reminded him. 'You knew all that, but it didn't make any difference.'

'No, it didn't,' he said, showing impatience. 'A lot of psychiatric bullshit about guilt in a five year old. You say I didn't love you, Stella, but, by Christ, you weren't easy to love! Ever think of that? Now we're being honest with each other, how would you feel when everything had crashed round you, and the only thing you had was a tearaway, hell bent on wrecking her own life in order to spite you?'

Stella said, 'It wasn't that. I was punishing myself. Jacob was the only one who made me feel I was worth anything. And then I lost him.' She came and sat opposite him. 'I want to tell you something. I don't want to keep it in, even if you never forgive me for it. I thought you were involved in his murder. I wanted to prove it . . . to destroy you. That's why I went after Reece. To get to you.'

Heyderman didn't say anything. He waited, as she did. Then he spoke in a very low voice. 'That's nice. That's what you think of me, is it?'

Stella felt the tears coming and tried to fight them back. It wasn't the moment for weakness. She knew him. He had no sympathy with frailty.

'That's how wrong I was about you,' she answered. 'So wrong, so twisted up.'

'I see,' he agreed. 'Something else to feel guilty about. You *are* going to be a bloody mess unless you stop all this rubbish and pull yourself together! You know something, Stella? You're more like me than I ever realized. I'd have done exactly what you did in the circumstances. I'd have gone out to get my father if I thought he'd done a thing like that. So what the hell are you crying about, eh? Because I didn't do it?'

'You're making fun of me,' she protested. 'I want you to forgive me.'

'Oh come on,' he heaved himself up from the sofa and came over to her. He put an arm round her shoulder. 'Yes, I am making fun of you, and it's about time you started laughing at yourself. All these years wasted . . . What the hell would Jacob think if he could see you? He bloody nearly made a grown woman of you, I'll give him that. You want me to love you, Stella? Then give me something to be proud of! Do something with your life. We're going home and it's all happening there. It's all to play for, whether the country goes down the pan into civil war or whether the new system works out. We've never been political as a family. The De Beers were liberals, they stood against apartheid. We just kept neutral. But you don't have to; you've got Yakumi's name to help you.'

Stella turned and stared up at him. 'You mean that? You wouldn't mind?'

'Would it stop you if I did?'

She hesitated. His arm felt warm and reassuring round her shoulders. Jacob, she thought. 'No,' she said. 'It wouldn't.'

'Good,' Heyderman said. 'That's my girl. Now for God's sake do something with your face. We're going down to get some dinner before the restaurant shuts. I'm starving.'

Jill Fairfax believed in exercise and fresh air. She had insisted on Elizabeth joining her when she walked her dogs, and it was a daily routine. It was a cold December day, with frost forecast for the evening and a faint mist coming up over the parkland. Elizabeth was looking better; she had put on some weight and said she was sleeping well. Outwardly she behaved normally, but her mother knew that she was miserable. She didn't use words like depression, they annoyed her, because she felt they were used indiscriminately for less fundamental states. Like plain unhappiness.

She strode out briskly. 'God, it's getting cold,' she remarked. 'I never like this time of year. Everything's dead, no leaves on the trees, flower-beds bare. Pop loves it because of the shooting. I'm just dying for the spring. I woke up this morning and thought, Good Heavens, it'll be Christmas before we know it!'

Elizabeth had the puppy on an extending lead. It

bounded off to the limit of the cord, thoroughly enjoying itself.

'So it will,' she said. 'I'd forgotten it was so soon. Actually Mum, Jean Pierre asked me to go over and stay with him. He plans to come here just before Christmas, and I could go back with him. Would you mind?'

Jill Fairfax stopped. She snapped a command and her Labradors came trotting obediently back to her, and sat waiting. She looked at her daughter, and said clearly, 'Yes I would. So would your father. If you won't go back and talk to your husband, then your place is here with us until you've made up your mind. Not going off with some bloody man old enough to be your father! He doesn't care, he wants you and James to split up for good. Sit, Dinki!' She shouted at the motionless bitch to relieve her feelings. Then she took a deep breath and said, 'I'm sorry, Lizzie. Of course you must go and do what you want to, it's none of our business. We'll just miss you, that's all. I was being selfish. We haven't had Christmas together for so long. I'd been making plans. Forget I said it. All right, walk on!'

They set off, crossing the broad park and turning towards the distant roof tops of the house.

'I'm not going back to James,' Elizabeth said suddenly. 'I've made up my mind. I'm going to get a divorce.'

Her mother didn't answer. She addressed her dogs instead. They were coming up the broad sweep of the front drive when she did speak.

'If you're sure that's what you want, that's it then. Dinki, Bizzi, heel . . .'

'I'm sure,' Elizabeth said. 'It's not what I want, but I know it's the only thing to do. James and I won't ever get back together, not as we were. It'd be some sort of compromise. It wouldn't work for either of us. I'm sorry, Mum darling, but I couldn't bear living like that. If we had children it'd be different. But we haven't. So . . .'

They walked round to the side door which was

under the archway of steps leading to the massive front entrance. Boots and waterproofs were kept there, with a giant bootscraper like a hedgehog, half its bristles worn through years of use. 'I thought of going to France because it might do me good to have an *affaire*,' she said. 'I'm not going to marry him, or anyone. Not for a very long time. I might feel happy for a change. But I can go after Christmas. There's no rush. So we'll be together, that's settled.'

She gave her mother a quick squeeze on the arm – Jill was not someone who hugged her children or felt comfortable with displays of affection – then Elizabeth hung up her coat, lodged her wet boots in the rack and went ahead upstairs. Jill began rubbing the dogs down to dry them. The puppy sprang up and rolled on its back to play.

'If you ask me,' Jill addressed it, 'you've got more sense, Bizzi, than my fool of a daughter. She's cutting off her nose to spite her face. Sleeping with some dirty old man won't stop her loving bloody James. Stay still, can't you!'

She went upstairs after a time to find her husband and tell him the news. A man in his fifties who slept with a girl of twenty-seven was quite simply a 'dirty old man'; modern trends had made no impression on Jill Fairfax.

Elizabeth didn't go into the library to have tea with them. She went upstairs and ran a hot bath. She felt chilled after the walk and the damp cold air was making her shiver. Divorce. The final severance of hope. I won't do it through a solicitor, she said out loud. I don't want to end up as enemies. I'll go and see James and tell him myself. After all, we were very happy. That must count for something. I'll go to London just before Christmas. There'll be a New Year and a new start. Then I'll be ready to face the office again. She had no feelings, as if her emotions were a set of nerves that had been severed. She couldn't even find tears for what was lost.

'I think you're a bloody fool,' Christa Harris said suddenly. She glared at her husband. He had his back to her and he was changing to go out to dinner. He never told her anything lately, and it maddened her to have to ask. He hadn't been able to exclude her from the coming fight because he had given her a substantial holding in the company as a wedding present.

'I know my dear. You've always thought so.' He was fastening his black tie and he went on tying it as he spoke.

'Why the hell must you have this fight with Julius?' she said. She had been saying it every time they saw each other, and it was irritating him more and more.

'What about Martin? You know perfectly well that you'll lose – where will that leave our son? Or don't you care about his future?'

'As a matter of fact,' Arthur turned away from the glass, 'I don't, my dear. I don't see anything about him that deserves my consideration. I'm thinking about myself, at the moment.'

'You won't win against my brother,' she said. 'You know you won't. He has most of the holdings and he'll get the shareholders on his side. Then what will you do?'

'Resign,' he said. '*If* he gets the shareholders on his side. But he won't. Tom Richfield is a good friend – he's a big shareholder – he'll back me. So will the old aunts, I know that. And you, my dear. We have a very good chance.'

'That's what I wanted to talk to you about,' she said. 'That's why I came in here. Not for a cosy little chat. I want to talk to you, Arthur. Seriously.'

He was slipping on his dinner jacket; he paused for a moment and looked into her face. The vivid blue eyes stared back at him, slightly narrowed and as hard as flint. It was strange how he no longer thought her good-looking, or noticed her in any way except to criticize. 'Very well, dear. Talk to me. But don't take too long. I'm meeting Hugh at the club.'

'Then you'll just have to be a little late,' she said. She went and sat down and crossed her elegant legs; she lit a cigarette and blew out the smoke. She had taken up the habit to irritate him.

'I've decided not to vote for you,' she said.

He didn't answer for a moment; he buttoned his dinner jacket and put his cigar case in the inner breast pocket.

'If you're trying to start a row, my dear Christa, I'm afraid I haven't got time. I'm going to meet Hugh.'

'I mean it,' she said. Her voice was quite calm; she sounded rather bored. 'I've been thinking it over carefully, and I've come to the conclusion that you're finished. You won't win, and even if, by some miracle, you did, you'll have to retire in a few years, anyway. I want Martin to have his chance in the organization. I don't see why you should lose it for him, just to satisfy your damned silly pride. I'm voting against you, Arthur, and that's definite. I spoke to Julius today and said so. I said pretty plainly that I expected him to look after Martin when he comes down from Oxford. I thought I'd let you know, that's all.'

'Thank you,' Arthur said. 'It's nice of you not to have kept it as a surprise. You've actually told him you'll vote against me?'

'Yes,' she said. 'I sent off a confirming letter this morning. You might as well give in. You haven't a hope of winning without me.' She looked up at him and smiled. 'You should have been a bit nicer to me, darling. It wasn't good policy to be so offhand with me lately. But then you're as rotten at policy as you are at business. Have a nice dinner with Hugh. Ask his advice. Maybe you'll listen to him.'

She got up, the cigarette between her lips, and walked out, leaving the dressing-room door open. He put his wallet in his pocket, made sure he had his door keys and the key to his car, and had a last look at himself in the glass. Then he switched out the light, an old nursery habit of economy which he had never lost, and went out of the room.

'I can't believe it,' Hugh Fuller said. 'It's impossible, my dear chap!'

'Oh no, it's not. I know Christa. She means it. She wants to make sure Martin gets in at the top and she'll sacrifice me to do it.'

They had reached the coffee and brandy stage and they had been talking about Christa's defection the whole evening. Fuller was genuinely distressed; he had never liked the woman, but this was outrageous. He said so, and Arthur shrugged.

'I never suspected it, not for a moment,' he said. 'We've drifted apart over the years, but I never thought she'd turn on me.' He gave a bitter laugh. 'I made over a hundred thousand shares when we were married, and I gave her another fifty-five thousand a few years ago. And she has a large personal holding from her father. It's more than enough to defeat me, in view of Julius's own holdings, and the majority of outside shareholders will follow him like sheep. What am I going to do, Hugh?'

'Look, Arthur, I'm one of your oldest friends.' Hugh Fuller leaned over the table and patted his arm. He felt quite emotional. 'I never liked the idea of this fight, but I thought it was a bloody shame that Heyderman should try and do you down. Anyway, I drew up that damned contract, and I've felt responsible.'

'Nonsense,' Arthur said. 'It wasn't your fault; nobody could have worded it better.'

'That's very generous of you,' the older man said. He brushed his white hair back. 'Can I give you a piece of advice? Real advice, as a friend?'

'Of course,' Arthur smiled sadly. 'I can do with it. I don't know where to turn at the moment. This has thrown me completely.'

'Give up,' Fuller said. 'Drop the fight. No, don't interrupt me for a minute, old chap. Look here, you've been working hard for the last thirty years. You're a rich man, Arthur, a damned rich man, actually. Why not call it a day? Look at me – I've got another three years, and then I retire. You've got about the same. I've been thinking lately that it isn't worth it. Arthur, why have a dirty fight in public? You haven't a hope of winning now – why not resign and cut your losses?'

'I can't,' he said. 'I can't be beaten like that.'

'You won't be beaten,' Fuller said. 'You'll have taken the initiative. After all, there's Heyderman, marshalling all his big guns for a fight, and you just say you don't think it's worth it. You retire. You could concentrate on sailing in a big way. That's what I'm going to do, anyway. Phyl and I have decided we want some time to ourselves, and I'm semi-retiring this year. Why don't you do the same? We could have a lot of fun. Phyl's devoted to you, you know that.'

'She's a wonderful woman,' Arthur said. Phyllis Fuller was a cheerful, sporty woman, passionately fond of sailing, and she never got on with Christa. Arthur had always liked her.

'I don't know,' he said. 'I don't know what to do. You've got your wife, Hugh. You've got someone to retire with.'

'That,' Fuller said, 'won't be a problem. Just get rid of that bloody wife of yours. I'll handle the divorce!'

'Don't worry,' Arthur said. 'That's the first thing I'm going to do.'

'Gentlemen,' Julius announced, 'I've called you in this morning because I've something to tell you.'

Every place at the Board table was taken except David

Wasserman's and Arthur's chairs. James and Kruger and Johnson and the man who had taken Andrews' place, a brilliant accountant called Bennett, were all seated round the long table. Julius had a young secretary beside him to take the minutes. Reece was away; he was said to be ill.

'This is a special meeting,' Julius said. 'We won't bother with the reading of the minutes of the last, or any company business, because we'll have our usual monthly meeting on the eighteenth of January as planned. I wanted to tell you that I have received a letter of resignation from Arthur. He has decided not to seek re-election at the Annual General Meeting. The Managing Directorship is now open, and we will elect the candidate at the next Board meeting and have the office approved by the shareholders at the Annual General Meeting.'

Arthur Harris's letter was quite short, and it was very dignified. It regretted the misunderstandings which had taken place, and reaffirmed that he had at all times acted in the best interests of the company. It expressed regret at leaving the Board in the circumstances in which he found it necessary to resign, but wished his successor good luck. He had decided to take this step rather than expose the company to the bad publicity which must result from a public fight to clear his name.

'So that's that,' Heyderman said. 'There's nothing else but to say that my personal nomination for the Managing Directorship will be James Hastings. I have here Wasserman's formal approval, and I take it that nobody will oppose at the next meeting?'

He looked round and for a moment his eyes challenged Dick Kruger. Kruger cleared his throat. 'I'm not at all happy about Arthur's resignation,' he said. 'I can't commit myself at the moment to voting for Hastings. I hope you understand.' He turned to James.

'Certainly I do. I shall be sorry if you can't change

your mind. I'd like to feel that I'd have someone as loyal to me as you've been to Arthur.'

It was a clever reply and it took Kruger off his guard. He reddened and said nothing. It sounded as if the vote at the coming meeting was just a formality. If he didn't come to a truce, then he would have to resign with Arthur.

As the meeting broke up, Heyderman called James aside. 'I think it's pretty well in the bag for you, Hastings,' he said.

'Yes, Chairman, thanks to you, I think it is.'

'Come and have lunch with me; one o'clock at the Savoy Grill. I want to talk to you about one or two things.'

James went out, holding the door for him; the rest of the Board members hung back, Heyderman went down the corridor and into his office. He felt relieved and full of his usual confidence. Problems always diminished when you faced up to them squarely. He wanted to get home and gear up for Christmas. Then go to St Moritz and ski over New Year. But there was one more thing he had to do. He buzzed his secretary.

'Call Ruth Fraser, please. Ask her to come up.'

Joy Reece didn't hear the front door bell the first time it rang because she was vacuuming the floor. Ever since the letter arrived by special delivery, she had been getting up at first light and cleaning the flat in a demented ritual, turning back the rugs, moving furniture, dusting and polishing every tap and metal surface till they shone.

Joy had brazened out the confrontation with Stella Heyderman, and in her judgement she had won. The woman wouldn't dare do anything. Not unless she wanted her father dragged through the dirt. Joy hadn't told Reece about the visit. She didn't want to worry him for nothing. He was so sensitive, and he took anything concerning them to heart. They had been sitting after a nice supper, watching a wildlife programme on TV, when the letter was delivered, at peace with the world and each other. When he opened it, he remarked, 'From Mr Julius . . . I wonder what's come up . . .'

And then he gave a cry like a stricken animal. Joy had rushed to him. He couldn't speak. He just handed it to her. He was dismissed on grounds of moral misconduct. He was barred from Diamond Enterprises' offices. Joy held him close, fierce as a tigress with a wounded cub. He had been the strong one, protecting her. But not now. He was broken and she knew it, feeling him break down and cry with his face hidden in his hands. It was her turn to support him.

She had urged him to go home, to catch the first flight back to Johannesburg next morning. He seemed incapable of doing anything. He didn't sleep all that night. He stayed in bed the next day; he seemed so ill, she hadn't the heart to suggest leaving. A day or two was what he needed, just to get over the shock. So she cleaned and polished to relieve the anxiety that was tearing her apart.

She shut the machine off and heard the bell ringing, long and insistently. She put a duster in her apron pocket and went to the front door. Two men were standing in the passage. One had a brown trilby hat on, and he took it off.

'Are you Miss Reece?'

'Yes,' she said. 'What do you want?'

'I'm Detective Sergeant Reynolds. This is Detective Constable Batchelor. We are making some inquiries. I wonder if we could have a word with you. And is your brother at home?'

13

'I hope you don't mind me leaving suddenly like this, Mr Hastings?'

James shook his head. 'No, of course not. It's a great opportunity. You deserve the chance, Ruth. You'd be a fool not to take it.'

She perched on the chair by his desk. He thought dispassionately that she looked glowing that morning, immaculately dressed as always, as bright and polished as the diamonds that would be more and more central to her life from now on.

'The Chairman gave me until Christmas to think it over, but I wanted to discuss it with you first.'

James smiled slightly. 'I think you've already made up your mind, Ruth. And good luck. Who knows where a job with Heyderman will lead you?'

'That's true,' she agreed.

Heyderman had no son to follow in his footsteps and the daugher was into politics. She had already established that he disliked his nephew Martin Harris through the office grapevine where most things were known. The boy had paid him a visit just before the Heydermans left for South Africa. He had been loutish and arrogant. The meeting wasn't a success.

'But it's exciting, anyway. I'm ready for a career change, and I've never worked outside the UK before. The salary and benefits are fantastic too. But I have to say, I'll miss working with you, Mr Hastings.'

'Not for long,' James said. 'You're set for big things, Ruth.'

'I hope so. The irony is,' she said, 'the Chairman told me it was Reece's report that made him offer me the job. He gave me a terrific write up over my part in the Paris operation. Mr Heyderman said he always trusted Reece's judgement. In spite of everything.' She tried to look sympathetic. 'What a terrible business that was.'

'Yes,' James nodded. 'Awful. God knows what was behind it.'

The news about Reece burst on the company like a bomb blast. A girl in the typing pool saw it first, and came rushing in with the newspaper. It was a small item headlined 'Brother and sister found dead.'

They had committed suicide. The caretaker had broken the door open when he saw newspapers piled up in the corridor. They were lying in the bedroom and they had been dead for some days. There was no note. At the inquest it was revealed that the police had been making inquiries. The verdict was suicide from barbiturate poisoning, and the case was closed.

'I'll say one thing,' Ruth went on, 'I'm glad to be out of Dick's way. Will you keep him on?'

'Depends,' James said. 'I want a good Board working with me. It's up to him. Any attitude problems and he's out. So when are you leaving?'

She smiled, pulled instinctively at her skirt, which only made it ride up higher. She just couldn't help using sexual body language, he realized, even though she knew it was quite meaningless to him.

'Well, I've put my place up for sale, and when I've sorted out what I want to take with me, I thought I'd go over as soon as possible. Find a nice apartment and get settled in. I really can't wait!'

Then, after a pause, she said, 'What are your plans for Christmas? Going away somewhere nice?'

'No,' James answered. 'I haven't thought about it. I expect I'll stay in London, there's plenty of work to do over the holiday.'

'Oh,' Ruth got up. 'Your wife won't be with you?'

'No, I'm afraid not.' He looked bleak, as if he resented the question.

'More fool her, then!' Ruth said suddenly. 'I'll come and say goodbye before I go. And I wish you every success, too. You'll make a great Managing Director. I'll be coming over with Mr Heyderman, so we won't lose touch.'

She gave him a little wave over her shoulder as she opened his office door and went out. Christmas. James had put it out of his mind. The Wassermans had invited him to join them in Nassau for five days. Friends had suggested skiing. His mother was staying with her niece in Canterbury. That was the last place he wanted to go; noisy children and carol services in the cathedral. He had made an excuse as soon as she mentioned it. He could survive Christmas if he kept busy. It would pass quickly, and then he would be back in his office with a whole new horizon ahead of him. Christmas meant nothing to a lot of people. It wouldn't mean anything to him from now on.

Ray Andrews had already taken a job as an adviser to a firm of commodity brokers. The salary and bonus were less than he had been earning, but he was happy. There was no travelling, and he and Susan had time to do things together. They planned to go to a small hotel in Cornwall with their daughter and their student son for the holiday. Ray had received a personal letter from James Hastings asking him to reconsider and rejoin the Board at his invitation after the meeting on 18 January. James expected his appointment as Managing Director to be passed by the Chairman and Directors. Andrews had been flattered but unmoved. He refused graciously, but firmly. He had made a new start in a new business he found interesting. He didn't believe in turning back once a break was made with the past. He sent James his sincere good wishes.

The gossip columns followed Arthur Harris into retirement. He was seen at smart restaurants and night-clubs like Annabel's and Tramps with various attractive women. He smiled when asked about his marital break-up after thirty years. He said he had decided to devote himself to sailing and having fun.

The South African press and television gave wide coverage to the arrival of Julius Heyderman's daughter after a long absence, and her announcement that during her stay overseas she had married the black lawyer and activist Jacob Yakumi. As his widow, she hoped to carry on his work in the new South Africa.

At Blackfriars Road, the work pressure was slackening before the start of the five-day break, followed by the hiatus of the New Year. James brought work home with him in the evenings. He had their old housekeeper, everything ran as smoothly as it did when Elizabeth was there, but it was different. The atmosphere in the house was impersonal, like a well-run luxury hotel. He couldn't wait to get rid of it. Spring was the best time to sell. He wouldn't buy another house. An apartment in St James's Place was on offer through a business contact. It had magnificent views over Green Park and a forty-foot reception room, ideal for business entertaining. Full service was available. Driving home in the December traffic, slowed to a crawl by shoppers and sightseers come up to view the Regent Street lights and decorations, James decided he wouldn't wait any longer. He might as well put in an offer for the pad close to the asking price because of its amenities and prestige position. He could move out of the house as soon as the purchase was completed. It was partly furnished, so he needn't denude his own property. He was surprised by his lack of sentiment. He'd bought the house just before he married; they had looked at it together, made plans for decorating and improving it.

Elizabeth had been so excited, matching colour schemes and scraps of material. It meant nothing to him now. That part of his life was over. Perhaps it was never meant to be more than an interlude, a painful lesson in the fragility of human relationships.

Like should marry like. They had had nothing in common but their love for each other, and, when the crunch came, it wasn't enough. He parked and opened the front door.

The house was empty; his housekeeper had gone out for the evening, he planned to have an early dinner at his club, and then go through some papers. The drawing-room door was open and the light was on. He knew she was there before he walked in and saw her. He could feel her in the house. She was sitting in an armchair by the unlit fire. He stopped in the doorway.

'Hello, James,' Elizabeth said. 'I let myself in. Mrs Glover said you'd be coming back around now.'

James took in the scene as if he was a spectator watching someone else playing himself. But Elizabeth was real.

'Liz? Hello. How are you?'

'Fine, thanks.'

He managed to say, 'You're looking well.'

Well, but not herself. Something had gone for ever; the lovely face had lost its innocence, its confidence.

'So are you. James, I'd love a drink.'

It sounded so forced and ridiculous it made him wince.

'Of course. Gin and tonic?'

'Please. Why isn't the fire lit? It's so gloomy.'

'I'm going out,' he said. He poured gin and tonic and dropped in ice, then helped himself to whisky.

'There's no lemon, I'm afraid. I only drink Scotch these days.'

He gave her the glass. Their hands didn't touch. He sat down opposite her. He had no idea he could still feel such pain. He had really imagined he was immune until he saw her sitting there, looking at him with those large grey-blue eyes. There were deep shadows under them now.

'Well,' he said after a long agonizing pause. 'This is a

surprise. Why have you come back suddenly like this?'

'I wanted to see you,' she said.

To ask for a divorce. He nearly said it for her. She wouldn't take the coward's way and hide behind solicitors. Whatever the cost to either of them, he knew Elizabeth would be straight, as she saw it. He just wished that, for his sake at least, she hadn't decided to be brave. He said, 'You want a divorce, I suppose?'

Elizabeth didn't answer. She picked up her drink and nearly drained it. She tried to smile at him but it didn't work. 'Dutch courage,' she said. 'No, I haven't come for that. I came up to London to see Jean Pierre and tell him it was never going to work with us. And I came here to ask you to forgive me.'

He said, 'Forgive you?'

She nodded. 'Yes. If you possibly can after the way I've behaved. If you can't, and I wouldn't blame you one bit, then I'll just go.'

She took a handkerchief out of her sleeve.

'Oh God,' she said. 'I don't want to cry, it's not fair on you.'

James said slowly, 'Elizabeth, what do you mean, forgive you?'

'Ruth Fraser came down to Freemantle to see me,' she said. 'She just arrived on the doorstep. She told me what happened. She took the message from Jean Pierre when I went into hospital. She stood there and told me right out that she decided not to tell you because you'd have come back to be with me, and ruined your chances.

'She said I was spoilt and stupid and didn't deserve you, and she only bothered to tell me because she liked you. She looked at me as if I were dirt. Then she just walked out of the house and drove off. Bloody tears . . .' She scrubbed at her eyes with the handkerchief. 'I wouldn't listen to you,' she went on. 'You swore to me and I wouldn't believe you. Oh James, what a terrible mess I've made of things.'

She reached blindly for her purse, stuffed the handkerchief away, and stood up.

'Look, I'll go now. Just try to forgive me, will you?'

He reached her before she could take a step. He held her firmly in his arms. 'You're not going anywhere. There's nothing to forgive, and if there is it doesn't matter. I still love you, Liz. Do you love me?'

'Yes,' she said. 'Yes, I do. But can we ever be the same after all this?'

He went on holding her. He said quietly, 'I don't know, darling. Not the same, no. But we can be together and work it out. That's what I want. Will you come back to me, and we'll try?'

Elizabeth looked up at him. 'Are you really sure, James? Do you think we can be happy again?'

James answered, 'I can't be happy without you, I'm sure about that.' He kissed her and they held tightly to each other. 'Ruth,' he muttered, his face in Elizabeth's soft hair. 'You never know anyone, do you?'

'Let's light the fire,' she whispered back. 'Make it feel like home again.'

Laura Karakov stretched; her thin arms were tanned a deep brown, but her face was shaded from the South African sun. She knew the damage sunlight did to ageing skin. 'What a climate,' she remarked. 'And everything's so cheap.' Ivan sprawled beside her in a lounger by the swimming-pool. They had spent a week as Julius Heyderman's guests in Johannesburg. The reconciliation was complete; they appeared at smart public functions together and Julius gave a dinner for them, inviting the top management of Diamond Enterprises SA and their wives. His wife Sylvia had been very gracious, taking trouble to show Laura the sights while the men talked business and made a show of friendship. All the fences were mended, Ivan was back in the family fold, and the misunderstandings of the past months were never mentioned.

'I don't like that city,' Ivan remarked. 'I was glad to get down here to the Cape. I feel like my mouth's been stitched up smiling . . . You were great, Laura. It was a good visit. We don't have to come again.' He hadn't enjoyed it. He had been defeated and humiliated and it would always rankle. Laura understood that. He was a proud man and a bad enemy.

'No,' she agreed coolly, 'we don't. But we were right to come here. Just remember he needed you, lover, or he wouldn't have moved his ass to invite you and make a big PR exercise out of it. You got the full treatment.' He stared at the shimmering blue pool. It was lunchtime and a lone girl was swimming up and down in a lazy crawl.

'It hasn't bought me,' he said.

'I know that,' his wife answered. 'And I'll bet he does too.' She wanted to reassure him and she flattered shamelessly to do it. 'You're Karakov,' she reminded him. 'You shook the hell out of Heyderman and he hasn't forgotten it. You want to order lunch out here?'

He grunted, his mind wasn't on eating. 'You order. Something light. That bastard Hastings, that's what sticks in my gut. Managing Director at his age. There was some dumb ass at dinner asking me about him and his "lovely wife" . . . After what he did to me. I get a pain just thinking about him.'

Laura said coldly, 'So do I. It looks like he's got it all. So forget about him. You've said it so often: business is business. Life has to go on.'

Ivan Karakov shifted so he could turn and look at her. He didn't often better her these days; he felt she was treating him too gently, as if he'd lost his edge.

'That's what it looks like,' he agreed. His eyes were bright with malice. 'But in Johannesburg I noticed a little something. I guess you must have missed it.'

She said sharply, 'Missed what? I didn't miss anything.'

'This time you did,' he said. 'Julius and his PA, Ruth.'

Laura had seen Ruth Fraser at all the official parties

and she'd been a dinner guest at the Heyderman's. Laura had been polite but chilling, remembering she had been James Hastings' secretary in Paris. A sharp little operator, oozing sex. If Hastings had hit the heights, so had she. 'You think they're screwing?' she demanded.

'I'd say so,' he said. 'I noticed little things. The way he looks at her. There's a communication there. Not just sex, sweetheart, something more. He's found a soul mate in the business. And she has ambitions, that girl. Big ambitions. I could smell it off her. She kicked Dick Kruger in the balls, remember? If she's humping Julius it's for promotion.'

He pulled himself up, let his legs swing over the side of the lounger. The swimmer had climbed out and was towelling herself in the brilliant sunshine. He noticed briefly that she had a good body.

He looked at his wife and he smiled. He reminded her of an old, sly crocodile. He said, 'There'll be a seat on the London Board when Kruger goes. And he's going, Julius told me. My guess is, she'll get it. If I was that bastard Hastings, I wouldn't sleep easy when she does . . .'

Laura closed her eyes, considering. Ivan was never wrong about people. He had an instinct. Over the years she had learned to trust it without question. She remembered a quotation she'd read somewhere, an old Chinese proverb. It had stuck in her mind because it appealed to her. Revenge is a dish best eaten cold. If Karakov was right, they'd feast on it together. She opened her eyes and touched him lightly on the arm.

'I'll go order us some lunch,' she said.

THE END

EXPOSURE
by Evelyn Anthony

Julia Hamilton was a high profile journalist with Western International Newspapers. When press baron Lord Western offered her a plum job with his flagship, the *Sunday Herald*, she could not refuse – she was to head a new riveting feature – Exposure – its aim, to root out corruption and malpractice in high places. Her first target was to go for the jugular of Western's enemy and rival, the business and media tycoon, Harold King, alias Hans Koenig. Koenig was a man of mystery, a man who had deliberately obscured the truth about his beginnings in Germany and who would go to any lengths to keep his past a secret.

Eager to meet her new challenge, Julia recruits her former editor, Ben Harris, a difficult, embittered man, attracted to Julia in spite of himself, and together they travel to Germany, unsure of what they might find. Their search leads them to Jean Adams, the niece of King's first wife, and witness to his sinister and ruthless exploitation. When Jean Adams becomes the victim of a savage sexual killing, Julia is even more determined to uncover King's past. Little realizing the extent of the danger she is in, Julia begins to uncover secrets that have been buried for fifty years, hidden not only by King, but by Western, her boss, who proves to be a far from innocent victim of this particular – EXPOSURE.

'Evelyn Anthony's best thriller yet'
Maureen Owen, *Daily Mail*

'She has carved out a niche of her own as the Queen of contemporary thrillers'
Daily Mail

0 552 13817 7

A SELECTED LIST OF FINE WRITING
AVAILABLE FROM CORGI BOOKS

THE PRICES SHOWN BELOW WERE CORRECT AT THE TIME OF GOING
TO PRESS. HOWEVER TRANSWORLD PUBLISHERS RESERVE THE RIGHT
TO SHOW NEW RETAIL PRICES ON COVERS WHICH MAY DIFFER FROM
THOSE PREVIOUSLY ADVERTISED IN THE TEXT OR ELSEWHERE.

☐ 14054 6	THE DOLL'S HOUSE	*Evelyn Anthony*	£4.99
☐ 13817 7	EXPOSURE	*Evelyn Anthony*	£4.99
☐ 13947 5	SUNDAY MORNING	*Ray Connolly*	£4.99
☐ 14227 1	SHADOWS ON A WALL	*Ray Connolly*	£5.99
☐ 12550 4	LIE DOWN WITH LIONS	*Ken Follett*	£4.99
☐ 12610 1	ON WINGS OF EAGLES	*Ken Follett*	£5.99
☐ 12180 0	OUR MAN FROM ST PETERSBURG	*Ken Follett*	£5.99
☐ 11810 9	THE KEY TO REBECCA	*Ken Follett*	£4.99
☐ 13896 7	GREAT FLYING STORIES	*Frederick Forsyth*	£4.99
☐ 09121 9	THE DAY OF THE JACKAL	*Frederick Forsyth*	£5.99
☐ 10050 1	THE DOGS OF WAR	*Frederick Forsyth*	£5.99
☐ 12569 5	THE FOURTH PROTOCOL	*Frederick Forsyth*	£5.99
☐ 13275 9	THE NEGOTIATOR	*Frederick Forsyth*	£5.99
☐ 13823 1	THE DECEIVER	*Frederick Forsyth*	£5.99
☐ 12140 1	NO COMEBACKS	*Frederick Forsyth*	£4.99
☐ 09436 6	THE ODESSA FILE	*Frederick Forsyth*	£4.99
☐ 10244 X	THE SHEPHERD	*Frederick Forsyth*	£3.99
☐ 13990 4	THE FIST OF GOD	*Frederick Forsyth*	£5.99
☐ 13598 4	MAESTRO	*John Gardner*	£5.99
☐ 13840 1	CLOSED CIRCLE	*Robert Goddard*	£4.99
☐ 13562 3	TAKE NO FAREWELL	*Robert Goddard*	£4.99
☐ 13281 0	IN PALE BATTALIONS	*Robert Goddard*	£4.99
☐ 13561 5	INTO THE BLUE	*Robert Goddard*	£4.99
☐ 13282 9	PAINTING THE DARKNESS	*Robert Goddard*	£5.99
☐ 13144 X	PAST CARING	*Robert Goddard*	£4.99
☐ 13839 8	HAND IN GLOVE	*Robert Goddard*	£4.99
☐ 13869 X	MATILDA'S GAME	*Denis Kilcommons*	£3.99
☐ 12433 8	A COLD MIND	*David Lindsey*	£4.99
☐ 13918 1	THE LUCY GHOSTS	*Eddy Shah*	£4.99
☐ 14145 3	MANCHESTER BLUE	*Eddy Shah*	£4.99
☐ 14143 7	A SIMPLE PLAN	*Scott Smith*	£4.99